*Too Young to Die: The Complete Cases
of MacBride & Kennedy, Volume 3*

Frederick Nebel

Frederick Nebel

TOO YOUNG TO DIE: THE COMPLETE CASES OF

MacBRIDE & KENNEDY

VOLUME 3. FROM THE PAGES OF BLACK MASK

FREDERICK NEBEL

Illustrations by
ARTHUR RODMAN BOWKER

Introduction by
EVAN LEWIS

Series Editor
KEITH ALAN DEUTSCH

Another Volume in the BLACK MASK LIBRARY

Boston • Philadelphia • New York
2013

© 2013 Altus Press • First Edition—2013

DESIGNED AND PUBLISHED BY
Matthew Moring

BLACK MASK SERIES EDITOR
Keith Alan Deutsch

PUBLISHING HISTORY
"Introduction" appears here for the first time. Copyright © 2013 David Lewis. All Rights Reserved.
Owing to limitations of space, permissions to reprint previously published material appear on pages 343-344.

Published by arrangement with Black Mask Press/Keith Alan Deutsch (keithdeutsch@mac.com).

THANKS TO
Ed Hulse, Evan Lewis, Ken McDaniel, Rob Preston & Ray Riethmeier.

Visit altuspress.com for more books like this.
Printed in the United States of America.

Another volume in the BLACK MASK LIBRARY.

Table of

CONTENTS

Introduction i

Rough Reform 1

Farewell to Crime 39

Guns Down 73

Lay Down the Law 107

Too Young to Die 137

Bad News 171

Take It and Like It 201

Be Your Age 231

He Was a Swell Guy. 267

It's a Gag. 291

EVAN LEWIS

THIS has been a long time coming.

Nebel fans like me have been waiting not just years—but *decades*—for this series to be reprinted.

In the heyday of *Black Mask*, two series stood head and shoulders above the rest: Dashiell Hammett's adventures of the Continental Op, and Frederick Nebel's saga of Richmond City. Both authors excelled in their mastery of the hard-boiled style, the depth and humor of their characters, the richness of their settings and the varied scope of their stories. But while Hammett is now a household name, Nebel has been largely relegated to the shadows.

The reason is simple. While Hammett and many of his contemporaries went on to write mystery novels, Nebel stuck to novelettes. As the pulps gave way to paperbacks in the 1950s, the novel became the dominant fictional form, rendering the novelette almost defunct. *Black Mask* writers like Erle Stanley Gardner, George Harmon Coxe, W. T. Ballard—and a guy named Raymond Chandler—remained in the public consciousness thanks to their books, while Nebel was remembered only by pulp collectors.

Nebel was a skilled craftsman who put his own stamp on the hard-boiled school of writing. His prose, packed with crackling dialogue and keen characterization, is as fresh today as it was in the 1930s. Altus Press has brought the bulk of his detective writing back into print. Now, at long last, they introduce new legions of readers to his most important body of work—the adventures of Captain Steve MacBride and his pal, reporter Kennedy of the *Free Press*.

When this series debuted in the September 1928 *Black Mask*, it was called "The Crimes of Richmond City." The title was appropriate because while this is the story of MacBride and Kennedy, it's also the story of a city. The series lasted nine years, and from first to last, Richmond City was portrayed as a living, breathing and growing metropolis—almost a character in itself.

Nebel's secret was simple. In writing about Richmond City, he was writing about his home town. The borough of Staten Island, New York, where he was born, was then known as Richmond. It comprised most of Richmond County, with Richmond Valley at one end, Richmond Terrace at the other, Richmond Creek in the middle, and joined by Richmond Avenue and Richmond Road. He took the harbor and residential areas of Staten Island and combined them with elements of the Bronx and Manhattan to create his own scaled-down version of New York. Richmond City seemed very real—because to Nebel, it was.

In the first volume of this series, comprised of stories published between September 1928 and February 1930, we saw Richmond City at its most violent. As the series began, crooked politicians and racketeers had such a stranglehold on the city that MacBride was powerless to act. It was only when his best detective quit the Force to fight fire with fire, that the grip is broken, and MacBride could start cleaning up. He did this with a vengeance. We saw pitched battles in the streets, usually with MacBride himself leading the charge, and the death toll was high on both sides of the law. While the worst offenders were weeded out, the corruption ran deep, keeping MacBride on the defensive. Things were so bad that the precinct house sometimes seemed the last bastion of law and order.

Now late in its second year, the Richmond City series was entering a new phase. In the second Altus Press volume, featuring stories published between April 1930 and February 1933, we saw MacBride on the lookout for new rackets and new forms of corruption, hell-bent to nip them in the bud. Though he took heat from other cops—and the commissioner himself—for overstepping his bounds, MacBride was on a crusade. And when his efforts finally earned him a spot at Headquarters, he faced the reality that some of his fellow officers were on the take.

The stories published between March 1933 and February 1935, collected in this third Altus Press volume, take on a more personal note. Rather than combating large scale corruption, MacBride and Kennedy often apply their talents to murder cases, and sometimes involving old friends. This group also includes "Bad News" (March 1934), in which MacBride is away on vacation and Kennedy takes the lead for the first time. This story, as you might expect, is the most comedic of the entire series.

With the series in its fifth year, MacBride is beginning to feel his age. He gets more and more frustrated with the job, particularly when men he considers friends don't support his actions. "It just breaks my heart with gratitude," he says. "Some fine day I'm going to start out and systematically change the shapes of a lot of schnozzles in this man's town." In "Rough Reform" (March 1933), he remarks, "The longer I work at this job, the more I think I should have taken up farming." He's tired of the long, irregular hours, and sick of "the blood and intrigue" that goes with police work.

In the fourth and final volume, featuring stories published between May 1935 and August 1936, we'll see secondary characters assume larger roles, and the introduction of two new regulars. By this time Nebel had come to think of himself as a novelist and wanted to delve deeper into his characters. This results in longer scenes, and sometimes longer stories.

MacBride's two best detectives, Ike Cohen and "Mory" Moriarity, were introduced early in the series, but in the final years their personalities grew stronger, providing more comic relief. They're often found sneaking drinks in the station or matching quarters in the back of the police car, and both spend a lot of time in speakeasies. The medical examiner calls them MacBride's cowboys. Kennedy calls them his stooges. MacBride calls them apes or tramps, but trusts them implicitly. "I've got two palookas working for me," he sums them up, "who think of me first and then the department."

The new regulars also add to the comedy. One of these is Kennedy's wacky bartender pal, Paderoofski. He's always ready to lend Kennedy an ear, and sometimes other essentials, like money or a gun. The other is MacBride's driver, Gahagan. He's an all-around dimwit and pays not the slightest notice to safety or traffic laws, but has an uncanny ability to get places in a hurry, and always delivers MacBride in one piece.

At this point in the series, the humor is welcome, because MacBride's moods have grown increasingly dark. He reaches the lowpoint of his career in "Fan Dance" (January 1936), when he finds himself suspended. "I ought to have been kicked in the head," he says, "the first day I ever put on a uniform." Kennedy's scenes are darker, too. Both the author and his characters seem to realize that Kennedy's drinking is out of control, posing a threat to his health and life.

Though Nebel had a long and varied career (a detailed biography appeared in Volume 1), his greatest legacy was the saga of Richmond City. To you who are about to enter the city limits and fight crime with MacBride and Kennedy, I offer a word of advice:

Hold onto your seat. It's going to be a wild ride.

Rough Reform

A young Italian girl saw hired killers do their stuff and was murdered— When Capt. Steve MacBride finished the job the whole of Richmond City knew he'd been at work.

TONY MATTEO walked up and down the length of the large living-room. He walked with a dogged, plodding persistence, setting his broad heels firmly into the thick body of the black and red carpet. He was a craggy man of middle years, a little bald on top. A large gold watch-charm swung against his stomach. There was sweat on his face, and his face now was peculiarly gray. Every time he passed the dark hardwood table in the middle of the floor his eyes slid sidewise towards it, he raised his chin and held his breath and afterwards his eyes rolled, showing the whites.

His wife sat in a rocking chair. She rocked to and fro with a nervous rhythm, and every so often a dry, hoarse sob wracked her throat. She was a little tubby woman dressed neatly in black, with a knot of hair piled high on her head. A boy of six and a girl of nine clung to either arm. The girl was crying and the boy was quiet, white-faced, staring away from the table with great effort.

Nick Matteo, the elder son, stood with his back to the mantel, stared downward towards the table. He was slim and dark, just rounding twenty years of age, and a little while ago he had laughed with fine white teeth and his dark eyes had sparkled. But now he did not smile, and a paleness had crept into his cheeks and given his face a ghostly, unreal look. No muscle twitched, not an eyelash flickered; he seemed scarcely to breathe. The ceaseless pounding of his father's heels, the hoarse sobs of his mother and the pitiful whimpering of his little sister seemed hardly to touch him.

Once his father said: "Mother of God!" in a broken voice, but his pacing did not slacken.

The sound of footsteps on the veranda did not rouse the woman. Old Matteo stopped pacing and clenched his hands, blinked. Nick Matteo raised his somber dark eyes, looked at his father, then said:

"I'll go, pop."

He moved slowly with a smooth young grace that was almost

1

catlike. He went into the large entrance hall where the wide dark banister came down from dark regions above. He laid his hand on the doorknob, opened the door, stepped back.

MacBride took his hat off and stepped in. His lean-boned face was ruddy from the cold, his squinted eyes flicked Nick, swung through the open living-room door. He said nothing. Moriarity and Cohen came in after him. Cohen snapped chewing gum between his teeth once. Moriarity flipped a coin into the air. It spun brightly, landed in his open palm. A uniformed cop came in last, closed the hall door quietly, twirled his nightstick on its leather thong. Nobody said anything.

Mrs. Matteo raised wet eyes and kept on rocking. MacBride tightened his lips, laid a hand on the woman's shoulder, patted it once; ran the hand over the little girl's head. He raised his eyes to Tony Matteo. Tony stood rooted to the floor, the sweat beaded on his face, his lower lip trembling. He raised his arms in a vague gesture, then let them drop limply to his sides, and his whole body sagged. MacBride went towards him, gripped his arm firmly for a brief moment.

"Buck up, Tony," he muttered.

Moriarity and Cohen had gone to the table. Cohen braced an arm on the table, pressed the gum against the back of his teeth with his tongue. Moriarity laid his hat on the table, dropped to one knee, picked up one of Rose Matteo's smooth white hands, then laid it down gently. The bosom of her white dress was red. She lay on her back and there was a white bandage over her eyes.

MacBride came over and stood beside him, thrust his hands into his pockets, stared down and shook his head grimly. Nick Matteo moved across the room and stopped at MacBride's elbow.

"Rosie," he said in a quiet voice.

Mrs. Matteo's sobbing broke out again, and Tony went to her, knelt down beside her and put an arm around her. The two children clung to him.

Moriarity rose with a congested face, said in a congested voice: "This is crummy, Cap."

"How many, Nick?" MacBride asked.

"Two."

"They just came in and let her have it, eh?"

"My little sister opened the door and they walked right past her and came and stood in the doorway there. I was sitting there reading the paper to Rosie. The one guy covered me and the other guy told Rosie to stand up. Pop was upstairs. Mom was in the kitchen. The guy who told Rosie to stand up said: 'I hear you're going to be able to see again.' She said: 'Yes.' And then he said: 'Maybe you'd be happier if you wasn't.' And he stood there and fired three times and Rosie fell against me and I held her. The two guys backed and went out and by the time pop came down they were gone."

Mrs. Matteo wailed: "She was goin' to be able to use da eyes maybe tomorrow!" and then clapped hands to her own eyes.

"Nick," MacBride's low voice said. "What kind of a slant did you get of these babies?"

"They were masked, Cap. Handkerchiefs—you know—over the nose and mouth. Hats yanked way down. Overcoat collars up. Only one of the guys did the talking."

"Anything strange about the way he talked?"

"No. Just a wiseguy. But I think the other guy was a dummy."

Cohen said: "A dummy?"

"Yeah. He never said a word all the time. But just before they started backing out this guy nudged the guy shot Rosie and did something with his fingers. The other guy shook his head no. I didn't move. I—I was standing holding Rosie. I think I could feel"— his eyes shimmered—"the way she got cold. I—" For the first time his deathly calm seemed to desert him. His voice broke and he stepped back, keeping his hands clenched at his sides, biting his lips to silence.

Tony came over with halting, heavy footsteps, clung to MacBride's arm. "I been whatcha call a good father, Cap. I raise good kids. My Rosie was lovely girl, no? And now—she's dead. My Nick—he's fine boy, too. Why da hell dey got to come here and kill my poor Rosie?" He dropped to his knees beside his dead daughter and prayed in Italian and Nick turned away and began to sob quietly.

Moriarity poked MacBride, said in a thick voice: "I—guess I can't take it any more, Cap. This kind of—" He stopped, then said: "Mind if I go outside and wait for the Medical Examiner?"

"I'd like to too, Mory." The skipper inhaled, hardened his bony jaw. "Sure, kid—go ahead."

Mrs. Matteo fainted and fell from the chair and the uniformed cop lifted her, carried her to a sofa and Ike Cohen ran into the kitchen for water. The little girl began crying and wailing again and MacBride picked her up and held her in his arms, put her head down against his shoulder.

The uniformed cop turned and said in a bitter voice: "By cripes, Cap, the guys that did this ought to be burned!"

MacBride was rubbing his big hand on the little girl's head. His shoulder muffled her sobbing.

"You're telling me?" he said.

THE murder of Rose Matteo hit Richmond City after a month notable for its lack of crime. It grated in the main bearings of the police machine which for several months had worked under the strenuous leadership of a reform mayor. The city's chief magistrate, Mayor Dan Mulvaney, had been swept into office as a peace offering to a harassed and indignant army of taxpayers. He had gone to work after the manner of a gale wind, cutting payrolls, eliminating soft jobs, breaking city contracts and going after municipal loans at rock-bottom interest rates. And he had landed, quite properly, on the neck of the new police commissioner, Joseph Eckhardt.

The murder, breaking as it did after the long calm, set Police

Headquarters to humming. The political press, opposed to the new mayor, took an I-told-you-so attitude. Lately cashiered departmental heads gloated and Eckhardt, the commissioner, received a long and pointed telephone call from Mayor Mulvaney and sat for long minutes afterwards gnawing his lip and cursing under his breath.

Kennedy of the *Free Press* sauntered into MacBride's office, cribbed a cigarette from a packet on the desk, lighted up and stood leaning wearily back on his heels while MacBride, having paid no attention to his entry, went through the morning mail.

Kennedy drawled: "Tough, that runout last night, Skipper."

"If you'd been around there after it happened, boy—seen the old folks and the little kids there—" He shook his bony head, frowned, growled out: "We got in the habit once of calling these heels rats. I've been thinking lately what an insult it is to a perfectly respectable rat." He nodded to a newspaper on the desk. "See the wisecracks in the *Morning Examiner?*"

Kennedy's face looked sad and a little bored beneath his lop-eared hat. "Just scanned 'em. That crummy sheet has to attract attention somehow. Its news value is nil. Who do you think slapped that lead into Rose Matteo?"

"I suppose if I knew I'd be sitting here like I am attending to routine. You sure start a day with a nice easy question."

Kennedy settled into an armchair, wrapped the skirt of his threadbare topcoat around his thighs.

"The reason, of course, is as obvious as the nose on your face. Maybe I should say as obvious as the nose on Ike Cohen's face. Anyhow, it was dead certain that she'd be able to see again. She was the only one on the scene when those wild bunnies walked into her father's office six weeks ago and bumped off the clerk there. They thought they'd fixed her by tossing that acid at her eyes. I guess they almost did, but Matteo had dough for the best doctors. Regaining her sight, she would have identified the guys did that job. Ten to one you've got pictures of them downstairs in the Bureau: that's why these muggs were panicky."

"Go on, tell me what I know."

"I'm just checking up for my own benefit. Our new mayor is hell on wheels. He's one of the most honest men I've ever run across. The death of Rose Matteo is one of the costs of victory and reform. For years Mike Dorshook has got the city paving jobs. He bid in for the

River Road job, sponsored by his district alderman. It looked like rosy sailing, but Mayor Mulvaney stepped in and found out that it was a frame on the city. He forced the Board to give the contract to Matteo because Matteo bid lowest. Matteo had his courage when he worked his way into taboo territory. It was Dorshook's territory."

MacBride sat back, scowled. "So now you want me to blame this job on Dorshook, huh?"

"I wouldn't be that foolish. Dorshook would keep his hands clean. He wouldn't have to do a thing. But he's tied up with a big crowd. A lot of graft was lost when the job went to Matteo. Guys that would have gone to work for Dorshook now have no work. Men that gave Dorshook other contracts before and robbed the city have been exposed and canned. It's not the only case. Mulvaney exposed the truck contracts, the city printing jobs, the crooked bus franchises.

"He's hated and feared and a lot more heads will fall before he's through. He said he would wipe out crime and corruption and he's on trial. If I miss my guess, the murder of Rose Matteo is only the first of a new series. There's a crowd in the city out to double-cross the mayor, to back him to the wall and to prove to the taxpayers that Mulvaney is a bag of wind. They can't get anything on him. He's too straight. But they can break down his morale. Find the master mind behind this crowd and you'll break the ring."

MacBride said: "Me, I like Mulvaney's guts."

"Well, old tomato, I'm no reformer myself, but my paper is backing the mayor and I can't afford to lose my job. I play along with you because I like your liquor."

MacBride gave him a drink and Kennedy, regarding the empty glass, said: "I think it's the first time in the history of this city that we've had a mayor willing to go the limit. It's the first time, I might add, that we've had a chief magistrate who's singled out old potato MacBride to carry his war through the streets."

"Leading up to what kind of a dirty crack?"

Kennedy smiled drolly. "You wrong me, Skipper. I've got big ears and I have a habit of putting them to door panels. There are a lot of door panels in Headquarters. Behind these panels are a lot of guys marking time. The fall of Mayor Mulvaney, they seem to think, will also inundate one Captain Stephen J. MacBride."

MacBride shot to his feet, laid a hard fist on the desk. "Who's out to whitewash me, Kennedy?"

"I can't afford to name names—or rather, to tag voices with imagined names. I can't see through door panels."

MacBride went around the desk and grabbed Kennedy's lapel. His voice was low, taut: "You know, Kennedy!"

"Listen, it's the only coat I have. Don't tear it."

"Just what did you hear?"

"You're not scaring me, Cap. Take your paw off.... Well, I heard a voice say, 'This leaves us sitting pretty.'"

"What leaves who sitting pretty?"

Kennedy shrugged. "Just before I heard that I heard the voices talking about the knock-off of Rose Matteo."

"When did you hear this?"

"Last night. Two hours after she was bumped off."

MacBride leveled an arm. "In Headquarters?"

"No—not exactly. A branch."

"Damn it," MacBride snorted, "don't waltz me around!"

"A branch, I said. The *Club Rendezvous,* in Lascar Street. Where H.Q. poobahs and political big shots quaff from time to time. I didn't know at the time that a murder had been committed. I didn't hear the word murder mentioned. I just heard Rose Matteo's name mentioned. I was very drunk last night. I was looking for the men's room upstairs at the *Rendezvous* and got in the wrong room by mistake. There were folding doors—locked. On the other side of the folding doors were the voices. I didn't think much about it. I had to see a man about a dog.

"So I sloped out again and it was later, over in Charlie Tirck's bar, that I heard about the murder. So when I heard about the murder I perked up and fell all the way back to the *Rendezvous.* I found the room again, but the voices had gone. It was slow at the *Rendezvous* by that time. Burt the barman and I rolled dice and I asked some dopey questions but he was dumb."

MacBride shook him. "Who would you say the voices belonged to? Come on, Kennedy—don't get lock-jawed now."

"We Kennedys are a thorough family, Skipper. Sometime maybe I'll hear a voice again. When I do, I'll be seeing you."

MacBride, exasperated, held on to his arm. "Kennedy, if you're holding something back on me—"

"Unhand the palsied arm, Skipper. You wouldn't break the arm that carries your banner, would you?" He broke away, teetered over on one foot, righted himself and sauntered out.

MacBride dived after him, nailed him in the doorway. "Just one question, Kennedy."

"Yeah?"

"What room were those voices in?"

"Well, you climb the stairway, go to the back of the hall. The last door on the left is the men's room—the one I missed first. I went in the one on the right. The room with the voices was in front of that."

"Okey. Scram."

"You took the intention right out of my mouth."

MacBRIDE slapped his way into the *Club Rendezvous* at a little before noon, went past the hat-check girl, knocked open a swing-door at the rear of the hall and entered the small, intimate bar. Two drunks were leaning against the bar. Behind the bar a fat bald man was shaking cocktails.

MacBride said; "Where's Tripp?"

"Office, I guess. Should I—"

"No."

The skipper crossed the bar, entered the rear lower hall, palmed a doorknob and pushed open a heavy door. Sam Tripp was counting bills. He used a wet sponge to moisten thumb and index finger and his lips moved as he counted. He looked up at MacBride, motioned to a chair, went on counting until he had finished with the stack before him. He made a notation on a pad of paper, shuffled the bills together and snapped a rubber band around them.

"Hello, Skipper. How's every little and big thing?"

"I let the little things slide and get headaches over the big ones, Tripp."

"I used to have headaches a lot, when I was young."

"So you stopped worrying."

Tripp laughed dryly. "That's about it." He was a blond man in well-fitting tweeds. His hair and eyebrows were almost white but not from age; he was really a blond. "Don't tell me you came down to make cracks about my liquor."

MacBride said: "To hell with your liquor. That's a crack, I suppose, about me cleaning out your slot-machines. That was orders, Tripp, and I carried them out."

"Duty struck old Skipper!" chided Tripp.

"Any game where the house makes a profit of ninety percent isn't on the level."

Tripp started counting more bills.

"Hold on," MacBride said.

Tripp said: "Oh, hell," hopelessly, and tossed the bills to one side.

"I want to know," MacBride went on, "who was in the room upstairs about ten o'clock last night."

"What room?"

"On the right, next to the last."

"You've got me there, Cap. Anybody I ought to know?"

"I suppose you let total strangers occupy those rooms?"

Tripp put his hands behind his head. "I might, if they spent enough."

"Come on, Tripp. Who was up there?"

"Frankly, I don't know."

MacBride leaned forward. "You'd like to go on doing business at this stand, wouldn't you?"

"Kind of—sure."

"Then don't hand me the high eyebrow when I ask you a question. Who was up there?"

"I told you, Skipper." Tripp put his palms on the desk, laid pale blank eyes on MacBride. "I told you I don't know. If that brings down a padlock, okey—it's my tough luck. And excuse the high eyebrow. I didn't know it was high."

"You not only lie like hell, but you have to crack wise in the bargain. You think you're the nuts in this neighborhood because a lot of big shots hang out here and practically support you. You ran your scatter high and handsome for a long time. I didn't like it but I couldn't do anything about it because I hadn't the administration behind me. But I've got a mayor at my back now who's got more guts than six previous mayors put together, and I'm not letting him down."

"So what has that got to do with me?"

MacBride said: "So you don't know who was in that room at ten last night?"

"I can't remember. There was a crowd here last night."

"Who's your upstairs waiter?"

"He don't come on till five this afternoon."

"I didn't ask you when he came on. I asked you who he is."

Tripp picked up a packet of bills, slapped it down. "His name's Apostos. A little Greek."

"Where's he live?"

"I don't keep an address book. If it'll make you feel better, I'll send him around when he comes in."

MacBride stood up. "I'll wait till five-thirty for him. Then I'll be down seeing you—if he don't show up."

Tripp stood up, shrugged. "I'll send him over in a cab. Don't get sore, Skipper. You know I'd help you if I could."

MacBride nodded ironically from the door. "I see that. You're just breaking your heart trying to help me."

CAPT. MacBRIDE stopped in a one-arm restaurant, grabbed a hurried luncheon and hopped a taxi back to Headquarters. He breezed through the central room with a nod to Otto Bettdecken at the desk, took the stairway up in a swift, long-legged stride and reached his office.

Moriarity was pacing up and down trailing great clouds of cigar smoke, and MacBride, making a neat pitch, hung his hat on the costumer in the corner and said:

"Where'd you get the lousy cigar, Mory?"

Moriarity pointed to a box on the desk. "You ought to know. They're yours."

"So now you're aping Kennedy, huh? Mooch, mooch—it's getting so around here that anything I don't lock up or nail down—"

"But what I was starting to say, and maybe this'll take your mind off the cigars—" Mory stopped and spat into a cuspidor, raised level eyes, lowered his voice. "I was just down to Tony Matteo's house. I ain't busting out in a rash of joy over what I picked up there."

"Spring it"

"Nick Matteo."

"What about him?"

Moriarity spread his palms. "He didn't come home last night."

MacBride, half out of his overcoat, stopped, said: "Go ahead, Mory."

"That's all there is. He walked out of the house while all the twenty-seven relatives were there. In the crowd he wasn't missed. They stayed there most of the night. Then he was missed. Tony the old man don't know what to think, but he's thinking the worst. One of the relatives remembered that Nick said he was going out for some butts.

Everybody was balled up, but this cousin by marriage said he thought it was about midnight. I like dagos when they're good people—and these are—but I go absolutely ga-ga trying to get a straight story. But it gets down to that: young Nick Matteo walked out of his house at midnight for a pack of butts and he hasn't showed up yet. If that ain't a monkey wrench in the machinery, knock me down with a feather."

MacBride took off his overcoat, hung it up and grabbed one of three telephones on the desk: "Hello, Davis. MacBride.... Get this. Nick Matteo, brother of Rose Matteo, murdered in her home last night, walked out of his house at about midnight last night. Last heard or seen of him. Broadcast that on the short wave and buzz all the precincts. That's all."

He hung up, grabbed another phone. "Otto, this is MacBride. Nick Matteo pulled a fade-out last night following the murder of his sister. Tell the Italian Squad to get the lead out of their pants. That's all."

He slammed the receiver into the hook, ran his hands back over his hair. "I don't go crazy about that news, Mory."

"Look. You remember Nick said that the dummy of the pair made signs to his pal just before the two scrammed?"

"Yeah."

"Might have been the dummy wanted to let Nick have it too. Might have been that after they scrammed they thought it over and figured it would be a good idea." He paused, inhaled cigarette smoke. "Kennedy has the right idea, I'd say. There's a lousy crowd in this town going to show the people that Mulvaney is a fake. Rose was only the beginning."

MacBride said: "Grab Ike, Mory. You and Ike slam through Little Italy and see what you can pick up."

Moriarity went out and MacBride dropped to his swivel chair, laid both fists on the desk and stared hard into space. He had thought all along, during that peaceful month, that crime was too silent, too inert. Systematically, thoroughly, he had cleaned out the more obvious crime nests of the city; had wiped the slot-machines out of speakeasies and poolrooms; had dusted out the notorious beer flats of the South Side. Progress, he reflected, had been too steady, too sure. He thought of the Matteo family and knew what another death in the family would mean to it. He was in his bitterest stratum of thought when the door opened and three men came in: Hovig, the Fourth Ward alderman; Samuels, commissioner for highways; Inspector Hartman of H.Q.

Hovig was bovine, pink-cheeked, as broad as he was thick. He had an ingratiating smile and an eloquent bow. "Hello, Captain. We thought you wouldn't be busy—"

"I'm always busy, gentlemen. What's on your mind?"

Inspector Hartman was a gaunt-faced dark man with a ramrod back. "Just a little thing, Skipper. Pete Hovig, you know, is the grandad of the Fourth Ward and likes to keep things nice and smooth over there. Tripp, the owner of the *Rendezvous,* called up and said you hit his joint this morning like a bat out of hell and got all steamed up."

"I guess Tripp never saw me steamed up."

Hartman waited a moment, then said: "No man blames you for carrying out your duty, Skipper, but it's kind of nasty to jump all over a guy just because he can't tell you what you want to know. Tripp's always been pretty peaceful—"

MacBride cut in: "I asked Tripp a question. I've been asking men questions long enough to know when I'm being kidded."

Hovig waved his fat body to and fro. "But look, Captain. Tripp didn't do no harm. You asked him a question and he couldn't answer because he didn't know and right away you heap all kinds of abuse on his head. For twelve years I've been a' alderman in the Fourth Ward and cops usually consult me when—"

"I don't have to consult anybody when I want to ask a man a few questions and I don't give a good damn whose ward it's in."

Inspector Hartman said: "MacBride, you can't run this police department. Lay off the Fourth Ward. Tripp's always been a decent guy and if you try to padlock his joint he'll open it inside of twenty-four hours."

"With the help, I suppose, of friends."

"Think what you want, but bear in mind that this is not a one-man police department."

Hovig held up his fat palms. "Please, gentlemen, don't get in no arguments now. Nobody wants to argue and make hard feelings. We all want to do right by Captain MacBride—"

"So I imagine." MacBride stood up. "I'm not asking for favors and I'm not giving any. The longer I work at this job the more I think I ought to have taken up farming. But I'm a cop, I've been a cop for years, and I've got a one-track mind. Murder's murder and I'll carry an investigation through any ward I feel like."

Hovig smiled, bowed, said: "But what on earth gave you any reason to believe that something was wrong at Tripp's last night?"

"I got a steer."

"But who—"

MacBride shook his head. "Nix, Mr. Hovig. If I let go the name of the man who dropped a bug in my ear I might be signing his death warrant." He turned away from the desk, strode to the window, leaned on the sill and stared somberly down into the street.

Inspector Hartman came over and said tautly: "You want to watch that loud mouth of yours, Skipper!"

Hovig complained: "He as much as said—"

MacBride stood up, swiveled. "If you men can't stand my loud mouth, then don't come around my office and try to tell me my job! And if you come around again—knock!"

THE working body of the Police Department dusted the length and breadth of the city in its search for young Nick Matteo. MacBride had a great affection for the uniformed force and for the common run of plainclothes men. He knew they could be depended on and he knew they were many and loyal to the shield they wore. Scores of them had worked with him during his many years in the precincts and at Headquarters.

The trouble, he knew, lay in the higher reaches of the department—close to him, close around him. Too many high police officials were reaching out and tasting of the political pie. Too many promotions were effected because smart young men worked with the unscrupulous politicos towards shady ends. MacBride had never been affluent; he was always in debt, there were bills always to be met; graft lay around him within easy reach but he scowled at it, went on driving a shabby car, went on being in debt.

Following an interview with the Police Commissioner at four that afternoon, he left Eckhardt's office with dull red color under his cheekbones and sweat in his palms. He thought it over for ten minutes in his office, then put on hat and coat and walked eight blocks to City Hall. Still he hesitated, and walked twice around the building before entering. Finally he walked into Mayor Mulvaney's office. Mulvaney, for all the storm and furor he had created, was himself an unostentatious man behind rimless nose-glasses. He had a quiet, crisp voice, graying hair and a grave, prelatic manner.

"It's good to see my chiefest ally," he said.

MacBride's face was grim, hard and stubborn about the jaw. "I'm doing something, Mr. Mayor, I've never done before."

"Come, come, Captain. You look guilty. Of what?"

"I've been a cop for years and I've taken orders and if I didn't like them I've closed my trap. I hate to do this, but I've got to." His voice was low, thick, constricted. "Commissioner Eckhardt's been a pretty square boss and I think he's doing what maybe he thinks is the right thing. But I can't see it. Do you know that Marvin case? About the big-shot forger skipped the city three months ago?"

"Go on."

"Well, I'm detailed to grab a ship for Europe and bring him back."

Mulvaney said: "H'm." He frowned studiously down at his hands. "I hate to countermand an order given by Commissioner Eckhardt. I've made a rule to let him do with the personnel of his department as he saw fit. I have given him orders, made explicit demands. But this—" He shrugged, took off his glasses, polished them while eyeing MacBride. "Don't want to go, eh?"

"I've never been abroad. I don't know the lingo. I think I ought to stay here."

Mulvaney placed his glasses back upon his nose. He said: "Did anybody see you come over here?"

"Your secretary saw me come in."

"That all?"

"That's all."

"Then keep it under your hat." Mulvaney picked up a telephone, called Headquarters. "Commissioner Eckhardt?... This is the mayor. Beginning immediately I should like to have Captain MacBride transferred.... Yes, transferred! To my office.... Yes. And he's to bring with him such men as he may see fit to help him in the duties of his transfer.... That is all, Mr. Eckhardt."

KENNEDY finished the tumbler of dago ink and the empty glass rang as he planked it to the white porcelain kitchen table upon which he sat, legs dangling. Guido Matteo, who was Tony Matteo's brother, refilled the glass from a pitcher and said:

"All around I have asked about da Nick. All over"—he waved a long arm—"heesa friends say, no, dey no see Nick. And-a my brud', my sis', my uncle—all around. Dis-a Nick no dere. Among-a twenty-six whatcha call relations"—he shook his shaggy head—"no Nick is-a dere. Whatsa man-a gonna do, huh?" He sighed lugubriously and let his broad shoulders sag.

Approximately fifteen of the relations were in Tony Matteo's living-room, and three young girls were engaged in washing dishes at the kitchen sink. Mrs. Matteo was abed suffering from collapse. Tony was in the living-room with his relations, at times quiet, at other times mad and excited. The male relations had been urging wine on him.

Kennedy tried some more ink, said: "What do you think about Nick, Guido?"

"Nick? Is-a fine boy. No drink, no run around wit' da women. Of course— shoo—some women, but not alla time. Study to be whatcha call-a de accountant. Be great-a help Tony's beezness."

"Not if these hot potatoes bumped him off, huh?"

"Sh!" Guido Matteo hissed and threw an apprehensive glance towards the other room. "No letta Tony hear dat!" He dropped his voice but it took on a savage, snarly tone. "I'm afraid dat whatcha joost say, Meester Kennedy, ain't all wrong. And if deesa guys did away wit' Nick..." He lifted a hand, clenched the fingers slowly, said: "Guido take out da knife he-bring from Italy thirty years ago. Guido go hunting, by jeese!"

Kennedy downed the last of the wine, stared sleepily into space for a long moment, looked at Guido, then looked down at the empty glass.

"Guido…" He slipped to the floor, took hold of Guido's tie, felt of the material. "Guido, you don't know these girls Nick ran around with?"

Guido jerked a thumb aloft. "Opstairs in Nick's room dere's a telephono. Hanging on de telephono is leetle book… got numbers in it. Come, you take a look."

It was ten minutes later when Kennedy left Tony Matteo's house. It was half-past four by his strap-watch. He walked four blocks, entered a cigar store, made his way into a telephone booth and drew a slip of paper from his pocket. He spent ten minutes making various telephone calls, hung up, bought a package of cigarettes and lingered on the curb for a few moments smoking and thinking. It was getting colder and he huddled his spare shoulders in his threadbare overcoat.

He flagged a taxi, climbed in, gave an address and rode for fifteen minutes. Alighting at a corner drug-store, he walked down a street of brownstone houses, entered one near the middle of the block and peered at the name plates in the vestibule. He pushed open the hall door and climbed a flight of stairs and in the corridor above he knocked at a door and stood teetering back on his heels.

Presently the door opened and a girl's face appeared there, indistinct in the dim light of the room.

"Hello, Maureen," said Kennedy lazily.

"Who—who are you?"

"I just called you up."

"But I said—"

"I know," he interrupted unhurriedly. "Don't be frightened, Maureen." He worked his way into the room, closed the door and leaned back against it.

The girl cried in a low whisper: "What do you want?"

"I'll tell you, Maureen. I called seven numbers and I came to this address because your voice sounded the most frightened of the lot."

He strolled across the room, raised the shades a little higher and sat down on the arm of an overstuffed chair. He spun his hat on a forefinger and after a while the girl came over timidly and sat down opposite him.

"What do you want here?"

"What do you know about Nick?"

Her voice rushed out: "I told you I know nothing. I told you over the phone—"

"I heard that. How long have you known Nick?"

"A year—about."

"See him a lot?"

"Now—and then."

"He like you?"

"What a question to ask me!"

"You like him?"

She said: "I like him."

Kennedy kept spinning his hat. "You wouldn't think of double-crossing him, would you?"

"I tell you—I tell you I know nothing about him."

"I didn't ask you that, Maureen."

Her hands were clenched. "I don't know what you think I am! Who are you? What right have you—"

"Calm, calm," he drawled.

"I haven't seen Tony for three days, I tell you! I don't know what you're thinking or what you're trying to find out!"

He started to say something—stopped, let his eyes slide to the floor, along the floor, and dropped his head way down. He rose quietly, looked at the girl, a hardness creeping into his usually slack mouth, an ember now in each usually placid eye. He turned and went swiftly on tiptoe across the room, grabbed hold of the doorknob, whipped open the door.

In the dimness of the corridor a shape wheeled away with startled outcry.

"Hey, you!" Kennedy clipped.

Feet drummed down the stairway and Kennedy darted to the head of the stairway, had taken four downward steps by the time the front door slammed shut. He reached the bottom, stumbled to the hall door, got it open and slapped his way out of the vestibule. Reaching the sidewalk, he caught sight of a coat tail vanishing around the corner.

He broke into a run. He was not a fast man on his feet and his legs wobbled a bit. There was nothing of the athlete about him. His breath pumped hoarsely from his throat and the strain of unnatural exertion told on his face. But he loped around the corner as a heel disappeared around the corner beyond. Later, in a catacomb of crooked, blind alleys, he stopped and leaned against a house wall, rubbed his chest and panted and used a handkerchief to rub clammy sweat from his face. Once, a long time ago, he had been a fairly good amateur boxer, but he had taken to the primrose path. Only his nerve, his brain, remained.

He turned at last and made his way back to the brownstone house. He did not go quickly, for his breath hammered his chest and his legs shook. He climbed the stairway and rapped on the door and when there was no answer he tried the knob. But it was an old-fashioned house, and there was a key on his ring that opened the door.

The girl had gone. He ransacked the closet and the bureau drawers and in one of the upper, smaller drawers he found a small cardboard box. After a moment he pocketed this, got a drink of water in the bathroom and left the small apartment.

He walked to the corner and climbed into a taxi. Twenty minutes later he alighted before Headquarters, held up a coin:

"Heads I pay you double, tails I don't pay at all."

"Nix on dat racket, bud. De fare's ninety cents."

"Tsk, tsk! No enterprise at all!"

He paid up and made his way into the central room and climbed to MacBride's office.

A clerk said: "Captain's not in."

"Where'd he go?"

"I think he went over to Tripp's *Rendezvous.*"

"In good humor?"

The clerk pointed: "Going out, he slammed the office door so hard he busted the glass panel."

"Swell! The old potato's back in form!"

He swung away and broke into a half-hearted, limping run.

A GIRL opened the door of Tripp's *Rendezvous* and MacBride strode past her, bringing into the foyer a gust of the cold outdoors and a tang of rich, strong pipe tobacco. The pipe was clamped in one side of his mouth and his fedora rode low over his eyes. He hit the swing-door with his fist and it whipped open and he struck his heels into the bar, shot keen, windy eyes over a dozen cocktail drinkers, looked into the dining-room, then headed for the rear hall and opened Tripp's office.

Tripp, in dinner clothes, had been on the point of coming out.

MacBride, kicking the door shut with his heel, took his hot pipe from his mouth, snapped a spurt of smoke downward.

"Well, that Greek —— didn't show up, Tripp."

Tripp was using a silk handkerchief to dust ash from a lapel. He was casual: "The hell you say. He left here at five sharp. I saw him in the car."

MacBride was unpleasant: "That's a lot of crap."

"Yeah? I hate to argue with you, Cap, but I went outside and saw Apostos get in the car. The hat-check girl saw me. I'd be a sap to say I sent him if I didn't. What would I gain?"

MacBride scooped up a telephone, called Headquarters. "Hello, Otto. This is MacBride.... Has that Greek turned up looking for me?... I get you. Thanks."

He hung up. "Nothing doing, Tripp." He made fists of his hands and jammed them against his sides and his pipe jutted uncompromisingly from one corner of his mouth. "That Greek knew who was up in that room last night and the Greek hasn't turned up to see me. The guys who were in that room knew about the murder of Rose Matteo and they were happy that she was murdered. Why? Because she was due to get her eyesight back and when she got it back she would have been able to identify guys."

Tripp flared up. "You're as much as saying that I'm going around town bumping janes off!"

"I said nothing of the sort. But I intend to find out who was in that room talking about the murder. Where's that Greek?"

"I tell you I sent him to your office at five!"

"Then where'd he go?"

"How the hell do I know?"

"Tripp—" MacBride went close to him, suddenly grabbed him by both lapels. "I'm a swell guy to play along with and there's no guy ever regretted playing along with me. You're lying, Tripp. You're lying all over the place!"

Tripp muttered: "Don't get tough, Skipper. You've got no right to come in here and manhandle me! Take your paws off!"

"You listen to me, Tripp—"

"Take 'em off!" Tripp wrenched free, stepped back, his eyes white and glassy. "To hell with your questions! I don't have to answer them and I won't! If you want me to, go round and try getting a subpoena! Outside of that, nerts to you!"

He spun on his heel, yanked open the office door and banged out.

MacBride did not move directly. He took the pipe from his mouth, spat into a cuspidor. He had drawn hard on the pipe and his tongue burned. He knocked out the bowl, blew through the stem to clear it, put the pipe away in the breast pocket of his overcoat. He was, momentarily, up against it. He ground palms together, took a yank at his hat brim, walked to the door. He opened it and passed into the hall, went on to the bar. He had no intention, really, of slamming a lock on the *Rendezvous*. It had been a threat and it had not worked. It had not worked, he reasoned, because Tripp was too heavily subsidized.

Reaching the bar, MacBride stood back on his heels, undecided, toying with thoughts that revolved in the back of his head. He was roused by the sounds of scuffling and angry voices in the front corridor. Hands in overcoat pockets, he went across the bar, shouldered aside the swing-door and saw a knot of men tussling near the front door. He went forward unhurriedly, planting one foot rhythmically after the other.

"Fight?" he asked.

Tripp swung around, his hard white cuffs protruding inches from his coat-sleeves. Two waiters were trying to hold down Kennedy. Kennedy's hat was on the floor and his hair, hardly ever parted, was a shambles now, and his tie was well over to one side of his collar.

MacBride said: "Are you drunk again, Kennedy?"

"I told the mugg—"Tripp began.

Kennedy snapped: "You big bum, isn't this a speakeasy? Aren't speakeasies open to the public?"

"Cut this out," MacBride chopped in. "You guys—take your hands off him.... You drunk, Kennedy?"

Kennedy regained his hat, punched the crown into shape. He drawled: "Nah, I'm not drunk." He was staring at Tripp. "So this watering-trough of yours—"

"Enough of that!" Tripp clipped. "I told you you can't come in my place and that stands!"

A slim young man in a natty derby, natty blue overcoat, leaned against the wall and calmly drew on a cigarette. Kennedy flopped around from one foot to the other, slapped on his hat, yanked at his tie. MacBride took a step, took Kennedy by the arm.

"Come on, Kennedy."

"Now hold your ponies—"

"Out, bozo!"

MacBride half-carried him out of the place and once on the sidewalk stepped him briskly up the street. When they reached the first corner, the skipper stopped, thrust hands into his pockets and eyed Kennedy sharply.

"So what, Kennedy?"

Kennedy leaned against a pole. "I was looking for you, old tomato— looking for you."

"And I'm looking for a Greek by the name of Apostos. When I find that baby I'll dust off the seat of his pants so thorough that they'll look like a mirror. By any chance, would you know this guy Apostos?"

"I never admitted knowing Greeks. But if you want to find out where the guy lives we can call up that Greek newspaper. But wait. I've got a nice bughouse fable for you—"

"What's the telephone number? Come on, come on—you're drunk and I'm in no mood to hear bughouse fables. What's the telephone number, baby?"

"Richmond 1001. But look here—"

"Hold that pole up till I come out."

MacBride barged into the cigar store on the corner, entered a telephone booth and spent two minutes at the instrument. He came out jotting down a number.

"Hotel Grecian," he said. "We'll get a cab."

"Now listen to me, you big flatfoot— I'm not drunk. I tell you that down at 112 Esmond Street is a girl—"

"Taxi! Hey, cab!"

"Is a girl that knows young Nick Matteo and when I quizzed her she got all stirred up and a guy was listening at the door and when I jumped him and chased him for six blocks and lost him and came back to land on the girl again she was gone."

"Okey, boss," said the taxi driver, pulling up at the curb.

"Wait a second," MacBride said. He looked at Kennedy: "Why didn't you tell me that?"

Kennedy slapped himself in the face. "Maybe I'm goofy!"

"In, Kennedy," MacBride said, and handed Kennedy into the cab, dropped down beside him. "Now what about this girl?"

Kennedy told him and when he had finished, withdrew from his pocket the small cardboard box he had taken from the girl's bureau drawer. He shook it and it rattled.

He said: "There are eight .32 auto cartridges left in it. She must have grabbed the gun and beat it while I was chasing this other guy. A gun-moll maybe."

"Esmond Street's on our way.... Okey, driver—112 Esmond Street and step on it.... What's her name, Kennedy?"

"Maureen McGivney. A wild Irish rose."

"Why did those muggs want to pitch you out of the *Rendezvous?*"

"Hell knows. They probably figured that I was the little bird flew to you with the crack about hearing voices in that room."

"I didn't tell them."

"Who said you did?... Did anybody pick up Nick Matteo's body yet?"

"No. I've got the river police on the job. They may have chucked him in the river."

Kennedy peered out of the cab window. "Say, I need a drink. There's Joe's—"

"Keep going, driver," MacBride said.

Five minutes later the cab drew up in front of 112 Esmond Street. Dusk had begun to settle rapidly and lighted windows shone, street lights glimmered in the wintry thoroughfare.

MacBride said: "Wait here, driver."

Kennedy joined him and they entered the house, climbed the stairs. MacBride reached the top eight steps ahead of Kennedy, waited with a hand on the banister.

"That one," Kennedy said, pointing.

MacBride walked down the corridor, rapped on the door and put his ear to the panel. There was no response. Kennedy came up beside him, took out his ring of keys, inserted a key and opened the door. The apartment was empty. It looked the same as when Kennedy had visited it before.

MacBride swiveled, said: "I can't waste time here. Come on." He headed for the door.

Kennedy locked it and they went down to the street.

"Listen, kid," MacBride said. "Suppose you keep an eye on this place. Stay here. I'll phone and have either Moriarity or Cohen come down to help you."

"But I need a drink. I've been running around—"

"I'll tell 'em to pick up a bottle on the way."

"Make it Scotch."

MacBRIDE climbed into the cab and drove off. He stopped at a drug-store three blocks farther on, made a telephone call, returned to the cab and gave the address of the *Grecian Hotel*. It was a ride of ten minutes through narrow, winding streets, hilly and badly lighted. Freemont Street was wider, brighter, noisier, and halfway down the hill the *Grecian Hotel* stood on the right, a drab three-storied building of rusty brick.

"A lad named Apostos," MacBride said to the fat, swart man at the desk.

"I'll call him."

"Never mind. I'm a cop." He showed a badge. "Room?"

"Upstairs—209."

There was no elevator. MacBride's heels rang on the brass strips that held down the staircase runner. The upstairs-hall was wide, low, paved with warped and faded linoleum and the lights were dim and far apart. The skipper headed down the hall, spotted 209 near the end. He was reaching a hand for the knob when the door opened and a man backed out carrying a suitcase.

MacBride grabbed him. "Going places?"

The man spun around, dropped his suitcase and reared back so violently that his head banged against the wall, his hat was knocked to the floor.

"Pick it up," MacBride said.

The man picked it up. His chubby little face lost color and his eyes became round, his mouth made a sickly grimace.

"Jeese, boss—"

"Yeah, I know, I know. Stand me up on a date, will you?... Go on, I've got a mind to smack you in the ear." He shoved Apostos against the door and the door sprang inward and MacBride said: "Inside, you." And scaled the suitcase in after him. He closed the door.

Apostos cringed backward across the room and croaked: "Now look, boss—now listen—"

"Sure." MacBride grinned ironically. "I intend to listen, so start your story."

"I tell you—"

"No hooey, Apostos. Why didn't you come to my office?"

Apostos choked: "I couldn't. I tell you—I couldn't!"

"Why?"

"Please, boss—it's all around town you're a tough cop and I didn't want to—I was scared outta my shoes—"

MacBride grabbed a fistful of Apostos' vest and plastered him against the wall, held him there with a rigid arm. "What I want, sweetheart, is information. Who told you to skin out of town? Come on before I lose my temper!"

Apostos cried: "Nobody, boss! Nobody told me to leave! Me—I just got scared. I didn't have the guts to go down there and face you, I ain't done nothing—only all my life I been afraid of cops account of when I was a little kid a dago cop beat me over the head with a nightstick."

"That'd make nice reading in a sob column, Apostos, but to me it's just a lot of bushwha." He shook the man violently. "Damn you, I haven't got all night! Talk!" He flung Apostos on the bed, leveled an arm at him. "Did Tripp put you in a cab at five tonight?"

"Y-yes!"

"Did he tell you to come to my office or did he tell you to fade away? I want the truth, Apostos, or so help me I'll wipe this room up with you!"

Apostos scrambled off the bed, grabbed MacBride's arm. "Listen, boss! For God's sake, listen! I got to get out of town. If I stay around here my life ain't gonna be worth a cent. Gimme a break, boss, and I'll tell you. I know you don't have to gimme a break, but I'm asking you. I ain't ever done a wrong thing in my life. All my life I worked for a living. Listen, boss—see me to the railroad station, will you?" He looked at his watch. "I gotta make a train that leaves in twelve minutes. Will you, boss? I'll tell you going over in a cab. I got to make that train—honest."

MacBride stared down at the pleading eyes, the shivering lips. He said: "Okey, Apostos. I get you. Grab your bag and step on it. Where you heading for?"

"New York. I'm grabbing a boat in the morning for the old country."

"Quick. Out."

Apostos lugged his bag into the hall and MacBride followed, slammed the door, and prodded Apostos towards the head of the stairs. They went down to the lobby, on through to the front door and out beneath the old glass marquee where light flooded the sidewalk.

MacBride yelled for a taxi and they stood on the curb waiting for one to draw up.

From the mouth of an alleyway across the street three jets of flame spurted, three explosions knotted with one another. Apostos was standing in front of MacBride. He fell against MacBride, dropping his suitcase, crying out—turned and clutched frantically at the skipper's coat, cried "Save me!" in a broken voice.

MacBride tried to get his gun out. He couldn't because Apostos was clawing at his arms, clinging to him. The skipper grabbed hold of Apostos, held him up.

"Easy, boy," he muttered grimly.

"Oh, Jeese—it hurts—it hurts—"

Automobiles had stopped. Pedestrians had stopped, horrified; some had plunged into nearby doorways. MacBride picked Apostos up, held him in his arms—backed up and went backwards up the steps into the hotel lobby. Heads appeared warily from behind chairs and tables.

"Get a doctor," MacBride said.

He laid Apostos down in a cracked leather divan. The Greek's eyes were rolling.

MacBride said in a clogged voice:

"I'm sorry, Apostos. Who did it, kid?"

Apostos' mouth worked, the whites of his eyes shone. He choked out: "Tripp—oughta—know."

His head fell back, rolled to one side.

A couple of uniformed cops came in on the run.

MacBride said: "There's a doctor on the way but I don't think he'll need one. Better buzz the morgue."

"Who did it, Cap?"

But MacBride was on his way out, hard-heeled.

DINNER and dancing at the *Club Rendezvous....*

The bar was alive, bubbling with good-humored conversation inspired by drinks mixed and delivered by two bartenders. In the dining-room off the bar an orchestra throbbed out a low, haunting blues song. Couples danced beneath a large multi-colored lamp that revolved slowly and bathed the dancers in a succession of changing colors. Waiters sped nimbly along the edge of the floor and the dreamy-eyed orchestra leader waved, dreamily, a thin shiny baton.

Everyone was in evening dress.

MacBride appeared at the bar, ruddy-faced, bony-jawed, something dark and threatening in his eyes. He looked about, pushed his way through the crowd, entered Tripp's office. Tripp was not in.

The skipper swung about and returned to the bar and blocked the headwaiter.

"Where's Tripp, you?"

"I guess he stepped out."

"Try to stop guessing."

"Okey. He stepped out."

"When?"

"I don't know. It must have been about an hour ago."

"Where'd he go?"

The headwaiter shrugged. "I'm damned if I know. He said he wouldn't be long. Will you excuse me? I got a big party to seat in there."

The man hurried off and MacBride stood biting his lip, darting his eyes angrily about the bar. He took a quick trip upstairs, fanned the rooms, found them empty and came down again. He again looked in Tripp's office, then left the bar, went out into the street and leaned there in the shadows. Cars drove up, people got out and entered the club and the cars drove off again. It was cold in the shadows and MacBride tapped his shoes on the pavement, crammed and lighted a pipe.

He waited half an hour and was about to leave when a limousine came swiftly down the street, stopped with a quiet complaint of brakes. The tonneau door opened and Tripp hopped out, sped across the sidewalk and entered the club. The man at the wheel of the limousine was in livery, and as he geared the car off, MacBride, instead of following Tripp, darted from the shadows and leaped on to the limousine's steel luggage rack.

It was not an uncomfortable seat, and he noticed that the car sped through dark, quiet streets. He watched the street signs and catalogued in his mind the limousine's course. Ten minutes later it slowed down in a dark street of two-and three-storied brick and frame houses, and presently it stopped. MacBride stepped from the luggage rack, crouched back of the car and saw the chauffeur enter a two-story frame house.

After a moment MacBride stood up, ran his eyes up across the face of the house. He thought he heard the scrape of a shoe across the street and spun around. But he saw nothing. He peered hard and listened intently. It occurred to him that if anything were wrong about the house, a lookout might be stationed nearby. He had no desire to walk up to the door and make of himself an easy target.

After a moment he walked away down the street, turned right at the next corner, walked a block and turned right again. Going up the street that paralleled the one in which the limousine had parked, he counted houses; and when he had walked half a block, scaled a wooden fence and prowled up an alley, into a backyard. He pried his way through a hole in another fence, entered another yard and went down an alley to where a wooden fence, six feet wide, made a dead end. Peering over the fence, he saw the limousine parked out front.

He retraced his steps up the alley, forced his way through a basement window and dropped into a damp basement. Groping, he found a wooden staircase and followed it to a door at the head. The door gave and he was in the street level corridor. He crept to the front of the hall and found the door secured by a snap-lock. There was also a chain bolt, unhooked. He hooked it and stood for a moment in the darkness.

Then he heard heavy footsteps coming down the stairway. He sped to the shadow of the stair-well, crouched there. The footfalls reached the lower hall and MacBride peered out. He saw a match spring to life, saw the face and uniform cap of the chauffeur in the brief glow of the match. Then the match went out and the slow footfalls moved on.

MacBride heard the door open, heard it grate against the chain-bolt. There was a moment of silence. The door closed and then quick footsteps sped on the wooden floor, sped up the stairway. MacBride came out of the shadow of the stair-well and crept to the foot of the stairway. He saw light in the hallway above.

A hoarse voice said: "Listen! Jeese, listen! When I just went down the chain-bolt on the door was on!"

A tense but quieter voice said: "You put it on?"

"No! That's why I come up to tell you! It got put on between the time I come up and went down! There's something screwy—something creepy about this!"

"Shut up! Keep your head!"

"I know, but—"

"Shut up! Get inside!"

"There's someone—"

"In, I said!"

MacBride hauled out his gun and rushed up the stairs and reached the top in time to see two men crowded in a doorway. The chauffeur threw a frightened look over his shoulder, ducked, put his hands behind his head and plunged on into the room. The other man fell down, cursing.

"Watch it, you!" MacBride barked.

He had his gun raised as he stopped in the doorway. The man on the floor wriggled into the room, stumbled to his feet. The room was large, well-furnished, comfortable. The chauffeur was standing by a blind fireplace, his back to the door, his hands still behind his head.

Alderman Hovig had made a blundering attempt to reach another door. Failing, he turned and seemed uncertain whether to show anger or red-faced embarrassment. Samuels, the commissioner of highways, had spilled a drink down his vest and was industriously drying it with a handkerchief. A box-headed man sat stonily at a table near a telephone and the man who had fallen down was now dusting and straightening his clothes.

MacBride pointed with his gun: "I've seen you before."

The man snarled: "I wouldn't fall over with surprise at that crack."

Highways Commissioner Samuels said: "Things have come to a fine state when policemen break into law-abiding houses—"

"Sing that song out the window," MacBride cut in.

"Now, now, now," Hovig chimed in, bowing. "There's no need for everyone to get excited. We must understand that Captain MacBride was pursuing what he thought was duty. We must consider." He shrugged, rubbed his fat palms together. "All of us make little mistakes—"

"Oh, so that's it! Now I'm making mistakes!" MacBride tightened his bony jaw and looked at the man who was still dusting off his clothes. "Didn't I see you in Tripp's tonight?"

"Did you?"

"In the hall there—when they were giving Kennedy the bum's rush." He nodded to himself. "Of course I did! And what was Tripp doing here tonight?"

Hovig stumbled from one foot to the other. "Tripp!"

"Yes, Tripp. Listen to me, you big shots and you other guys here— you little rats. I saw Tripp get out of that car at his joint and I tailed the car to this address. Apostos, his Greek waiter, was bumped off tonight—right on my hands. He was bumped off because he was the guy served a crowd in one of Tripp's rooms a couple hours after Rose Matteo was given the works. Apostos was to come to my office at five-thirty this evening. He never came. He was warned not to. Rose Matteo's gone. Her brother's gone. Apostos is gone—"

"Please—please!" implored Hovig. "What has all that to do with us?"

"This, my prize alderman! Samuels here wanted that paving contract to go to Porshook. So did you, Mr. Alderman! So did a lot of other grifters in your lousy Fourth Ward. Matteo got the contract. A lot of you guys were gypped out of about forty thousand dollars. So one day some heels walk into Matteo's office intending to wreck it. His clerk started to grab a phone and got lead in his belly and died and then one of the heels thought it would be a swell idea to toss a vial of acid in Rose Matteo's face—"

Highways Commissioner Samuels thumped the table. "I refuse to stand for these insinuations!"

"Refuse and see if I care! You tried to keep me from landing on Tripp. You tried to have me shipped to Europe to bring a guy back. All you birds are trying to make a jackass out of the finest mayor this city's ever had! And out of me! Matteo's place was jumped, his daughter was blinded, because Matteo had the guts to try to turn an honest deal—"

The man whom the chauffeur had knocked down said: "This cop is raving mad!"

The box-headed man seated at the table began drumming with his fingers.

Hovig mopped his face and said: "Captain, if you would only listen. If you would only calm yourself—"

"What I'm going to do," said MacBride, "is pinch Tripp. And I'll tell you why. Apostos, just before he croaked, said Tripp ought to know who bumped him off. Now all of you stand just where you are. Not a move out of any of you. Tripp's no killer, but his place has been a port of call for a lot of you thirsty guys—and Tripp will talk."

He stood with his gun leveled. "You at the table there. Grab that phone and call Headquarters. Ask for either Cohen or Moriarity. Whoever is there, tell him I said to slam over to the *Rendezvous* and pick up Tripp. And send the wagon here."

The box-headed man leaned back, smirked, laughed shortly and lit a cigarette.

MacBride ground out: "Pick up that phone—"

"I'll phone," Hovig said. "Once and for all we'll clean this nonsense up—"

"You'll stay right where you are," MacBride told him.

"But if I'm willing—"

"I told you what to do!"

"By ——! MacBride, I'll have you broken for this!" Hovig cried out.

"You"—MacBride was looking at the box-headed man—"pick up that phone and do what I told you."

The box-headed man's smile faded and a shadow swept down across his face. He growled hoarsely and slashed a hand through the air.

"What's the matter with you?" MacBride said.

The man growled again and started to rise and the chauffeur said: "Watch your step, Hen!"

The box-headed man roared and raised his hands and his fingers worked furiously.

MacBride clipped: "Okey, Hovig. You call. This is the guy I want. This is the dummy helped bump off Rose Matteo. Come on, Hovig, call Headquarters!"

The dummy roared, picked up the phone and hurled it savagely. The wires broke. He roared again and knocked over the table, bared his teeth and rolled his eyes. Then suddenly whipped a big revolver from his coat.

"Good ——! don't!" screamed Hovig.

MacBride's gun spoke once. The dummy reeled backwards, his arms dropping. His gun went off and put three bullets in the floor. The chauffeur dived behind a chair. The man MacBride had seen at Tripp's snapped an oath out of the side of his mouth and kicked out. His foot hit MacBride's gun-hand and the gun clattered to the floor.

The skipper brought up his left fist but the man ducked and lunged for the gun and they went down together.

Hovig cried: "Don't!"

Highways Commissioner Samuels said: "Quiet, Hovig! This cop found things out and he's been working alone. He knows too much. Stay out of it!"

"But—"

"Stay out of it or else. We can't expect too much of Tripp. He'll talk if he's pressed too hard." He crossed to the chauffeur. "Run downstairs. Get the car away before anybody hears this. Bend up the plates to make sure. Quick!"

The dummy had lost his gun. He was bleeding, sagging around on his feet. He sagged across the floor, braced a hand against the wall and drove his foot at MacBride's head. MacBride groaned and fell sidewise, the gun beneath him. His opponent struck him behind the ear and tried to roll him over, tear him away from the gun. MacBride's hands groped on the floor. The dummy kicked out again, but he was weakening, his aim was poor, and he missed. Then he threw himself on MacBride and his weight flattened MacBride on the floor.

Samuels whispered: "They'll finish him, Hovig. Come on—we'd better get out of this. The back way. Through the basement. It's our only chance!"

Hovig hesitated but Samuels grabbed him by the arm and rushed him through the door.

The dummy, dying, had his hands around MacBride's throat, but MacBride had hold of the gun. He could not use it because his hands and the gun were pinned beneath him and he was pinned beneath the dead weight of the dummy. The other man was trying to yank MacBride's arms from beneath his flattened body. He was panting and growling:

"Get off, dummy! I got it if you get off!"

The dummy sighed and relaxed and his companion heaved him off MacBride, grabbed for the skipper's arms again. He punched MacBride in the head and the head banged down against the floor; the skipper groaned and shook all over. The gun was ripped from beneath him and the man stood up.

"Dummy," he cried hoarsely, "can you make it?"

The dummy lay on his back, his mouth and eyes open.

MacBride sat up, turned over and got to his knees, rose to his feet, dazed, reeling. He fell against the wall and braced himself and blood was running down his cheek.

"Okey, Skipper. You knew too much, huh? You knew the dummy and me bumped off Rose Matteo, huh? A hell of a lotta good it'll do you because you're going to get what's been coming to you for a long time. I'm going to—"

A gun blazed twice in the doorway. The man stopped talking, looked stupidly at MacBride, at MacBride's hands. Then his head moved slowly to the right. His knees buckled and his eyes rolled upward. His knees struck the floor and for an instant he was poised there in a prayerful attitude. Then he pitched forward on his face.

Young Nick Matteo stood in the doorway, somber-eyed.

MAUREEN McGIVNEY sat in the swivel chair in MacBride's office, and Moriarity paced up and down, his hands behind his back, cigarette smoke spurting from his lips. Maureen McGivney was pale and red-eyed and her hands were folded in her lap.

Moriarity was irritable. "Maybe I can't make you talk, sister, but the skipper will. And I promise you that you'll hang out in this chateau till you do come across."

"I've done nothing wrong," she said.

"Ha! I sure like the way you put that, little one."

"I tell you—"

"Cut it! You've told me enough for one sitting! I—"

The door opened and MacBride walked in. His overcoat was torn and his hat was crushed in and there was blood caked on his face. He walked to the desk, opened a drawer, pulled out a bottle of Scotch and took a long drink straight from the neck. He corked the bottle, looked at the door.

Nick Matteo appeared there, his young face grave and a little haggard.

Maureen jumped up. "Nick!"

"Hello, Maureen," he said dully, his eyes on the floor.

MacBride held the bottle up. "Drink, Nick?"

"No, thanks, Cap. I don't use it."

"Nick!" the girl cried. She ran across the office, gripped Nick Matteo's arms. "Nick—are you hurt? Is anything—"

He smiled wanly, put his hands on the girl's shoulders. "I'm all right, sugar."

The skipper dropped heavily to his swivel chair, tossed his hat on the desk. His hair was plastered down over his forehead and his eyes stared hard into space.

Moriarity tossed away his cigarette. "Hey, Cap, where you been? What you been doing? I picked the jane up in front of her house and come back here and I can't find you—"

"I got the guys killed Nick's sister, Mory. They almost got me. We're going to have a new alderman, I think, in the Fourth Ward—and a new Highways Commissioner."

Moriarity said: "I'm damned!" Then he looked at Nick, at the girl. "Where does the jane come in? I frisked her for a gun but she didn't have one."

MacBride waved a weary hand. "We had her wrong, I guess. Seems she's kind of sweet on Nick."

Nick Matteo said: "It wasn't her fault. After Rose died, I went out of the house. I had to go. All I could think of was my dead sister. I walked the streets for a while and then I went to Maureen's. She lived alone and there'd been some housebreaks in her neighborhood and I knew she kept a gun.

"So I went and got her gun. She tried to stop me but it was something no one could stop. I could think only of my dead sister. So I made Maureen promise to tell no one she'd seen me. And I took the gun and I went out and I started after the men who'd killed Rose. I wasn't known in the speakeasies. They didn't know me by sight. I kept going around and around looking for a dummy. I knew if I went long enough I'd find the man.

"And I did. Tonight. I was standing on a corner and saw two men come out of a cigar store and the one spoke and the other talked with his hands. I wasn't sure, so I followed them. I followed them to down in front of the *Grecian Hotel* and I saw them kill a man as he came out. They ran and I followed them again and they went in a house where a limousine was parked out front and I—"

MacBride said: "He saw me come down there and he followed me around the back. I busted in through the basement. He followed. I nailed these guys in a room upstairs and when I was battling the two heels Samuels and his chauffeur and Hovig slipped out. They were sure I was finished.

"Nick saw them go out the back way. He's going to be the state's star witness. Then he came upstairs. I tell you, I'm here now, Mory, only because Nick came upstairs. The dummy's dead and his pal's dying at the city hospital."

Kennedy appeared in the doorway and said: "Will Hovig's face be red?"

"Red?" MacBride chuckled harshly. "As soon as I get some ham and eggs under my belt, Kennedy, I'm going down and see Hovig.

And if you think his face'll be red, you're color blind. It'll be black, honeybunch—and blue."

"Old tomato! Old tomato!"

Farewell to Crime

Cap. Steve MacBride, the hard-boiled, can still be sorry for a man who knows how to take it.

MISS WEBB stood in the middle of the floor, man-style, feet spread and arms jammed firmly akimbo. She wore low oxfords. Her dark suit was severe and followed a severe leanness of frame. She had a long jaw, dead-white skin, black hair that was combed tightly to her head and parted on the left. A black string tie hung from the collar of a silk blouse.

She said, "Stop it." She said it in a detached, preoccupied manner.

Tessa shut up, pursing her lips so tightly that little muscles bulged at the corners of her mouth. She was younger than Miss Webb. She had loose flaxen hair, a robust figure, milky skin that was flushed now on the cheeks. She had not the cool poise of Miss Webb and moved about nervously. Her hands and feet were large.

She ventured "Shouldn't I—?"

"No." Clipped, curt, final. "Nothing. Touch nothing. Do nothing."

"It seems, Gwen—it seems I ought to do something."

"Nothing… nothing. If you're going to blubber all over the place, you might go downstairs. It's too bad about the new Aubusson, but…" She shrugged.

She bent her left arm sharply, glanced at a wrist-watch. From a pocket of her jacket she took a packet of cigarettes, lighted one, blew smoke through her nostrils. She went to one of the front windows, clasped her hands behind her back, looked down into the quiet street and squinted one eye against the column of smoke that rose from her cigarette.

Presently she said: "Here they come."

"What—what shall I do?" Tessa stammered.

Miss Webb turned, stared. "Let them in, of course. What did you think?"

"Yes, yes."

Tessa opened the door, stepped into the hallway and closed the

39

door quietly. She sniffled, wagged her head. The heavy green runner muffled the fall of her feet. She thumped down two wide flights of stairs, heard a buzzer sounding somewhere distant in the house. The halls were large, high; the walls were of old dark wood and the massive banisters shone darkly beneath high amber lights. She reached the hall door, opened it, her eyes wide and staring.

Kennedy was saying: "In those days Clement McKnight owned it. He used to follow the horses, but after a while the horses he followed, they followed other horses, so he lost all his money and his wife, the former Nancy Pelham ran away with a jockey.... Good evening, madam."

MacBride said: "Just a minute, please," to the girl and then called down the steps: "Come on, come on."

"Of course," Kennedy drawled, "that was before my time."

Moriarity and Cohen came across the sidewalk, up the steps. They had been matching quarters in the rear of the police phaeton and had dropped one down back of the seat.

"Finder's keepers," Cohen said.

"It was my quarter, though," Moriarity argued.

Impatient, MacBride growled: "In, in, you apes. Always I've got to waste time collecting you tramps."

The quartet passed into the hall. Tessa closed the door and the men straggled towards the staircase.

"Upstairs," panted Tessa.

She went ahead of them, heavy-footed, and her hand gripped the banister. With her other hand she brushed strands of loose flaxen hair from her forehead. They reached the third floor and Tessa slowed down as she neared the door. She threw a frightened look at the men. They followed in a drawn-out line, Kennedy last.

Tessa opened the door. "In here."

MacBride walked in with his hands in his overcoat pockets. His eyes flicked the room, landed on Miss Webb, stopped there. Moriarity and Cohen wandered in and Kennedy, closing the door, strayed across the room and plucked a grape from a green glass bowl.

Miss Webb nodded to an open door. "In there."

MacBride went hard-heeled to the doorway. He stopped there for a brief moment. Then he entered the other room.

Kennedy had taken possession of a bunch of grapes. He said to Miss Webb: "This is the old Clement McKnight house, you know."

"I know," she said.

He popped a grape into his mouth. "How'd it happen?"

"I'm sure I don't know."

MacBride came to the door. "Take a look at this, gang.... Did you call a doctor, Miss Webb?"

"There was no need. I used to be a nurse."

"What would you say she died of?"

"Strangulation."

He nodded, said: "The Medical Officer is on the way over."

He turned and looked at Moriarity and Cohen. They were kneeling beside the dead woman on the floor. Cohen, his face smooth and swart and expressionless, was rhythmically tossing a quarter in the air. Moriarity was gingerly running his fingers across the woman's throat. The bedroom was large, a little flamboyant, and there was the cloying odor of perfume. The woman's head lay near one leg of a large bureau. She had bled from a gash on the head.

Cohen pointed: "She fell. You can see where her head hit the leg of this doohickey. Cut her open like an ax."

Kennedy, in the living-room, had picked up a small glass object to which he was now affixing a metal top. He sneezed.

"Pepper," he said.

"What?" said Miss Webb.

"Pepper. There was pepper in this—"

He sneezed again.

Tessa gulped: "That reminds me. I heard a man sneezing—"

Miss Webb's cold dark look seemed to silence her.

MacBride came into the room saying: "What?"

"Pepper," said Kennedy. He put the pepper shaker down on a coffee table. The remnants of a brief meal remained there.

"You said?" MacBride shot at Tessa.

She seemed about to weep. "I heard a man sneeze in the hall."

"Well," said Moriarity, bobbing into the room. "I guess she's about forty five. She wasn't bad to look at in her day."

"Not very," added Cohen, appearing, tossing the coin.

"If you don't quit that," Moriarity said, "I'm going to take it away from you."

"Boo," chided Cohen.

"Hey," MacBride said, "cut it out. Shut up a minute. And you, Kennedy, stay the hell away from that fruit bowl.... Now, Miss Webb."

She ground out her cigarette in a tray, looked up at MacBride with a candid, impersonal stare.

He said: "Her name?"

"Hazel Noonan."

"Miss or Mrs.?"

"Miss."

"Lived here long?"

"About a year."

Tessa had begun crying.

Miss Webb said: "You'd better go downstairs."

"Let her stay," MacBride said. "We don't mind…. Know any of her acquaintances, Miss Webb?"

"No."

"What do you know about her?"

"Nothing. She paid her rent regularly and I rarely saw her otherwise."

"She live alone?"

"Yes."

"Have many callers?"

"I wouldn't know the number. I never watched the halls."

"Did you hear any outcry tonight?"

"No."

"What made you come up?"

"The radio was playing pretty loud here. It never had before. I sent Tessa up to ask Miss Noonan to tone it down. Tessa came running down babbling and I went up and found her dead."

"How long was the radio on before you sent Tessa up?"

"Half an hour."

"From what time to what?"

"I first heard it about eight o'clock, so it must have been about eight-thirty when I sent Tessa up."

MacBride turned on Tessa. "You said you heard a man sneezing in the hall. What time?"

"It was—it was about eight, I guess, or a little after."

"Was he going up or down?"

"I—I heard the front door slam afterwards."

Moriarity said: "It wasn't theft. There's seventy-two bucks laying on the bureau. Maybe she cut corners with a guy and he just sloughed her."

"Don't touch anything.... Mory, get a fingerprint man over here. Call the morgue, too.... Miss Webb, how many other tenants have you?"

"Three apartments rented and three single rooms."

"Any on this floor?"

"No."

"Any beneath this room?"

"An apartment like this. But the occupant's away."

"Take Mr. Cohen with you and wake everybody in the house. You, Ike—ask 'em if they saw anybody in the halls between eight and eight-thirty. Where'd Kennedy go again?"

Kennedy appeared in the bedroom doorway holding a small wooden box in his hand. "Funny thing about that old Queen Anne desk, Cap—had a secret compartment in it." He held up the box. "And look what papa found there."

"What?"

"Heroin."

"Ah!" said Moriarity from the telephone. "Happy powder!"

"Decks and decks of it," Kennedy drawled, pleased as a small boy who has found the hidden button. "Give a look, Skipper. Ten—fifteen—twenty decks of it. A dope plant, old tomato. A—huh—m'm—*Ka-choo!*"

MacBride growled: "Damn it, sneeze the other way! You think I want to catch cold?"

"Not cold. Not cold," Kennedy wheezed "Pepper...."

ABEL KANTZ, one of the Deputy Medical Examiners, telephoned MacBride next day and said: "About this Hazel Noonan. We place her death at approximately eight p.m. She fell or was pushed first and opened her head. I say this because one of your cowboys—Ike Cohen—said the leg of a bureau was bloody and that the wound bears the imprint of the bureau leg. I mean I say this because the fall, the cut dead, while it caused a lot of bleeding, didn't cause her death. She was strangled. She was strangled after she fell by a pair of strong hands. In *re* the heroin angle: she was not a user. No indications of her having ever used any kind of drug. She used alcohol. For your information also: there was blood on her teeth. Not her own blood. She must have bitten her attacker.... How is Mrs. MacBride these days?"

"Swell. And thanks for the report, Abe." The skipper hung up, chopped off: "So that's that."

"What about her?" Ike Cohen said.

"She wasn't a user. And that means only one thing." MacBride rose, made a complete circuit of his office and sat down again. He glared at Cohen but said reasonably: "It means, Isaac, that what we first thought was just an everyday bump-off is not, Isaac, an everyday bump-off. She wasn't a user. She didn't use the stuff. But she had enough stuff on hand to give a big gang the feeling that the depression's over. So what does that mean? It means, as even a sap like me can see, that she was the queen bee in a dope ring. She had the stuff—"

"I get you. And somebody wanted it. It was bunked. Kennedy found it by accident. What do you mean, guys came there and bought it?"

MacBride shook his head. "No; not in that neighborhood. She was—well, call her the wholesaler. Somebody else retailed it to the users. On the outside. She would have been a sap to have had a lot of users filing up to her apartment."

The phone rang and MacBride answered it, nodded, said: "Go ahead, I got you." He made notes. Then he hung up, said: "Mory. That was Mory. He found out she has a total in the Westminster Bank of fifteen thousand bucks. She opened an account there eleven months ago with two hundred bucks. She deposited since then twenty-five thousand and has a balance of what I said—fifteen thousand and a few cents. Not bad, huh?"

"Any will? Any legal connections?"

"No. And that"—MacBride pointed—"is going to stump us. That—and other things. Where'd she come from? We didn't find one thing in her apartment that'd lead us back over her trail. Her clothes— she had lots of them—were all bought here in Richmond City. Good clothes—but from department stores. No store in town has a record of her on a charge account. Apparently she paid cash for everything. We found no letters. No cards. She didn't even keep a list of telephone numbers. Her account at the bank was the only thing. And Mory just said that as far as he could make out all her deposits were in cash. Catch on? No names on checks no way of tagging her down that way. No pictures of herself around the place and no pictures of anybody else. And her face was so distorted at death that we couldn't get one of her then. I rushed her fingerprints to the Washington bureau by air mail, but I got a hunch that's a dead end.

"I say this. She came to Richmond City a year ago. And from the looks of her bank deposits she went right into business. What does that mean? No—don't stop me. It means that within one month she was in solid with somebody. She had her clients located and she had access to a sure supply of dope. Who'd she meet here? Who gave her the big in? Who—"

The door opened and Jahraus, a fingerprint man, came in and said: "A flock of prints, but one set's yours, one's Mory's, one's Ike's here and about nine o' them are of Kennedy's."

"Sure. He always balls things up mooching things. Grapes or apples or cigars. What else?"

"One strange pair?"

"Maybe those women."

"Nope. I got those." He laid a photographic copy down and said: "These were taken off one of the black patent leather pumps the dead dame had on. I got no record of them."

"Send a copy to Washington?"

As Jahraus went out the phone rang and MacBride hooked it towards him. "Oh, it's you, Kennedy!... What?... I get you. I'll be right over." He rose as he pronged the receiver. He said to Cohen: "Kennedy's always under foot, Ike, but he keeps his nose to the ground."

"What's he got now?"

"His words were: 'Palsy-walsy, I've been places, seen things and met people. I'd like to introduce you to a few of the facts of life, you ripe tomato.' Like that." He was into his overcoat. "Keep an eye out here, Ike. I may be right back. There's a chance that he's drunk."

He went down to the central room, found Otto Bettdecken, on desk duty, complacently munching a braunschweiger sandwich. He went on downstairs, past the pistol range and into the garage. Duffy was polishing the phaeton's bright work.

"Let's go, Duffy," the skipper said.

He found Kennedy sitting on the top step of the stone stoop that led to the vestibule of number 10 Jermine Street. Patrolman Schwartz-brau was leaning against the rail, twirling his stick.

"Who's upstairs?" MacBride asked.

"Fitzgibbons. We take turns."

"Remember, if any mail comes for the dead Noonan woman, I want it."

"I gotcha."

Kennedy finished eating an apple and tossed the core to the gutter. He stood up, a pale, slight, slouchy figure in his lop-eared hat and threadbare topcoat.

"What I thought," MacBride said. "Drunk again."

"Keeps out the germs. Besides, I was thirsty."

"D' you ever try water?"

"Once. It gave me stomach trouble." He waved languidly towards the façade of the house. "They say Clement McKnight used to throw the swellest parties here—real hi-de-ho stuff. That was before his wife run away with—"

"I don't give a damn about Clement McKnight. What did you get me down here for?"

Kennedy snapped fingers, remembering. "That's right; I did call you, didn't I?... Well, let's go."

He fumbled into the phaeton. MacBride followed briskly, slammed the door shut. He darted a sidewise, suspicious look towards Kennedy.

"Your move," he said.

Kennedy said: "Duffy, old duffer, roll the barouche to Grand Drive and Williamson."

"Huh? That's just around the corner—"

"One block north, two east. *Allez!*"

DUFFY poked the car into gear and they rolled off, turned left at the next block and swung into Grand Drive traffic. At the northwest corner of Williamson Street the phaeton stopped and Kennedy fumbled to the sidewalk. He looked at his wrist-watch.

"Just a minute or two to wait, Cap. They never did know whether Clement McKnight killed himself. He just vanished. Left the old house, plenty mortgaged, to a half-wit second cousin. Old houses, to me, are like old songs, full of the flavor—"

MacBride had taken hold of his arm. "I'd like to know, Kennedy— I'd like to know what the hell we're standing on this corner for."

Kennedy moved his chin. "It's up a bit, really. Come on."

They moved along the curb to a taxi stand. Three taxis stood in single file and the driver of the foremost nodded to Kennedy and then looked at his watch. Then he craned his neck.

"Here he comes. I go off duty now."

He climbed out of the cab and said: "Hi, Burt," as a short, red-faced man came up to the cab. He added: "Hey, Burt, mind you told me about that fare had the sneezes last night."

"Huh?"

"Burt," Kennedy said with lazy familiarity, "this is Captain Stephen J. MacBride, Police Headquarters, and I'm Kennedy of the *Free Press*. Charley means about that man you picked up at about eight-thirty last night—the man couldn't stop sneezing."

Burt brightened. "Yop. Oh, yeah—yeah; that guy. Sure. I thought he'd blow his dome off—"

MacBride pried in with—"Okey, now, Burt. It seems you picked up a sneezing man. Where'd you take him? What did he look like?"

" 'Bout tall as you, sir. Little heavier. It was cold out and he had his overcoat collar up and his hat turned down. It was one of the worst cases of sneezing I ever seen. I took him to a place in Jockey Street. A house. Maybe it was a speak. After I let him out I dropped some change and was feeling around for it. So I could hear him. He knocked on the door and it opened and he said: 'Hello, Pietro,' and went in."

"Where'd you pick him up?"

"Right here at the stand. I was parked here."

"Remember the address?"

"No. But I remember the house."

MacBride turned to the other driver. "Do me a favor, will you? Stick with the cab for about an hour. I need Burt."

"Okey, Captain."

"Come on, Burt."

They returned to the phaeton, climbed in.

MacBride said: "Jockey Street, Duffy."

By day Jockey Street was drab, dusty. Its pool-halls were silent, its garages noisy. Women in shawls leaned out of tenement-house windows and watched the produce trucks roll up from the river. Peanut roasters whistled shrilly. An old scissors grinder went up and down clanging his bell.

"That there's it," said Burt.

It was a two-story frame house wedged in between two four-story brick houses. It was an old house, with paint peeling and windows dusky with steam. Two wooden steps led to the front door. Duffy stopped the phaeton and MacBride stepped out, flexed his arms, cleared his throat sharply, strode across the sidewalk. Kennedy followed, hunched in his threadbare topcoat.

MacBride heard a heavy bolt thrown back. The door opened. A man looked out placidly. He was a broad man with a mane of black and gray hair and he stood comfortably on bowed legs. His face was large, ruddy on the cheeks, and many wrinkles spread fanwise from the corner of either eye and seemed to lift his shaggy eyebrows upward towards the temples. The broad mouth uncurled slowly in a smile, the almost hidden eyes twinkled.

MacBride turned back the lapel of his coat, showed his badge. "Headquarters," he said.

The man's expression did not change. "I am Pietro," his low, dreamy voice said.

"Swell. I'm MacBride. Want to talk to you, Pietro."

The big face radiated. "Shu… come in."

They entered a low hall, moved into a room that contained three oilcloth-covered tables. On each table was a bowl of bread-sticks, a sheaf of paper napkins. There was a piano against one wall. A horse-hair sofa. A lot of biblical pictures. A second-hand store had furnished this room and there was a shabby but cozy geniality about it. Pietro leaned back on his bowed legs.

He said: "I have notta met dis gentleman…"

"He's a reporter. Kennedy."

"Ah… so… yes."

MacBride said: "What do you do here?"

"Spaghet'… de raviol'—"

"And dago red, huh?"

"Ver' good steaks, Cap'n. You come around some time—Pietro show you wan swella steak."

A little black-haired boy of about five appeared in the doorway.

Pietro said: "Dat's my bambino. Go in to you moth', bambino. Scramma, Pietro…. You lika de raviol' Cap'n?"

MacBride had a hard, caustic eye on the Italian. "I'm looking for a guy landed here between eight and nine last night, Pete."

Pietro lit a twist of an Italian cigar, grinned while doing it. "Whatsa kinda guy, Cap'n?"

"A guy with the sneezes."

There was a crunching sound. Kennedy was sitting on one of the tables eating a breadstick.

"Pepper," said Kennedy.

Pietro grinned broadly, dreamily at him. He finished lighting the black twist, pursed his lips, blew gently at the match until the flame died.

"I'm a-scared I no see dat kinda guy," he said slowly, smiling. He remained smiling at MacBride. He let smoke drift sluggishly from his mouth and through it his teeth shone.

MacBride said: "I have a man who saw this guy come here. He saw your door open and heard the guy say: 'Hello, Pietro.'"

Pietro beamed. " 'S lotsa dagos in dissa street, Cap'n. Pietro she's a lotsa dagos' name. So whatcha call sorry."

MacBride lifted his chin. "Oh, so you're sorry. A real big-hearted, sympathetic Italian." He stopped short, darkened, and his mouth hardened, his brows came together. But suddenly the shadow left his face. He cracked a tight, lop-sided grin, swung on his heel. "Come on, Kennedy," he snapped and left the room like a blast of wind.

He reached the hall door, drew a cigar from a vest pocket, nipped savagely at the end of it. Kennedy arrived beside him. MacBride gestured aloft with the cigar.

He said: "There's one palooka I couldn't scare in a million years. He's got what it takes."

He strode across the sidewalk, heaved into the phaeton. "Headquarters, Duffy."

Kennedy got in beside Duffy.

"It's this way, Burt," MacBride said to the taxi man. "I want you to look over some muggs at Headquarters. Do you think you'd remember this guy if you saw him again?"

"I think I might, Cap'n. I can't just describe him, though."

MacBride took Burt down to the Bureau of Criminal Identification and set him loose in the Rogues' Gallery. But Burt turned up nothing. They went up to the central room and MacBride left Burt standing near the desk and crossed to Dr. Carl Lestrange, the Chief Medical Examiner, who was on his way out.

MacBride said: "I think we're going to run into something big on that Hazel Noonan kill."

Lestrange had his hands in his overcoat pockets. "Good."

"Dope ring stuff, Doc."

"She wasn't a user, you know."

"I know. That's why I think it's dope ring stuff."

"That's a thought, Cap. Go to it!"

Lestrange slapped MacBride's shoulder, strode off. The skipper returned to Burt and said: "Okey, Burt; you can scram for the time being. I'll need you again though and— What the hell are you staring at?"

Burt gulped: "Who—who was that?"

"Who was who?"

"The—the guy you was just talking to!"

MacBride looked towards the front door, which had just swung shut.

"Oh, that," he said, chuckling. "That's Doc Lestrange, the Medical Examiner."

Burt ground out hoarsely: "B' jeepers, if it didn't look like the sneezing guy I picked up last night!"

THE skipper sat in his office. He sat doing nothing. His palms were on the flat-topped desk, at arms' length. His eyes were vacant, transfixed with thought. No one else was in the office. It was very quiet, very still. A slantwise bar of sunlight broke at the back of the skipper's head, bent over it like a white band and leveled out across his hands.

He was not especially pleased. The unpleasantness that brooded inside him appeared, presently, at the corners of his mouth, dragging them downward. It appeared, too, on his forehead, fell shadow-like to his brows, bending them inward. A sigh escaped him and ended in a rasping, baffled grunt. He shot upward suddenly from his chair, towered warmly, darkly, his fists clenched, his eyes boring keenly into space.

The door opened and Kennedy lolled in.

"Get out," MacBride said stiffly.

"Phooey on you, Skippery-wippery—"

"Get to hell out!"

Kennedy stopped, blinked. He turned around, said in a quiet aside: "M' gawd, he's nuts!" and lolled out of the office.

MacBride relaxed, folded his arms, rubbed one hand along the side of his jaw. He took a turn up and down the office, his head bent. He stopped, looked at the clothes tree in the corner. Then he crossed to it, put on his hat and overcoat and went out.

He didn't call out Duffy with the phaeton. He walked for a while, hitting the pavement hard with his heels. Presently he entered a drab graystone building, opened a door and found a girl hammering a typewriter.

"Captain MacBride to see Dr. Lestrange," he said.

She bounced up, entered a connecting office and reappeared in less than a minute. "All right, Captain MacBride."

Lestrange was tall and heavy but not fat. There was a hard roundness about his head and body. He was about fifty, clean-shaven, and close-cropped gray hair gave him an athletic appearance. He did not wear glasses.

He was casual, cordial. "Hello, Captain. This is a surprise."

MacBride sat down, grumbled half to himself: "You're telling me, huh?"

Lestrange had neat, white strong hands. He lit a cigarette, snapped smoke through an amused half-smile. "You look in the dumps, old-timer."

MacBride held a palm a foot from the floor. "Way down." He had avoided looking at Lestrange, but now he raised his keen blue eyes and sighted like a man looking along a gun barrel. "This thing I've got on my mind, Doc, is not so hotsy-totsy. I've turned up so many slimy things in municipal bureaus in my time that a lot of guys are beginning to think that's my specialty. It isn't. It's just my tough luck that after a lot of clowning around somebody walks up and hands me a slice of information on a silver platter. I usually take it and begin to juggle it like a hot coal. One thing I hate, Doc; I hate scandal. I hate it especially when it's in a municipal bureau. It's like being in the family. I lose weight, sleep and my appetite over it. Do you get me?"

"I think I understand what you mean."

"Well, a guy walked up to me today and said he picked up a guy that looked a hell of a lot like you last night at Grand Drive and Williamson."

"That's interesting, Cap. It's always interesting to find you've got a double in town."

MacBride was still sighting.

Lestrange leaned forward, showed amused interest. "In connection with what, Cap?"

"This man—this taxi chauffeur—picked up a man that was doing a hell of a lot of sneezing. He picked him up three blocks from number

10 Jermine Street."

"Jermine Street?"

"Address of the late Hazel Noonan."

Lestrange warmed to the subject. "Tell me more."

"A girl in the Jermine Street house heard a man going down the stairs last night sneezing to beat hell."

Lestrange leaned back, made a wry smile. "That kind of puts me on the spot, doesn't it?"

MacBride was not humorous. "This driver drove the man to number 211 Jockey Street and the man went in a house occupied by a dago named Pietro Piolo. Pietro says no, but he's that kind of dago."

Lestrange was in good humor. "The whole thing is interesting, Captain. Interesting, I mean, in the nature of circumstances. The circumstances being that a man resembling me should have done all this. Of course, it's absurd, and you needn't worry yourself sick about it. It's simple. I was home last night. My daughter and I were home."

"Swell," said MacBride, but he was still sighting. "Do you know Pietro Piolo?

"That Italian you mentioned? No."

MacBride paused for a moment. Then he said: "I suppose your daughter would swear you were home last night?"

Lestrange laughed. "You're a great one, Captain!… But yes, if she had to."

"You know," MacBride said, "we picked up an odd fingerprint in the Noonan apartment."

"So I heard."

"Would you be willing to let us take your prints?"

"Nonsense! This is becoming ridiculous! What makes you suppose I'd run around town killing people?"

"Hazel Noonan, we think, made her money wholesaling dope."

"Well?"

"No man in this town would have been able to supply her better than you."

There was a long minute of silence. Then Lestrange rose. "This ought to make me sore, Captain. But it doesn't. I forgot for a moment that I was dealing with old skipper MacBride. You want my prints?"

"That's what I came here for."

Lestrange went around the desk, capped MacBride on the shoulder. "You're a great one, Cap—a great one!" He put on his overcoat, his hat.

MacBride was standing. "I'm the only one in the Department knows this, Doc. I won't take you down to the Fingerprint Bureau. I'll take 'em in my office."

"That's thoughtful. Let's go."

When they walked into the central room at Police Headquarters, MacBride said: "You go up to my office, Doc. I'll run down and get a copy of those prints."

Lestrange seemed unconcerned. "Be seeing you," he said, and took the stairway up.

MacBride did not go directly to the basement. He went down the main hall, opened a door. "Mory... Ike!"

There was a group around a table. "In a minute," Cohen said. "I'm holding a royal flush."

"You heard me! Come here!"

Moriarity and Cohen came out and MacBride spoke briskly, in a low voice, for several minutes. The two detectives hopped for their hats and MacBride went downstairs. He climbed, later, to his office and found Lestrange enjoying a cigarette.

MacBride said: "I used to be a fingerprint man."

Lestrange smiled, held out his hands. "Take 'em, Captain, and I wish you luck."

It was five minutes later that MacBride laid down a magnifying glass, sat back. He actually grinned.

"Nope, Doc. Not yours."

Lestrange chuckled, swung from side to side, easily, in the swivel chair. "Lost your man, eh, Captain?"

"And glad of it, Doc."

Lestrange did not leave directly. That was because MacBride opened a box of cigars, poured out a generous tot of brandy. The two men talked, conjectured about the case. It was MacBride who, glancing from time to time at the clock on the wall, kept driving the conversation.

Presently the door opened and Moriarity walked in with Pietro Piolo. Pietro was leaning back comfortably on his bowed legs, wearing his dreamy smile. Lestrange leaned back in the swivel chair and showed only a casual interest in the arrivals.

"You wanta me, Cap'n, yes?" Pietro said in his low, unruffled voice. MacBride swung a leg over a corner of the desk. "Know him, Doc?"

Lestrange looked up, peered keenly. "No."

"This is Pietro," MacBride said—and watched.

"So that's Pietro!" Lestrange said.

"Dissa boss say you wanta see me, Cap'n."

MacBride shrugged. "Take him out, Mory."

Moriarity took Pietro out, closed the door. But in a moment the door opened again and Ike Cohen came in carrying Pietro's five-year-old. The child was frightened, wide-eyed. But suddenly he reached out his arms.

"Doc!" he cried. "Doc, you take me from bad mans!"

Lestrange was standing. His shoulders drooped. He reached out his arms.

"All right, little bambino—come to Doc."

MacBRIDE did not gloat. He said to Cohen: "Take the kid back home, Ike. Tell Mory to hold Pietro." His voice was low, a deep growl. Cohen took the child out.

Lestrange lighted a cigarette, strolled to a window, stared down into the street. He seemed detached, unmoved. He was incredibly cool and self-possessed.

MacBride said in a throaty voice: "If you think I'm pleased about this, you're nuts!" He was angry, his shoulders hunched, a sour look on his face. "It's like I'm holding a bomb and don't know what to do with it."

Lestrange said without turning: "I daresay you know what to do with it."

MacBride took four long strides, spun Lestrange about and bit him with a dark glare. "I'm in no mood for drawing-room cracks, Doc. If this doesn't upset you, it does me. And why? Because it's going to give a lot of lousy newspapers in this city a chance to make lousy passes at the administration. And not only in this city."

He turned, walked as far as the door, came back again. "Sweet—sweet as the roses in May! My grandmother's eye!... Chief Medical Examiner revealed as chief source of supply for enormous dope ring. How does that sound? Chief Medical Examiner convicted of murder of Hazel Noonan, dope queen. Swell, huh?"

"Except that you're premature, Captain," Lestrange said quietly.

"The fact that the Piolo child knows me is not an indication of guilt—"

"So now you're—"

"As," Lestrange cut in, "a murderer. Obviously I lied about knowing Pietro. I do know him. Very well. I've been used to going to his place for excellent T-bone steaks with mushrooms. The moment you mentioned Pietro in my office, I said I didn't know him because, as it happens, I know him so well. He's a valued friend. I pretended ignorance to avoid saying anything that might incriminate him. It's enough that I've been dragged into this thing. I didn't want to drag Pietro into it."

"But you went to his place last night."

"Yes, I did."

"You went to his place from Number 10 Jermine Street."

Lestrange smiled indulgently. "I was not at Number 10 Jermine Street last night."

"You ever been there?"

"No."

"Doc, you're a damned liar!"

Lestrange smiled. "Naturally I'm used to the wild ideas your good friend Kennedy springs from time to time. A man was heard sneezing in the hallway of the Jermine Street house. Three blocks away I climbed into a taxi-cab. I was sneezing. Coincidence. Striking coincidence." He picked up his hat. "Captain, I've things to attend to at my office. You'll know where to find me if you have a warrant sworn out. Good-day."

Lestrange walked out.

MacBride stood with his head bent, his stare fixed on the closed door. Five minutes later he went down the hall, pushed open an office door and said: "Mory—" He stopped short.

Moriarity was sitting on the floor. His eyelids drooped and there was a silly sag to his mouth. MacBride strode forward, lifted Moriarity up and set him down in a chair.

"Now what happened to you?"

Moriarity wet his lips. "The dago socked me."

"Where is he?"

"You're asking me?... Hell, we were standing here and he was wearing that innocent, harmless grin of his and then all at once—zingo!—and the Irish collapsed."

"You fat-head, what did you want to let him do that for?"

"Let him! Don't be dumb all your life!"

"Now cut out the insults! Who the hell do you think you're talking to?"

"Okey; suspend me."

"Suspend you? I'll suspend your neck. Get up and stick your head under some water and then sail down to Pietro's joint and warm your pants on his front doorstep. And stay there!"

MacBride spun on his heel, returned to his office and jammed into his overcoat. He went downstairs, reached the garage and broke up a crap game in which Duffy was the big winner.

"Number 10 Jermine Street and if I catch you again rolling the bones in H.Q. I'll bounce you back in harness. Between one thing and another around here—Bettdecken with home-brew under the central room desk, you rolling bones in the garage, and the vice squad sergeant running a handbook—this is getting to be a hell of a Head-quarters!"

He slammed the phaeton's door violently and the car boomed out of the garage. He sat alone in the rear, while the car hummed through the streets. Duffy brought it neatly to a stop in front of Number 10 Jermine Street. MacBride heaved out, slammed the phaeton's door shut and went up the steps. He was admitted by the girl Tessa.

"Miss Webb," he muttered.

Tessa led him to the rear of the lower hall and into a large, comfort-able living-room where Kennedy and Miss Webb sat facing each other across a small table. Neither looked up. They were intent on a chess game. Tessa closed the door and remained standing in front of it. MacBride, his face bleaker, took slow measured steps across the resilient carpet and stopped beside the table.

His approach had not been detected. The two were deeply, pro-foundly absorbed in the game. Miss Webb's face seemed whiter, more drawn, and there was a feverish glow in her transfixed eyes. Her hands, tense as her body, seemed to vibrate and there was a faint shine of perspiration on her face. Kennedy was slouched in his chair, his eyes half-shut, not a muscle twitching. He seemed half asleep. Miss Webb reached a shaking hand towards a black knight, paused, drew back her hand.

MacBride knocked on the table, said: "Time out!"

Miss Webb almost fell off the chair. Her eyes blazed as she sprang to her feet. She stood shaking all over, her face dead-white and drawn with anger. Her mouth worked.

She screamed: "Just when I had the move figured out!"

"Trouble, trouble, trouble," sighed Kennedy, and then took a swig from a square-faced bottle of Gordon's.

Miss Webb ran across the room, threw herself on to a divan and burst into loud weeping. Tessa padded across the room on big feet, knelt down beside the divan and patted Miss Webb's head. Miss Webb struck out and Tessa fell back with finger-marks on her cheek.

MacBride stood rooted to the floor, bewildered. He stared at the crying woman, at the girl sitting on the floor. He looked down at the chess board, where Miss Webb had had but one move to make to avoid being checkmated.

Kennedy smiled drolly, sent a knight hopping haphazardly about the board. "King and queen and knights in armor and grave, cleft-headed bishops and castles and pawns... pawns. Life is a play...."

"Shut up. You're drunk."

"She had but one chance. Her black shining knight would have saved the day though himself dying on the field of honor. She had but to command. She hesitated. She should have sacrificed the knight, but yonder lay a castle containing that which she wanted most. Not that she loved the knight. She loved his peculiar kind of exchequer which is here represented by the castle. Ergo, will you have a drink, palsy-walsy?"

"Please, Kennedy—please shut up! Shut up, will you? I ask you—"

Miss Webb was on her feet again, her smart haircomb disheveled, her eyes rolling, her breath coming hoarsely. She was grinding her palms together and shaking her head from side to side. But she said nothing. She seemed robbed of the power of speech.

MacBride strode towards her, grabbed her by the arms, held her rigid in his strong hands.

He muttered: "Say something."

She stared up at him with horror-stricken eyes. Then she began laughing hysterically. She threw back her head and he watched the muscles beneath her chin working.

Tessa clapped hands to her ears and barged out of the room.

Suddenly Miss Webb collapsed. MacBride laid her on the divan and watched her body convulsing. He turned around and went across the room and grabbed Kennedy by the throat.

"Listen, you mugg!"

"Puh-lease, Skipper! Is this gratitude, you horse's neck?"

"And what should I be grateful for?"

"Miss Webb."

"What did you do to her?"

"Lemme go before I kick you in the belly."

MacBride let him go but stood threateningly over him.

Kennedy said: "Chess is an odd game. Great mental strain. It has driven people crazy. So what did little old Kennedy do?"

"Never mind bragging. What did you do?"

"I got Miss Webb into a game of chess. She's the type can't stand it. You may remember how cool and composed and matter-of-fact she was when we first met her. Swell acting that was. But I knew she was not naturally cool and composed. I noticed the veins near her temples, the tiny wrinkles around her mouth that came from violent grimacing. The transparency of her skin. A neurotic case. I upped and handed out a stiff test of her coolth and composure." He tossed a limp hand negligently. "She's a user, Cap. She uses dope. If you don't believe me, have a medico look her over. Meantime, she may know things that may interest the Police Department. I beg pardon... you do work for the jolly old Police Department, what?"

CAPTAIN MacBRIDE entered his office swiftly, took off hat and coat, hung them up. He stalked to his desk, sat down, yanked open a drawer, withdrew a bottle, poured himself a stiff jolt and downed it neat. He rasped his throat, knocked the cork into the bottle with the heel of his hand and replaced the bottle in the drawer. He crammed tobacco into a battered pipe, lighted up and puffed so hard for a full minute that his head was completely enveloped in smoke. He rose, plowed out of the smoke screen and made a hard-heeled circuit of the room with a hand clamped tightly to the back of his neck.

Then he went down to the H.Q. detention ward for women. The ward consisted of three private rooms, each furnished after the manner of a hospital room. Two women attendants were struggling with Miss Webb. A police doctor looked on.

He said: "I'd better give her a shot."

"Not yet."

The doctor shrugged.

MacBride frowned. "I know, I know—it's tough on her. I don't pan these people. Every time I have to do with one I get sick at my gut. I feel sorry as hell for them. But I've got a job of work to do."

"She's a pretty bad case."

"I never would have thought it the first time I met her."

"You sometimes never know because you meet them on their good behavior."

"That guy Kennedy uncorks the wildest schemes of any guy I ever knew. First off they seem goofy—but when you look back, when you check up, you find out how sane they are. Drunk or sober, on his feet or on his back, that guy *always* uses his head."

"I'll hold off, then," the doctor said.

MacBride pointed: "When I ring, I want her brought up to my office and left there with me."

He returned to his office. Five minutes later he was knocking out his pipe when Lestrange strode in.

"Look here, Cap. What about Pietro? Haven't they found him yet?"

MacBride reached the phone, called an extension. "Send her up." He pronged the receiver. "Sit down, Doc."

Lestrange bored him with a blunt stare. "I want to tell you this: there's nothing wrong with Pietro. He must have become frightened. Pietro's all right."

"Moriarity doesn't think so. Ask Moriarity. Sit down."

Lestrange sat down.

MacBride got up, went to the door, opened it and passed into the corridor. He returned in a moment marching Miss Webb before him. Her eyes were bloodshot and her face was distorted. MacBride got her into the office and kicked the door shut. Gripping her firmly, he said:

"Maybe you know her, Doc."

"I'm afraid I never saw the woman before."

She was sobbing and her short hair lay in tattered bangs across her eyes. She brushed it back and stood swaying and breathing hoarsely and staring at Lestrange.

"Is this the man?" MacBride said.

She choked: "Yes. Yes."

MacBride said: "Know her, Doc?"

"I repeat, I never saw her before."

"She's the owner of that rooming-house. She saw you."

"Really? I don't believe she did."

She rasped: "I did! I—I saw you come down from her floor. I—I listened at her door while you were in there. I heard her. I saw you come out."

MacBride shook her. "Why didn't you spring this before?"

"Because—because I'd found out who—who her supply came from. I wouldn't have told—not even now. But they promised me a deck downstairs when I came back."

Lestrange stood up. "Young woman—"

"Don't young woman me. I tell you I wouldn't have told. Why? Because it would have been worth more not to. I—I could have got all I wanted from you. I—I got it from her—at a stiff price. I wanted to find out where she got it, but I never did. And I couldn't squeal on her—because then my supply would have been shut off. But last night—I heard you rowing with her. I—I heard her fall and then there was silence and then you came out—and I hid!—and saw you go downstairs—and Tessa heard you sneezing. And then I went down and kept my mouth shut. Because I knew you would have supplied me for nothing—to keep my mouth shut. But things went wrong. I'm caught. I—I need it right away—this minute!"

She began struggling again. MacBride pressed a button on the desk and a cop came in.

"Take her down," the skipper said.

The cop took Miss Webb out.

There was a moment of silence while the two men regarded each other.

MacBride's face was sunk. "Murder, you know, Doc."

"I know."

"So what?"

"I was there."

"And killed her."

Lestrange spread his hands. "You wouldn't believe me."

"What's that piece of adhesive tape doing just above your left wrist bone?"

Lestrange looked down at it, grimaced, said nothing.

MacBride said: "One of your assistants said there was blood on her teeth. I suppose that could be yours."

Lestrange moistened his lips, lifted his chin, took a breath. "Well, what are you going to do about it, Cap?"

"What the hell can I do, Doc?"

"You can let me go to my office and get a gun."

MacBride considered this with one eye asquint. He said: "Doc, I never really liked a murderer until I met you. You know, I never knew much about you. We never met much in the course of our duties. I always worked with one of your assistants. I've been laying into you hard today—and I've come to like you. You can take it. I never saw a guy take it the way you can."

"Thanks—if there's any virtue in being able to take it."

MacBride shook his head. "You shouldn't have killed her."

"Will you let me go and get my gun?"

The skipper eyed him steadily. "Doc, I've never gypped the law since I've been a cop. If it was anything but murder—I'd give you a break. But it's murder. I've got a one-track mind regarding murder."

The phone rang and he picked it up, spoke briefly. In a moment he set the phone down.

He said: "I've still to put this on the books."

"I appreciate the way you've tried to keep it to yourself."

"I've got two palookas working for me who think of me first and then the department. I'm going to get one of them in here now. He's going to sit with you till I come back." He picked up the phone and rang.

Ike Cohen came in a moment later.

MacBride went down to the central room, headed for the garage. He ran into the police doctor.

The doctor said: "What do you think?"

"Shoot."

"The woman died."

MacBride stared vacantly at him.

The doctor said: "Heart attack. She had a bum heart."

MacBride went on to the garage.

THE *Hotel Exeter* was a tall, narrow building on Broad Boulevard, on the fringe of the better shopping district. Leaving the taxi, MacBride stretched his legs across the broad sidewalk, slapped his way through the revolving door and entered the high, modernistic lobby. A chubby man with thick fingers gestured, kept his voice low.

"In my office," he said.

"You the house officer?"

"Yeah. Switzer."

"Okey."

They took a corridor down back of the marble desk, and Switzer stretched out an arm towards a doorknob, opened a glass-paneled door and jerked his chin. Moriarity was sitting on a chair holding his chin. Pietro was sitting in an armchair, strapped to it. Switzer's assistant stood behind him.

Switzer said: "This dago here sails into the lobby, sails up to the desk and grabs the register. The clerk grabs it, too. I'm coming in the lobby and see the row. The dago's getting tough. I call Merkel here and just then this man—Moriarity here—comes hitting it across the lobby and the dago turns and smacks him out of a clear blue sky. Then me and Merkel jump the dago."

MacBride said: "Thanks. Will you men leave us here a minute?"

Switzer said: "Look out for the dago."

"I'll handle him."

Switzer and Merkel went out and MacBride stood spread-legged, fists jammed to hips, neck straight. He looked from Moriarity to Pietro.

He said to Moriarity: "How did you get here?"

"Well, I got tired of hanging around Jockey Street. I took a walk and I saw a cab shoot by with the dago in it. You could have knocked me over with a feather—"

"I believe it."

Moriarity reddened. "Okey, razz me. Anyhow, I grabbed another cab and followed him here."

Pietro began fighting the strap that held him down. MacBride unfastened the strap and Pietro heaved up and MacBride punched him in the chest, seating him again. Pietro's big hands gripped the sides of the chair and his eyes rolled darkly, viciously, and his thick brows bent and unbent.

"And you needn't make faces," MacBride said. "What the hell were you doing here?"

Pietro applied thumb to nose and spat on the floor. Then he said: "Dat's my beezness!"

MacBride slapped him violently on the cheek and Pietro surged up and MacBride slammed him back into the chair.

"Pietro," he said, "you came here looking for somebody. Who is it?"

"Dat's my beezness, my job!"

MacBride regarded him for a long minute. "Pietro, you're running around wasting time. Lestrange has confessed and it's all over. He killed Hazel Noonan. So there's no damn' use in you high-tailing around here. Come on, I'm taking you back to Headquarters."

Pietro scowled fiercely. He rose quietly and raised his palms, shook them, shook his head and smiled sinisterly. "No, no, Cap'n. Dissa what you say she's one big lie. Doc no killa dat woman, Pietro know."

"You're a liar. We've got a witness saw him come out of the woman's apartment."

Moriarity said: "Has it occurred to you, Skipper, that we haven't taken this guy's prints? Look at them hands. Maybe he killed her."

"Me!" howled Pietro, striking his chest.

"No, it was Lestrange," said MacBride, feeling his way, watching Pietro. "Lestrange killed her and he'll hang for it. It's open and shut. We take Pietro back to Headquarters right now. We'll lock up his wife, too, and send his bambino away to a home. He'll never see the bambino again. Neither will his wife."

Pietro's eyes widened. "My little bambino! Whatsa dis you talk? My bam—"

MacBride took out a pair of handcuffs.

Pietro shrank back. "No! No! Notta my bambino!"

MacBride was cold, clipped: "Talk, then. What did you come here for? No stalling. No wasting time. Spring right now or I'll slap the cuffs on you! Come on, spring!"

"Ukkey, boss—ukkey. But please, boss—please"—he shook his head—"not my little bambino."

"Talk."

Pietro pawed at his own chest. His eyes rolled. The bambino threat had weakened him and fright moved in his eyes. "I—I been look around—find people—ask da questions—and I come here. I looka for guy whatcha call Tim Hickox."

"Hickox," MacBride said. "Know the name, Mory?"

"Nope."

"Go ahead, Pietro."

"I looka—grabba de book outside to looka de room—"

"What for?"

"Getta dis guy Hickox. I'm know—see?—I'm know he bomp offa de woman. Please, boss, letta me go opstairs—"

"How do you know he bumped off the woman?"

"I'm know!" Pietro roared. "Doc Lestrange he know, too! But he can't tell—see? He tella me no tell! See?"

MacBride turned to Moriarity. "Keep him here, Mory. This sounds goofy but I'll find out. And for crying out loud take your gun out of hibernation and hold it on him."

He stepped out of the office, found the two house officers waiting in the corridor.

"See if there's a man named Hickox living here," he said.

They went around to the desk and the clerk said: "Oh, yes. Permanent guest. Timothy Hickox. Room 616."

"We'll go up with you," Switzer said.

"No," MacBride said. "This sounds too goofy to make a grandstand play. I'll go up alone."

He crossed the lobby and entered a waiting elevator and it lifted him to the sixth floor. He got out and walked down the corridor with his hands in his overcoat pockets and his hat riding low over his brooding forehead. He was baffled and angry and his face was a reflection of the unpleasant state of his mind. He reached the door marked 616 and rapped loudly with his knuckles. He scowled up and down the hall and then brought the scowl fixedly to the door and rapped again.

It opened while he was knocking and a tall man in a blue silk shirt and gray braces stood there drawing on a cigar and saying:

"Yes?"

MacBride could see beyond into the room. Several men sat around a folding card-table. Smoke hung congenially above their heads and there was the sound of low, good-humored conversation.

The skipper moved forward a step, turned his lapel back. "You Hickox?"

The man turned. "Hey, Tim."

MacBride walked into the room, shouldered the blue-shirted man aside, elbowing the door shut. He leaned back against it. The room was large and had a disappearing bed. There was plenty of furniture.

One of three men at the table had risen and stood now with hands thrust into hip-pockets and chin raised.

"Yeah?" he said.

He was big, thin-legged, with sloping shoulders and a paunch. His hair was thin and fuzzy, grayish. He had wet eyes half-covered by pulpy lids. Like the others, he was dressed well. The cigar smoke, MacBride thought, smelled swell.

The skipper said: "I wish you'd put your coat on, Mr. Hickox, and come with me."

One of the seated men shuffled a new deck of cards. He chided: "You're honored, Tim. Hurry back for the next hand."

"Where to?" Hickox said.

"Downstairs."

Hickox squinted quizzically. "If you'll pardon me, I don't get this."

MacBride was weary. "Never mind, never mind. Come on. I don't understand it myself, so we'll both start from scratch."

"Who wants to see me?"

"A dago named Pietro Piolo."

Hickox dropped his wet eyes about the room. He laid down his cigar carefully. Taking his coat from the back of a chair, he put it on, brushed off lint with his fingers. He was still quizzical.

"Pietro Piolo? That's a new one on me. What's he want?"

"Let's go down and see."

"Sure."

Hickox came towards the door and MacBride slapped his pockets, removed a chubby .32 automatic.

"I'll mind this for you," he said.

"Thanks." Hickox opened the door, turned and said to the men in the room: "Be seeing you right away, fellows."

"Okey, Tim," the blue-shirted man said.

The door closed. MacBride squinted at Hickox, squinted at the door. He prodded Hickox and they moved off, passed a staircase, turned right at an L and came to the elevator. The car was at the lobby floor. MacBride buzzed it up. He watched Hickox closely as they entered.

"Down," he said.

A light blinked for a stop at five, the floor below.

"Don't stop," MacBride said, eyeing Hickox.

Hickox looked sidewise at him.

The car dropped to the lobby floor and the door slid open. MacBride gripped Hickox's arm and marched him out of the car, headed him across the lobby. Hickox walked rapidly, eagerly. But suddenly his left foot shot sidewise. MacBride tripped, tried to regain his balance; but the floor was slippery, like glass. He ended in a sprawl.

Hickox was running, pounding his feet down hard. MacBride did not bother to rise. Lying flat, he waited until Hickox was in silhouette against the lobby door. His gun exploded. Hickox hit the revolving door head-on, spun it with his dead weight and went sliding on his face across the sidewalk.

The three others had come down the staircase and were deploying to cover Hickox's escape. The clerk ducked down behind the desk. MacBride lay in the center of the lobby. Switzer peered around the corner of the desk. A gun blazed from the door. Switzer fired. The gang crowded through the revolving door and MacBride, rising, fired twice. Heavy glass fell, ringing on stone.

Moriarity went past him like a streak, braced his legs and slid six feet into the doorway, belted his way through. A man was dangling on the curbstone. He was trying with all his might to raise his gun. The strain showed on his face. It seemed as though he were trying to lift a great weight. Little by little he got the gun up.

"Who's that?" Moriarity asked.

"One of them."

"Well, then...."

Moriarity drilled the man's middle and the man flung down into the street with great violence and was then suddenly still. Hickox was crawling away. There was something ridiculous about the way he crawled—with his head down, a wary look on his face.

MacBride walked over and stood in front of him. Hickox merely changed his course and went to the left of MacBride's legs, and then kept crawling. MacBride turned, took two long strides and lifted him up.

"Give me a hand, Mory. He's flabby—but he's heavy, too."

"What did he do?"

"Started playing tag-you're-it. He knew the other guys were coming down."

"What do you make of it?"

"I'm still in the dark, Mory. Grab his legs."

THE fingerprint man said: "Yes, that's right. This guy Hickox's print matches the one we took off the dame's patent leather slipper. Absolute."

MacBride said: "Thanks." He hung up the receiver and shoved the phone to the middle of his desk, leaned on his elbows, his fingers interlaced. "That checks," he said. "His print's on the slipper."

Lestrange nodded. "Pietro, you see, lost his head. His only thought was of me. He knew Hickox from the old days. Just as he knew Hazel Noonan. And me. What Pietro was interested in mostly was saving my life. He didn't give a hang about my reputation.

"That was the only time I went to Hazel's apartment. I was full up, you see. I went there to offer her thirty thousand dollars to clear out of the country. She laughed at me. She was a little drunk. I guess I became kind of angry. And then Hickox came in and she told him about the money. He urged her to take it. I had it with me and I gave it to her and she promised to leave the country. Then she laughed again. I didn't like it. I grabbed hold of her and shook her and she bit me. Then she threw the pepper shaker at me and the top came off. The pepper almost blinded me. I tried to grab her again, to prevent her throwing a bookend. She fell and hit her head on the leg of the bureau. Hickox stood by and chuckled. She lay there unconscious and Hickox said: 'You better scram. I'll take care of her.' I did. I went out, sneezing. I couldn't seem to shake off that pepper."

"And you supplied her with dope since she came to Richmond City?"

Lestrange was white-faced, his eyes fixed on space. "Yes. I had to. It was a form of blackmail. It was blackmail. I—I had to, Cap. I supplied her regularly. Met her or Hickox on country roads—in my car. And I couldn't—I didn't tell you about Hickox being there last night because I knew—I knew he'd strangled her for the money. And I knew I couldn't tell because then he would also tell something I would have bartered my life not to have told. Turn about, you know.

"It was twenty years ago I met them. I was young, but not too young. I went down to Porto Rico to get a thorough grounding in tropical diseases. One of my first experiments was on an itinerant pedler. I saved his life. His name was Pietro Piolo. He afterwards helped me in the great plague there—he always had a good stomach.

"Then I met Hazel and fell in love with her. Pietro never liked her, but I was blind, I guess. Then I found that she was stealing narcotics from my supply. I found she was supplying—you guessed it—Hickox. He was selling it. That finished us. It was only last year she found me again. She'd become more degenerate than ever—" He broke off, stood up. "What's the use, what's the use!"

MacBride's chin was sunk to his chest. "You ought to've bluffed her."

"I would have. But you forget I have a nineteen-year-old daughter."

MacBride looked up, his eyes becoming very round.

Lestrange's voice was low, hushed: "Hazel Noonan's daughter."

MacBride stood up and said: "Cripes!" bitterly.

"That, Cap, was the whip she held over me. The revelation, which she or Hickox could have made, that would have ruined my daughter." He struck the desk, suddenly furious. "It will ruin her if it ever should come out—" He stopped, white and shaking.

MacBride said: "Were Hickox and Hazel the only ones knew where the dope came from?"

"Yes."

"Well, Hickox died on the way to the hospital. Hazel's dead. Miss Webb, who saw you come downstairs—she died this afternoon of heart failure. The taxi-cab driver wasn't sure of you—he only thought. The fingerprint on the dead woman's slipper was Hickox's. So that's that. Hickox killed Hazel Noonan. That's all I wanted to know. I won't say you were right or wrong in supplying her with dope. But I've got kids and I'm touchy about my kids, too. I can see your point. I set out to find a murderer. Through a lot of lucky breaks I found him. My duty's done, as I see it."

Lestrange did not say anything. Standing, tall, white-faced, a peculiar shimmer came into his eyes, a shaky smile appeared on his lips.

MacBride had the bottle out.

"You've been through hell, Doc. Sock this into your belly. It's the real McCoy—from a boat we raided last week. And were those guys sore!"

Guns Down

Capt. Steve MacBride may be "slow on the uptake, but he's sure hell on the downpour."

Chapter I

IT was quiet now. The orchestra members sat on their dais, beneath the huge inverted glass tulip. Their instruments lay beside them. The dance-floor was a bright, deserted field. Tables, row on row, surrounded it, and at these tables men and women sat, waited. Occasionally there was a faint flash as someone raised a glass to his lips; the flash instantly drew the attention of scores of eyes, and the drinker lowered his glass with a guilty, self-conscious look.

At the wide entrance, which was shaped like an enormous keyhole, Sanarens stood with Rigardo. Sanarens owned the *Keyhole Supper Club*. Rigardo was his steward. They stood side by side, Sanarens, with his mouth appearing and disappearing behind a white handkerchief; Rigardo, with his hands locked behind his back, his chin down, a dark up-from-under look in his eyes. The waiters, scattered about, stood like images. The cigarette girl had not moved during the past five minutes. The oldish man who lay face down on a table near an open window had not moved in six minutes. Nor would he move again. Ever.

Sanarens raised one ear in a birdlike, listening attitude. Rigardo, keeping his hands locked behind his back, swiveled neatly and peered down the wide corridor that led towards the lobby. There came the sound of feet shuffling and striking on the tiles, and the careless mutter of voices.

Then Sanarens turned, patted his lips with his handkerchief, thrust the handkerchief into his breast pocket. He inhaled deeply, held his breath. A straggling group of men came towards him; the group was led by a tall, bony-looking man in a dark suit and a gray fedora, shoes polished so highly that every time one swung forward it caught and reflected the lights in the corridor. A uniformed cop walked beside him. A short fat man, carrying a small black bag, followed the cop.

Two plainclothes men came next. Last, and well in the rear, came a small, spare man in nondescript clothes; he swayed gently from side to side, hummed absent-mindedly, and seemed to take a passing, foggy-eyed interest in the swooning murals on the walls.

Sanarens said: "Hell, MacBride—hell..." and made a vague, sickly gesture.

"Added attraction, huh?" MacBride said.

Rigardo said in a clipped, lipless way: "Guy got it, Skipper."

"Lovely murals!" the fat assistant medical examiner chirped.

"Lousy, you mean," Kennedy said.

"I maintain they're lovely."

Kennedy sighed: "Maintain, then—maintain. Who cares!"

MacBride walked across the dance-floor as he would walk down a street—firmly, matter-of-factly, objectively. Behind him, the assistant medical examiner—Oscar Hirsch—bobbed on his short fat legs; his nose-glasses danced on his nose and flashed brightly, hiding his eyes. Sanarens walked sidewise, pointing.

The skipper nodded. "Yeah, I see."

He came to a dead stop beside the table, reached down, grabbed the back of the dead man's neck and lifted the head. Two tables away, a woman smothered a scream. But MacBride looked at the dead man's face, tightened his lips, let the head drop back on to the table.

"Go to it, Doc."

"Right, Steve!" Hirsch said cheerfully.

The skipper turned, put his hands on his hips, leaned back on his heels and let his dark, weary eyes cruise around the large room. Moriarity was snapping gum with his tongue and teeth and MacBride said out of the side of his mouth:

"Cut it, Mory."

Sanarens was trembling—he had the handkerchief out again—and Rigardo was still standing with his hands locked behind his back, his face a smooth, swart mask.

Ike Cohen, rubbing dice in his palm, dropped one; he bent and picked it up and found MacBride's hard, disapproving eye on him. Cohen shrugged and drifted away, and Kennedy stood erect now but swaying ever so gently from side to side—quite placid, quite drunk.

MacBride said to Sanarens: "Joe Sibbold, of course."

"Y-yes. He was sitting there and—"

"Everybody here?"

"I—I don't think so. When the shot came, there was a grand rush. You know how there would be a grand rush and—"

"How many got out?"

"I couldn't tell. How could I tell? There was a grand rush—"

"Ah," sighed Kennedy, sleepy-eyed, "a grand rush."

MacBride said: "Where'd the shot come from?"

Sanarens pointed to a small window above the table. It was open. Several other windows, equally small, were open.

Rigardo said: "It was that window. The lights were out—all except those little table lamps—and there was a spotlight on Flossie Doane—she was dancing. I saw the gun flash at that window. Before we got the main lights on, there was a rush for the doors. At least half a dozen got out before we could close the doors."

"Get a doctor?"

A man stood up. "I looked at him. I'm an M.D. I happened to be dining here. He was dead when I looked at him."

Hirsch bobbed his head. "I guess he was dead, all right!"

MacBride spoke to Rigardo: "What's outside that window?"

"An alley."

MacBride turned. "Mory—Ike, take a look at the alley."

The two detectives went out.

Kennedy said: "There were three at that table, Rigardo. Who besides Sibbold?"

"A guy and a jane—both young."

"Names make news, you know."

Rigardo lit a cigarette. "The jane's Louise Maybanks. I don't know the guy. They had a table over there by themselves. Sibbold came in, sat down, saw them and asked them over to his. They went over."

Moriarity and Cohen came in and Moriarity said: "Nothing out there. The window's pretty high, about eight feet from the ground. A guy'd have to stand on something."

"Another's guy's shoulders, maybe," Kennedy offered.

Hirsch, bending to the floor to snap shut his bag, said: "Look what I found."

"What?" MacBride asked.

"The bottom side of a cufflink."

"Look for the top. The top might have an initial on it."

They all looked, moving the table and the body, but found no more. The part that MacBride took from Hirsch was shaped like a miniature egg, of solid gold. He slipped it into his vest pocket.

"Get the morgue, Mory," he said; and to Sanarens: "Okey; take away that table cloth. The City will pick up the body."

Sanarens was rubbing his palms against his handkerchief. "Is—is there going to be any trouble for me?"

MacBride dropped his voice: "Better close till this blows over—say about a week. You'll be in the papers and the Federals may take it into their heads to knock you over."

"B-but no trouble from the Bureau?"

"What the hell do I look like?"

"Jeese, thanks, Skipper!"

"Forget it and—" He stopped short, took three slow but purposeful steps and gripped Kennedy's arm.

Kennedy shrugged, removed a pint flask of liquor from his pocket and replaced it on the table from which he had taken it.

"Sibbold," he explained, "always had good Scotch."

"Mugg!" MacBride grunted.

SLUMPED in a chair in MacBride's office, Kennedy let cigarette smoke dribble from his nose. Half of his face and most of his nose were hidden by the downward slouch of his shapeless, faded fedora. The smoke mushroomed against the underside of his hat brim, oozed around the edge, flowed upward. His right leg was jacked over the left knee; a garterless sock was wrinkled and twisted down to a worn oxford.

MacBride was pacing the office, trailing fragrant pipe smoke from an old briar.

His voice came husky, hard: "Poor old Sibbold...."

"He brewed the best beer in this man's town—the best three-point-two, I mean. There was a character for you. When Prohibition hit this country, the Sibbold Brewery closed down—and I mean closed down. Sibbold had an unusual respect for the law. He said then, 'I'll close now. But it won't be long. This law can't last long. Then I'll open again.' Well"—Kennedy sighed—"he sure had a long wait. And then, by the grace of God and thirsty senators, we were allowed to have three-point-two. And Sibbold's brewery was ready. The old braumeister came back from Munich at Sibbold's expense. The wet, pungent tang of malt and hops again on Exeter Street... Sibbold in his glory, sitting in his great office, with a picture of Lincoln on one wall and one of Frederick the Great on another. A lonely old mutt... ever since his wife and daughter were wiped out in the Long Beach 'quake. It was lucky he had his old business to turn to, or he would have gone ga-ga. So endeth the house of Sibbold... so endeth a dynasty. Finis," he sighed, with a weary gesture of his hand, and let his body slump deeper into the chair.

MacBride stopped pacing, took his pipe from his mouth, jabbed the stem in Kennedy's direction. "It's a smack in the jaw to me, Kennedy—it's a kick in the gut. Only the other day Sibbold sent me a case of lager, with his compliments. In the old days, I was in harness, with a beat past his brewery. We wore helmets then. It was in the days when hoodlums used to toss bricks at us from roofs.

"And this is lousy, reporter. Ever since Prohibition hit us, ever since the bootleg song-and-dance began, mugg after mugg, gang after gang, tried to muscle into Sibbold's brewery. But not a chance. He kept three men there; they kept it clean, polished, swept, scrubbed—while Sibbold waited for the return of legalized beer."

Kennedy stood up, yawned, stretched. "Old horse, there's more bootleg beer being sold in this city today than ever— more, by far, than your legal three-point-two. The Chicago Era beer barons have got to keep the ball rolling. They've got to think of their women and children—yowssuh, Skipper, their women and children. Our old palsy-walsy Sibbold was killed because he refused to play marbles: that's a guess, but it's as good as any and if you—"

The phone rang and MacBride grabbed it. "Yeah, Charlie.... Uh-huh.... Swell and thanks, kid."

He hung up, crossed to the clothes tree, took down his hat and overcoat. He put on his hat, hung his overcoat on his arm. He cleaned out his briar, placed it on a tray.

"Going home?" Kennedy said,

"I can always go home, Kennedy."

"Where to?"

"Just places."

The door banged behind him.

Chapter II

HE sat alone, in a corner of the back seat of the new Bureau sedan. It was a long black machine, shiny, powerful, with eight competent cylinders beneath the lean-flanked hood. He watched the lights of mid-town wheel past—red, green, blue, white; moving lights and stationary lights; lights that commanded you to buy this and that. The bleat and blare and drone of traffic beat upon his ears—the clash of gears, the whine and whir of accelerated motors.

Joe Sibbold's mangled face danced against the background of shifting, gyrating lights. Old Joe Sibbold—a little quaint, with fixed ideas, sharp scruples. Once in a blue moon he used to put on evening clothes, go to a supper club, dine by himself. A lonely old guy.

The skipper moved in his seat, muttered a congested oath. Benninger took a left turn sharply, made a taxi brake suddenly; shot down a narrow side street between lean buildings with smart façades. Braking easily, the car edged towards the curb, came silently to a stop. MacBride left his overcoat in the tonneau, climbed out and said:

"Pull up a bit and wait."

The lobby glowed with a mellow radiance; light poured gently from hidden nooks and crevices. A black marble desk stood at one side, with several phones on it. The clerk looked up.

"House call," MacBride said, and picked up one of the phones; and to the operator—"Miss Maybanks." He waited, staring absently at the black sheen of the desk. And then he said: "Miss Maybanks?... This is Captain MacBride, Police Headquarters. I'd like to see you a moment.... Yes, now.... Thanks."

He pronged the receiver, crossed the lobby and entered a black lacquer and chromium elevator that lifted him noiselessly to the seventh floor. Walking down the corridor, he carried his hat in his hand. His hair was black, thick, wiry; he was well-dressed in a quiet, plain man's way. Lean and straight and bony on the nape.

There was a door, tan in color, with a knocker shaped like a crouching tiger. He raised the knocker, let it fall, and stood pinching his lower lip between thumb and forefinger, waiting with his eyes downcast, dark and brooding. In a moment a latch clicked, the door opened. He looked up at a tall, black-haired woman.

"Yes... come in."

She backed into a small foyer, and he entered, holding his hat with both hands now. He saw that she was lovely, with a fine columnar neck, eyes dark as her hair but more luminous, full red lips, a figure that did well with the long black evening dress she wore. And she was a little frightened, a little expectant, with her dark eyes flickering back and forth across his face. She indicated the living-room with a slim white hand, long, tapered fingers.

He dipped his head, went past her into a large room lit by scattered floor- and table-lamps. In a high-backed chair sat a large, high-chinned man smoking a cigar. Rising, he was very straight, big-chested, neatly groomed. His cheeks were flat, his forehead broad, and from it a mane of darkish hair swept backward without a part, and was dappled gray above the ears. He had, MacBride saw, a striking presence, a sound self-assurance.

The woman was saying: "This is Mr. Boyd."

Boyd made a slight, brisk movement of his head. "Hello, Captain MacBride."

In the gloom at the farther side of the room MacBride saw white curtains blowing inward, kiting and flopping. The woman moved, hovered beyond the radius of glow of the nearest lamp. He could see her white face floating above the slender length of black dress.

She said quietly, almost in a whisper: "You wanted to see me."

"About this *Keyhole* shooting. You know Sibbold was killed." He turned to Boyd. "You were there with Miss Maybanks?"

"No, I wasn't. I just dropped by here...." He made a half-turn, stared towards the blowing curtains, moved his cigar. "Fellow over there—Hendricks."

MacBride peered hard.

Boyd explained: "Drunk."

The woman's voice pleaded: "Please don't wake him. I put a wet towel on his head. He's frightfully drunk. He drank too much."

MacBride made his way slowly across the room, turned on a floor-lamp. The man lay on a divan beside the open window. A coverlet had been thrown over him, and a wet towel, padded, covered his eyes and forehead.

"Please," the woman pleaded in a hushed voice.

MacBride shrugged, turned. "Why did you run out of the *Keyhole?* Why didn't you hang around?"

"God knows. That shot. Well, everyone jumped up and ran. I grabbed Tom and ran with him, and out in the street we ran and ran until he began stumbling so much I had to call a cab. I brought him here. I didn't think I was doing wrong."

"You knew Sibbold well?"

"Not at all. Tom knew him."

MacBride turned. "You knew him, Mr. Boyd?"

"No." Boyd was looking at his cigar. "Only of him."

MacBride said to the woman: "Did you see a face at the window?"

"No. I only—heard—the shot. I jumped up—everybody jumped up and there were screams and—" She clapped hands to her face, buried her eyes. "It was awful—awful. For an instant I saw Mr. Sibbold's face—" She choked, shook her head violently.

Boyd was matter-of-fact: "Don't you think, Captain, you ought to give her time to pick up?" Without bending, he rubbed ash from his cigar into a tray.

"You're a good friend of Miss Maybanks, I suppose."

"Kind of, yes. Too good, maybe. I disapproved of this fellow Hendricks. Not bad, I suppose—but drinks too much."

"You live in this burg?"

"Yes. Boyd's Investments. My office is in Race Street. I live at the *Williamsport.* Hendricks used to work for me and I had to fire him because he drank too much. Liquor's all right—but in its place." He smiled wryly. "Try to tell Miss Maybanks that!"

She said: "Tomorrow, Captain. Would tomorrow be all right? I know nothing—and I'm sure Tom knows nothing. We were just sitting there when it happened. But I'll tell him—tomorrow. Please?"

MacBride looked at the inside of his hat. "All right. Tomorrow morning—first thing—at my office." He moved towards the door. With his hand on the knob, he turned to say: "Take it easy, Miss Maybanks. I don't bite." A tight smile cracked his left cheek.

She was standing with her hands folded on her breast, her eyes wide, all expression suspended in her lovely face. She nodded slowly, like a mechanical doll. Back of her, and to one side, Boyd stood looking down at his cigar, rolling it round and round between thumb and index finger. He seemed enwrapped in thought.

The skipper took his hand off the doorknob. His brows bent, coming down and together above his nose. His nostrils twitched ever so slightly, and he sucked against one cheek, drawing his face awry for an instant, then letting it snap back.

Boyd looked up candidly, then curiously.

MacBride said: "What's the matter?" to the woman.

"I—I feel just a little ill."

Boyd took hold of her arm. "Lie down. You'd better go in and lie down. I'll wait till Hendricks wakes up. I'll take him home. Come." He put a firm pressure on her arm without seeming to do so, turned her about. "You'd better."

MacBride said: "Wait." He took a few steps, tossed his hat on to a chair, said again: "Wait."

Boyd said: "I'll take her in and then—"

"Shut up. Wait, I said."

Boyd shrugged and was calm, leisurely when he replied: "You're the doctor, officer."

"That's settled, then. Good. Miss Maybanks—" He walked towards her with his fists on his hips, his elbows jacked high and wrinkling his coat collar. "Come on; what's up, what's the matter? Is this an act or are you sick?"

She held her face in her hands, looked between her hands with dark, shining eyes. "I want to be alone," she sobbed. "I want to be left alone. Please leave me alone."

"I'd like to. You may be sick. Okey. But you're sick about more than just a little thing. Listen, girl; for crying out loud, I'm an old cop and

I've been around and I've seen girls go and come, and I can tell when something's wrong.... You want to be alone! Spill it, girl. What's wrong?... Okey, you're sick. Now what's making you sick?"

Boyd offered: "No doubt the shooting at the *Keyhole*—"

"Stay out of this?" MacBride said. "I'm talking to the girl."

"Of course, but on the other hand—"

"Will you for cripes' sake keep your mouth shut! How many times do I have to tell you?"

Suddenly Louise Maybanks burst into tears, turned, ran across the living-room, into the bedroom, slammed the door.

Boyd shook his head, made a regretful face. "She does that, Captain—frequently. Do me a favor, will you? See her later—tomorrow. Remember, she saw a man's face half blown off. She's a sensitive woman—hardly more than a girl."

"Tomorrow might be too late. You may have been around with women a lot, and I haven't—but I know 'em. I know the signs. This one's got that nutty look in her eyes that spells trouble—suicide. And why? *Why?*"

"I'll—"

"You'll do nothing. A tip for you, Mr. Boyd, would be to get the hell out of here."

MacBride went hard-heeled across the room, palmed the knob of the bedroom door, pushed it inward.

Boyd called: "I'll be going then, thank you."

"Good-night!" MacBride snapped.

The woman was lying on the bed, face down. The skipper sighed, wagged his head. He crossed to the bed, bent down and tapped the woman on the shoulder; but she did not respond. He turned her over, saw that her face was bathed in sweat. Her eyes were closed. She had fainted.

He felt a twinge of conscience. She was lovely to look at, and he thought he might have been a bit rough with her. He went into the bathroom, soaked a towel with cold water, brought it to the bed and bathed her face, left the towel on her forehead. Standing up, he scratched the back of his neck, wandered back into the living-room and over to the divan where Hendricks lay. He stood on wide-planted feet, pinching his lower lip.

Something hit him on the head and instantly he was unconscious.

Chapter III

THE taxi clanked down the street, cut around a sedate limousine, swerved sharply towards the curb and came to a violent stop in front of the tall, narrow hotel. The handle on the rear door clicked and rattled but did not open, and finally the chauffeur climbed out, grabbed the outside handle, twisted and yanked and finally whipped the door open. Kennedy fell out and took the chauffeur down with him. It was a full minute before the two men became sufficiently straightened out to rise, and it was the chauffeur who helped Kennedy to his feet.

"I gotta have the handle fixed, bud."

"You ought to have more than the handle fixed, Casanova. Tariff, please?"

"I don't getcha. Huh?"

"Fare—fare!"

"Oh! Seventy-five!"

"Ought to have the meter fixed too." He entered the lobby diagonally. His hat was crushed on the back of his head, one of his shoe-laces was untied, his tie-knot did not quite meet the inverted Y of his collar. In his face was a sodden, wasted but good-humored expression. He hiccoughed twice, half-heartedly, before he reached the black desk.

"Good-evening to you," he said to the well-groomed clerk. "Press… Kennedy. What apartment's Louise Maybanks in?"

"You want to see Miss Maybanks?"

"Oh, no. I just want to know where she lives."

"Seven-O-seven."

"Thank you very kindly. This is a nice chateau you have here."

He made a dizzy swivel, zigzagged across the lobby and slid side-wise into an elevator. He was very drunk, but genial, good-natured and polite.

"Seven, please, my lad."

"Seven, sir."

"Nice boy.…"

The elevator rose, stopped quietly and without a jar. Kennedy flip-flopped into the corridor, turned left and teetered leisurely on his way, singing in a husky, cracked whisper, "Life is just a bowl of cherries…." He found 707 and used the knocker. He stood teetering from foot to foot, backwards, sidewise, and hummed placidly to himself; tried the knocker again, violently this time. Finally he gave it up, grabbed the knob and sailed in with the door. Reeling around recklessly, he accidentally banged the door shut. And then he shot into the living-room, covering half of it in a perilous headlong stumble that did not end in a fall. Because MacBride stopped him; the skipper stopped him with a hard right hand, held him up, while he used his left hand to hold a wet towel on his head.

"Omar Khayyám! By God, if it ain't Omar Khayyám!"

MacBride backed him across the room, lowered him into an armchair, said; "Drunk as a coot again. Swacked. Plastered." The skipper stood holding the huge wet towel on his head; beneath it, his face was severe, hard-lined. "What are you doing here, fat-head?"

"See Louise Maybanks…. S'listen, d'you have to wear that turban or—"

"Pipe down," MacBride growled. He lowered the towel, balled it, pitched it through the bedroom doorway so hard that it hit with a wet smack against the opposite bedroom wall. He brushed his hands. "I just came to about three minutes ago. I was beaned, sweetheart—I went out like a light."

He made a sharp turn on his heel, crossed to the telephone and scooped it off the table. "Gimme Police Headquarters." He looked at Kennedy and laughed bitterly, harshly. "Taken for a sleigh-ride, I was. What I get for being human to people. I ought to have my pan kicked in. I ought—"

He broke off, said into the mouthpiece: "Otto?… MacBride. Listen, Otto. I want a broadcast for three persons: Louise Maybanks, Thomas Hendricks, and a man named Boyd. This guy Boyd owns Boyd's Investments, office in Race Street, and he lives at the *Williamsport Hotel.* The dame is about five feet seven, about twenty-five years, about one-thirty pounds, black hair, wearing a black evening dress. I don't know what Hendricks looks like. Put that on the short wave. Send Moriarity or Cohen out to the *Williamsport* for Boyd. I'll be seeing you." He whanged the receiver into the hook, flexed his arms, his legs, tightened down his jaw as a hard glitter came into his eyes.

"So she's mixed up in it," Kennedy said.

MacBride was pointing. "The guy Hendricks was drunk—and out—on that divan. He's the guy must know something. The jane fainted. I was standing in front of that divan when—bingo!—I'm beaned. The guy Boyd had left a few minutes before. I guess he did. Maybe he didn't. But if he did, then I was conked by somebody hiding in a closet or something. When I came to, everybody was gone—even the drunk. But the jane, the jane"—he held up his fist—"she was scared, scared about something. So scared, so damned sick with fright, that she passed out. And me—I was out for at least twenty minutes."

He picked up his hat. "Come on." He hauled Kennedy out of the chair, steered him to the door and on into the corridor. They walked to the elevator bank, and when the door slid open MacBride shoved Kennedy in and said to the operator:

"Do you know Mr. Boyd?"

"No, sir?"

"Do you remember taking down a tall, heavy-set man, gray around the ears?"

"About half an hour ago?"

"Was it half an hour ago?"

"I took a man like that down about half an hour ago."

"Was he alone?"

"Yes."

"Did you take Miss Maybanks down later?"

"No."

"Is there another elevator?"

"Only the service."

"Man on that?"

"Not this late. This late, it works automatic. You press a button and it comes up, or down. You know, just like—"

"I get you."

The skipper helped Kennedy from the car, hung on to his arm and piloted him to the desk. He said to the clerk:

"Got a house officer here?"

"Why, yes, sir."

"Get him." MacBride jerked his thumb. "Tell him to park in 707 till a cop gets here. Meantime, if anyone comes in the apartment, they're to be pinched."

The clerk stammered: "All—oh—uh—b-but...."

And by that time MacBride was hauling Kennedy through the door. Up the street, he found Benninger snoring at the wheel of the police sedan. The man's rubicund face was a study in peace and well-being.

MacBride said to the night at large: "Sure—I could die and be dead for hours, and Benninger would pound his ear just the same. I could be— *Benninger!*"

Long training made Benninger snap awake, choke the motor and step on the starter—all in an instant.

"Ah!" hiccoughed Kennedy. "A robot, by God!"

"In, drunk. And you, Benninger—Headquarters."

The sedan rolled quietly through the dark streets.

"How's the knob?" Kennedy asked.

"Lousy," MacBride said. He went on, "The jane—I wouldn't call her a broad, because I don't think she is—"

"Getting sentimental in your old age?"

"I can do without any wisecracks from you, Kennedy. A nice girl—breeding, poise: things a mugg like me likes because I don't run across them any too often. I don't say she knows anything, but I've got a hunch this young guy Hendricks does, and she knows he knows—and she loves him—and that's why she's frightened stiff. It could be that she played 'possum—that when she saw me standing by the divan she sneaked up and let me have it; then she woke him up and got him out of the apartment."

"And now where is she?"

MacBride slapped his knee. "We'll get her. Through her we'll get Hendricks. Hendricks will know who killed Sibbold. The more I think of it, the more I believe it!... That's the third red light you went through, Benninger. Did somebody steal your brakes?"

"Oh, hell," Kennedy chided. "Boys will be boys, Stevie."

WHEN MacBride entered the central room at police headquarters, Otto Bettdecken, the man at the desk, was having a midnight snack consisting of pumpernickel, liederkranz and lager. His mustache was creamed with foam, his apple cheeks glowed.

"Any news?" MacBride said.

"About that what it was you called up about?"

"Yeah."

"Nope. Mory and Ike shot right out, and the roof put it on the short wave. Your wife called up and said when you come home you should pick up a bottle of milk of magnesia, I think it was milk of magnesia."

"You're sure it wasn't citrate?"

"Well, now that I think of it—"

"Call her back and check up."

He went on up to his office, and Kennedy trailed in after him, looking very white and drunk. MacBride took a long look at him, then opened his desk drawer, took out a whiskey glass. Into the glass he poured equal parts of Worcestershire sauce and Scotch.

"Try that."

"Thanks."

"It either picks you up or knocks you down completely."

"If it'll stay down it'll do me good."

"If you think it's not going to stay down, go in the washroom and be decent about it."

"Ah," said Kennedy, setting down the empty glass, "I think it'll stay down."

The phone rang and MacBride picked it up. "MacBride, yeah…. The Fourth?… Okey." He hung up. "They want me over at the Fourth Precinct house. You stay here."

"The air'll do me good."

"Come on, then."

They went downstairs, and MacBride was halfway across the central room when Otto Bettdecken called:

"Hey, Cap! That was bicarbonate of soda your wife wanted!"

Chapter IV

THE Fourth was a tough, ragged precinct. The precinct house stood in a narrow street of ancient brick houses, its twin green lights making a ghostly glow. It was a frame building of two stories, with six wide wooden steps leading up to two swing-doors. The central room was dim, the walls a dull drab brown, the desk high and pulpit-like.

Entering, MacBride saw that the room was filled with cops, a few detectives, some newspapermen. There was more activity in the rear.

Bollingay, the detective-sergeant attached to the precinct, said from the crowd:

"Got something back here I thought you'd like to see."

A red-head said to Kennedy: "Got anything on your hip?"

"A bruise—private, brother."

MacBride went through the crowd, following Bollingay's heels. They turned right into a narrow corridor, then left into a large room. Bollingay stopped and nodded to a cot upon which a man lay. MacBride nodded also, crossed the room and gazed down at the wide eyes, the dead pale face.

Bollingay said: "Automobile license," and passed MacBride a yellow card.

MacBride looked at it and said: "What happened?"

"Melcher was on beat along River Road. Found him laying alongside an ashcan in Hilt Street—dark as hell there, and Melcher fell over him. He rang in and I ran down. A doctor was there when I got there, but the guy was dead. I ran him over here for the time being."

"Shot?"

"Nah. Socked on the head. In the back. It's split."

"Anything else on him?"

"Thirty bucks and some change. I put it in an envelope."

"Anything else?"

"Nah."

Kennedy came in and said, "Who's he?"

"Hendricks," MacBride said.

"Sick?"

"Dead."

There was a moment of silence and then MacBride stirred, said to Bollingay: "Okey. Shoot him to the morgue and tell 'em to get to work on him right away."

"This connects with the Sibbold job, huh?"

"There's a connection, Al. There's got to be. I was counting on finding things from this bird. Come on, Kennedy."

The Bureau sedan carried them out of the ragged neighborhood. MacBride sat in the darkness, chewing on his lip, saying nothing. He had been certain—dead certain—of extracting valuable information from Hendricks, and he had been certain of apprehending Hendricks in a very short time. His main balloon of hope had burst: Hendricks was dead.

Inside, deep down, he felt a sense of guilt. He should have roused Hendricks in the first place. He should have been deaf to the importunate pleading of the woman; it would have saved the man's life—obviously it would have saved Hendricks' life. The skipper inhaled deeply, let the breath out slowly, bit by bit. Was Kennedy right? Was he getting sentimental in his old age? His hand became a fist on his knee. His lips came together tightly over his teeth. Maybe the woman knew something too. Maybe she would be found dead also. A lump rose in MacBride's throat; it was with an effort that he downed it, swallowing hard.

Police work: he was tired of it, sick to death of the blood and intrigue that went with it. Long, irregular hours. When he was a harness bull, he had regular hours on and off. Now, as head of the Detective Division, he had no hours at all. He should have been in bed long ago.

When he swung into Headquarters, Otto Bettdecken said: "Mory and Ike came back with a guy."

MacBride nodded and climbed the stairs, went down the corridor and pushed into his office. Kennedy drifted in after him.

Boyd was sitting on the desk, swinging his feet, rolling a walking stick between his palms. Self-possessed, calm, he said:

"I'm in the limelight, eh, Captain?"

The skipper was not in a facetious mood. He hung his hat on the clothes tree, blew his nose; his eyes had a dark inward look and there was a tautness around his mouth.

He said: "When you left Miss Maybanks' apartment, where'd you go?"

"Home."

"Right home?"

"Right home."

MacBride said: "It ought to interest you to know that Miss Maybanks has disappeared."

Boyd stood up, dipping his head, placing a curious direct stare on MacBride. "Perhaps she took Hendricks home."

"Hendricks is dead."

Boyd dipped his head a little more, made his stare more intently curious. "My Lord!" he said with quiet concern.

Moriarity was shaving down a match. Cohen was shuffling dice in his hand.

"In Hilt Street," MacBride said in a dull, drab voice. "He was found dead in Hilt Street. When you left Miss Maybanks' apartment—a few minutes after you left—I was knocked cold from behind. When I came to, Miss Maybanks and Hendricks were gone."

Boyd was grave. "That's curious."

Came Kennedy's voice from a far shadow of the room: "Mr. Boyd, what's your specialty in investments?"

"General investments—no specialty. It's hard to specialize in these parlous times."

"Beer stocks, for instance, are swell now."

"I believe they are."

"Aren't you handling blocks of Wesserbrau, Red Band, Hilderbrau, and Black Prince?"

"Experimenting, yes."

"Didn't you have a long interview with Sibbold?"

"I had no interview with Sibbold."

"Didn't you suggest a combine with Sibbold and didn't he refuse flatly to go into any combine?"

"I had no interview, suggested no combine." Boyd bowed. "I'm sorry if you've been misinformed." He turned to MacBride. "Is there anything I can do for you, Captain?"

MacBride said: "It keeps pounding in my head, over and over again, that you know what lays behind all this. Just what were you to Louise Maybanks?"

Boyd shrugged. "A friend…" He mused a little, flexed his lips. "And like a friend, I catch trouble for my pains."

"She's got dough," Kennedy drowsed. "Dough. Were you her financial adviser?"

"Naturally, since I'm her friend."

"You advised her, I suppose, to plant a lot of dinero in these brewery stocks?"

"I suggested that, did not urge. Naturally I would have suggested that."

A match flamed, lit up Kennedy's worn and sallow face, brought out clearly the marks of self-indulgence, the stamp of an intemperate man killing himself by inches with drink.

MacBride snapped: "If you've anything to say, Kennedy, say it. Don't fandango all over the place."

"Let it slide," Kennedy said. "I was just talking through me hat. I don't know anything. Not," he added, with a curious intonation, "a thing."

Boyd revolved his walking stick between his palms, said slowly to MacBride: "I regret this embarrassing position—but I don't regret having tried to offer Miss Maybanks some advice. I only hope she is safe. I know nothing, Captain. I'm sorry I know nothing. I regret I did not urge you to wake up Hendricks. That I do regret."

"And me too," MacBride muttered.

"I should like to catch some sleep."

"Okey. You can go."

Boyd made a leisurely exit.

Moriarity clipped: "Ya-a-ah—Kennedy making left-handed cracks again—like all the time."

Kennedy was languid: "Nerts to you, darling—precious nerts to you."

"F'r two cents—"

"And who did you say your father was?"

"Stop it!" MacBride barked. "You're like a lot of damned hoodlums! All of you!"

Cohen rolled the dice on the desk, showed a seven, snapped his fingers.

"Take those dice, Ike," the skipper said sulphurously, "and get the hell out of here. Mory, you go too. Hang downstairs. And I said downstairs—not down the street in the Greek's."

The two detectives went out and MacBride landed in his swivel chair, filled his briar, lit up and puffed furiously. His dark, hunted eyes danced back and forth across the desk's bright surface; his fingers worried the pipe bowl.

"It's like this, old tomato," said Kennedy wearily, hardly above a husky whisper. "This Boyd may be okey, and maybe he is. But he dug into the beer stocks when the brewers opened their shops. He handles power, railroads, steel. Okey. But he dug deep into beer. Sibbold was in beer. Hendricks worked for Boyd and was fired. Boyd was a financial adviser to Louise Maybanks. It connects—all around, link by link.

"Boyd says he knows nothing. He's in the clear. But watch him, Skipper, watch him. The betting was that this state would stay dry. Bootleg breweries went full blast up to the last. Then the state went wet. Think of thousands of barrels of beer, the thousands of bottles of beer, that were on hand at the time. Think of the dough sunk in all that beer. And where goeth that bootleg beer?

"Listen. Sibbold was killed for a definite reason. He was killed because he wouldn't play ball, wouldn't get in line, or he was killed because he found out something and was primed to spring what he knew. Nail this guy Boyd. He's smooth, polished, and he can take it. But how long can he take it? Nail him! Hold him as a material witness. Frame him. But nail him—get him in the jug. He knows something. Uncle Kennedy says he knows something."

MacBride said: "You're guessing. You believe in a hunch. I never frame a guy. I wouldn't frame Boyd."

"You're getting weak-minded. Damn it, you're getting weak-minded!"

MacBride said nothing.

Chapter V

L OUISE MAYBANKS: missing. The morning newspapers said so. From dusty files they had rooted out pictures of Louise Maybanks—taken five or six years ago, when she made her debut. Sibbold dead. Hendricks dead. Louise Maybanks missing. Once she had spun in the social whirl of the swank West End. The winter of 1929 and '30 had killed her father, and his death had killed her mother; between them, they'd left heavy insurance to Louise Maybanks. Some phrased it this way: "And then Louise went native." By that they meant that she had moved out of the West End, taken a suite in a sleek hotel, run the gauntlet of nightclubs, night life, men by the score. Erratic, unreasonable—but perpetually lovely; a moth badgering a flame.

These headlines haunted MacBride. He saw them wherever he looked: Louise Maybanks Missing. He was not only a conscientious policeman, he was a conscientious man. It occurred to him that the blood of Louise Maybanks might already be on his hands. He thought of it that way. If he had acted properly in her apartment, Hendricks would have been saved, Louise Maybanks would not now be missing.

"Oh, hell," Kennedy said, "don't go around looking like Macbeth—or maybe it's Othello I mean. What's to be, will be."

"In your mind maybe; not in mine."

"If I'm walking down a path and I come to a tree and the tree's in my path, I walk around the tree; I don't bust my head against it."

"I've got a one-track mind, Kennedy. I'm the kind of guy brainy people make jokes about. But I'm what I am. You're wasting your breath, sweetheart."

He sailed out of his office like an ill wind, pounded his heels down the stairs, went out and walked to the morgue. The morning was bright, crisp; people looked happy; a hurdy-gurdy played *Valencia* and kids danced. But MacBride wore a face as long as a mule's.

He spent ten minutes in the morgue, and when he came out his hat was jerked an inch lower on his forehead, his jaw jutted a fraction of an inch more than when he had entered. And he was cursing behind tight lips. He had made a phone call from the morgue, and in a few minutes Benninger arrived with the Bureau sedan and MacBride climbed in, snapped an address, sat back with a somber look and folded his arms.

The sedan sped west, went through the park, came out on the Boulevard and followed it for half a mile. It turned right into a wide street, stopped in front of the *Williamsport*. MacBride swung out, hiked up the long cement walk and slapped his way into the lobby. He reappeared in a minute, slammed into the sedan and rasped out another address. Benninger, looking very alive, whipped the car into gear and MacBride folded his arms again and continued to look very somber. The way led east, bearing northward. Benninger used the siren and jumped the stop lights.

Race Street was on the fringe of the financial district, and halfway down it there was a seven story brown building in front of which Benninger stopped. MacBride's coat tails flew as he crossed the sidewalk, and entering the revolving door violently, he floored a man who was on the way out. He didn't look around.

An elevator lifted him to the fourth floor, and he went up the fourth floor corridor stabbing dark looks at the names on frosted door panels. Then he grabbed a doorknob, opened the door, and saw a youth pounding a typewriter. A connecting door was open, and through it he caught a glimpse of Boyd. The youth was saying, "Yes? You want to see—" but by this time MacBride was in the inner office, and he slammed the door behind him.

Boyd looked very neat, very well groomed, self-possessed behind the large, flat-topped desk. And he was cheerful, though offhand:

"Good morning, Captain."

MacBride did not loose a flow of language. He pulled up, tightened down; he was suddenly calm and cool, but with an effort. He placed both hands on the desk, leaned on his straightened arms.

Boyd said: "Indications are you know something about Miss Maybanks. Please don't keep me in suspense."

"Mr. Boyd, how drunk would you say Hendricks was last night?"

"Drunk? Well, quite drunk. Very drunk. When a man can't stand on his feet, he's very drunk, isn't he?"

"Yes, he's very drunk when he can't stand on his feet. You say then that he was so drunk he couldn't navigate."

Boyd nodded leisurely. "He was very, very drunk."

"That's all I wanted to know. Good morning."

He turned on his heel, left the office and made a phone call from the lobby. "Mory," he said. "You and Ike grab a cab and shoot down to 45 Race Street. Snap on it."

He stood outside the lobby, tapping his heels. Ten minutes later Moriarity and Cohen alighted from a cab, and MacBride said:

"You guys plant yourselves here. If Boyd comes out, tail him. Tail every move he makes."

He crossed the sidewalk, climbed into the Bureau sedan and shot Benninger another address. It was five minutes' ride to the *Flower Apartments,* on Winscott Street, and MacBride was out of the sedan before it completely stopped. Inside, he had a few words with the elevator man, and was then lifted to the fifth floor. A door marked 510 was the door that felt the rap of his knuckles.

Sanarens, the *Keyhole* owner, puffy-faced from a long night, opened the door, pulled his robe tighter about his beefy stomach. His eyes flickered and he said:

"I just got up and—"

"That's all right, Sanarens," MacBride said, pushing in, closing the door. "It's this: how much did Hendricks drink last night?"

"Hendricks?"

"The guy was with Louise Maybanks."

"I—oh, that fellow. Well—"

"He drank a lot, didn't he? He was cock-eyed drunk, wasn't he? He was swacked, plastered—wasn't he?"

Sanarens' puffy white face jounced. "I guess he was pretty drunk, Cap. But I told him, I advised him—"

"You told him to lay off, huh?"

"Yes. Personally I told him. My place is a nice place and I don't like to see—"

"You don't like to see a guy get so swacked he can't walk. Is that it, Sanarens?"

"Y-yes."

"Then you'd say Hendricks was so lousy cock-eyed drunk he couldn't walk. You'd say that, huh?"

"Uh—yes."

MacBride roared: "You'd swear to that, would you?"

Sanarens went backward across the living-room, flopping his hands, making a round startled O of his mouth. MacBride went after him, dogging his backward footsteps; and he yelled:

"You will swear to that, won't you?"

"My God, Skipper—you look crazy!"

"I am crazy! I'm nuts! I'm out of my mind!" And then he snarled in a low, contemptuous tone: "Yes I'm out of my mind, I am, I am!" He caught hold of the lapels of Sanarens' robe, heaved the man on to a divan, growled: "Sit down, mugg!"

Sanarens not only sat, but he shook also—he shook from his puffy jowls down his arms and down his chest to his fat stomach; nor did his legs escape. And sweat came so suddenly to his face that it seemed to have been pumped there.

"So I'm crazy, am I!" snarled MacBride.

"Jeese, Skipper, what's the matter? Ain't I always been a decent guy? Ain't I been square, on the level?"

"Like a corkscrew you have.... Listen, Sanarens," the skipper went on in a low deadly voice. "I'm looking for Louise Maybanks. I want her. I've been gypped and double-crossed, and I want her."

"You're asking me!"

"I'm asking you. You're a lousy, two-tongued bum, Sanarens, and you're going to come across or I'll make a hospital case out of you. You hear that? A hospital case!"

"Now look, Cap! Now wait! Jeese, now wait!"

"I'm waiting. And to speed you up, I'll tell you something you already know. This: Hendricks wasn't drunk. The autopsy showed that there wasn't a drop, not one drop, of liquor in his system. Not one little drop, Sanarens! You hear that?"

Sanarens jumped up. MacBride gripped him, held on to him.

"That's a lie," Sanarens choked. "You can't kid me. That's a lie!"

"I'm suddenly beginning to hate the sight of you, baby. Spill it quick! What's the hook-up? What happened to the jane?"

"I tell you—"

"I'm telling you I've got no patience. Where is she?"

"I don't know—"

MacBride hit him with the flat of his hard hand. The sound of the blow frightened Sanarens as much as the blow itself.

MacBride's voice was thick: "I gave you every break a guy in your business could get. I never grafted. I never took a cent from you. I let you run your place wide open and I tipped you when the Federals were hot. I was a white guy to you, Sanarens, and you gypped me."

He planted his fist in Sanarens' face, drove him toppling across the room. The skipper's face was red with rage. He watched Sanarens fall, take a table down with him; and he went after the man, picked him up and hit him again and again—and he meant every blow. Sanarens flopped to the floor, his face bloody. He crawled on hands and knees, in a circle, gibbering, a grotesque figure in a silk robe, silk pajamas. Finally he stopped crawling and lay sprawled on his back, only half-conscious.

MacBride picked up the telephone. "Emergency Hospital," he said. His breath was laboring, his eyes humid. "Emergency Hospital?... *Flower Apartments*, Winscott Street. Apartment 510.... Yeah, a mad dog bit a man named Sanarens."

Chapter VI

AS the skipper walked down from the lobby of the *Flower Apartments*, he saw Benninger beckoning excitedly. MacBride lengthened his stride, and Benninger said:

"Mory and Ike just went past in a cab, tailing another cab."

"What'd they say?"

"Nothing."

"A cab drew up here, but the guy instead of getting out, he went on again. Then Ike and Mory came along—and followed."

"Boyd." MacBride was looking at the ambulance.

"Huh?"

MacBride jumped into the tonneau. "See if you can pick up Mory and Ike. Step on it."

Benninger pointed. "They're just making a left, way ahead there. See?"

"Get after them. Just tail them."

"Oke."

Benninger squared off behind the wheel, got the motor into high gear and stepped on it.

"No siren," MacBride said.

"I gotcha."

The skipper sat in the middle of the rear seat, his hands braced on his spread knees. The knuckles were a bit sore, a bit chafed. It was madness to have hit Sanarens the way he did, but the old boy could stomach almost anything but a double-deal. He was still warm under the collar, his blood had not yet cooled off. His body was rigid, his face granite-hard, pale now rather than red, for his purpose, despite the heat of body and mind, was a cold and deadly one.

Benninger picked up the tail easily, followed the taxi across a broad plaza, down a boulevard, left into a commercial thoroughfare. Traffic offered obstacles, but Benninger, fully awake now, was an able driver, worming his way in and out of line, browbeating other cars out of the way. His siren would have cleared the way instantly, but MacBride did not want the siren.

They cut south and east towards Little Italy, but turned sharp east before they reached it, and went over a short but abrupt hill, down a street of decent-looking dwellings, small second-rate apartment houses, rooming-houses: a German district, sedate, busy, not blatant.

Suddenly the cab stopped in front of a drug-store, and Benninger drew up behind it. Moriarity and Cohen remained seated in the cab, leaning forward, peering hard. After a moment they moved, opened the door and stepped out. MacBride walked up to them.

"Good work, kids."

Mory spun, shrugged. "Hello, Cap."

Cohen said: "He just left that gray cab and went in that frame house there with the hydrant in front of it. We'll wait and see when he comes out."

"I'll go in." MacBride said. "I'm going to nail that baby."

"What was the ambulance doing in front of the *Flower?*" Moriarity asked.

"I poked Sanarens."

"Why don't you wait till Boyd comes out?"

"I'm through waiting. Come on."

"Should we knock?"

"No. We'll take the door down."

"Bust a window instead," Cohen offered. "You can always say you fell against it by accident."

MacBride nodded. "Idea."

He led the way because his legs were longest. But Moriarity and Cohen were right behind him as he turned into the short flag walk leading to the low veranda. MacBride did not pause, did not slow down. There was no second thought. He put his feet on the veranda, took four steps across the boards and put his elbow through the nearest window. Then he put a leg through, followed with his body. He did not draw his gun, but his hand was on it. Moriarity and Cohen joined him. The room was empty—a small, stuffy sitting-room with a door at the left.

"This way," MacBride said.

They went through the doorway into a square hall. A stairway led aloft. MacBride went up on the run, two steps at a time. He heard a door bang, heard quick voices, sudden movement. He reached the upper hall as a door opened. Instantly the door slammed shut. Cohen went past him like a streak and hit the door with his right shoulder. It did not give. There was excited movement behind the door.

MacBride said: "Open it."

There was the sound of running feet.

"Where's that?" Cohen muttered.

They all looked around but did not know.

"Open it!" MacBride rasped.

A door banged somewhere distant in the house.

"If there's a back stairway..." Moriarity said.

Cohen dashed to the rear of the hall, opened a window there, looked down into a large yard; the yard had a field behind it, a street beyond the field.

MacBride drew his gun and put two shots through the door's lock. He grabbed the knob. It fell apart in his hand and the door opened and the skipper stepped in, stopped short in his tracks.

Boyd stood in the middle of the room, unarmed. Two small men, one a blond, the other a red-head, stood on either side of him; both were armed, with the guns leveled at MacBride and Moriarity. A tall bald man stood holding Louise Maybanks in front of him; he held her with one hand, with the other hand he held a gun to her back. He had white eyes, brown skin—or his skin was so brown that it made his eyes seem white.

"This is the situation," Boyd said. "You cornered us, but the book's not closed. Not by a long sight. One move out of you or that fellow with you, and the woman gets killed. That plain?"

MacBride lowered his gun. "Plain enough. So what then?"

"We're leaving town. We've got to. We're taking the woman with us. We want a head start out of this building, and if you throw a squad out after us, the woman gets killed. I want to make it clear that she gets killed just as soon as any attempt is made to apprehend us. I saw the ambulance in front of the *Flower*, drew my own conclusions. I hope I've made myself plain."

Louise Maybanks' hair was tousled, as though she had struggled. There was a bruise on her lovely white face and there was a kind of dead terror in her eyes. She uttered no sound. She stood tall and straight, a convulsive movement in her breasts, an intermittent pulse in her throat. But her lips remained shut, tight.

The blond little man and the red-haired little man had faces like masks of wax—cold, bloodless. The bald man kept lifting and dropping his upper lip, and his left hand held Louise Maybanks in a grip of steel.

MacBride grunted: "Put those guns down, you pups. How far do you think you'll get with this?"

Boyd said: "It all depends on you. If you want the woman killed now, start now. If a week from now, start then. If a month from now...." He shrugged. "It's up to you."

Louise Maybanks' lips opened. "Start now," she said in a dead voice. "This minute... now." And then she screamed: "Now! Now!"

Heat rushed over MacBride and he said to Boyd: "A swell spot you put me in—a swell spot."

"Her life is in your hands, Captain."

MacBride backed up. "Okey. It won't be on my hands."

"My God!" she cried. "Make them kill me now!"

"I'd like to get them now," MacBride said. "I could—the little rats there, the two little punks—and Boyd—and the lug holding you. But it's guns down with me—though your face'll haunt me, girlie, till I nail these babies."

Moriarity muttered: "Come on, Cap—before you blow off."

MacBride backed up to the threshold.

At that instant Cohen appeared on the threshold of the doorway leading to a room beyond. Cohen stood quite easily on his feet. He did not shoot from the hip because that is chance shooting. He aimed. His arm was up, level. He sighted. He fired. The shot broke the bald-headed man's gun-hand at the wrist. The room shook.

MacBride had no time to aim. But the two little men were close and they erred in looking towards the other doorway. MacBride fired four times, lightning fast. He knocked down the red-head with two shots, hit the blond with one. Moriarity put three shots into the blond as Boyd drew sluggishly.

"Down, Boyd," MacBride said sadly. "Gun down, Boyd—"

But he had to shoot Boyd. He nailed Boyd's hand to his chest while the red-head threshed around on the floor and called to God.

Louise Maybanks stood very tall, very straight, with her eyes closed tightly, her back arched, her hands doubled at her sides. She did not collapse, but her slender body shook, vibrated, and every bone in her jaw was visible.

MacBride said thickly: "You get around, Ike."

"Yeah," Cohen said. "Before you shot that door open I dropped to the backyard and came in the back way, and up. I guess I walked into something…. Catch the girl, Cap. I think she's going to slam down."

MacBride caught her.

KENNEDY poured himself a generous portion of the skipper's Scotch, raised it, said: "I suppose this is because I didn't say, 'I told you so.' Well, down the hatch, tomato!"

"Boyd—yeah, Boyd." MacBride muttered. "One of the smoothest articles I ever ran up against. It was like this. Boyd had his foot deep in beer. He got these bootleg brewers on the string and he made a tie-up with most of the legal brewers. But not with Sibbold. He explained the racket to Sibbold, but Sibbold wouldn't get in line.

"The bootleg breweries had thousands of gallons of beer on hand and the hookup was this: the legal brewers were to let their labels be slapped on the bootleg beer and they were to get a cut. It was explained to them by Boyd that this would hold only until the bootleg beer was used up. But Sibbold saw the catch. He knew that once he'd get in it, he'd have to stay in it. He'd have to keep slapping his labels on bootleg beer, because the racket was too good to let go—for the bootleg crowd.

"Then some of these guys got wise, sneaked a batch of Sibbold's labels and slapped them on their bootleg brew. Boyd fired Hendricks because Hendricks took Sibbold's part. Then Sibbold threatened to bare the whole scheme. Boyd urged him to think it over and urged him to have supper at the *Keyhole.*

"Sibbold went there, but Boyd hadn't arrived yet—though he'd reserved a table by that window. Sanarens was in on it. By accident Hendricks and the woman were there, and Sibbold asked them over for a drink. Hendricks didn't drink but he went over, and Sibbold offered him a job. The kid was glad to have it. Sibbold was on the spot.

"Hendricks saw that hand come through the window and he grabbed, but not soon enough. The shot was fired. But he tussled with the hand, broke a cufflink. He got the top part but not the bottom. I got the bottom. He ran out and the girl ran after him, and they ran several blocks after what they thought was the man. But they lost him. The girl didn't want to go back to the *Keyhole* because she'd got a glimpse of Sibbold's face. Hendricks took her home. They were followed by the red-head and the blond, and by Boyd, who'd picked up his two muggs.

"Boyd thought it would be easy with Hendricks. It seems the blond—the guy who actually killed Sibbold—had helped himself to a pair of Boyd's monogrammed cufflinks.... Well, they finally slugged Hendricks. But just then I turned up. When I went into the apartment, the two punks were hiding in the closet. Boyd had threatened Louise Maybanks that if she didn't talk the way he told her to, the two punks in the closet would kill me and her. So she acted—and damned well.

"After I was beaned, the two punks carried Hendricks to the service elevator and made the woman go with them. She went gladly. She thought Hendricks was only unconscious. She didn't know he was dead. Imagine—while I was in that apartment, Hendricks was on that divan—dead! Ought my pan be red!"

Kennedy said: "Boyd and his muggs sure balled things up."

"Of course they did. But they couldn't help themselves. Their only out when I entered Louise Maybanks' apartment was to pretend that Hendricks was dead drunk. They had no time to think of the consequences. And they fooled me—boy, how they fooled me! Two hot rods in the closet and a dead guy on the divan!"

Kennedy grinned. "You may be slow on the uptake, old tomato, but you're sure hell on the downpour.... I'd drink to you, but the glass is empty, and I never hint for a second drink, even though at present I'm unusually dry."

"That's what I like about you, you bum. You're so bashful. Here, souse!"

He slid the bottle across the desk.

Lay Down the Law

Kennedy, newshound extraordinary, goes on a bender and puts Capt. MacBride and his whole force on their ears.

Chapter I

SHE was pretty tight. Mike, the blond bartender, very neat and dapper in his starched white monkey jacket, put a bright shine on the glass he had been polishing for several minutes and at last planked it down with a gesture of vanishing endurance. It was between ten and eleven, and most of the regular customers were at the bike races or the theater. There was no one standing at the bar. The woman, sitting at a small bar table against the opposite wall, was the sole customer.

Mike slapped down the bar rag, clipped: "Clam it! Pipe down! Sign off!"

She fanned the air limply with her plump white hand. "Take a hay ride, bar boy. Just because you came up out of the spittoons is no reason you should get high hat."

"Nobody's getting high hat, funny face."

"Lay off and gimme a drink—double Scotch."

He shook his head, made his lips taut. "Nix. You're swacked now. You came in here swacked. We're getting a crowd in here soon and I ain't gonna have you sitting there cockeyed and shooting your mouth off. This here is a respectable joint and the dame at the door ought to get her slats kicked for letting you in. Go on, scram."

"Yeah?" She opened her purse and yanked out a roll of bills, flaunted it. "I've got what it takes, kid. Look at it! Why, damn it, I could buy this dump, lock, stock and barrel!... Huh, funny face, am I?" She rose, swayed across to the bar and fell against it, her mouth twisting sullenly and her eyes glittering. "I wanna drink," she hiccoughed solemnly. "T' hell with your lip, bar boy. Gimme a drink. Duh-double Scotch."

Mike's eyes snapped, and he braced his arms on the bar. "You heard me. Take the air before you get given it."

"Ha. Chuck me out, will you!"

"Hey—" Dave Rood came in through a rear swing-door. "Hey, who's making all the noise?"

She looped around on one heel. "Oh, 's you, Dave. Hello. Tell this rat to give me a drink."

Rood lifted his white, hard chin towards Mike, queried with his pale eyes.

Mike said tightly out of the corner of his mouth: "Beefing. Shooting her mouth off. She's unkdray, Dave, and noisy. Shooting her jaw off. Like this: 'I'm back in this burg and I'm staying. Because why? Because I know enough to burn a lot of guys and I'm cashing in.'" He bent his hard stare on her. "Plastered when she hit here."

"Nerts to you!" she flung at Mike; and to Rood: "What the hell is this here, a saloon or a tea garden? Am I asking for a hand-out? No! I'm asking for a drink. And this dumb slob keeps making cracks."

Rood remained cool, unmoved. "We don't want to hear what you know, Bertha. I'm running a bar, not a hall."

"Jeese! So now you're starting on me!"

"I'm telling you things, Bertha."

"To hell with you then, too! Gimme a drink!"

"You're tight now, Bertha. Take a walk."

"Take a walk my eye! I'm gonna—"

"This way," Rood said, taking her by the arm.

He was not rough. He was firm and determined, marching her from the bar into the hall before she quite knew what it was all about. Then she began to struggle, holding back, digging her heels into the rug. He dragged her on, saying nothing, while she began heaping dark and blistering invectives upon him. Reaching the door, he opened it, gave her a brisk little shove, closed and bolted the door behind her.

She went down the flight of six stone steps slack-legged and miraculously did not slip on the snow. She was still cursing and muttering, and she stood on the sidewalk, teetering back and forth. The snow fell silently, small wide-spaced flakes that came out of the dark above and made a moving haze about the street lights.

She was still teetering back and forth and muttering dire imprecations when a taxi drew up. The driver reached back and opened the door, and she swayed towards it. Kennedy flopped out and both collided and went down heavily. Kennedy sighed philosophically, and the woman, heavier, lying on top of him, let out an exasperated breath. The driver swung down and helped them up and Kennedy made a deep, exaggerated bow.

The woman was swaying. She said: "Who's going in this cab, you or me?"

"I," said Kennedy, "am going in Dave Rood's."

" 'S no use. They ain't serving liquor in there."

Kennedy mumbled: "Quaint. Well...." He sighed and swung back towards the cab.

The woman started at the same time and both became wedged in the door of the cab. Kennedy backed out, muttered an apology, and the woman climbed in. Then Kennedy climbed in after her and flopped down beside her.

"So what?" the driver said.

The woman hiccoughed: "Let's go to Brick Square."

The cab started, rolled down the dark street, its tires crunching drily on the packed snow.

The woman said to Kennedy: "You own this car?"

"Yeah. My town car."

"Swell of you to gimme a lift."

"Glad to. Have a drink." He passed her a pint flask and she took a long swallow.

"Say," she said, "this stuff's good. Why'd you wanta go to Rood's?"

"They have good ginger ale there," he muttered.

He was sitting with his elbows on his knees, his head in his hands. He could not see very well because when he was very drunk a film always danced before his eyes. He was always either slightly drunk or very drunk, and on this night he was very drunk. When the cab stopped, the woman hauled herself out of the seat and leaned past him towards the door. But he moved and opened it himself, and since both tried to get out at the same time, both had difficulty in keeping upright when they landed sprawling on the sidewalk. The driver jumped down and Kennedy thrust a dollar round and round until finally the driver made a desperate thrust and landed it.

The woman said: "C'm up an' have a drink."

"Please' to meet you," Kennedy replied, and taking her arm, staggered with her up the street. Passing through a door, they went rubber-legged across a high, narrow and deserted lobby. It was an automatic elevator, and the woman said half aloud, "Eighth floor," and jabbed one of the buttons. After having missed the eighth floor three times, she finally succeeded in punching the right button, and Kennedy zigzagged down the hall after her.

It was a two-room apartment, large and modern, but Kennedy saw little of it, even as he saw little of the woman's face; he merely knew it was a face by the pale blur he saw, and he knew it was a woman by the sound of her voice.

"Sit down," she said, and sloped off towards the pantry.

He shook his head. "No thanks. Sit down, you never get up. Stand, and you never have to get up. Simple as ABC, only most folks never realize it, never realize. That's life, though. Look it up, if you don't believe me. Page ninety-two of the telephone directory."

The woman reached the pantry, sat down and passed a hand across her forehead. "Whew!" she breathed out. One leg gave, and she fell sidewise, then downward, and lay on the floor. She rolled over and lay on her back, looked at the ceiling calculatingly for a moment, then closed her eyes and passed out.

Time means nothing to a drunk, for a while at least, and Kennedy remained swaying in the center of the floor for at least fifteen minutes. Then he jerked up his head, looked about, and muttered, "Huh. Giving me the go-by, huh?" He did a few broken-kneed steps, then teetered towards the door and muttered, "To hell with you." He opened the door, chuckled, broke a match stick and imbedded one piece of it in the keyhole. "That," he mumbled, "is for giving me the go-by."

He reached the elevator, found it to be still on the eighth floor, and entered. After several futile attempts to get it all the way down, he left it at the third floor and walked to the lobby, punched open the lobby door and went unbalanced out into the street. A strong arm stopped him and he vaguely saw two dark figures standing in the snow.

One said: "Take it easy, buddy. You'll kill yourself."

"Thanks, friend. Doubtless you saved this city's star reporter from concussion of the brain or housemaid's knee."

"Name's Kennedy, ain't it?"

"Such is fame! Can't go anywhere without being detected.... You are right, my friend. Kennedy. Excuse me now. I have to rush back to the office and write it up."

"Write what up?"

"Story. Big story. I've just interviewed a very famous character."

A third voice muttered: "Let him go ahead."

Kennedy swung off, making crooked tracks in the snow. Every now and then he stopped and raised bleary eyes in search of a cab; saw none, and went on, bent way over, seeming at all times about to stumble but miraculously holding to his feet. He turned a corner and a figure sidled up alongside him and quavered:

"Bud, c'n you help out a guy?"

Kennedy said: "You look cold, my good man. Here." He removed his tan coat, said: "Put this on.... Ah, it fits! And the hat—here."

"But looka, mister—"

"Nothing at all. And here's a buck. Buy yourself a cup of coffee."

Hatless and coatless now, he swung on, swerved right at the next corner and found a taxi standing a few yards farther on. He fell into it.

"Louie's," he said. "Louie's in Race Street."

"Okey, chief."

The cab jolted off and Kennedy slid down on the seat, fell asleep.

He did not hear the three shots that rang out. He did not see the panhandler in the tan overcoat and gray hat stop suddenly, turn half around with a shocked, open-mouthed look. He did not see the man fall against a pole, claw at the pole, slip with agonizing slowness down to the snow and lay there while new snow fell softly upon him.

Chapter II

THE emergency ambulance had red-tinted headlights and these sprayed a roseate glow on the snow. Its spotlight, not tinted, was flung across the curbing, and men moved within its radiance. A motorcycle with the police insignia stood jacked up on its standard, its putteed officer standing spread-legged before it. The cop on the beat was writing in his book, bending downward and sidewise to take advantage of the motor-cycle's headlight. The snow continued to fall, softly, unobtrusively, and men's boots crunched in it; voices, even the low ones, were sharp and clear in the cold, and breath spumed.

"Here, here and here," said the ambulance doctor.

"Didn't have a chance, huh?"

"Nah."

"Looks like a bum."

"Smells like one."

New headlights swung into the street, the sound of a big motor purred, big tires made a lazy swishing sound on the snow and a long black phaeton, curtained front and rear, drew up behind the ambulance. MacBride got out, bent to tap his pipe empty on the running-board, and then went forward scraping its bowl with a penknife. Moriarity and Cohen followed, straggling.

The cop on the beat made a half-salute. "Hi, Cap."

"Schumacher. What happened?"

"Ask me. I don't know. I was mopin' along Wellington when I heard three shots bust out. I ran around and around account of I didn't know where they come from. But finally I walk up and find this guy crammed down against that pole."

MacBride moved closer, pried into his pipe-bowl and said down towards the doctor: "Stiff?"

"What do you think?"

"Never mind what I think."

The doctor looked up. "Oh… thought you were somebody else!… Stiffer than I'd want to be." He stood up. "Some bum, he looks like. Except the benny. The benny looks new, like the hat. Otherwise, he's rags and I guess he ain't had a bath since the Johnstown flood."

The cop on the beat said: "Here's his hat. Got initials in it there."

MacBride looked. "J.X.K.," he said.

"Lotta busted pencils in the pockets too."

"J.X.K.," MacBride repeated, looking upward into the falling snow.

He turned back to the doctor. "Okey; run the stiff over the morgue, it's on your way. And let me have that coat. I'm taking the hat too. What time did this happen, Schumacher?"

"The shots, you mean?"

"Yeah."

"By my clock, ten to eleven."

"Okey. When you ring in the house, tell 'em I picked up these duds…. Ike, Mory, come on."

He led the way back into the phaeton and Dugan, the man at the wheel, stepped on the self-starter.

"Stop at the first telephone," MacBride said.

The car started off and Moriarity said: "Why the duds?"

"They're Kennedy's."

"How d' you know?"

"The hat's got J.X.K. in it."

"What's X stand for?"

"It doesn't stand for anything. When he joined the army, he said his name was John Kennedy. They asked him for another initial and he said he didn't have any. They said he had to have one, so he said, 'All right; make it X.' They asked him what it stood for and he didn't know, but he said offhand one of those gadgets you play with sticks sort of."

"Xylophone," Cohen offered.

Moriarity leaned forward. "What the hell do you think happened to him?"

"Damned if I know. He rang me about eight-thirty tonight and he was tight I knew by the way he talked. Wanted to know if I'd join him in a Turkish bath. That meant he was pretty tight. When he's pretty tight he either wants to go to a Turkish bath or ring strange doorbells.... Okey, Dugan, this'll do."

The skipper climbed out, strode through the falling snow and entered a cigar store. From a booth he telephoned Kennedy's paper and said: "Kennedy there?... Has he called in within the past hour?... Any idea where he is?... Any idea where he might be?"

He hung up, growled, shook his head and returned to the phaeton, "Not a sign," he said. "Okey, Dugan; drive to Nick Valente's. He phoned from there."

A Negro band was making things lively at Nick Valente's. The crowd was loud, drunk but good-natured. Nick Valente, fat and round and short, was drinking Perrier straight at the end of the bar when MacBride walked in.

"Kennedy was here tonight, wasn't he, Nick?"

"Yeah. Stewed."

"You're telling me? When'd he leave?"

"About half-past nine."

"Say where he was going?"

"Turkish bath."

MacBride used Valente's phone, knowing the Turkish bath that Kennedy patronized. "Captain MacBride, Police Headquarters.... Yeah, I'm looking for Kennedy again. He been there?... Hasn't? Okey."

He returned to the phaeton and said: "Dugan, make the rounds."

MacBride visited many speakeasies. In a few Kennedy had been, and MacBride managed to check up on his movements until ten o'clock. From then on, he had no luck. He walked in on Dave Rood at one o'clock and said:

"I'm looking for Kennedy, Rood. Seen him tonight?"

"No. I haven't."

"He was in this neighborhood."

"Not here, Cap. What's up?"

"I'd like to know. We picked up a dead bum wearing Kennedy's hat and coat. The thing now is—find Kennedy."

"Was he drunk?"

MacBride said: "Is he ever sober?" and walked out

He made another stop down the street and the owner said: "No, he isn't. I guess that was the kill I heard about over the radio—late news flashes. Unidentified man, about fifty. In Welch Street, wasn't it?"

"Yeah."

The skipper went out, climbed into the car. "Headquarters, Dugan. There's a chance he may be at his room, but I doubt it. I'll phone from there."

Chapter III

WHEN they reached Headquarters the man at the desk said: "*Free Press* phoned you, Cap." MacBride telephoned Kennedy's paper and spoke for a few minutes with the night city editor. Hanging up, he turned to Moriarity and Cohen. "At about midnight," he said, "some guy phoned the paper and asked if Kennedy was there. The editor tried to trace the call, but it came from a dial phone, so there was no go."

He turned, grabbed the telephone and called Kennedy's room. As he had expected, he received no answer.

Cohen said: "Maybe he's there but too drunk to answer it."

"That's an idea. Come on."

The skipper stretched his legs across the central room, went downstairs and into the garage. He buzzed Dugan, and the chauffeur appeared getting into his overcoat. MacBride and Moriarity and Cohen climbed in back and the car shot out of the garage. Stuffing his pipe in the darkened tonneau, MacBride said:

"I'd hate to see Kennedy pass out of the picture, though I've always had a kind of feeling that on one of these drunks of his he'd get in trouble. You never can tell what he'll do next. Got a match, Ike?... Thanks." He lit up, filling the curtained car with a rich aroma of strong tobacco. "And I tell you, if he's come to harm, I'll turn this town upside down. He's a souse and a pest and a nuisance and he's always razzing me; but the guy's got something. I don't know what it is, but he's got it.... Take the turns slow, Dugan. Maybe you'd like to pile us up. And we're not in England. Try the right side of the road for a change. And it might help if you turned the lights on."

"Hell, I was just thinkin' the battery'd run down!"

Cohen sing-songed: "We're all out of step but Dugan. How'd you ever get a driver's license, Dugan?"

"I pestered me mudder till she give me one." He turned his head completely around and said: "That hold you?"

"Look where you're going!" MacBride yelled.

Dugan tugged on the wheel, grazed an iron blinker in the middle of an intersection and said: "Jeese, how they keep movin' them things around!"

"Right next," MacBride said. "On two, and then left. It's in the middle of the block."

It was a three-storied frame house in a dark, quiet street of similar frame houses. There were a few trees, scattered street lights, and most of the houses advertised furnished rooms for rent. The phaeton stopped and MacBride said:

"You guys wait here. I won't be a minute."

He hopped across a low mound of snow, crunched across the sidewalk and up a short flight of wooden steps. He opened the vestibule door, then the inner door. A night-light glowed in the hallway and there was a table with a basket containing a number of letters.

He climbed the stairway of the quiet, sleeping house. His feet made no sound falling, but every now and then a board creaked beneath the old runner, and when he took hold of the banister, it creaked. He reached the second story corridor and took the next stairway to the top. He knew Kennedy's room was in the rear, on the right, and above his door a small yellow light hung suspended from the ceiling.

He knocked. Looking down, he saw patches of wet on the linoleum and knew that Kennedy must be in.

"Kennedy," he growled.

There was no answer. He palmed the knob, opened the door and peered into the darkness.

"Kennedy!" he rasped. "It's MacBride, fat-head!"

He stepped in, groped around for a switch. There was sudden movement in the dark, and instinctively he ducked his head. Something hard landed on his shoulder, made his left side give and his left leg buckle. He crashed into a chair and felt it spin away and heard it crash into something else. His right hand shot towards his gun, but was stopped in mid-career by another hand that locked on his arm.

He turned and bucked with his head, struck something that gave and grunted, and then he was attacked from the opposite side and knew that more than one fought him. He used his right knee, then his foot. He bore heavily towards the right, felt a blow glance off the rear of his head. He kicked out backward. He tried mightily to free his right, his gun hand, but it was locked in a strong grip. His jaw met a wild, short blow, and the blow hurt and he cursed and heaved, taking his unseen opponent with him and crashing into the other. Something toppled, fell with a crash. He landed on a bed, heard the springs creak, felt a weight upon him.

"On the bed!" a voice near his ear panted.

He heard quick footsteps.

"Where?"

"I got him here—"

The skipper turned his body, turning one of the men with him, and heard the sound of something striking the metal bed post. He tried to heave off the bed, but other hands, groping, scratched down across his face. He chopped with his left hand, hitting a head that ducked, getting an elbow in the mouth as he jerked his own head around.

Then the hard thing came out of the dark, landed on his head, and his breath shot out; he let go and covered his head with his arms, fell from the bed and hit the floor hard.

"Scram now!" a hoarse voice panted.

"Okey!"

The skipper was dazed but not out. He heard running feet, heard the door slam. He groped to his feet, yanked out his gun and lunged across the dark room; his legs struck something and he slammed down. Up again, he clawed for the door, clawed along the wall and found the light switch and snapped it. Light sprang upon the room. One glance revealed that it was empty, and he pulled open the door, raced down the corridor and bounded down the stairway. He reached the hall door, opened it and yelled:

"Ike, Mory—two guys!"

Mory's voice drifted up from the phaeton: "Where?"

MacBride ducked back into the hall, saw a door open in the rear. He ran to it, stepped into a yard, found the snow falling tranquilly and peacefully. Footsteps came running behind him, and he saw Moriarity and Cohen. He cursed and slushed around in the yard, found a fence with several boards missing, went through the opening and saw that he was in an empty lot. Beyond was a street. He ran to it and looked up and down and saw no one.

"What the hell?" Moriarity asked.

"I walked into Kennedy's room—on a couple of guys. So they walked all over me.

"Know them?"

"It was dark. Come on up. We'll look it over."

By this time Dugan was in the lower hallway, more an onlooker than an active agent. A few men and women were also in the hall, half-dressed, asking questions.

"It's only the cops," MacBride said, striding.

A fat woman said: "It sure sounds like a troop of elephants."

"And who are you?"

"I'm the owner. I'll have you know."

"Have me know, if it makes you feel better.... Dugan, what are you doing in here? Get outside. The last time you left the car, you left it running and a couple of muggs swiped it."

"He left it running this time," Cohen said.

The fat woman said: "Police. Humph! A lot of rowdies, making a disturbance in a respectable house like this!"

"Listen, lady," Cohen said. "Do you knit?"

"No."

"Do you play parchesi?"

"No!"

"Do you have bad dreams, spots before the eyes—?"

"And I won't be ridiculed!" she cried.

MacBride shoved Cohen. "Quit it, Ike. Upstairs. Mory, after him!... Listen, lady, pipe down, will you? Give your ears a chance. If you don't shut up, I'll run you in for disorderly conduct, resisting an officer and using profane language in a public place."

"Ridiculous!" exploded a small, bath-robed man.

"And who are you?"

"Her huh-husband!"

"Well," MacBride said, "you got one tough break out of life, so we'll let it slide."

Chapter IV

MAcBRIDE, sitting at his office desk, spoke into the boxlike annunciator: "Gabe. I want this put on the short wave. We're looking for Kennedy, the *Free Press* newshound. He was last seen in a Dowd Street cafe at ten p.m. He'll be wearing a gray suit, and we're sure no hat. He'll be intoxicated. About five feet eight, about one-thirty-five pounds, blond, sallow complexion. Precincts, patrols and cruisers and also the river squad."

He clicked off, rubbed sleep from his eyes. He unlocked his private drawer, hauled out a pint bottle and took a stiff bracer, slid the bottle across the desk and said to Moriarity and Cohen:

"You guys, too."

Cohen took a swallow, passed the bottle to Moriarity, who tilted his head way back, gurgled. MacBride stood up and snatched the bottle away from him, locked it up. He said:

"Give you an inch, you take a mile."

The phone rang and he grabbed it, sat down, snatched up a pencil and sat on the edge of his chair. "Go ahead.... I get you.... Sounds like him. That's all, huh?... Okey." He hung up, sighed hugely, wagged his head.

"That was the Third Precinct calling. A taxi driver came around and said he picked up a guy of Kennedy's description near the scene of the shooting, at about eleven. The guy told him to drive to Louie's in Race Street. They drove there, but the guy didn't go in. He told the driver to go in and buy a quart of rye and then, when he got the bottle, they drove to a second-hand store down in Fish Street and the guy bought a second-hand overcoat and a hat. Then he bought a bag of peanuts and told the driver to drive him to Hio Park, where he said he was going to feed the squirrels. That's the last the driver saw of him, at eleven-thirty. That sounds like Kennedy. I'll swear it was Kennedy. The Third sent a couple of guys through the Park, thinking he might have folded up, but they didn't find anything."

The squad cars and patrol flivvers were cruising the snow-swathed city, stopping, searching late-wandering automobiles. Plainclothes men, singly and in pairs, looked in at restaurants, speakeasies, questioned the known madames, tried the dance halls, all the Turkish baths. They talked with taxi companies, went around and quizzed taxi drivers at random. The order had been given: "Communicate directly with Captain MacBride."

The skipper was snatching forty winks when the phone roused him. Patrolman Abell, Second Precinct, was calling:

"I was just talkin' with a guy that drives an independent taxi down here in Clove Street. He says he was drivin' a guy around a lot that sounds like Kennedy, only this guy was wearin' a hat and overcoat but he thinks it was Kennedy account of once when he come out of a speak he yelled back to a guy, "See you get your muggs in the *Free Press*, old kid." Sounds like he was a newspaper guy, see? Well, finally they drive up in front o' Dave Rood's place and this guy gets out and bumps into a jane 'd just come out of Rood's. They're both tight, and this guy gets back in the cab with the jane and the jane says, 'Drive to Brick Square.' Which he does. Then the jane and the guy get out and he last sees 'em walkin' down Granite Street at about he thinks ten-thirty. They was both pretty tight."

MacBride hung up, flexed his lips and said across to Moriarity and Cohen: "It looks as if he got mixed up with a woman." He stood up, strode to the clothes tree. "Get your duds on. This is the first lead that's worth a damn. Come on."

Moriarity and Cohen grabbed their coats and marched after him, and on the way down the hall MacBride said:

"It figures this way. Kennedy hooked on to something. What, hell knows. These guys I ran into in his room were looking for something too—something he's got. We've tapped every place where he might be, and he's not there. The answer is that he's in trouble somewhere. And that's bad. If he has got something, he won't talk—and they'll beat him; and a good beating would kill him. This woman may mean something and she may not."

It was almost three in the morning when the police phaeton drew up in front of Dave Rood's. Dugan stayed at the wheel. Moriarity and Cohen went in with MacBride. The place was empty but for the hat-check girl, Mike and Rood. The girl was getting ready to leave and Mike and Rood were counting the cash at the bar. Only a few lights were burning.

"Don't you ever sleep, Cap?" Rood asked.

MacBride said: "We think we've got a line on Kennedy. He was around here before midnight."

Rood was counting bills. "Not here, Cap."

"Outside, I mean. There was a jane in here around ten. She was tight and when she went out Kennedy was getting out of a cab. He was tight and the jane was tight. They got in the cab together and drove off."

Mike bent his brows, tightened his lips, and Rood finished counting in silence, made a notation and then looked straight at MacBride.

"Where do I fit in?"

"Ten's usually a slack time here. It wouldn't be hard to remember who was in here around ten."

Rood was still regarding the skipper levelly. "I like to see nothing, hear nothing, Cap. You know that. You know it's the only way I can stay in business and run it respectable."

"I know. But this guy Kennedy happens to be a kind of pal of mine and it's time for you to break an old custom."

Rood shrugged, looked down hard at the bar. "There was a jane named Bertha Kohlman in here about that time. She didn't get tight here. She lit here tight and got noisy and nasty and I gave her the gate."

"The late Ben Kohlman's wife?"

Rood nodded soberly. "Yeah."

"How long's she been in town?"

"I dunno. About a week, I guess."

"She come in here often?"

"She was in a few times."

"Alone?"

"She always came in alone."

"Was she in the dough?"

"She had plenty."

"Where's she living?"

Rood tapped his fingers, pursed his lips.

"Come on," MacBride said. "This is between you and me."

"I don't know where she lives except she made a crack several times she was living in Brick Square." He put his pale eyes on MacBride again. "If there's a kick-back on this, I'll know who to thank."

"Did I ever cause a kick-back on you yet?"

Rood shrugged, shook his head.

MacBride pivoted. "Come on, gang."

Moriarity and Cohen followed him out. The flakes were larger, closer together and made a soft hissing sound in the dark street, and the hot hood of the phaeton steamed. The skipper and his two men climbed in.

"Brick Square, Dugan."

A match flamed and Cohen lit a cigarette. "So Bertha Kohlman is back. Well, well and well! It was a year ago that Ben Kohlman took nine slugs in his gut and never got over it. That's one of the jobs still on file, Cap."

MacBride slapped his knee. "Kennedy was in on something. I'll bet my shirt he was in on something!"

"I understand Ben left his wife flat broke."

Moriarity said: "I kind of smell closed books for Kennedy."

"Where should I stop in Brick Square?" Dugan asked.

"At the corner there," MacBride said, pointing, "and we'll work around it. She lives in one of these hotels or apartment houses. Dugan, you kind of drift along. Ike, you start left and take the hotels. Mory, you start left and take the apartment houses. I'll start right and take both. If you spring the dope, join Dugan, and you, Dugan, give a low one on the siren, so we'll all know. And remember, I said a low one. Keep drifting round and round the square."

Chapter V

THE car stopped. The men got out and separated and MacBride walked into a dim, sleeping hotel lobby and roused the clerk. He asked questions, scanned the guest list and left. Next he entered an apartment house, leaned on a bell till the manager, in pajamas, answered. Briskly, he went down the manager's list, thanked him and left.

A milk truck rolled past, clanging; and at the other side of the Square, a late trolley-car grated around a curve. MacBride entered two more hotels, three more apartment houses. He saw Dugan drifting past leisurely, on the wrong side of the street. He entered another apartment house and had quite a time getting an answer. He was not so many blocks distant now from the spot where the unidentified man had been shot down.

"I'm Captain MacBride, Police Headquarters," he said to the sleepy-eyed man who opened the door in the rear of a lobby hall. "Got someone here named Kohlman—a woman; Bertha Kohlman?"

The sleepy man was peevish. "How should I know offhand?"

"What are you supposed to do then; look, aren't you?"

"Oh...."

He put on a bathrobe and went to his office, thumbed his register. "Yes," he said. "Eight-fifty-five."

"Got a pass key?"

The man was waking up. "What is this?"

"It may be a pinch and it may not. I may not have to use the pass key, but I'll want it anyhow. You come along."

He walked to the front door, looked out but did not see Dugan. He shrugged and came back in again, joined the manager at the elevator and rose with him to the eighth floor. By this time the little man was full awake.

"Goodness, what *is* the matter?"

"When I find out, I'll tell you."

They reached the door of 855 and MacBride promptly knocked, stood waiting and tapping his toes on the floor, chewing on his lower lip. When no reply came, he knocked again; and after a couple of minutes he said: "Let's have the key."

He found immediately that it was impossible to insert the key due to the fact that a matchstick was lodged in the keyhole. He grunted at this, then took out his penknife, opened the smallest blade. This did not work; he could not push the stick through, neither could he withdraw it

"I wonder what the hell's the idea of this," he said.

He stood back on his heels and looked the door over as if calculating its strength. There was no transom. He tried his penknife again but seemed only to imbed the stick more securely.

"I could," he said, "get this thing out eventually, but I'm in a hurry. I suppose you'd crab if I busted the door down."

"Well, I'd certainly rather you wouldn't."

"Okey. You offer a bright idea then how I'm to get in this place."

"Perhaps we could wait."

"I thought so. You're insured against this stuff, aren't you?"

"Oh, yes."

MacBride grunted, walked down the hall, yanked a fire ax from the wall and came back. He motioned the manager back. He struck at the panel nearest the outside edge of the door, pierced it, twisted the ax and pried a strip outward. Then he reached in with his arm, found the snaplock and turned it. The door opened and he walked in.

The manager followed timidly, suicide of the occupant being mainly in his mind.

MacBride saw clothing scattered about the living-room floor. In the bedroom, on the bed, he found the woman clad in a pink slip but with her stockings still on. He turned her over. She sighed, moistened her lips, yawned in her sleep.

"Tight," he said. And to the manager: "Okey. Go downstairs and stand in the door and when you see a big black car pass slowly, hail it. You'll find a cop at the wheel. Tell him to call the others."

The manager hurried out and MacBride stood looking wooden-faced down at the plump, scantily clad woman. He shook her, but she did not rouse, so finally he went into the bathroom, got a glass of water, returned to the bed and pitched the contents in her face. She started, gasped, but she was drugged with liquor and roused slowly, opening one bleary eye first, then the other, then covering her eyes with an arm, against the bright glare of the lights.

"Holy Moses!" she blew out. "Whew!" She struggled around to a half-sitting posture, leaning on her braced arms, her hair hanging down over her face.

MacBride strode to a closet, found a silk negligée and tossed it at her.

"Snap out of it, Bertha."

She looked up slowly, a sullen droop to her lips and her eyes foggy. "Yeah? Who're you?"

"Bum memory, huh?"

"Say, who're you anyhow?"

"MacBride. The cops."

Her tongue was thick, listless. "Whatcha want, huh?"

He grabbed her, stood her on her feet and thrust first one of her arms, then the other, into the silk negligée. He held her at arms' length, while her head flopped this way and that. He shook her and she lifted her head and looked dully at him.

"Gimme a drink. Stiff one. Bit o' the hair o' the dog...."

He set her down in a chair, went into the pantry and poured a stiff dose of rye into a water glass, brought it to her and watched her down it. It burned, made her gasp for breath, pant a bit.

"So what?" she said.

"So I'm looking for a guy named Kennedy."

"See him around here?"

"No."

She shrugged. "Tough."

"Where is he?"

"Where's who?"

"Kennedy."

"Who's Kennedy?"

"The guy was with you."

She scoffed. "Ah, nobody was with me. Been alone. Lone wolfess— that's me. Heh—heh! D'jevr-r hear o' the lone—?"

"Snap out of it! I tell you this guy Kennedy was with you!"

"Says you. Don't remember. Don't b'lieve you."

"This guy," bit in MacBride, "is a newspaperman—a reporter. He was with you sometime before midnight. Last year he worked on the killing of your husband. So did I. He was with you tonight. He was up here in your room."

Her head snapped back. "Who was?"

"Kennedy."

Her nostrils quivered, her lips hardened and a glassy but somewhat steady look took possession of her eyes. She pushed herself up to her feet. She looked jerkily around the room, then swung her face back towards MacBride.

" 'S lie! 'S lie!"

He grabbed her arm. "Listen, sister. This guy happens to be an old pal of mine. He's disappeared, see? He disappeared after he left you! What did you tell him?"

She grimaced and her eyes widened, borrowed a touch of horror from her numbed senses. "What did I tell him! By God, I didn't tell him anything!" She tried to break loose but MacBride held her. She yelled: "It's a trap! I never seen the guy! You lemme go!"

"You saw him, Bertha, and after you saw him he disappeared. You probably told him about the killing last year of Ben Kohlman. You never did tell us all you knew about that. But you got tight and told him and maybe there were some guys hanging around who didn't want him to know. So they took him in tow." He gripped her hard, straightening her. "Who are those guys? You'd know the guys, sister, and you've got to spring!"

She gasped: "Honest to Gawd, MacBride, I don't. I tell you I never seen the guy. I don't remember. Look out—you're hurting my arm!"

He was grim, laconic. "I might break it."

She could not recall having been with anyone, least of all a reporter. Try as she would, she could not remember. But inside, deep inside, she was numb with horror. She must have been awful tight, she reflected, not to remember anything. She didn't remember coming home, undressing.

MacBride was saying: "You were sober enough to jam your keyhole with a match."

"I didn't.... I don't remember."

"Get some clothes on. Headquarters may help refresh your memory."

"Listen, MacBride—"

"Clothes—get 'em on."

He gave her five minutes to dress, then marched her out of the apartment and down the corridor to the elevator bank. He pressed the button that brought the elevator up, opened the door and prodded her in. The elevator descended slowly to the lobby floor. He opened the door, took hold of her arm and marched her out into the lobby. He saw the manager lying on the floor, and at the same instant two men, masked, stepped in his way with leveled guns.

"Quick, skipper—let go the dame."

The woman cringed. MacBride looked from the two masked faces to the manager, saw the welt on his forehead where a blunt instrument had struck.

"This won't get you far," he said.

"Let her go, Skipper—quick. We're in a hurry."

MacBride let her go, the hair on his neck bristling. One of the men grabbed the woman and hurried with her to the front door. The other backed up, keeping MacBride covered. He stopped at the door through which the other man and the woman had gone; he waited, motionless, while the other two crossed the sidewalk to a snow-swathed automobile. MacBride could see past him, knew by the sound of an accelerated motor that a third man was at the wheel. When the woman and the man had disappeared inside the car, the man in the doorway hooked the door open.

"Stay where you are," he said. "One move before I get in the car, and you get it."

MacBride said: "Get a good head start, lug; you'll need it."

The man backed out, his gun still leveled. The car began moving; it moved out of range of the doorway. The last man suddenly turned and ran, hopped in. The car roared off, its rear wheels spouting clots of snow.

MacBride bent over the manager, saw his eyelids flutter, heard him moan. The skipper reasoned he would come to soon. He drew his gun and ran to the doorway, ran out into the snow. He fired a shot in the air.

The police phaeton came moping down the street, and MacBride, standing on the curb, motioned Dugan to hurry. Dugan swung the car in and MacBride yanked the door open.

"That car just swinging right. Follow it."

He landed on the rear seat, slammed the door shut. Dugan gunned the motor and the phaeton boomed off. Fifty yards father on, Moriarity and Cohen came out of a small hotel.

MacBride snapped: "Siren, Dugan—and stop."

The siren moaned and Moriarity and Cohen lifted their heads. MacBride let the door swing open.

"Hey, you guys!"

They picked up their heels and dived into the phaeton, and Mac-Bride slammed the door and Dugan gunned again, squaring off behind the wheel.

"Open it up," the skipper said.

"What's doing?" Cohen asked:

"I found the jane and two guys took her away from me. Get out the machine-gun, Ike—just in case."

Chapter VI

THE white flakes fell, large, heavy; they fell with a kind of unhurried calm, wrapping themselves leisurely around telephone poles, building ridges on windowsills and steps. There was little traffic at this hour to churn up the fallen snow; the streets were white in the dark, deserted and peaceful until the fleeing sedan screamed through them. Silence folded over behind it, but was startled a moment later by the speeding police phaeton.

"What'd she say about Kennedy?" Moriarity asked.

"Nothing."

Cohen had climbed into the front seat beside Dugan; he sat now holding the submachine-gun, a dead butt cold on his lips. The wind drummed the canvas top. Twin windshield wipers kept shaving the snow off the windshield. Clots of snow kept drumming up against the mudguards.

"They doused their lights," Dugan said.

"Douse your own. Snap the spotlight on now and then if you lose sight of them, but snap it right off again. No use being a target."

"That buggy can step," Cohen remarked.

"Three guys and the jane," MacBride said. "We don't want to hit the jane."

Cohen leaned forward, snapped on the dashlight, snapped it off again.

"Sixty-two," he said.

They roared down a wide street parallel with street-car rails. Ahead, they saw a street-car, and then the sedan plowing past it. Beyond, snow and darkness gobbled the sedan, and Dugan switched the spotlight, fanned it back and forth, picked up the fleeing sedan and snapped the spotlight off as two shots rang distantly, muffled. A whanging sound snapped off the car.

"Left mudguard," Dugan said.

Cohen said: "Suppose I let 'em have a few, low, Cap."

"Nix. I want that jane."

"I'm gainin'," Dugan said monotonously.

Wind billowed out of a side street, struck the car, rained snow upon it and battered the curtains.

"Made a left," Cohen said.

Dugan nodded, gripped high on the wheel with his left hand. Then cut the corner, the tires biting into the snow.

Dugan said: "Guy drivin' that's a pretty good driver."

"Look," said MacBride. "Lean on the siren. Stay on it. The sound of it might scare 'em, make 'em reckless."

The siren started with a low moan, grew, expanded, burst in terrifying volume through the dark city streets and remained screaming. The sedan sped faster and Dugan, hunching over the wheel, flattened the pedal against the floor. Churned snow beat furiously against the mudguards.

"If we gotta stop sudden," Dugan said out of the corner of his mouth, "it's gonna be funny."

Two tiny jets of flame appeared ahead, and close at hand glass shattered. "Headlight," Dugan said.

MacBride said: "There's a bad curve ahead where this street shoots into Triangle Place. Watch it."

The words had barely left his lips when the men heard the frantic screech of brakes up ahead. Dugan had braked partially and was doing about fifty. He took the twist on the outside, saw the square ahead, well-lighted, the snow drifting and waving like white curtains. And among the curtains a swerving, snaking sedan. Dugan braked a little more, hugging the right-hand curb.

The sedan ahead seemed to straighten out. Spurting snow, its brakes rasping, it skidded, slid, turned completely around. Dugan swung to the left to avoid hitting it. The sedan, still spinning, lifted to one side, poised for a moment, slammed back to all four wheels again so violently that snow was dislodged from its roof. It ricocheted off a pole with a sound of torn metal. Its motor thundered, its rear wheels burned into the snow.

Dugan was braking, rapidly but at the same time cautiously. A block beyond, when the speed was down to ten, he gave a twist on the wheel and skidded the car neatly in an about-face. The sedan was starting diagonally across the square. It smacked into an iron traffic standard, knocked it down and went slewing across the sidewalk. It tore its metal against an iron fence, bounced back into the street, and digging its rear wheels into the snow, grazed a mail box, left the street entirely and went barging into the small park, crashing benches and hedgerows beneath it. A tire blew and the car lunged drunkenly to the left, skidded about and stopped. Doors whipped open and four figures piled out.

Dugan had stopped.

MacBride clipped: "You stay here. Ike, Mory! And, Ike, leave the Tommy. We got to run."

He was the first to start off, leaping over the low iron fence into the park. For a brief instant he saw the four figures pass beneath the hazy radiance of a floodlight in the center of the park. Moriarity and Cohen came pounding up to join him. They found a wide footpath and raced along it. The park was quiet; the snow fell tranquilly. The running feet made little sound on the soft snow.

MacBride and his men came out on the other side of the square. MacBride fired in the air. They could see the figures running along the sidewalk opposite. The figures were bunched and MacBride did not want to hit the woman. He started off again, stretched his legs, with Moriarity and Cohen on either side of him.

"In there," Moriarity snapped.

MacBride squinted: "Where?"

"That hotel."

They came upon a swing-door that was still swinging slightly. They crashed into the lobby, saw elevator doors at the far end closing. They saw a petrified clerk at the desk.

MacBride yelled: "Can you run that other elevator?"

"I—I—"

"We're cops. Come on." He looked up at the indicator above the door of the car that was rising. He saw the needle stop at the last number. "They went in that car, didn't they?" MacBride snapped.

The clerk gulped; "Y-yes."

"Okey. Run us up. Run us up to next to the last floor. Mory, you better stay down here. If this car that went up comes down again, threaten to shoot if they open the door."

The clerk ran MacBride and Cohen to the ninth floor and MacBride said: "What's upstairs?"

"Solarium and roof garden."

"Okey." He looked up at the indicator of the other elevator, saw that it was still at the top floor. "Good. Now take your car down and shut off the power that runs these things. Then call the nearest police station. Scram. Ike, let's go!"

They ran up the stairway, reached the roof floor and found themselves in a large foyer. They crept from this to a wide doorway, saw a large lounge where a few amber lights glowed. It was quiet up here, remote and removed from the street and the snow. They returned to the foyer and saw one elevator door open, the car empty but for the unconscious operator.

"Outside," Ike said.

"Not the door," MacBride said. "That looks like a switch box. Try it."

Cohen tried it and all the lights went out.

MacBride said: "Okey. Give me three minutes. I'll go through the lounge and out a window. After three minutes, spring the lights on. Watch that door. If anyone comes in it, let him have it."

"Okey."

MacBride groped his way into the lounge, across it, found a window and opened it. He listened for a half minute, then stepped out and closed the window. The snow was deep up here, soft. He edged along the wall to the end, peered around it, moved on and then made a quick dash to a ventilator. He slipped and crashed into the ventilator, heard movement beyond, and then muffled footfalls running.

The lights sprang on. Light streamed from a window and showed a man half-twisted in surprise.

"Drop it," MacBride barked.

The man dived away and MacBride fired. There was a rush for the door. Cohen fired and smashed glass. The group turned and flung back and MacBride yelled:

"Dopes, don't you know a trap when you see one? Drop those rods! Bertha, scram!"

He spoke from a triangle of shadow, seeing but not seen. One man held on to the woman and the other two rushed, their guns breaking in flame. Lead chipped the brick ledge behind MacBride and he pulled his trigger and felt the big gun fight his hand. One of the men slammed down, spreading snow beneath him, and the other jumped back towards the door. Cohen kicked the door open and fired point-blank and came out on the bound, shooting again at close range as the man brought his gun up. The man jerked and fell clumsily and Cohen stepped nimbly aside. The third man yanked Bertha to the door and went in with her, and MacBride went bounding past Cohen and shouted:

"Stop!"

He stopped inside the doorway, held his gun raised. The woman fell and the man looked down savagely at her, snarled and cursed and snapped his gun level with her body. MacBride put a hole in the center of his chest and said:

"Okey, Ike. Drag those other lugs in. The precinct men'll be here any minute. Wait. First go over to the phone, phone downstairs and tell 'em to send Mory and an elevator up."

The woman was crouching on hands and knees, staring fixedly up at MacBride. He leaned down and hauled her to her feet but she still kept looking fixedly at him.

"All this," he said, gesturing to the floor and to the roof garden, "happens to be an example of laying down the law. I've got everything I want but one thing—Kennedy."

She shook her head. "I—I don't know where he is—honest to gawd I don't."

"For two cents, Bertha, I could smack you down right now."

"I tell you I don't," she said slowly, breathlessly. "I don't remember ever seeing him. These guys thought I saw him too and told him things. If I did, I don't remember. I told them I didn't. Bugs, this guy on the floor here, was hunting all over town for him, thinking he knew something."

"Knew what?"

She stared hard at the floor, felt her throat. "Knew what I know. I came back to this town knowing Bugs knocked off my husband. I told Bugs that to his face and then I told him there was no use in him bumping me off because I had the whole thing down in black and white in a safe deposit vault. I said, 'If I'm bumped off, the vault is opened. I left instructions.' And on top of that, I made him come across with dough—Bugs said he saw this guy Kennedy come out of where I live and that him and Joe John took some shots at Kennedy up the street. But it turned out to be a bum. And then they heard on the radio the cops were looking for Kennedy. They went to where Kennedy lived and—"

"Walked over me. Yeah, I know."

She whimpered. "I ain't done nothing, Captain. I just got drunk. I didn't shoot anybody and I didn't do anything. But Bugs was scared—scared of Kennedy and of what he swore to hell I told Kennedy. And scared of me. He thought I was two-timing. He wanted to kill me right there in the car but he was afraid of what I said about the vault." She giggled hysterically. "And that was a joke! I ain't got anything in a vault. It was just my idea, though I knew Bugs knocked off Ben. But there was nothing I could take into court. Ha! Wasn't I cute?" she cackled.

MacBride made a face, then snarled: "Shut up cackling! I hate the guts of these heels we just polished off, but I hate yours worse. You could have saved all this lousy bloodshed by coming across when Ben was killed. But no. You figured to go off a while, mark time and then come back and call for a pay-off. And you're the kind of bum good cops get shot up over."

She threw her head back, laughed lustily. "And what a pay-off! Fifteen grand, and I would have got more! Poor Bugs, I sure had him going nuts!"

He was looking past her. He was watching Bugs. Bugs, lying on his belly, was trying to raise his gun. Pain and agony and hatred twisted back and forth across his face, and he seemed to be making a super-human effort to raise that gun. MacBride took a step, put his foot down on Bugs' gun and hand.

He said: "My sentiments are with you, guy—but there's always a law to lay down."

THE skipper stood in his office at half-past four that morning. It was deserted but for himself. He figured that an outbound trolley would reach the corner in fifteen minutes, and he would board it and go home to his wife. He stood spread-legged, wrapped in thought, and stuffed a pipe which he would smoke on the walk to the corner and while waiting for the trolley.

When the door whipped open, he looked up, wrenched from his revery, and saw Kennedy reel in. Kennedy wore a hat too large for him and a very long black overcoat that also was too large for him.

"Hello, old tomato. You've got to come with me. Come on, come on; no use arguing."

MacBride looked bleak. "Kennedy, where have you been?"

"Places, places—oh, lotsa places."

"You're drunk."

"Very drunk. Come on, come on; you've got to come along with li'l' ol' Kennedy."

MacBride was unimpressed, very dour. "Where you been all night?"

Kennedy's eyes were almost shut, his legs rubber-kneed, his mouth slack. "Well, can't recall very much. But did get to ringing doorbells. Lotsa fun, ringing doorbells. So finally I have exceptional good fortune. I ring a doorbell where big house party is in progress. Oh, great fun, great fun. Been there for hours, playing games, having little drinky. So then li'l' girl decides we play Scavenger. Very good game. Everybody is sent out to get something—ice-box, old horse, bellows, complete works of Shakespeare, Maltese cat, and so on— Oops!" He teetered, lost his balance and fell into a chair that stood conveniently near.

MacBride looked down at him. He was sorry and angry and bitter. He listened to Kennedy cough and looked at Kennedy's wet shoes, his ghostly face. He used the telephone.

"Jake," he said. "Send a couple of boys up.... I want them to put Kennedy to bed. Hot rum punch and so on. Right away."

Kennedy gestured. "Hey! Playing Scavenger! I was sent for police captain and you've got to—"

"Bed for yours, sweetheart. And a couple of cops to stand by and shoot the pink elephants you'll be seeing before daylight."

Too Young to Die

Capt. Steve MacBride, hard as they come, discovers a streak of sentiment.

Chapter I

THE house dick, Lackman, came out of 909, closed the door quickly but with a reverent quietness, and then stood for an instant getting out a breath that must have gagged him for several moments. Buttoning his coat, he headed for the elevators.

He was a medium-sized man, almost uniformly gray—hair, skin, clothes—and he would have gone unnoticed in a crowd, even in a small crowd. He was neat but not neater than the average man, and hurrying now, he kept hiking his elbows up behind him while his forearms moved backward and forward like the side rods on a locomotive.

The corridor turned sharp right, and a little beyond, Lackman came to the elevator bank, caught an empty down-bound car. The operator looked anxiously at him, seemed several times on the point of asking a question but in the end did not. The bronze door oozed open and Lackman strode into the suave tranquillity of the lobby. A couple of clerks at the desk craned their necks, followed him with quizzical stares.

He pushed open the heavy swing-door at the main entrance and went out to stand beneath the glass marquee. The entrance was on a private half-moon-shaped driveway, and between the driveway and the public boulevard was a billowing mass of shrubbery, white-cloaked now with snow. The snow, very dry, fell in large, leisurely flakes, landing silently but sighing faintly as it came down out of the dark.

The huge doorman cleared his throat and began: "You look like you seen a ghost, you look like."

Lackman said with a kind of anguished bitterness: "I wish to hell it was a ghost instead of—"

He stopped short as he saw a long curtained touring car whip into the driveway. It took the turn of the driveway swiftly, leaning a bit, and then brakes, sharply applied to wheels with skid-chains, brought the car to a definite, violent stop. Behind, a flivver coupé, squealing, whanged its front bumper into the rear bumper of the touring car. A loud oath was heard within the coupé and then Baumlein, the medical office man, hopped out as Kennedy drifted languidly from the touring car.

Baumlein cried: "You nuts, you nuts, you! What you doing, trying out new brakes or something?"

"Hey, Finnegan," Kennedy called to the touring car's chauffeur, "you trying out new brakes?"

"Yowssuh!"

"Finnegan says," Kennedy told Baumlein, "yowssuh."

"Look at my bumper!" Baumlein yelled. "Look at it!"

"You look at it. What's the sense of both of us looking at it? Consider—"

MacBride stepped down from the touring car and elbowed Kennedy aside. Moriarity and Cohen followed and Moriarity said: "You know, if this keeps up there'll be good sleigh-riding. I ain't been sleigh-riding since I was so"—he held out his hand, palm down—"high."

"Look at my bumper!" Baumlein cried.

MacBride, the collar of his overcoat turned up, went straight towards Lackman while Kennedy and Moriarity and Cohen went into a huddle over the bumper.

"Gawd! MacBride," Lackman said in a thick, hushed voice, "it kind of got me for a minute—" He gulped. "Just lost my kid last—"

MacBride took his arm. "Come on."

They were halfway across the lobby before MacBride realized that his entourage was not with him. He stopped, turned, curled his lip. "Wait a minute," he said. He headed for the entrance with one eye dangerously asquint. He found his entourage grouped around the broken bumper in animated conversation.

"Muggs," he said, dragging out the word wearily.

They turned.

MacBride said: "I suppose I ought to remind you that we're here on a murder case. Maybe you haven't been told."

Baumlein grabbed his bag out of the coupé and with a hurt, resentful look at MacBride went bobbing into the lobby. MacBride herded the others in. They entered the elevator and on the ride up there was a self-conscious silence, while MacBride, still a little angry, eyed each man in turn with a dark, exasperated stare. Lackman led them to 909, his elbows working.

The cop on the beat was standing in the apartment foyer. He touched his nightstick to the visor of his cap. A short stocky woman, oldish, with iron gray hair puffed at the ears, sat on a high-backed chair and stared at the foyer wall with glazed, transfixed eyes.

Lackman whispered to MacBride: "The mother."

MacBride looked down at her, his eyes clouding.

Baumlein, impatient, said: "Well, where is it, where is it?" in a querulous voice, and the cop on the beat pointed lazily with his nightstick. Baumlein bustled irritably into the living-room.

The skipper swung his stare away from the woman sitting on the chair. His long, bony face had a hard cast, but in his eyes there was a transitory brooding look. Saying nothing, he went on into the living-room and saw Baumlein at the farther end, kneeling beside a body. MacBride jammed his arms akimbo, stood where he was, gnawing on a corner of his lip; and after a moment Kennedy dawdled up beside

him and let a mildly appreciative eye wander haphazardly about the sumptuous room.

"Done," he said absently, "in excellent taste."

MacBride bent a dark, disapproving eye on him.

"The room, I mean," Kennedy explained. He made a delicate, undulating movement with the fingers of one hand. "I like the chaste motif. They're going in strong for pastels these days. Have you noticed?"

The skipper growled out of the side of his mouth; "Lay off, lay off."

Kennedy meditated for a moment, then proceeded: "The chaste motif goes very well with the personality of our late"—he sprayed fingers towards the body—"Lily Carewe. Poor, dear Lily Carewe—"

"Lay off, lay off," the skipper muttered way under his breath.

Moriarity came in snapping gum with his teeth and Cohen took a seat on a smart divan, helped himself to a cork-tipped cigarette and lit up.

Baumlein snapped shut his black bag, rose and came back across the room. "Strangled, of course," he said. "About two hours ago."

"Anything peculiar about it?" MacBride asked.

"There's a mild abrasion on her chest, as though the guy that did it got her down and knelt on her chest while he let her have the old gag act."

"That's all, huh?"

Moriarity went over to the body and then came back saying: "Hell, she must have been beautiful."

"She was."

They all turned and looked at Lackman. His face was unusually gray, drained of all color, and there was a choked look in his eyes, a kind of weary anguish about his mouth.

Lily Carewe's long blond hair lay in waves on the carpet. Her peignoir was of a fragile blue color, her legs were long and beautiful, slender.

"She certainly was beautiful," Kennedy droned. "She knocked down two grand a week on the radio, singing lullabies. You've got to be good to do that. She was on the air three times a week and all the kids went nuts about her, and not only the kids. They say she had the kind of a voice that made you feel you wanted to be a kid again. And they say she was as good as her songs, living the simple life with her mother. Well, that's life: here today, gone tomorrow."

Lackman muttered: "She was too damned young to die."

"Nineteen," Kennedy said, plucking a grape from a fruit bowl.

MacBride went across the room, unbuttoning his overcoat. He knelt down, stared bitterly at the dead girl. He had seen a lot, too much, of life and death and mostly death, and since it was mostly death, he was often angered by the seeming futility of his job. He hated to see the young die, and it especially moved him when the young was so beautiful as Lily Carewe. Gray had come into his tough black hair, bits of it, here and there.

"WELL," Baumlein called petulantly across the room, "I'm on my way."

MacBride rose, crossed to him and said: "Okey."

"And about that bumper: it's my own car and you guys are going to get me a new bumper."

Kennedy drawled: "Of such small incidents are nicknames born, and henceforth you shall be known as 'Bumper' Baumlein. Good old Bumper Baumlein."

Baumlein colored. "As for you—phooey!" He spun on his heel and went out.

MacBride wandered into the apartment foyer, leaned against the wall and looked down at the blank-eyed woman. She sat with her hands locked in her lap. She looked very plain, almost old-fashioned.

MacBride said: "Mrs. Carewe...."

She did not look up at him. Her eyes seemed unalterably fastened on the blank foyer wall, but presently she said: "Yes?"

"I've got a kid too. I can understand this kind of thing, and I'm sorrier than I can tell you, and if I start asking questions right off the bat—well, it's because that's my business." He looked at his watch. "It's half-past eleven now. When did you find your daughter?"

"About half an hour ago."

"You live here—I mean, in this apartment?"

"In a room adjoining it—the other side of the bathroom."

"There was a struggle—must have been. Did you hear it?"

"No." It seemed impossible to shake her out of her trance. "I heard nothing. I was going to bed—about to—and I came in to see if Lily's headache was better. That's what I found. I—I called the desk and they sent up the house doctor and Mr. Lackman came up too."

Lackman said in his constricted voice: "Mrs. Carewe was walking around in circles. The doctor had to give her something."

MacBride addressed the woman: "Was anybody in your daughter's apartment this evening?"

"I don't know. I went to my room about eight. There may have been, but I don't know."

"She have any men friends?"

"She"—the woman nodded, inhaling—"knew a few men."

Kennedy said from the living-room entry: "There are some pipe ashes in one of the trays, Skipper. The ads say, though, always trust a man who smokes a pipe, so that's out. It wasn't a pipe-smoker."

The woman's eyes widened at this levity.

"Don't mind him," MacBride said. "He reads the humor magazines all the time.... Lackman, ask the elevator boys if they saw a guy leave this floor at about—well, between nine and ten. I mean, a guy that looked excited or something."

Lackman went out and MacBride took a meditative tour of the living-room. Near the body, he bent down to pick up a small particle that reflected the glow of one of the floor lamps. It looked, in the palm of his hand, like a small filing, a mere sliver. He picked up a blank envelope from the secretary and in it deposited the tiny filing. Lackman reappeared with one of the elevator boys.

"He—" Lackman began.

But MacBride said: "Let him tell it."

"It was about nine-thirty, I guess, but I ain't sure. Anyhow, it was between nine and ten: I'm sure of that. This man kind of slammed into the elevator with his hat on crooked and a wild kind of look in his face. His face looked flushed. He was very excited."

"Describe him."

"About as tall as you, I'd say. Only younger. Oh, I guess he was maybe twenty-one or two. He wore a light tan coat; it looked like a trench coat only it wasn't. He was very fair complected, his cheeks were very red at the time, like I said."

The woman stood up, her lips trembling and her hands folded tightly. She stared at the elevator boy and then she stared at MacBride.

"Know him?" MacBride said.

Her lips were still trembling. "It couldn't have been!" she cried in a thick, clogged voice.

"Who is he?"

"His name is Leonard Barnsdale. But it couldn't—"

MacBride silenced her with a quick movement of his hand. "Where's he live?"

She began shaking her head, but at the same time she said: "At the *Hotel Bradford.*"

MacBride turned. "Mory, Ike—you guys stay here." He grabbed up his hat and strode hard-heeled towards the door. When he reached the elevators, he found Kennedy beside him.

"Listen, Kennedy, I'm tired of having a stooge along. Why don't you try night school or something?"

"Why, when I know everything already?"

They rode down in the elevator, and as they stepped into the lobby one of the managers accosted MacBride and led him to the desk.

"Mr. Skayne," he said, indicating one of the clerks behind the desk, "just came back on duty. He had to leave earlier in the evening because his wife is at the hospital, very ill. He said that just before he left, at about nine-thirty, a man came up to the desk and asked for the number of Miss Carewe's apartment. Of course, Mr. Skayne asked who was calling, and the man smiled and didn't care to give his name. He tried to pass Mr. Skayne a five-dollar bill. Mr. Skayne, of course, refused and the man went away."

MacBride looked at Skayne. "What did he look like?"

"In his forties, I'd say. He was in evening clothes but looked rather hard—not the type of person who would be apt to call casually on Miss Carewe. He was quite tall, very broad, with a dark, smooth face and a hard, slow, kind of husky voice. I'd know him if I saw him again."

MacBride said: "Thanks." He pointed. "Keep memorizing what he looks like. I may need you later."

He pivoted and strode out of the lobby and found Kennedy drowsing in the tonneau of the police touring car.

"Finnegan," MacBride said, "the *Hotel Bradford.*"

Chapter II

THE *Hotel Bradford* was a narrow building of red brick, eight stories tall. It was unpretentious and for men only. It had a reading-room and a gymnasium and catered to students and business men of good reputation, and its rates ran from one-fifty to two-fifty a day, but usually rooms were engaged by the month.

There was no roof garden, no view—the hotel was in the palm of the business district—and no marquee, no doorman. The doorway in front of which the police car stopped was large, plain, slightly recessed. The street—North Water—was deserted at this hour. Halfway up the face of the building, there was a scaffolding suspended by a series of ropes from the roof.

Kennedy lolled out of the touring car and MacBride, in a hurry, shoved him out of the way and went pounding his feet across the sidewalk. He yanked open the door, climbed three inside steps to the small, plain lobby and headed for the desk. His heels made loud, rhythmic sounds and he blew his nose and was shoving his handkerchief into his overcoat pocket by the time he reached the desk.

An oldish man, thin, bald, looked up at him and MacBride said: "I'm MacBride from Police Headquarters. What room's Leonard Barnsdale in?"

"Uh—who?"

"Barnsdale—Barnsdale."

The man blinked, looked right, left, blinked again. "Uh—you wanted to see him?"

MacBride nodded wearily. "Yes."

The man fidgeted with his lip. "Uh—well—well, of course." He made a vague gesture with his hand. "Room seven-two-six. Uh—could I be of any assistance?"

"Yes. Stay here."

MacBride pivoted and crashed into Kennedy. Kennedy held his nose and said "Ouch," quietly.

"Well, you will get underfoot all the time." MacBride swung off towards the single elevator. It was open, its attendant standing alongside. MacBride entered and Kennedy followed, still holding his nose.

The elevator rose leisurely and at the seventh floor MacBride shoved Kennedy out, then went striding off ahead of him. He came to a door painted 726 in plain white lettering, and knocked. There was the sound of a chair being moved, a quiet voice, and in a minute the door opened and a youth's face peered out anxiously.

"Hello," MacBride said.

"Hel-lo."

"You Barnsdale?"

"N-no."

"Where is he?"

The youth moistened his lips. "Who—are you?"

The skipper pulled his badge out of his pocket. The youth took a backward step, reluctantly, and MacBride, putting his hands back into his overcoat pockets, opened the door wide with a neat twist of his shoulder. He saw another youth lying on a single bed with a wet towel draped over his eyes and forehead. Kennedy drifted in and closed the door with a kick of his heel.

The room was very small, very plain, with one narrow window. The bed was of iron, painted white. There was a small bureau, one chair; there was no bath.

MacBride pointed with his chin: "That Barnsdale?"

The youth who had opened the door nodded.

The skipper drew out his battered pipe. He stood back on his heels, unhurried now. Back of him, Kennedy stood holding his nose. The skipper worked roughcut tobacco into the pipe bowl and said:

"And what's your name?"

"John Atwood."

"Live here?"

"Y-yes. Downstairs a bit."

MacBride lit his pipe, said: "What's the matter with him?"

"He's—well, he's asleep now."

"I can see that…. Wake him up." Atwood went to the bed—he had to move but a step—and shook Barnsdale, said in a low voice: "Leonard, Leonard…."

Barnsdale heaved a vast sigh, raised his hands and dragged the wet towel from his face. He blinked. There was a blue welt on his forehead. He sat up abruptly, looking from Atwood to MacBride with suddenly harried eyes.

MacBride carried the solitary chair to the bedside and sat down. "Well, Barnsdale, I'm from the cops. Been in an accident?"

"No. No."

"Walked into a doorway, I suppose." Barnsdale shook his head. "No."

"Been over to see Lily Carewe tonight?"

Barnsdale grimaced and looked away. There was a subdued fever in his eyes, a torn look about his mouth; his hair was disheveled and his hands shook. He was young, MacBride saw, and not bad to look at. The skipper drew on his pipe, letting the smoke dribble upward from one corner of his mouth.

"You were over there, weren't you?"

Barnsdale, still grimacing, nodded. MacBride took a few more puffs, keeping his narrowed-down eyes fastened on the working agony in Barnsdale's face. Then MacBride said: "You'd better get dressed, boy."

"Why—why? Oh, I'm tired, tired."

"He's a recluse," Kennedy chimed in. "He wants to be alone."

"Come on, Barnsdale," MacBride said. He stood up, replaced the chair. "Maybe you thought you just smacked her, but as a matter of fact, boy, you killed her."

"Killed her!"

Barnsdale pivoted on the bed, his feet hit the floor and he stared up at the skipper with bulging eyes,

"What are you saying?" he cried.

"Come on, get dressed."

Barnsdale jumped up and grabbed MacBride by the lapels. "But what are you saying, what are you saying?"

"I'm saying," MacBride explained, "that Lily Carewe is dead."

Barnsdale backed up, clutching at his throat with one hand. He kept backing up until the wall stopped him. Atwood started towards him, his face anxious, one arm half-extended. MacBride stopped him.

"Mind your own business," MacBride said.

"But I tell you—"

"I told you to mind your own business.... Barnsdale, get your pants on."

"Lily... Lily... Lily," Barnsdale moaned, and wagged his head loosely, hopelessly, from side to side. "It's not so. It isn't true. Lily can't be dead."

MacBride took his pipe from his mouth and sighted along the stem at Barnsdale. "Lily Carewe is dead. It was a tussle and she was strangled and in the tussle you collected that welt on your head—"

"No, no! I didn't. I got this welt—" He stopped short, shook his head violently. "I tell you I didn't! Please believe me! I—I'd be the last person—"

"Get dressed. Cut out this act. You're going over to Headquarters.

That's final," MacBride snapped. "Any more talk out of you, I'll take you the way you are."

Barnsdale looked stupefied. In a stupor, he began dressing. Atwood, watching him, kept swallowing frequently, and color began to creep over his face and presently he spun on MacBride and said:

"He didn't! I'll tell you how he got the bump on the head!" He leveled an arm at the window. "See that window? Well, he jumped out of it. He tried to commit suicide. He intended smashing himself on the street below but a story and a half down there's a scaffolding and he landed on it. I live one floor below. I heard the sound and looked out and there he was on the scaffolding, just below my window. I jumped down.

"He was stunned and I held on to him, and just then another fellow, who'd heard the sound also, looked out and I told him to help me. He went in my room and knotted two sheets together and hung them out. I tied one end around Leonard and we hauled him into my room. We had to borrow some smelling salts from the desk-clerk, and he was curious and he came up, too. We all decided to keep it quiet. We brought Leonard back to his room and I stayed with him. We can prove that by the desk-clerk."

Barnsdale had stopped dressing. He was hanging his head, his body limp.

"Of course," said Kennedy, "what you say is likely true. You can prove that Barnsdale tried to commit suicide. You can't prove that he didn't kill Lily Carewe. Naturally, sometimes, when a guy hauls off and kills a jane and then thinks it over, he figures the quickest way out for him is to do the Dutch. Say you did prove how he got the bump on the head. Okey. But how the hell can you prove he didn't choke the girl to death?"

Atwood's mouth fell open.

MacBride moved, tapped Barnsdale's shoulder. "Come on, boy; the pants on."

Chapter III

IT stopped snowing during the night. It was a cold, clear morning when MacBride returned to work. The cold nipped at his cheeks, his nose, reddened them, and he came striding into his office with snow still clinging to his rubbers. He hung up hat and overcoat, sat down, took off his rubbers and opened both windows a few inches from the top. He sat down at his desk, yelled: "Rheingold on deck!" into the annunciator, and began thumbing rapidly through a batch of bulletins and reports.

Detective-Sergeant Rheingold came lazy-footed into the office and MacBride said:

"What did you get out of Barnsdale?"

"Ever try to get water out of a stone?" He spread his palms, shook his head. "Nothing doing."

"What do you think?"

"I think he's either a sap or he don't know a thing."

"Lay a hand on him?"

"Nah. But everything else we put him through. You can't seem to raise the guy out of the dumps he's in. It sorta bores me after a while."

MacBride said: "Send him up."

Rheingold went out and the skipper rose, took a turn up and down the office, placing his hand on the back of his head and drawing it down his nape. In a little while Rheingold reappeared with Barnsdale and MacBride said to the sergeant:

"You wait outside the door." And to Barnsdale: "You sit down there."

Barnsdale dropped limply to a chair, let his hands hang between his knees. His collar was open and his tie undone. The skipper prowled about the office, slowly, measuring Barnsdale with a keen, unwavering stare. At last he sat on his desk, bracing one foot on the floor, letting the other dangle. He thrust his hands deeply into his trousers pockets.

His low, gruff tone was intended to chide: "Come on, boy; open up. You've got to realize you're in a tough corner, that everything's against you. Come on, come on; give us a line."

Barnsdale mumbled: "I didn't kill Lily."

"See? Same old story, same old tune. The words and music are ancient, boy. Lily's found choked to death. You were there at about the time. You go home and dive out a window." He raised his arms. "Do you blame us for snagging you?"

"I didn't kill Lily."

MacBride folded his arms, "What was the fight about?"

"There was no fight."

"Sure there was."

Barnsdale, staring weakly at the floor, shook his head. "No. Lily—well, Lily told me we were through." He picked the palm of one hand with the forefinger of the other. "Lily said we were through. It was so sudden, out of a blue sky. I—I did get angry a little, I was so surprised. And yet—I don't know, maybe I shouldn't have been. Who am I? A forty-dollar-a-week piano player."

"Where'd you meet her?"

"In a radio broadcasting station."

"When?"

"Six months ago."

"When'd you start going with her?"

"Well, about a month ago."

"Any other man in the case?"

"No, I don't think so."

He withdrew a pipe from his pocket and fidgeted with it. MacBride passed him a pouch of tobacco and Barnsdale stuffed the pipe and the hard-boned skipper struck a match.

"You see," MacBride said, "I'm not going out of my way and trying to hang something on you. But, hell, look at the way the cards read."

Barnsdale took a few drags on his pipe and then forgot it. His whole body sagged hopelessly in the chair. He began talking as if to himself, in a small remote voice: "I can't understand it. I can't believe Lily's dead. It doesn't seem right, it doesn't seem possible." He wagged his head. "I—I can't even believe I'm here being charged with—" He stopped, wagged his head again and covered his face with a hand.

MacBride rocked to and fro on the desk for a long minute, chewing on his lip, keeping his keen, speculative stare bent on Barnsdale. Presently he stood up, went to the door and opened it and said to Rheingold:

"Okey; take him down."

Rheingold raised an inquisitive eyebrow. MacBride shook his head, turned, said to Barnsdale:

"Okey, boy."

The door closed and the skipper walked slowly to his desk, laid his hand on the telephone. After a moment he picked it up and called the hotel where Lily Carewe had met her death. He asked for the manager.

"This is Captain MacBride," he said to the manager. "Is your clerk Skayne there?... Well, phone his home and tell him to come over to Headquarters immediately.... Understand, I said immediately."

He hung up as Kennedy lolled in. The reporter drifted to the radiator, tapped his wet shoes against it.

"Why the hell don't you wear rubbers?" MacBride frowned.

"Make my feet sweat."

"Humph!"

"And I always said I'd rather freeze to death than sweat to death.... And how is our youth Barnsdale this fair morning?"

MacBride scowled at the desk. He rapped the desk lightly with his knuckles. "Shot to hell. You know," he went on, peering down at his knuckles, "I'm beginning to believe the kid is on the up and up."

"Going soft-headed in your old age, huh?"

"Maybe." MacBride sat down. "Maybe, Kennedy. But I've been in this business so long, so long, sweetheart, that I can almost smell the truth. No reason for it, no reason you can lay a mitt on. It just—well, you just smell it. I've seen heels come and go, and I've seen guys that've gone cuckoo over a dame and sloughed her. I've seen, I've picked up eighteen-year-old punks that were as old as the hills in other ways; kind of ageless. But a kid like this—a kid like this kind of impresses you with his youth. He hits a jam like this one and he seems, well, like he was just born."

"Stop," cried Kennedy dramatically, "you're going to make me bawl any minute. I'm just going to break down and—"

"Yeah, I know how you are. I've been around you a long time, Kennedy, and I've come to know your front. Anything for the wisecrack.... But I'm getting on in years."

"You're telling me?"

"And the older I get, the more I want to give a guy a break. My reputation's made. I don't have to build myself up any more. Looking back, I figure I've hung two-to-five-year raps on guys that didn't deserve 'em. I was younger then, hell-bent to make a record."

Kennedy grinned, opened a telephone book. "We will now both break into a hymn."

MacBride stood up, struck the desk briefly, said in a brief, blunt voice: "That kid's innocent."

"May I print that?"

"Print it now and I'll print your puss."

SKAYNE, the hotel clerk, went down into the basement of Police Headquarters with the skipper. Here were large metal books bracketed to the walls; these books contained many metal pages and the pages contained many pictures of men who had been booked on criminal charges.

"This is our Rogues' Gallery," MacBride explained, opening the first metal book. "The idea is to find a likeness of the man who asked for Miss Carewe's apartment number. We figure that after he left the desk he may have found her apartment number from someone else. Pick out any picture that even looks just a little like this guy. Take your time. Go down this aisle and up the other. I'll be over by that desk. Call me if you see anything."

The skipper left Skayne and went over to the desk. Mullins was taking fingerprints of a suspect, and in a few minutes Bachman, one of his assistants, appeared in shirt-sleeves and said:

"Well, Steve, we went over that apartment. We found Barnsdale's prints, a maid's, the mother's, the dead dame's, a bellhop's—this was on the door—and then we found a thumb print that don't match up."

"Where'd you find it?" MacBride asked.

"On a sterling silver cigarette humidor. The dead dame's is on it and then this other one—a guy's. I've put Bickle on the files, to see if maybe we can spot anything, but I don't think so."

MacBride said: "Good work."

About twenty minutes later Skayne called him and MacBride rapped his heels up the aisle and found Skayne pointing to an old picture.

Skayne said: "I don't know about this. It doesn't look very much like the man; in fact, it looks very little like him. But at the same time, there is a resemblance. The man on the picture is much younger, and the chance is so wide that I'd hate to swear to it."

MacBride made a note of the file number and said: "That's what I want. Keep looking till you've seen 'em all."

He gave the file number to Bachman and in a few minutes Bachman returned with a memorandum.

"It was taken twelve years ago, Steve. It's a picture of Sam Cebra—"

"Sam Cebra!"

"You got it, Skipper. He's never been up since, and as a matter of fact, according to this record, he beat that rap. At that time, he came here from Cleveland and was picked up for sticking up a lunch-room on River Road—"

"Hey," Bickle said, coming over, "I just tailed down that thumb print you picked up in the Carewe place. It's Sam Cebra's and we got his print about twelve years ago."

"Why all the hullaballoo about Sam Cebra?" Kennedy asked, drifting down the stairway.

Chapter IV

SAM CEBRA is one of the institutions of Richmond City, but one not to be whispered in the same breath with, for instance, the Cabot Memorial Library or the Town Hall. Cebra hit Richmond City in his late twenties, a lad on the make, but in a tinhorn way. He figured the city a pushover in those days, and on his first job, much to his amazement, he never got to first base.

It was the lunch-room job. He cracked it on his lonesome and was hiking around the corner towards the docks when he ran smack into a then first-grade detective, Steve MacBride.

In those days MacBride hit first and asked questions afterwards, and he opened Cebra's scalp with a blackjack to the later tune of eleven stitches. That blackjack may have put a great deal of sense into Cebra's head, for he was never caught red-handed again. Possibly, too, it was the smart shyster who got hold of him, beat the rap for him, and of course emptied his pockets.

But Cebra rose. Not openly. His shadow grew rather than the man himself, and while from time to time killings occurred up his alley, none occurred on his doorstep. An alley and a doorstep are much different from each other in the legal catch-as-catch-can. So Cebra rose, making his power felt first here, then there, looking always before he leaped and then many times preferring not to leap.

He was known to the cops and to the District Attorney's office as a smart fellow, a generally sane fellow. He was of course a public enemy, one of the most powerful gang barons the city had ever endured. He had wide political influence, but he was not a loud-mouth. They took it for granted that he was a killer, but they could not hang anything on him. The know-it-alls said that probably in the end a woman would be the cause of his downfall....

It was at about noon that MacBride stepped from the police sedan, walked across the sidewalk, which had been cleared of snow, and entered the lobby of the white stone apartment house. To the elevator operator he said:

"Sam Cebra's."

"Who's calling?"

"Never mind ringing him, boy. I'm from the cops." He showed his badge as he walked into the elevator.

"Penthouse A," the boy said.

The elevator rose swiftly, silently. It stopped. The door slid open and MacBride stepped into a private corridor. He pressed a white pearl button beside the door. A small, rocky-looking man in black livery opened the door.

"Hello, Snoozer," MacBride said.

"Strike me, as I live and breathe if it ain't—"

"You live and breathe; Snoozer," MacBride said, walking in. "Live your way to Sam and breathe to him I'm here."

"Honest, I ain't seen you since—"

"I caught you with your paw sunk in a drunk's pocket back of Union Station."

"Jeese, I been off that stuff for years, I come up in the world."

"What, fourteen stories?"

"Hah?"

"Let it slide. Where's Sam?"

"Just taking his bath."

"Me after you."

They went down a corridor, then down a short circular staircase whose steps were padded with carpet an inch thick. This brought them to a triangular foyer off which three doors opened. MacBride found Sam Cebra in the blue-and-white tiled bathroom, sunk in a tub of steaming, scented water.

"Hello, Steve."

"Hello, Sam."

"I'll be out in a minute. Run in the living-room. Hey, Cornelius, mix the skipper a drink."

Snoozer said: "What you having, Cap?"

"Nix."

MacBride wandered into the tremendous living-room. At one end was a fireplace, at the other a small, chromium bar with four high stools standing before it. Every bit of floor space was covered by dark green carpet. There were three divans.

In a few moments Cebra entered, yanking tight the belt of a gray silk robe. His feet were encased in straw sandals, and, saying: "Well, of all people," cheerfully, he went to a humidor, plucked a cigarette, lit up. "Yes, of all people. How are you feeling these days, Steve?"

Cebra was tall, a little taller than MacBride and much broader. His face was big but it had a dark satin smoothness and his eyebrows were sleek black, his hair lay back smoothly on his big head, partless. His hands were huge, but well-kept.

MacBride unbuttoned his overcoat and said: "Sam, I haven't seen you in a long time because I haven't had cause to. I mean, I guess there's been plenty of cause but—"

Cebra smiled. "I get you, Steve."

"Now, though..." MacBride sat down. "Now, though, Sam, there's something up your alley."

"There've been a hell of a lot of things up my alley."

"This particular alley looks like a sure bet to your doorstep. I'm speaking of Lily Carewe."

Cebra dropped casually on to one of the divans, lounged back comfortably. His unconcerned "Let's have it" was accompanied by a tranquil stream of cigarette smoke.

MacBride leaned his elbows on his knees. "You were in her apartment last night, Sam."

"Was I? Tell me about it. I'd like to know."

"Smooth, aren't you? I like 'em smooth, Sam. They're easier to wrinkle.... Well, we picked up a fingerprint of yours in her apartment and fingerprints have a habit of wandering around with the guy that owns 'em."

"They have, Skipper. Nonetheless"—he sat up, tapped a yawn—"you're just a little nuts." He twisted his head. "Cornelius, bring me some black coffee.... As I was saying, Steve—"

"I know: I'm nuts. Hang your ears on this bit of wisdom, Sam. You stopped at the hotel desk last night and tried to buy your way up to Lily Carewe's apartment. The clerk turned you down. Who else did you bribe?"

"What do you mean?"

"Who told you her apartment number?"

Cebra brought his eyebrows together. "Listen, what the hell are you trying to hang on me?"

"Murder, Sam."

"Okey, I can take a joke."

"It's no joke."

Cebra stood up, jamming his big hands into the pockets of his robe. "Listen, I have a hell of a time as it is enjoying my breakfast, without having you busting in here with something you heard in your sleep."

MacBride rose slowly, flexed his legs and then placed them wide apart and jacked his hands on his hips. "Sam, you've come up in the world. I met you on your first job in Richmond City and it looks as if I'm seeing you on your last."

"Oh... so I knocked off Lily Carewe. Why, will you tell me?"

"I don't know why. But you were clowning around her hotel and we picked up your print in her apartment."

Cebra's eyes darkened, his mouth hardened. "I tell you I never saw her apartment."

"Don't be a dope, Sam. Why did you try to chisel at the hotel desk? Why did you want to see her?"

"I'll not tell that."

"You admit you stopped at the desk, then?"

"Yeah."

"Why?"

Cebra's eyes narrowed down. He shook his head slowly. "I guess it was just an idea I had."

"Now I've got an idea, Sam. Get dressed. Come down to Headquarters. You haven't been there in a long time. We've made a lot of alterations."

Snoozer came in with a cup of black coffee and Cebra said: "Thanks, Cornelius." And to MacBride: "I never did like Headquarters and I don't think the alterations'll interest me. I wasn't in that girl's apartment and that stands."

"Your fingerprints stand, too, Sam."

"I smell a double cross somewhere."

"Finish the coffee and we'll go."

Cebra took a few quick gulps, set down the cup. There was a sting in his tone: "For a one-track mind, Steve, you take the cake. Damned if you don't."

THE skipper was sitting in his office when Lewiston, a laboratory man, came in and deposited the tiny sliver of gold which MacBride had picked up in Lily Carewe's apartment.

Lewiston said: "It looks, near as I can figure out, like it came from a clasp pin. It's so damned small though, it's hard to tell, but I'd say it's part of some design. It's very fragile. Rings are usually stouter, so I don't think it came from a ring."

"Okey, thanks," MacBride said, and Lewiston went out.

Sam Cebra turned from the window, sighed. He was obviously bored, though he was also a little worried. He was a fine figure of a man, dressed now in decorous blue.

In a few minutes Rheingold brought in Barnsdale and MacBride said: "Barnsdale, did you ever see this man before?"

Cebra and Barnsdale looked at each other, and after a moment Barnsdale shook his head and mumbled: "No." He looked haggard and drawn, listless.

MacBride went on: "Did Lily Carewe ever express fear of someone? Did she ever seem scared?"

"Only—well, when she told me we were through, she seemed a little queer. I don't know whether it was fright or what it was. I guess I didn't think much about it at the time."

"Who's he?" Cebra asked.

"Another suspect," MacBride said. "Okey, Rheingold; take Barnsdale away."

When they had gone out, Cebra bent a curious eye on the skipper. "How does the kid figure in it?"

"The kid was in love with Lily Carewe. I thought I picked up a red-hot when I picked him up, but I began changing my mind. I changed it completely when things worked out in your direction. Sam," the skipper said, standing up, "I ought to have a motive nailed to you, but I haven't. Are you going to do a little talking or am I going to book you right off the bat?"

"I guess maybe you'll have to book me."

"Sam," MacBride went on roughly, "you're dumb to take this thing easy. Fingerprints don't walk into a place without fingers. We've got your print. We got it in Lily Carewe's apartment—it was plain as day there on a silver cigarette humidor."

Cebra's eyes steadied; they narrowed down and a shrewd look, almost a look of cunning, captured them. After a moment he said:

"I sent that humidor to Lily Carewe."

"Be your age—"

"I am. I sent it to her yesterday morning."

"Sam, quit stalling."

"I'm on the up and up."

"Why the hell would you send her a humidor?"

Cebra smiled slowly. "I kind of liked her singing."

"Did you send your card with it?"

"No. I just wrote out on a white card, 'From a fan.'"

"Then why did you go to the hotel desk last night?"

Cebra chided MacBride with his slow smile. "I don't know. It was just an idea, just a kind of impulse."

MacBride snapped: "Sam, you're a damned liar. You can't even prove you sent that humidor."

"Can't I? Put on your duds and come with me."

They went to a jewelry shop in Spruce Street, a smart, very fashionable shop, and MacBride saw instantly that Cebra was recognised. A tall man in a cut-away bowed and said:

"How do you do, Mr. Cebra?"

Cebra idly slapped his gloves in his palm and said: "What kind of purchase did I make yesterday morning?"

"You mean the silver humidor?"

Cebra smiled sidewise at MacBride and continued: "I had it sent to a young lady from here, didn't I?"

"Of course, Mr. Cebra. I recall you asked for a chamois and brushed the humidor, inserted a card and placed the humidor in our special blue velvet gift box, which we wrapped and sent to the address indicated."

Cebra again smiled mockingly at MacBride.

MacBride said: "Let's go."

They stopped on the sidewalk outside.

Cebra said lazily: "I get crazy ideas sometimes, Steve. That was one of them. It ought to make it plain that just because you find a guy's fingerprints in a place is not evidence complete that the guy was there…. I've got a date now. Or do you want to book me?"

MacBride was peering keenly into Cebra's face. "One of us is crazy, Sam." He tightened his lips, trying to keep down the color of chagrin that was working up his neck. "I can dish it and I can take it, though. Keep your date. But watch your alley, Sam."

Cebra chuckled and mockery again touched his voice when he said: "Why should I, when you're watching it?"

"Little razzberry, huh?"

Cebra said: "Well, toodle-oo, Steve." He strode leisurely off, hailed a taxi and climbed in. As the taxi moved past the skipper, Cebra grinned sardonically at him, raised his hands, clasped them and gave a prize-ring shake.

MacBride's face got very red.

Chapter V

BARNSDALE was sobbing. There was a trickle of blood on his cheek, a cut on his lip. He was breathing quickly, thickly, the sobs intermingled with the hoarse, grating breath. A couple of cops held him in vise-like grips. They had torn one of his coat-sleeves, ripped his tie. His eyes, harried and terrified, kept jerking from side to side.

MacBride walked in on the group, stopped, rasped: "Who the hell's been beating up this kid?"

Moriarity was sitting on a tipped-back chair. "No one beat him up, Skipper. Downstairs, Jake got careless with the cell and left it open for a minute, and what does this kid do but try to lam. He makes it upstairs and is heading for the garage when he runs into Grosskopf. Grosskopf tries to stop him, but he's slow, and the kid makes the garage as Wayne and Simmonds"—he indicated the cops who held Barnsdale—"come up the ramp. They nail him and he fights like hell, so they have to sock him a couple of times."

Kennedy drawled: "It was like this. Barnsdale didn't like the confinement. He started out on a little road work and Wayne and Simmonds mistook his purpose—"

"You," chopped off MacBride darkly, "for once keep your oar out of this." The skipper looked suddenly malignant; with a quick stride he reached Barnsdale, took a fistful of Barnsdale's shirt and shook him violently. "What the hell do you mean by pulling an act like that?... You guys let him go."

Wayne and Simmonds stepped back and MacBride shook Barnsdale again, backed him across the room and flung him into a chair. "What I get for being decent to you, huh? I ought to get my pants kicked off!... Listen to me, boy. I kind of went soft on you. I tried to treat you right, didn't I? What the hell was the idea?"

Barnsdale stared stupidly at the floor. MacBride hit him with the flat of his hand, snarled:

"Snap out of it!"

Barnsdale cringed in the chair. Above him MacBride towered, his face dull with rage and his fists knotted and pressed hard against his thighs. There I was a muggy, dangerous look in his eyes, a savage twist to his mouth. He reached down, grabbed hold of Barnsdale's hair and snapped back his head.

"Answer me? What was the idea?"

"I—I don't know."

"Well, well, well," chuckled Kennedy.

"Shut up!" MacBride flung over his shoulder. And then to Barnsdale, furiously: "Answer me!"

Barnsdale croaked: "I don't know. I—I just saw the door open. For a minute—for a minute I guess I went mad. I was afraid. I walked out and then I ran and then I couldn't stop. I—I just ran on and on—"

"And what were you afraid of?"

Barnsdale was panting, wagging his head. "Everything."

"The murder of Lily Carewe, for instance?"

The boy screamed suddenly: "I didn't murder her! You're trying to make me say I murdered her! But I didn't!... I ran because—because, I don't know, everything seemed so hopeless for me, so terribly hopeless. I—I wasn't in my right mind. I'm not now. But you can't, you can't," he cried desperately, "make me say I killed Lily!"

MacBride said in a deadly voice: "You killed Lily Carewe. You strangled her. She turned you down and you went mad, just as you say you went mad when you ran out, and you jumped on her and choked the life out of her!"

Barnsdale heaved up, his eyes bulging. "No. No!" He struggled, he fought MacBride with a wild, unreasonable desperation. Moriarity started to jump him. MacBride said: "Stay back!" And he swung round and round the room with Barnsdale until at last Barnsdale collapsed, sagged to the floor.

MacBride stepped back and said: "Take him out. Lock him up and see he stays locked."

Wayne and Simmonds took Barnsdale out and the skipper withdrew a handkerchief, mopped his face, the back of his neck and up beneath his chin.

Kennedy sighed. "And so our dear old skipper has another illusion broken. He goes ga-ga over a nice young boy and the nice young boy repays him by trying to lam. Tsk, tsk; well, well; so, so. Blessed is the earth, for it shall inherit the meek."

"Razz me, Kennedy. If it makes you feel better, razz me."

"The trouble is, old tomato, that you're letting up. You got too meek. Just because this kid has a nice face and a sad story, you forget all you ever learned. He came to you as a suspect on a gold plate, well seasoned, and just because you got sentimental you go waltzing around town trying to drag in folks like Sam Cebra. You're losing the old grip, you're losing the old grip."

MacBride made a fist and looked down at it. "Am I?" he muttered. He remained silent for a long moment, looking at his fist. Then he opened it. The palm was damp with sweat. He swiveled and strode out of the office, went down to the garage and climbed into his sedan.

"Drive around, Finnegan," he said.

"Where?"

"Just around."

The skipper sat in the back of the sedan and Finnegan drove it out of the garage. Riding on, MacBride tried to consider himself. Was he going soft? A few more breaks like this last one and he'd wind up in some outlying precinct. He had come out bluntly and said that he did not believe Barnsdale was guilty, and then Barnsdale had tried to break jail. Going off on a tangent, he had landed on Sam Cebra with a feeling that here was the man. He had been dead certain about Sam Cebra. And Sam was an old offender, worth the catch. But how easily and how smoothly had Sam Cebra turned the tables on MacBride! Up Sam's alley again, but not on his doorstep. An old joke!

He leaned forward and told Finnegan to drive to the hotel where Lily Carewe had been murdered. And leaning back again, he remembered Lily's young loveliness. Too young, too young to die. Like Barnsdale. He also was too young.

When MacBride walked into the hotel lobby he ran into Lackman, the house dick, and Lackman was perturbed.

"Listen, Captain," he said. "I was just about to phone you. It's about Lily Carewe's mother."

"What about her? I was just going up to see her."

"Well, look now. The maid was up in Mrs. Carewe's room, cleaning, and the old lady said she was going around the corner to a drug-store and would be back in ten minutes. She told the maid to leave the door and windows open, to air the room good. Well, the maid did, and about half an hour later she was going down the hall and she saw the door still open. It kind of puzzled her, because the old lady hadn't come back.

"But she didn't say anything and went on about her business; only when she passed the door an hour later, well, it was still open and the old lady wasn't in yet. Then she told the housekeeper and the housekeeper told me. That was about fifteen minutes ago. I hunted all over the hotel, but nobody saw her come in. I went down to the drug-store, and they said she hadn't been in today. So I was just about to give you a ring. It looks damned funny."

MacBride squinted into space, said after a moment: "It does, Lackman, it does. If she turns up, ring Headquarters. If I'm not there, leave the message."

He returned to the sedan, placed his foot on the running-board and crammed tobacco into his pipe.

"What's up?" Finnegan said.

"Lily Carewe's mother walked out of the hotel about two hours ago and kind of vanished. Got a match?"

"Yeah."

The skipper lit up, staring thoughtfully over the bowl of his pipe. He tossed the match away, said: "Drive to Sam Cebra's, Finnegan," and climbed in.

"Cebra's?"

MacBride said in a hard, absent-minded drawl: "Yeah."

HE got out of the elevator, took two slow steps and jabbed his forefinger against the pearl bell-button alongside the door. He plunged his hands into his overcoat pockets, tilted his pipe upward in one corner of his mouth and rocked gently to and fro on his heels. After a full minute, the door opened and Sam Cebra said:

"Twice the same day."

"Twice the same day, Sam," said MacBride laconically. He heard swift running feet somewhere—on the spiral staircase, he thought. The sound vanished soon.

"Come in," Cebra said.

"Intended to."

The skipper strolled in and Sam Cebra closed the door, gestured with an open palm. "Before me, Steve."

MacBride nodded and they moved on, walked down to the living-room. Snoozer was standing behind the bar, reading a newspaper.

The skipper called out: "You always sprint down stairways, Snoozer?"

"Cornelius," Cebra said, "maybe the Captain'll have a drink now."

"Can that," MacBride said. "I didn't come here to drink."

Cebra chuckled. "Well, I can see things have gone wrong again, Steve. What brings you up here this time?"

"Just a hunch this time, Sam." MacBride opened his overcoat. "I thought I'd like to look your place over. They say it's a swell layout. I'd like to see it"

Cebra, lighting a cigarette, lifted his eyes to MacBride's face, lowered them. "Don't try to be funny, Skipper. What's on your mind?"

"Any objection to me seeing the dump?"

"Don't horse around. What do you want?"

MacBride put his tongue in his cheek. "Just see the place—the rooms, the furnishings. You know, see the place."

Cebra began to look very grave. "After a while I get tired of horse-play, Steve. We've got on well for years but if you're going to begin to get nasty, that's okey by me, too. I was just going out. Come up some time when I'm not busy. It's a big place and it takes time to do it justice."

"I'd like to see it now."

"Some other time."

"What's the idea, Sam?"

"I just hate being made a goat."

MacBride blew his nose. "Okey. You go on where you're going. I'll wander around myself."

Cebra grabbed his arm, spoke very close to MacBride's face: "You heard me, Steve."

"Take it off."

"You heard me."

"Take it off, Sam."

Cebra removed his hand and MacBride stepped quickly backward, tripped over an ottoman and fell down. Snoozer hit the bar with the flat of his hand, burst into laughter.

"Cornelius!" barked Cebra, disapproving.

Snoozer's face froze.

MacBride got up, a little flustered, and with a humid look in his eyes. He turned on his heel and made for the spiral staircase.

"Where you going?" Sam Cebra called.

"Look your place over."

Cebra broke into a run and caught MacBride halfway up the stairway. "You can't pull that stuff here, Steve."

MacBride snarled down into his face: "Can't I? What the hell am I doing now?... Leggo, Sam!" He broke from Cebra's grip and reached the top. But Cebra was at his heels and caught hold of him again.

"Steve," Cebra said in a grating voice, "you're not going to act the cop in my place. Get out or I'll throw you out."

"Listen," Snoozer said anxiously, "kind of stop and reason it out kind of like."

"Cornelius," Cebra said, "you stay out of this.... Steve," he went on grimly to MacBride, "if you don't get out of here—"

MacBride spun Cebra against the wall. Anger flared in Cebra's eyes and he rebounded and hit MacBride hard on the side of the jaw. The skipper careened, lost his footing and went down the staircase; but halfway down he caught himself, rose and came back up the steps with a vicious glint in his eyes.

Cebra panted: "For cripes' sake, Steve!"

MacBride, about to punch Cebra, stopped short at sight of Lily Carewe's mother coming out of one of the rooms beyond. At the same time there was a small sound from Snoozer, who started swiftly towards the woman. His hand was outstretched, as if to placate. Cebra was in MacBride's way, and the skipper could not see what actually happened; but in an instant he saw Snoozer groveling on the floor.

MacBride grunted: "So you did kidnap her, Sam!"

The woman came on the run and MacBride held out his hand. The next instant he found himself on the floor. He caught a glimpse of the woman going down the staircase. Cebra was bounding after her. MacBride jumped up and followed. In the huge living-room he saw Cebra dive at the woman, saw her shift, brace herself and throw Cebra off sidewise. Then she darted for the small door behind the bar. It was locked. She spun and gripped the bar, looked down, her lips tight. She made a grab at something back of the bar.

"Look out!" Cebra cried.

MacBride said: "Mrs. Carewe—"

She was leveling a gun across the bar. MacBride now found that his left arm, the one with which he had tried to stop her, was quite numb.

He said: "Put down that gun. In the name of the law—"

"Get back," she said. "I'm going out."

Suddenly she shifted, fired. Snoozer fell from the lowest step into the living-room.

MacBride yelled: "Drop it, woman!" and started towards her.

She fired, missed MacBride. He saw there was nothing else to do. His own gun leaped in his hand, roared. The bullet turned the woman half around, slammed her backward. She struck a shelf of glassware and the glasses came down, shattering about her. Her feet kicked around back of the bar as she went down, and her body, heaving, crunched the fallen glassware.

MacBride went to her, bent, took hold of her and dragged her out into the living-room. She was quite heavy. She tried to get away, fought with her left hand; her right was useless.

"Cut it out, cut it out," MacBride kept saying.

Cebra said: "She drilled Cornelius clean."

MacBride finally had to fling her roughly to the floor. One of her stockings had fallen down and the skipper, reaching to yank her dress down, saw that her right knee bore a small stain. An iodine stain. The stain covered a small cut.

"My God!" he muttered.

He stood up, stared at Cebra.

Cebra said: "She's not Lily Carewe's mother."

"She's not—"

"No," said Cebra. "Hell, I ought to know. Lily was my kid." There was a glaze in his eyes, but his voice was almost offhand. "I just found that out. Yes, Lily was my kid. Lily Cebra was her name, though she didn't know it. This is Hortense Carewe. 'Babe' Carewe she used to be when she was a tumbler in a circus, years ago.... Should I phone a doctor?"

"Yeah," MacBride said in a dull, vacant voice.

Cebra walked away. He stopped and looked down at Snoozer. Snoozer was quite dead.

"Poor Cornelius.... His name wasn't really Cornelius, Steve. I just called him Cornelius."

He went on to the telephone.

KENNEDY came into the skipper's office and the skipper, sunk in thought, did not look up for the space of a full minute. Then he blinked, roused himself.

Kennedy gave a sigh of relief. "Why the brown study?" he said.

"It was the first time I ever deliberately drilled a woman. I was just thinking it over. I had to drill her or she'd have drilled me." He rubbed his jaw. "She was strong. Stronger than you. Hell, she'd have tossed you over her shoulder."

"What did she say?"

MacBride leaned back, clasped his hands on his nape. "She killed Lily because Lily wanted to marry Barnsdale. She didn't kill her deliberately. It was an accident, fit of rage; she didn't know her own strength.

"Lily was determined to marry Barnsdale. The old woman was determined she wouldn't. Why? Because the old woman was getting most of the dough Lily made and she didn't want anyone else cutting in. Barnsdale made very little dough. It came to a head when the old woman finally told Lily that she was not her daughter. What's more, she told Lily who her father was—Sam Cebra, one of the most notorious public enemies. And she told Lily that if she married Barnsdale she would be through as a high-priced lullaby singer—because the old woman said she'd spring the truth on the public.

"Imagine how the girl must have felt. She'd never seen her father and therefore had no affection for him. She realized that Barnsdale didn't always work; not because he didn't want to, but because of conditions. Also, she was afraid of the notoriety. You can't blame her. So she sent him away. Then she remembered the awful look in his face and was afraid he'd commit suicide. She told the old woman she was going to Barnsdale's hotel and tell him the truth. The old woman argued; they both argued; and in a fit of rage the old woman lit on Lily. Knelt on her, broke the lavallière Lily was wearing—with her knee, of course."

"Whew!"

MacBride went on: "Lily's mother ran away from Sam when Lily was a year old. She got a job in a circus dancing, met Babe Carewe, told Babe about her life. Six months later she died and Babe brought the kid up as her own, never told her.

"A week ago Sam saw a picture of Lily in the newspaper and remembered his wife. Lily looked a little like her, not much, and Sam didn't really think Lily was his kid. But he got sentimental and sent her a cigarette humidor anonymously. He even got so sentimental that he wandered around to the hotel. When Lily was murdered, he began to take a great interest. He remembered that his wife had gone with a circus, and so he phoned Babe Carewe and said: 'Were you ever with a circus?' She hung up on him. This made him figure she had been, so he got Snoozer and they watched the hotel and when the old woman came out they waltzed her into Sam's car. She was scared stiff, and went along without a fight. Sam got very curious and got tough with her and she went to pieces. He was trying to get the whole truth out of her when I turned up. He didn't want me butting in. He wasn't sure yet."

Kennedy grinned. "I guess my face ought to be red, huh?"

"No redder than mine. When I walked in on Sam, I was dead sure of him. I never figured the woman at all." He stood up, stretched. "Too bad. I'm getting to like Sam Cebra. But some day Sam's going to miss his step. Tough. Too bad. I'll walk up his alley, find something on his doorstep, put the cuffs on Sam and help the State burn him. I won't like to do it, because Sam's a nice guy. Tough. Too bad."

Bad News

Kennedy, wise and whimsical newsman, pinch hits for Capt. Steve MacBride.

Chapter I

SHE was a big brunette, forty-odd, but her good lines had not faded away. Five feet seven, she weighed about a hundred and fifty, but it was pretty evenly distributed; she had nice ankles and feet big enough to carry her weight. Her face was broad, but high cheekbones gave it an elongated look, and there was only the shadow of a double chin. Sway-backed, flat-stomached, she nearly approached the hour glass motif. Her name was Nora Hourihan, but everyone called her Babe. She had married twice and both her husbands had gone out by the hot route: the first on Fife Street one winter's night—his stomach shot wide open; the second near the river—the top of his head blown off. They began to say after that that she was bad news to men.

Taking the bottle of Scotch from the sideboard in the dining-room, she carried it into the living-room and planked it down on the glass-topped tea wagon. Marino, the plain-clothed sergeant from the precinct, was leaning against the wall, his hands in his pockets. Babe Hourihan looked a little white and when she lit a cigarette her hand shook.

She said: "Okey, Joe; measure your poison."

"I'll take the same as you," Marino said.

"I'm not drinking."

"Go ahead. Maybe you need it."

"I guess I do."

March sleet was driving against the window panes, making a thin, brittle sound like dry twigs burning. But the apartment was warm, cozy, comfortable. Marino had not removed his blue Chesterfield. He was a broad, dark man, with startling white teeth and bright brown eyes. He wore good clothes, dark; and crisp white linen, and his hair was thick and shiny black, without a part. His voice came from deep places, with a not unpleasant slurring sound.

"To you, Babe," Marino said.

"Down the hatch."

They drank.

She coughed, made a face and sat down on the cretonne-covered divan. Marino put down the glass, touched his lips with a handkerchief and said almost confidentially:

"You're giving me the straight of it, huh?"

"My gawd, Joe, why shouldn't I?"

He pursed his lips, nodded, grave-eyed. He walked to one of the windows, his footfalls solid but elastic—he was a heavy, powerful man, and gave the impression of being in complete control of all his muscles. He watched the sleet sparkling against the window pane.

Babe made a little sound and put her hand to her forehead, holding it there.

Marino was saying: "Now, Babe…." He came over and sat down beside her, fiddling with his big hands. "Maybe we'll head him off before—"

"Maybe—maybe!" she cried hoarsely. "That's it—maybe!" She blew her nose. "What if you don't?"

He slapped his broad, strong knees. He was a little older than she was and had lost his wife five years before. The baby had died, too. His eyes clouded. He slapped his knees again and then stood up, buttoning his overcoat. Crossing the room, he picked up his hat.

"I'll run along, Babe. Sit tight. If you get a buzz let me know. Meantime"—he was at the door—"I'll keep fanning the town."

She croaked: "Thanks, Joe. Thanks a million."

The door closed quietly behind Marino and for a few minutes Babe cried, the tears running down her cheeks. The sound of the driving sleet chilled her. Johnny was out in it somewhere—hunting, hunting, with a gun in his pocket. She had lost two husbands and now she was afraid she would lose her son: the mad streak that had run through his father had now, at last, cropped up in Johnny. She rose and pulled down all the shades, hoping they would mute the sound of the crackling sleet.

MARINO walked into *Enrico's,* a quiet place in Flamingo Street. *Enrico's* was famous for good food. The bar was in a small room at the rear of the restaurant. It was Monday night. Every night except

Monday night there were a piano player, a violinist and a guitar player in the restaurant. Troubadours. They were very popular. Johnny Hourihan played the guitar and sang. Monday nights it was dead, except for the gourmands. Kennedy was the only one standing at the bar. He was matching dimes with Paderoofski: it was a nickname, because sometimes he used to play the piano; his real name was Bennie Iammaranzio.

Kennedy had taken off his wet shoes and placed them on the radiator to dry. He was now wearing a pair of carpet slippers which Paderoofski had lent him: they were many sizes too big. When Marino wandered in, Kennedy said to Paderoofski:

"I feel there is a dark man hovering near; he is of Latin extraction and does not play the harpsichord."

"Hi yuh, Sarge," Paderoofski said.

Kennedy wobbled about, said: "See? Didn't I tell you? You don't play the harpsichord, do you, Joe?"

Marino kept his hands in his overcoat pockets and stood about a foot from the bar. He wore a sad-eyed smile. "Hello, Kennedy. Thought you were on the wagon."

"I was. But it got stuck in one of those alleys off Jockey Street and I had to get off. Hated to."

"Yes, you did."

Paderoofski raised his flamboyant eyebrows. "Whatcha drinkin' t'night, Sarge?"

"He doesn't drink," Kennedy rambled on. "He's a vegetarian. Nothing but vegetables all the time. Phooey!"

Marino said: "I'd like to talk to you, Kennedy."

"By me it's agribble."

"Over here."

Marino went to one of the booths at the farther end of the bar and Kennedy followed, walking in the overlarge carpet slippers as a man walks on snow-shoes. His pale hair was tangled, his pale eyes looked foggy and marks of dissipation lined his young-old face. There was something ageless about Kennedy—something worn and battered and washed-out; and also, something wise and good-naturedly wicked, like a benign satyr. He took nothing seriously—least of all himself. He had nothing of the southern intensity, the dark gravity of Joe Marino. A little round-shouldered, a little hollow-chested, he looked as if a good wind might knock him over.

He flopped down at the table, facing Marino, and said: "Match you dimes, Joe."

Marino, lighting a cigarette, shook his head. He blew a stream of smoke downward; it hit the table, flattening out, and Marino said in a guarded low voice:

"You know everything, Kennedy. What's the chances of finding Johnny Hourihan?"

"What's in it?"

"Glory."

"You take the glory and I'll take the cash."

"On the level," Marino said, studying his palms.

Kennedy hiccoughed. He sat back, looking very weary, his eyes half-closed. "What are you doing, Joe, pulling a fast one on Babe? I thought you were on the make there. What did she do, give you the merry air?"

Marino said in his guarded voice: "I could just as well smack you down, Kennedy."

"You're telling me, huh? You know why I stay out of drafts? Because drafts always knock me down. It's not the knocking down I mind, Joe; it's the job I have getting up again. Myself, I believe in kindness. Cast your bread upon the waters and it will come back all wet."

Marino said "Nerts!" in a quiet, exasperated voice and stood up, started off.

"Wait," said Kennedy. "You're a white dago, Joe. Sit down and tell the old padre what's on your mind."

Marino said: "Then cut out horsing." He rarely raised his voice. Sitting down, he leaned on his elbows, clasped his hands together, looked at the wasted gray-white face of Kennedy, the dozing eyes.

"Are you listening?"

"Sure."

"I was just over to see Babe. She called me up about noon and I went over and seen her and she said Johnny was out gunning for a mugg named Mike Jakoboin. Well, I chased all over town on the look for Johnny or Mike. I don't care who I get, so long as I get one of them. They're both playing hide and seek with each other and if they meet it's fireworks."

Kennedy looked sound asleep, but his lips moved: "What's the matter with Johnny?"

"Dame trouble. He got himself in a sweat over a girl named Louella Wynant and it seems Louella sees Jakoboin one night and something goes wrong and Jakoboin makes a pass at her. He knocks her cold and messes her up generally and a little later Johnny comes in and sees her and goes off his nut. He makes tracks for home, raving to Babe, and then he grabs her gun out of the bureau and lights out. That was last night. He's not been seen since. We can't locate Jakoboin either. It's bad news for Babe, Kennedy. If these guys meet—one of them goes up for murder, with the edge on Johnny."

"So what?"

"You're supposed to know this town like nobody else. You're supposed to know more people in it than anybody else. I want a steer, that's all. Jakoboin or Johnny: I don't care which I get, so long as I get one of them."

"Doing this for Babe, huh?"

Marino chuckled. "Why not?"

"Why not?" Kennedy echoed. "I always said she had the swellest pair of hips this side of Topeka, Kansas."

"Don't get personal."

"I never got personal with Babe in my life. I think something of my life. But I can still admire her hips…. Paderoofski, my shoes!"

Chapter II

FLAMINGO STREET makes a left jog near the top of the hill, and then ends abruptly at Wickwire Square. It always used to be Flamingo Street north of the Square as well, but the year Kurt Du-hammel was made mayor he went in for changing names a lot. A friend of his who lived north of the Square wanted the whole street named after himself—he'd given a lot to the campaign fund. This raised a great row and finally there was a compromise made: they renamed only half of the street. Hence north of Wickwire Square, where the old mansions have bay windows, Flamingo Street becomes Brenstuhl Drive. "This is not," Kennedy used to say, "poetic justice."

He came out on Wickwire Square, ten minutes' walk from *Enrico's,* and stood there in the eye of the sleety wind. He shivered to his marrow. His threadbare coat was really a spring coat. He never wore gloves. His socks were silk and his shoes were thin. Rubbers he never used. He looked like a scarecrow or like the shadow of an emaciated tree. He kept tapping his feet in the slush while the sleet drilled him. *Enrico's* was warm, a friendly place, and Paderoofski was a lay philosopher, and Kennedy cursed himself half-heartedly for having been taken in by Joe Marino. But Joe was a white dago. Besides, Kennedy had a weakness for Babe Hourihan, even though he knew she was not for him.

A taxi, whaling across the Square, braked and slid up to the curb; its wheels shot a geyser of slush into Kennedy's face and the driver said cheerfully:

"Taxi, sir?"

Kennedy spat the slush from his lips. "You annoy me," he said, and bending his head into the wind he walked away. Several blocks farther on, he stopped on another corner. Things were beginning to simmer in his mind, but they were not quite clear yet. A taxi slammed into the curb, doused Kennedy with slush, and the driver said cheerfully:

"Taxi, sir?"

It was the same driver.

"I'll bet," Kennedy said, "you're taking a correspondence course in salesmanship."

"I did once. I give it up account of my wife didn't want me on the road all the time. How'dja guess it?"

Kennedy sighed, opened the door and climbed in. "You win. Drive me to 408 Hurd Street."

"Yes, *sir!* Number 804 Hurd!"

"Number 408."

"Yes, *sir–r!*"

It had occurred to Kennedy that it might be a good idea to go to Mike Jakoboin's apartment first. Marino had gone there first also but had not been there since. Jakoboin ran books in a number of pool-halls and cigar stores in Richmond City and was in the dough. He also owned a part interest in Lady Fair, who had been doing well recently at Agua Caliente.

The apartment house was at the quiet end of Hurd Street. Kennedy entered the small lobby and went directly to the elevator. You operated it yourself. He pressed the button marked five and the car wheezed to the fifth floor. He had dropped around to see Mike only a month ago and knew the apartment number. It was at the end of the corridor, a mahogany stained door with a white push-button alongside it. He leaned on the button for a few seconds and then waited. His shoes were soaked again, his feet cold, and the sleet, melting on his hat, dribbled from the brim. He rubbed his chilled hands together and his teeth chattered.

There was no answer and he rang again, heard the faint sound of the buzzer inside. He shrugged, rattled the doorknob as a parting gesture. To his surprise, the door was not locked, and he went in. The lights were on and the living-room was very warm and Kennedy went to the nearest radiator, warmed his hands on it and tapped his feet against the bottom of it. He heard a low humming sound and noticed that the radio was turned on, but apparently the particular station had gone off the air. He didn't bother to turn it off.

He found Jakoboin lying on the floor just inside the bedroom doorway. He could tell by the dilated eyes that Jakoboin was dead.

When he felt Jakoboin's heart, he knew he was dead. The wound was in the center of the chest. Jakoboin had his overcoat on, even his gloves. There was a suitcase lying open on the bed, but packed. He must have had his derby on too, for it lay a few feet away, upside down. A few bureau drawers were open. Possibly Jakoboin had sneaked in to pack hurriedly and then to breeze. He was a big man, fortyish, handsome in a leonine way, and a smart dresser.

Kennedy muttered "M-m-m" absent-mindedly and wandered about the apartment. In the pantry he found a bottle of Scotch. He took the bottle and a glass and carried them, one in either hand, into the bedroom. Standing near Jakoboin, he poured a generous portion and downed it neat without batting an eyelash.

After a few minutes he rambled about looking for the telephone; found it and called the Eighth Precinct house.

"Joe Marino there?... Who am I? Why Father Mullaney.... Yeah." He waited, moving his feet inside his soggy shoes. Then: "Joe?... Kennedy. Come around to Jakoboin's. Come alone.... What do *you* think?" He hung up slowly, hummed abstractedly to himself and returned to the bedroom.

From a closet there he took a pair of slippers, sat down and removed his shoes. He put on the slippers and placed his shoes on top of the radiator. Then he found a copy of *Variety*, and dragging an armchair over to face the radiator, he sat down and propped his feet on top. His back was towards Jakoboin. He lit a cigarette and read *Variety*.

MARINO came and stood in the bedroom doorway and Kennedy, turning a page, looked over his shoulder and said:

"Greetings, Joe."

Marino said nothing. He stood with his hands jammed in his overcoat pockets. His eyes were humid and his mouth was hard and there was gray color beneath the swart of his face. There was no sound but the clicking of the sleet against the window panes and the sound Kennedy made turning the pages of *Variety*.

Then Marino said in a thick low voice: "How'd you find this?"

"Oh. I just thought I'd beard the lion is his den, if the lion was in. The lion was in but in no shape to be bearded. That's life; here one day, gone the next."

Marino raised an ear. "What's that?"

"What?"

"Humming sound."

"Radio. Maybe the station was on when the shot was fired. It's since signed off."

"D'you touch it?"

"No."

There was a moment's silence and then Marino muttered "God!" in a deep, choked voice.

Kennedy stood up, stretched. "Bad news for Babe is right. Her luck always did come in bunches, like bananas. Does anyone besides you and me and Babe know Johnny was gunning for him?"

"No. Maybe Louella Wynant, too."

"So what?"

Marino raised his dark grave eyes to Kennedy.

"Hell," said Kennedy. "I can keep my mouth shut."

Marino dropped his eyes.

Kennedy poured another drink and again downed it neat. He looked at the empty glass. "This is out of your precinct anyhow, Joe. MacBride's on leave. Who's over H.Q. tonight?"

"Langard."

Kennedy, weaving a little, considered.

"If Mac was on, we might get a break. Hic—I guess I've got the hic-cups."

"Try some water. Bend over and drink it kind of upside down, from the far side of the glass."

"I can't stand water. That's why I can never go to sea. I always get seasick. Hic." He headed for the bottle, tripped in the slippers he wore and slammed down.

Marino helped him up saying: "You're plastered."

"Who, me?"

Marino's voice shook. "For God's sake, Kennedy, stay sober."

"Don't let it get you, Joe. Hic—whoops, dearie!"

Marino shook him, half-pleading, half-angry. "You hear me, Kennedy!"

"Listen, Joe. The best thing we can do is just walk out of here. What have you touched since you came in?"

"Just the knob."

"Okey. I've touched the knob, the phone, that chair, this bottle and glass, and the pantry doorknob and the shelf in the pantry. I'll wipe 'em off. Wait. I touched two radiators too."

Marino stood with his hands in his pockets, his eyes clouded, his forehead wrinkled. He felt thick in the throat, a little dazed, a little uncertain just what to do. In the ordinary course of events he would have known what to do; he had a good head on his shoulders and was no mugg in cop's clothing. He was also human. He was under the spell of Babe Hourihan.

Not moving, he watched Kennedy zigzag about the apartment wiping off those articles he had touched. He knew Kennedy was drunk and he only feared that he would become too drunk; and Marino regretted having drawn Kennedy in. Not that he mistrusted Kennedy, but it stood to reason that no drunk was as able as a sober man. At least, records proved that much.

"Now that that's done," Kennedy said, "we'll toddle along. We can't help Jakoboin, so let him lie. Somebody 'll find him and I don't suppose it matters much to Jakoboin when. He makes a nice, clean appearance.

No blood. I guess the heavy overcoat soaked it all up.... Well, brother Marino, to horse and away."

They met no one on the way down; met no one in the lobby. Kennedy's shoes were moist and hot from having stood on the radiator, but the slush in the street promptly cooled them.

He said: "Okey, Joe. You beat it over to Babe and break the news. I know it's lousy, but that's your job, not mine. I'm going on a tear of my own. If anything turns up, I'll call you at the precinct house."

"What are you going to do now?"

"Try to get a line on Johnny."

Marino's voice was dull, flat: "I'll go tell Babe then."

WHEN she opened the door of her apartment, Marino stood looking at her with his eyes out of focus. He felt awkward and clumsy and his body was immovable, it seemed, like a rock. His face was grave; it seemed that all but a profound sense of gravity had been drained from his system. He could not smile. He could not smooth things over. He was not that kind and knew it.

"Joe...."

He walked in, his eyes looking straight ahead, and she closed the door. He turned and looked at her again and said:

"Jakoboin—" He couldn't get it out.

But she knew what he meant. Her shoulders sagged and she dragged her feet across the floor and dropped to the divan. She did not cry. Her eyes settled on the floor and remained fixed on the floor and she said liplessly:

"Where?"

"Jakoboin's place."

"When?"

"I don't know. Kennedy found him and called me."

"Kennedy!"

"I needed somebody, so I went to Kennedy. He knows the town up, down and across. You can count on Kennedy."

"He never stays sober long enough—"

"I know, but—"

"Oh, Joe!" she cried, breaking a bit.

"Steady," he said. "Nobody knows but you and me and Kennedy. I didn't report it."

"They'll break you for it, Joe!"

He said grimly: "If they find out."

"Joe, you mustn't—"

He was still grim: "I've done enough for them. I carry three wounds I got in line of duty. I've served them straight and square for eighteen years. I've got a right to this deal."

She grimaced. "I got you into it, Joe. I shouldn't have, only"—she made a feeble gesture—"I had no one else to turn to, to go to."

"I'm glad you didn't, Babe."

She put her face in her hands. "Oh, Joe, Joe!"

His eyes glistened sadly. "Don't cry. Listen now, don't cry, will you? It'll be all right." He sat down beside her, patted her knee. "Don't, Babe. Kennedy's a funny guy but he's okey. He won't get too drunk."

"Johnny, Johnny," she moaned, "why did you do it?"

Marino patted her knee.

Chapter III

BROAD STREET is a bright street at night. It begins quietly enough, on the north side of Richmond City, but traveling south it gathers speed and finally bursts into a constellation of lights, a hodgepodge of traffic. Here are the theaters, the chop suey joints, the dance halls, a flock of cut-rate drug-stores, cut-rate ticket sellers, commercial and theatrical hotels, cafeterias, noisy cabarets, chiselers, tramps, has-beens and comers.

Buck Street is one of the feeding arteries, a narrow street, an old one, remodeled and rehashed so often during recent years that an old-timer, returning, would scarcely recognize it. Halfway down this block from Broad stands the *Grenadier Hotel*—white brick for the first two floors and red for the remaining eight. It is the narrowest hotel in the block. Its lobby is narrow, too, but rather deep, with the desk at the extreme end. Kennedy, coming in through the revolving door, got somehow caught in it and went round with it twice before getting actually into the lobby. His shoes dripping, his coat buttoned wrong, and his hat looking like a wet mushroom, he steered an irregular course for the desk.

"Miss Louella Wynant," he said sleepily.

"Who's calling?"

"That's fame for you…. Oh, well, let it slide. Kennedy of the *Free Press.*"

The clerk turned to the switchboard and said: "Buzz Miss Wynant."

The operator snapped: "I thought she just checked out."

"Wynant?"

"You ought to know. You told me about two minutes ago."

"You're right; I did." He turned to Kennedy and said: "She just checked out." He grinned, bowing.

"Things like that make you happy, huh?"

"Beg pardon."

"Forget it, forget it," said Kennedy, waving his hand limply. "Know where she went?"

The clerk bowed again, grinned with his teeth shut. "So sorry, but I don't."

"Happy one minute, sorry the next. A quick-change artist."

The clerk did not smile but he said very distinctly: "Are you by any chance drunk?"

"Not by any chance, darling. If you're getting tough, stop it. Just because you're out of knee pants is no indication that you're grown up. Respect age, my son; respect age."

He swiveled sharply, almost lost his balance and went teetering down the lobby. Out front he said to the doorman:

"Did a young girl check out with bags?"

"Ask the clerk."

"I asked him. Working in a theatrical hotel has gone to his head. He tries to imitate Barrymore. For two cents I'd break something over his head."

"Make it five bucks and I'll do it for you."

"Like him, huh?"

"And how…. A young girl? Dark? Good-looker?"

"A big mouth and a toothpaste smile."

"About five-minutes ago. I put her in a cab for Union Depot."

"Here's two bits. Grab me a cab, will you?"

The doorman whistled and a taxi drew sharply into the curbstone, spattering up slush.

"Yes, *sir!*" the driver said cheerfully.

"Oh-oh," Kennedy said. "It's you again."

"Boy, I sure get around!"

"I'll bet you're good to your mother and everything. Okey. Union Depot, wild man."

The railroad station was at the dark heel of the town, a large barn-like structure, slate-gray, with a row of sooty lights out front. Here the wind and the sleet whined, blew in great penetrating blasts. As Kennedy went in through the door he said to a redcap:

"Train out in the last ten or fifteen minutes?"

"No, suh. Last one left about half hour ago. New York."

"Okey. Thanks."

He went past a newsstand into the dimly-lit terminal. A couple of train boards were lighted for departures. One for Boston, in twenty minutes; another for Montreal, in thirty-five. Here and there were groups of people, one group clustered for an arrival. The terminal was drafty, cold, and Kennedy shivered. Faces were not very distinct. He could hear the sleet driving against the metal roof, and sometimes trainmen came in from the platforms, their rubber coats shiny wet.

He made his way towards the lighted sign that said Waiting-Room in large block letters. The door was old, huge, heavy, and worked on a pneumatic spring. He had to pull hard to get it open, and when he squeezed in the warmth of the waiting room was a pleasure to his chilled marrow. The room was drab, painted an ugly shade of brown, and there were long, hard, high-backed benches.

On one of these benches sat Louella Wynant. Kennedy recognized her instantly. He would have recognized her instantly in a large crowd; she had an attractive shape, a baby face with large pool-like eyes, a wavy mouth, very full, very red. She had all the physical attributes of a musical comedy girl, but she could neither sing nor dance, she had no stage presence and was too high-hat to hit the burlesque circuit. Kennedy'd last seen her in the *Club Turk*, where she'd made a hit as a cigarette girl. For the sport of it he'd given her a few lines in the paper.

He looked a wreck and here, in the waiting room, he had all the chances of being thrown out for vagrancy. But he had an air: drunk or sober—and he was very drunk now—he had the air of a man unconcerned with the material present. Wandering round the back of the bench, he sat down beside the girl and said:

"What train are you making, Louella?"

There were two suitcases at her feet. She wore a dark red-shaped something like a fez; it rode jauntily over one eye. Startled, she turned, placing her large liquid eyes full on Kennedy.

"I beg you-ah pahdon—"

"Nix on the overseas accent, Louella. It's ham to me. I saw you sitting here and thought I'd sit down and see how you're getting on in the world—"

"Oh, Kennedy. I didn't recognize you at first."

"I don't blame you. I'm wearing my disguise. So that when I buy chewing gum out of slot-machines I don't have to look at myself. Just my sentimental nature."

She talked with pursed lips, her voice babyish: "You say the funniest things. They don't ever mean a thing. Are you going somewhere?"

"I don't really care one way or another. Where are you going?"

"Just on a little trip."

"Waiting for someone?"

"Oh, no," she tossed off. "Just going on my lonesome-wonesome, just." Her smiles were rapid, kittenish, her large swimming eyes coy, dancing.

He sagged where he sat, looking very weary and dejected. But his eyes, though hazy, droop-lidded, observed that her hands were gripping her purse tightly and that her breast was expanded. He had a momentary feeling of sentimental remorse. He thought of Johnny, dark, slender young kid; intense, earnest: he thought of Johnny going haywire over Louella. Back of that exquisite, babylike face he doubted if there dwelt a single sensible thought. Vain. Coquettish. Why wasn't she some rich man's darling instead of a girl waiting here for—Johnny.

He muttered: "Come across, Lou? Who are you waiting for?"

"But nobody. I'm really waiting for nobody. What makes you think I'm waiting for somebody? Can't a girl sit in a railroad station without waiting for somebody? Can't a decent, honest girl take a train alone without somebody is with her? Can't—"

"I didn't mean to wind you up that way, Louella. Pipe down. You'll be drawing a crowd."

She shrugged, blinked her eyes, pouted. "The idea. A poor girl nowadays can't—"

"All right, all right, all right. But please lay off the High C. You're taking the train alone. That's settled. I just thought if you weren't, I'd like to meet the new boy friend, because you know, Louella, I was always interested in your welfare."

"I'm sorry, Kennedy—s-sorry." She looked as if she were going to cry.

"Don't," he urged, "I'll go. Well, have a good trip and don't look out the window when you come to tunnels."

He made his way as far as the newsstand and pressed himself into an alcove there. From this point he could watch the gates of the two impending departures. She did not take the Boston train. It left on time and the board was darkened and now he kept his eyes on the one remaining lighted board. In a little while Louella came out of the waiting-room and stood at the gate of the Montreal train. A porter carried her bags. She peered about intently, tapping her foot, moving impatiently from one to the other. A half dozen persons went through the gate. The porter spoke with her and she shook her head and then she kept looking frequently at the terminal clock. The porter addressed her again, pointing to the clock, then to the gate. She stamped her foot, wrung her hands. The big gate slid shut. The board was darkened. In a moment there was the tolling of a locomotive bell.

Then Louella snapped something to the porter and left her bags at the checkroom; walked out with her head up. Her face was crimson and her high heels drummed rapidly on the floor. She did not see Kennedy. He watched her go out. Then he went as far as the door and saw her climbing into a taxi-cab.

Johnny had not come. Kennedy figured that something must have leaked, that Johnny must have been picked up by the cops. And he thought of Babe Hourihan. He remembered how he used to drop around there on cold nights, sit up till all hours and play Russian Bank with her. He remembered the good stews she could make and how many times when he got so tight his legs gave 'way, Babe used to get dressed and take him home; throw him on his bed and pull off his shoes and then give him a ring in the morning, so he'd have time to get to the office. All these familiar, homely thoughts fought at Kennedy's whiskey-soaked consciousness.

He stumbled through the door, skated precariously across the sidewalk and clawed at the handle of the nearest cab.

"Tail that one just left," he said.

"I ain't tailin' no dames for no wise-guys."

"You college graduates make me sick," Kennedy said, and teetered to the next cab.

"Yes, *sir.*"

"My gawd, me and my shadow!"

"I grabbed some chow while I was down here account of—"

"Okey. Tail that cab just left."

"Boy, I'll tail the tail off it!"

"A man of spirit, eh? Go to it, old tomato!"

Chapter IV

IT was not a long ride, but it was a fast one. Kennedy was knocked all over the tonneau and spent most of the time picking up his hat. The driver was an expert at skidding, gauging his skids to a nicety, adding those little touches so dear to any cab driver's heart. Presently he slowed down, came to a stop and said:

"They just stopped. You want me to pull up or—"

"No. I'll get out here. Have you driven taxis long?"

"Me? No. For years I drove a hearse."

Kennedy paid him. "Now you're letting go your suppressed desires, eh? Carry on, pal. Life's never dull while driving with you, and that's something." He was looking up the street while talking.

He saw Louella leave the cab and enter a building. He slushed along and coming to the building she had entered, realized it was the apartment house where Jakoboin had lived. For an instant he stopped, puzzled; then he went forward and sagged through the doorway.

Reaching the elevator bank, Kennedy saw the marker on top moving, heard the sound of the elevator's mechanism. He did not wait for it, but took the stairway up. It was not well-lighted and several times he slipped and banged his shins. When he reached the fifth floor, the corridor was empty. He saw that the elevator was at this floor, its outer door closed. Grinning complacently, he zigzagged down the hall, sometimes turning over on one heel, his legs wobbly.

As he reached for the doorknob of Jakoboin's apartment the door flew open and Louella ran into his arms. He made a pass at her arm, caught it and held on.

He smiled crookedly, his eyes drowsy. "What's the rush, Lou? You missed your train."

"B-b-b-b—"

"Greek to me."

"S-s-s-s—"

"Still Greek."

"Oh!"

"That's better," he said, working her back into the apartment, closing the door. "Your eyes are so big, grandma."

"K-k-k-k—"

"You probably mean Kennedy. Yes, Louella?"

She panted: "Let me out! Let me out!"

"You're on High C again. Have you no regard for the neighbors? Consider all these people who have to get up early, get to work."

Her eyes horror-stricken, she clapped her hands to her cheeks. "You're mad," she groaned. "Mad. I always knew you were a little mad!"

"A little. My sugar plum, I'm completely nuts. Who is that in the other room giving such a good imitation of a corpse?"

"Don't talk like that! It ain't religious."

" 'Is not religious,' Lou. Not 'ain't' ever."

She groaned: "Oh gawd! Oh mother!"

"Oh, hell, stop it."

"He's dead!"

"Who?"

"Mike!"

"Mike who?"

She flung towards the door crying. "Let me out! Let me out!"

He caught her and they both fell down. Sitting on the floor, they looked at each other. Louella's face was chalk white, her lips hueless, her eyes stark with terror. Kennedy looked drowsy, reminiscent, a little droll.

"All is vanity, Louella. Death is no stranger. Dust unto dust. Do you remember Hiawatha?"

Her teeth chattered. "Mad! Mad!"

"Where's the gun you used?"

"Me!" she cried.

"Mike's dead, isn't he? Or did you stab him?"

She scrambled to her feet and made another try for the door. Kennedy caught her and whirled her about. His hand made a loud slapping sound as it gripped her wrist.

"I didn't!" she panted. "I didn't kill him! Johnny Hourihan did it!"

"Don't say things you can't prove, Lou."

"He told me he was going to."

"You can't prove he did it."

"He said he was going to beat Mike up."

"And then meet you and elope."

"Meet me! You're crazy! Mike was meeting me tonight! Mike and me were going to Montreal! And I come back here and find poor Mike dead! That damn' fool kid had to—"

"Easy, Lou. If Johnny did this, he did it for you."

She cried: "Can I help that? Is it my fault if he goes off his nut? No!"

Kennedy let go her hand. He looked very dejected. He leaned back against the door, his mouth sagging, his face very gray and worn by years of drinking, late hours, little sleep. The world seemed to him then a very cockeyed place, full of more wrongs than rights. He looked up at Louella's pretty, babyish face; and he thought he saw in it that above all things she cherished Louella. Avarice, fear and cunning were interwoven there with all her child-like prettiness.

He said disgustedly: "You're a moron, Louella. A guy goes the limit for you and you crab." He grabbed her wrist. "You're going with me."

"Where?"

"To see a friend. Act ladylike or I'll sit on your neck. Life may have been all a bowl of cherries for you; now try the pits. Out. And keep your mouth shut."

"Listen, Kennedy," she blubbered. "I didn't do it. You know I didn't do it. Listen, I can't afford to get mixed up in this. It'll hurt my career."

He laughed. "What career?"

"I'm going to be a great actress some day. Listen," she panted on, clutching at his frayed lapels. "Be decent. I'll treat you square, Kennedy. You must come around sometime. Honest you must. I mean it. On the level."

"I've got a pash now, Lou. She wins me with her Melba toast. Thanks just the same."

"But I can make the duckiest absinthe frappé."

"You would. Think of what you've touched in here—"

"I've got gloves on."

"Okey. Out, then."

HE made her walk. No taxi-cabs. And he chose a way that was dark, gripping her arm hard, half forcing her along.

"My poor feet! My new shoes! I'll catch a death of cold!"

"Here's hoping."

"My hat! My new hat!"

"I like the Russian motif."

"Poor Louella," she whimpered, "always gets a bad break."

"Poor Polly, poor Polly," he mocked. "Polly want a cracker?… Keep your voice down," he snarled, "or Polly will get a crack on the coco!"

"Such humiliation for a poor girl…."

By back streets, through slush-ridden back alleys he hauled her; and at last walked her into a brownstone front and marched her up two flights of stairs. He knocked on Babe Hourihan's door. It was Marino who opened it.

"I guess maybe I came for a little advice," Kennedy said.

Joe Marino raised a finger. "Sh! Babe's laying down. I just dropped in a little while ago. I've been walking my feet off."

Kennedy shoved Louella into the living-room. Babe was lying on the divan with a damp towel over her face and there were some cups and saucers on the tea wagon; there was the smell of coffee making. Marino had his coat and vest off.

His voice was a husky whisper: "She's worn to a frazzle." He then nodded towards Louella, saying to Kennedy: "What are you doing with her?"

Louella seemed to be on the verge of the jitters again. She had met the plainclothes sergeant before.

She squeaked: "I—I d-didn't."

"Didn't what?" Marino said, scowling.

Kennedy had gone to the kitchenette. He returned carrying a bottle and a glass. "Didn't kill Jakoboin. You see, Joe, in my very ineffectual way I tailed her to Union Depot. She was waiting for Jakoboin. She and Jakoboin were heading for Montreal. It was to have been very ducky-wucky. So says she."

Louella turned harried eyes on Kennedy. "Why did you bring me here? Where am I?"

"You must be talking through your hat," Marino said darkly to Kennedy.

Kennedy drank. "Science has proved that while one is wearing a hat it is utterly impossible to talk through said hat. I take my hat off. There… I place it on the table. It is now also utterly impossible to talk through that hat."

"See?" pleaded Louella. "He's ga-ga!"

"Listen, Joe," Kennedy said, dropping his voice. "This piece of fluff was down at the station waiting for Jakoboin. When he didn't show up for the train, she checked her bags at the station and lit out for his apartment. All the time I figured she was waiting for Johnny. I even figured she was going looking for Johnny, when she left the station. Much to my astonishment, what does she do but walk smack into Jakoboin's apartment. I bumped into her as she was lamming and after a little scrimmage she tries to win me to silence in the boudoir manner. You get me, don't you, Joe? She was planning to leave with Jakoboin. Johnny apparently was just a kind of doormat she wiped her feet on, so to speak."

Babe Hourihan sat up, her eyes wide open, her face very white. She had wakened a moment ago, had lain listening, motionless. Marino did not notice her sit up. His dark eyes, darker with turmoil now, swung on Louella.

Kennedy said idly: "And she told me she knows Johnny bumped off Jakoboin. Figure it out."

"Oh, Mr. Marino," Louella chattered, "I didn't do a thing. I'm entirely innocent. Mike just got rough with me and slapped me down, but he didn't mean it. Then Johnny came in and I was crying and I guess very angry and told him Mike slapped me down and I wish he'd beat Mike up for me. I didn't really mean it, but I guess Johnny took me seriously. Johnny got very angry. Johnny was always sappy on me, but is it my fault if I'm very beautiful? Am I to blame if he gets silly and shoots Mike?"

"He did it for you," Babe Hourihan said dully.

They all turned and looked at her. She was leaning forward, her arms braced, a gray shadow on her face, a dismal up-from-under look in her eyes.

"For you he did it," she said in the same toneless voice.

"I beg your pardon," Louella said haughtily, "but whom—who are you. I may—may I ask?"

"You may ask," said Babe dismally.

Marino muttered: "She's Johnny's mother."

"Oh!" squeaked Louella, her pretty hands fluttering. Her eyes expressionless.

"He was ready to die for you," Babe went on forlornly. "You encouraged him. You played with him. I saw one of your letters, full of stuff that would drive any kid nuts. And meantime you were fooling Mike Jakoboin too. Poor Mike—poor Johnny!... You rat, you little rat! Oh, you heartless trollop!"

Louella spun on Kennedy. "You brought me here! You fiend!"

"Ah! Now I'm a fiend!" He clapped his hands. "Goody!"

Louella made a dive for the door. Marino took a long step, grabbed her, wheeled her about, lifting her clear off her feet and planking her down again.

His voice was low, bitter: "I've run across a lot of broads like you, kid. Teasers. Do you realize what you you've done?"

She babbled: "I'm the victim of a trick!"

Kennedy took another drink. He sat sleepily on a chair, helping the drink along with a cheese sandwich, his attitude that of one taking a mild, passing interest in the proceedings.

"You can't hold me!" Louella cried. "I didn't do anything! Johnny did it! You can't hold me! What can you hold me for?"

Marino closed down hard on her wrist: "How long 've you been playing around with Jakoboin?"

"I've known Mike a year. He was good to me, except he had temperament. In a ditch now, she was beginning to fight back. Her head went up, she showed her handsome teeth. "If you think you can get me to take Johnny's part, you're crazy. What could he give me? I didn't tell him to kill Mike. I didn't mean it when I said he ought to bust Mike's jaw. I was just nervous, upset and humiliated. Mike's been good to me. Mike even made out his insurance to me and then this fool kid has to go and bump him off. Even if I said he just should bust Mike's jaw, was that meaning he should kill Mike?"

Babe's voice shook: "You told him Mike beat you with his fists, kicked you around, hauled you by the hair! That's what you told him!"

"Mike didn't mean it!" Louella shouted back. "It's his temperament. He always used to say afterwards I was just a little child—a little bitsy-witsy, he would say, a little bitsy-witsy child! And then—"

Babe ran her hands through her hair, dug her fingers into her scalp. She cried hoarsely: "Take her out! Take her out! Before I do something to her! My God, take her out! She's no human being! I don't know what she is!" She fell forward on the divan, moaning: "Oh, Johnny, my poor Johnny!"

Marino was gritting his teeth. He said to Louella: "When did you last see Johnny?"

"Just before I left for my train."

"What!"

"Well, he came up and I didn't want to be hard, I just told him it was all a mistake and that Mike and me were friends again and that I was leaving town. It was funny. He didn't say a thing. He just hung his head dopey-like and walked out…. You might have thought he'd at least tell me he'd bumped off Mike, so I wouldn't have to wait in that dirty railroad station!"

Babe beat upon the divan with her hands. "Take her out!"

The phone rang and Marino looked at Kennedy, then went across the room and picked up the instrument. "Hello…. This is a friend. What d' you want?… Yeah. When?… Um…. Okey. Hold it there."

Joe Marino put down the phone. Babe was looking fixedly at him. Kennedy was lounging on the small of his back, his eyes almost shut, but not quite. The cigarette butt he held was singeing his fingers but he did not drop it. Marino's face seemed to swell; his hands were at his side, his fingers splayed, stiff. Babe got up, her lips parted, one hand outstretched, like a sleepwalker's. Marino crossed to her and put his arms about her, pressed his swart cheek to her hair and stared fixedly down at the divan. He patted her back. It was a broad, a solid back. He could feel her body begin to shake and he said:

"Nora… Nora," in a thick, clogged voice.

The cigarette was burning Kennedy's fingers.

Babe choked: "Johnny—Johnny—did it…."

"They picked him up—in Jockey Street—by his own gun—he was dead."

She said with a strange tranquillity: "He thought he had nothing more to live for. If he'd only known. Oh, Joe, what have I to live for now?"

They seemed unaware that anyone else was in the room.

"Me, maybe," Marino muttered. "I ain't much, Nora, but—well, you need a man around, and I need a wife around. I get lonesome as hell sometimes. Dagoes weren't made to be bachelors, I guess. Don't cry, Nora. Don't cry now."

She sobbed: "You like me, huh, Joe?"

"You put it mild."

"I never knew you were that way about me, Joe."

"I did." He rubbed his cheek against her hair. "Try to be brave, Nora. Try hard. Johnny did the only thing; it was the only way out. He took it on the chin."

Chapter V

KENNEDY dropped the cigarette butt and looked blankly at his charred finger.

Louella said: "Of course I'm sorry it happened, but you can't blame me if—" Marino took his arms from around Babe. His chin went down and he walked across the room, raised his hand, drove the hard flat of it against Louella's cheek. She went down. Marino stood over her, his lips wet, a dark brown hatred in his eyes. His solid body trembled and his fingertips worked nervously against his palms, sweat stood out on his forehead and the color drained from his face.

"Oh, oh, oh," whimpered Louella. "You hit me."

"I'd like to break your neck," grunted Marino.

Babe said weakly, hoarsely: "Don't, Joe; don't. Maybe she can't help if she was born without a heart. Leave her alone. Take her out, Joe. Get her out of my sight."

Marino turned and went to the telephone saying: "I'll get my sister over."

"I'll be all right," Babe said.

But Marino telephoned and in a little while his sister came.

"Rose," he said, "stay here with Nora. I've got things to do. Johnny— " He dropped his voice to a whisper and his sister looked shocked, gripped his arm. He patted her hand. "Do that for me, will you, Rose?"

Kennedy emptied the bottle and looked very drunk. Louella was standing with her face to the wall, sulking. Marino put on his street clothes and grabbed his hat. He grabbed Louella's arm.

"You go out too.... Coming, Kennedy?"

The three of them walked downstairs. The sleet was still driving and the street was glazed, slippery. The blast of the wind drilled to Kennedy's insides and he huddled in his threadbare overcoat.

"Dragging me around on a night like this!" complained Louella.

The wet sleet left silvery lines on Marino's swart face. His eyes glittered as though wet with it too. "I don't suppose," he growled, "this will ever make any impression on the thing you call a mind of yours. We can't do anything to you, and that's the hell of it. Crimes of your kind are not down in the code. Guys die all the time for dames like you. You drive 'em nuts and then laugh it off. There ought to be a law against it. You played around with Johnny because he worshiped you and you played around with Mike because he had the dough."

She tried to tug her arm free. "Let me go. I got to get out of this wet or I'll catch a death of cold."

"If I could depend on that, sister, I'd plant you down in the nearest puddle and make you sit there all night."

Kennedy, swaying precariously on his feet, took the attitude of a mildly interested spectator. He stifled a yawn, leaned so far forward that Marino thought he was going to fall and gripped him, righted him.

"Much obliged," muttered Kennedy.

They began walking towards a main boulevard, Louella between them.

"I want a taxi," she said. "Please summon me a taxi."

Kennedy, plodding along, his head bent forward, his eyes almost shut, mumbled on and on to himself. Joe and Babe. He didn't think much of Johnny; Johnny was dead and that was over with. It had to be that way. Johnny would never have gone free. Murder. No one would have understood. They would have said cold-blooded murder. The chair....

Marino was saying doggedly, in a deep passionate voice: "I hope some day, Louella, you'll get a guy that will break your pretty neck. Or a guy you love who doesn't love you. Though I doubt that like hell. It's not in you. You—"

"I don't have to listen to that crap!" she cried. "I can make my own way! Johnny was a sap, a dope! I'll never be down and out, copper. Because Mike left me a lot—a lot! To hell with you—there, it's out—to hell with you!"

She rushed away from them, heading across the sleet-glazed street.

KENNEDY went to *Enrico's* and sat at the bar and Paderoofski, who was closing the cash register, mixed him a drink.

"Leave the bottle out," Kennedy said. "Lend me your slippers."

"But look, Jeese, I'm closin' up any minute now."

"Okey. Then just leave the bottle out." He drank. "Paderoofski, let's match dimes."

"Plees, look, now, Meester Kennedy. It's vera late. You better go home an' get some sleep."

"I have no desire to go home, my friend. I have a keen desire to match dimes. One can always go home. Besides, you know my home. I've always been a hall-room boy, Paderoofski." He poured another drink, looked dreamily at it. "Joe Marino may get married soon."

"Yeah? Good!"

"There's a dame might have straightened me out." He chuckled, said, "Ah, nerts," and downed the drink. "Charge this. I'm broke."

He passed out, dead drunk. Paderoofski took him home and put him to bed, undressing him down to his underclothing. He emptied Kennedy's pockets and hung up his clothes. The pockets had given up only six cents, a few keys, a box of matches and a penknife.

Paderoofski set the alarm clock for seven next morning. Then he took half a dollar out of his own pocket, laid it on the bed table. He stood for a moment looking down at Kennedy's tired, wasted face. He shook his head woefully.

"Jeese," he said. "Jeese."

He went out.

Take It and Like It

*Kennedy takes a murder rap
and makes the best of it.*

Chapter I

KENNEDY was standing on the corner of Hallam and German Streets when he saw the girl pass rubber-kneed beneath a street light halfway down German. There was a moon somewhere in the April sky but its light did not reach into German Street. German Street was narrow, barricaded on either side by two- and three-storied houses of brick or wood, many of them untenanted. Kennedy lived a block up Hallam in a rooming-house. He had moved into it a week before and had started out tonight, ten minutes ago, for a place to eat. Someone had said there was a good chili joint in the neighborhood and he was trying to get his bearings.

He was moderately sober, and leaning indolently against the pole, he saw what he took to be the shape of the girl coming back up the street. He could tell by the sound of her heels that she walked irregularly, but he was not greatly interested. She had the gait of a drunk, and being drunk, he often said, was one's own business. He did not remain leaning against the pole because he was in any way interested in the girl but because he was puzzled how to get to the chili joint. The wine there, they said, was excellent, and if wine is excellent it doesn't matter much about the food. The girl was coming up on the opposite sidewalk and he hoped she would stay on the opposite sidewalk; but presently she crossed the street and came staggering on towards him. He thought of moving on, but he wasn't sure yet about the chili joint and he had no notion of going out of his way, even for a block. When he was drunk he would wander all over Richmond City, but being practically sober, it was a different matter.

She came on towards him and she must have seen him, for the pole against which he leaned had a light halfway up; and in the pool of light he was a slight, frail figure in an unpressed gray suit and a gray fedora whose brim was pulled down all around. He had about

him an air of languid, washed-out decadence. As the girl came closer, staggering, coughing in the silent street, he turned his head the other way.

But she crashed into him. She coughed as she crashed into him and he turned around casually and saw her careening backwards. She was bent over a bit, her legs were bent and she gave the impression of staggering flat-footed. He hoped she would not fall but made no move to prevent her doing so.

She did not fall.

"I—I b-beg your pardon," she muttered hoarsely.

"It's all right, kid. Only why don't you grab a cab and go home? Slamming around the streets this way—"

"I can't go home."

She was braced against a house wall now, her hands pressed back against its rough surface, her fingers splayed. Her hat was cocked over one eye; it wasn't cocked over one eye because of any trend of style but because it appeared to have been shunted that way. She wore a

dark coat with a thin band of some dark lightweight fur around the collar.

"You see," she panted hoarsely, shaking her head, "I—I just can't go home."

"Drink," he said, "has always been the curse of the going-home classes. But what's the sense of slamming around the streets all night? Choose a convenient doorway, park yourself and let it pass."

"Please," she begged, "do something."

"I'm sorry, madam. I'm trying to find a chili joint. Do you happen to know of a chili joint around here where the wine's supposed to be the nuts?"

"Please!" her voice begged from the shadow her face was in.

"Please what?"

"Help me. J-just—well, haven't you a place where I could—well—lie down, rest?"

He lit a cigarette. "You've got a nice voice."

"Thank you."

She pushed herself away from the building. "I—I didn't mean to bother you. I'll go on." She staggered and her knees were no good and she fell down and cried a little, not much. She remained on her knees, bracing herself with her arms.

Kennedy moved across the sidewalk, bent over not farther than he had to and took hold of the girl's arm.

"Snap out of it. A couple of more headers like that and you'll get your face lifted. Try helping yourself. Come on. I'm no heavyweight. Let's go. One... two... *three.* That's a girl. Hold it now." She was on her feet.

He did not release her arm. She did not look at him but looked away as though ashamed. Her hat was a little more over one eye; patches of hair sprouted unbecomingly from beneath it but she was not a bad looking girl. She was very good looking.

He sighed. "Okey, come on. I've got a room up the street where you can sleep it off. But don't expect me to stay there with you. I've got to find this chili joint. Come on."

She hung her head as they walked up Hallam Street. Her feet dragged and her breath still came out hoarsely, sometimes with a transient sob. Kennedy walked her up the four steps of the wooden stoop, held on to her with one hand while he used the other to get out his keys. He unlocked the hall door and prodded her into the corridor. His room was on the main floor, in the rear, and on the way down the corridor she stumbled and suddenly giggled. It was a mad little giggle, hysterical, and Kennedy muttered:

"For crying out loud, shut up. I just moved in here."

He got her into his room. It was a large room, old-fashioned, with a brass bed against one wall and an old roll-top desk against the other. There was a table in the middle on which stood a couple of bottles, rye and gin, and there was a Morris chair and a Boston rocker.

He let her fall on the bed, then took hold of her legs, lifted them on to the bed and rolled her over to the middle of it. She lay panting and sobbing a little, but he had had crying jags himself and did not mind. He unrolled a blanket and tossed it over her.

"Stop it! Stop it!" she cried, and kicked the blanket off.

"Yell like that again," he told her, "and I'll toss you out."

She began sobbing loudly. He had no intention of trying to talk her out of crying; it would have been useless. So he sat down, sighed, called himself a fool and poured half a water glass of rye. He drank it from time to time, savoring it with pursed lips. When at last her sobbing sounded subdued and far away he drained the glass, rose and went out, hoping she would be gone by the time he got back.

He walked down to Hallam and German again and leaned against the pole and in a few minutes the cop on the beat came along. He was a young cop, rosy-cheeked, and twirled his nightstick with a self-conscious arrogance.

"You got a home?" he said to Kennedy.

"Sure," drawled Kennedy, unimpressed.

"Go to it, then."

"This pole private or something?"

"Crackin', huh? So you're crackin'?"

"By the way, do you know where there's a chili joint around here?"

"I don't like chili."

"Neither do I. But I heard they serve swell wine there."

"And I don't like wine."

"What do you drink?"

"Milk! Three times a day!"

Kennedy pushed himself away from the pole. "Take a tip, copper. Give it up. It probably sours on your stomach and makes you that way."

The cop growled threateningly: "Little man—"

"What now?"

"Scram outta here!"

Kennedy sauntered off singing under his breath: "You're a big meany...."

Chapter II

MacBRIDE was working overtime, trying to catch up on matters that had accrued during his leave of absence. He and his wife had toured the Southern States in the new flivver. In Richmond, Virginia, he had driven through a red light, crashed into a truck and lost his right fender and in Philadelphia he had been arrested for driving the wrong way on a one-way street. But all in all they had had a nice time and the skipper looked fit, brown, and got rid of the matters on hand, one by one, with a swift, hard precision.

He barked into the inter-office annunciator: "Bogardus on deck!" fanned a cloud of pipe smoke from in front of his face and puffed new clouds—strong, Burley tobacco—into its place.

Sergeant Bogardus came in holding a half-eaten ham sandwich behind his back and MacBride said:

"I'll not waive this charge!" and jabbed at a memorandum on his desk. "The bird drove through the red light and red lights are put up to stop, not to drive through. If we put up red lights and people drive through them, what the hell's the use of putting up red lights?"

"Yes, sir, Cap'n."

"And you, Bogey—either swallow what you're eating or spit it out."

Bogardus swallowed, the effort making his eyes bulge.

"And what," MacBride wanted to know, "is that racket upstairs?"

"That's Moriarity, I think, trying a new back flip."

"Tell him to lay off. A person'd think this was the Y.M.C.A. instead of police headquarters. I go away for a while and come back and find a lot of clowns around.... Okey, Bogey. Beat it. How's the new kid?"

"Swell, Cap'n."

"Great. See he eats lots of spinach."

Ike Cohen poked his head in to say: "You busy, Cap?"

"I'm always busy."

"Well, a call just came in. Murder or something over in the East End. Bettdecken's just getting it over the wire."

"Get—" MacBride winced at the sound of a heavy thump on the floor above; he looked up at the ceiling and said: "Get Mory. The potato's upstairs flipping back flips. Get him before he lands on his pants and knocks his brains out. Tell Gahagan to get out the car. You and Mory be down the garage. I'll shoot down in two shakes and pick up the full dope from Bettdecken. Who was it?"

"Who was it what?"

"Murdered."

"I just heard Bettdecken saying something about a jane."

"Who's calling in?"

"Chatterson. A new cop on the beat."

"Okey. Mory. Gahagan. The car. I'll be down in a shake."

"Oke."

IT was a cool night, but not too cool. Spring was in the air, the first flush of it, and though the police car sped along on dry cement the haunting smell of lush earth was somehow in the air. The moon could be seen from this broad avenue. The stars winked, some broadly and some faintly. The skipper took his pipe from his mouth so that he might better fill his lungs with the night air. His cheeks were ruddy in the glow of the dash-light, his jaw brown as a nut and hard as a nut and his eyes made two bright glitters beneath his wiry brows.

"Where's Kennedy been keeping himself?" Moriarity asked. "That guy's usually as familiar around the place as a spittoon."

"He got fired," MacBride said.

"I know he got fired but that wouldn't—"

"Did you hear why?" MacBride said, looking over his shoulder into the darkened tonneau.

"No."

MacBride gave a short, guttural laugh. "Boy, if that guy ain't a lulu! He takes the cake and the berries that go with it. Well, it was like this. I heard it. Just today. I called up Flannery, the editor, trying to get him to give Kennedy his job back. So what? So this: They put Kennedy on the dramatic page for a spell and what does the bunny do one night but get tight and go to review a play at the Channock Theatre. In the first intermission he goes out and goes across the street to a bar for a drink. Well, he met a friend. Sure, he's always meeting a friend.

"So he takes about six highballs aboard and is plastered to the eyes when he leaves. He toddles across the street and sits till the end of the show. He writes next day that it's a lousy show; that he can't make head or tail of it; that in the first act the heroine's a blonde and in the last act she's a brunette; that in the first act the hero's a Scandinavian and in the last he's a wop. Well, what do you think? When they check up they find that Kennedy was so tight that he went back to another theatre, the one next door, and saw the last act of another show, thinking it was the show he'd gone in to see first. Can you tie that! Can you!"

Cohen roared. "Boy-oh-boy-oh-boy!"

"I always figured," Moriarity said, "that guy would grow up to be a bum."

"Ah-r-r," growled MacBride, half-defensively. "He's no bum. He's got more brains than you can shake a fist at, only he rents them out all the time."

Moriarity insisted: "He'll wind up cutting paper dolls."

"Anyhow," MacBride said, "they'll be the best paper dolls."

Gahagan said: "This 's the street, ain't it?"

"Yeah, make a right," MacBride said.

The car swung right, went up a slight grade. They could see the red-tinted headlights of the ambulance, and when they drew up on the wrong side of the street, facing the tinted headlights, they saw a crowd on the sidewalk. Patrolman Chatterson was standing on the wooden stoop. He was young, rosy-cheeked, and possessed of a self-conscious arrogance.

MacBride swung out. "You Chatterson?"

The cop touched his nightstick to his visor. "Yes, sir, Cap'n Mac-Bride."

"Who's upstairs?"

"Ambulance doctor. It ain't no use, though."

A roadster braked sharply at the curb and Rube Wilson, Assistant District Attorney, hopped out and rapped patent leather dancing shoes across the sidewalk, sharply elbowing people out of his way. He was a small, wiry man, young, with a tight jaw and a black velours hat raked over one ear. He wore a topcoat over a tuxedo.

"What's to it, MacBride?"

"Let's go in and see. You too, Chatterson. Mory, Ike, shoo these folks off."

When they went into the room the ambulance doctor and the ambulance chauffeur were placing the girl on a stretcher.

"Hi, law," the doctor said. "Vespers will be sung. Hey, copper, why didn't you call the morgue bus?"

"It says in the book of rules and regulations, page forty—"

"Forget I mentioned it. When'd you get back, MacBride?"

"Who is she?" Rube Wilson said.

"Am I a mind reader?"

MacBride said: "Drunk?"

"There's the odor of liquor."

MacBride turned to Chatterson. "Who called you?"

"The woman runs the place."

"Where is she?"

"She just went in her kitchen before you come account of she's baking some bread. I was moseyin' along and I seen her run out on the stoop and she seen me and calls me. So I run up and she says, 'There's a woman inside. I think she's dead or somethin'.' So I run in with her and, sure enough, she looks dead."

"How long's she lived here?" Rube Wilson tossed in.

"She don't. She—"

At this moment the rooming-house mistress appeared in the doorway. She was large, fat, with neatly plaited gray hair and a red face, big red hands.

"What's your name?" MacBride said.

"Hannah Mecklinborg. I tell you, officer, it's an outrage!"

"Never saw her before, huh?" MacBride asked.

"Never! But—I heard her come in. Anyhow, I think it was her. She came in with the fellow rents this room. They sounded drunk. She was giggling and when they got in the room there must have been a fight. I heard her yell, 'Stop it! Stop it!' Just like that. I—well, I was in the hall at the time, and I thought I ought to knock on the door, but then they calmed down, so I went on about my business. Intending, though, you understand, to give the fellow a piece of my mind tomorrow. Then after a while I thought I heard them going out. But then after a while again, I was in the hall and I heard a thump in the room. I don't know why, but I was scared, and I knocked, and when I got no answer I tried the door. I opened it and, well, there she was, on the floor alongside the bed."

"Was she dressed?"

"Yes, all dressed. I thought maybe she'd managed to get dressed and then fainted. So it must have been the fellow went out alone."

Rube Wilson flung at the doctor: "What do you make of it?"

"One thing, she was beaten up. Her body's full of bruises and there's a lump on her head. I'd say she died from the beating, offhand. Possibly a blood clot on the brain."

MacBride turned to Hannah Mecklinborg. "What time would you say they came in?"

"Seven-thirty. I know because I was putting a cake in the oven."

"And what time did you hear the fellow go out?"

"About, I guess, half an hour later."

"And what time did you open this door and find the woman?"

"At about nine."

"And what's the guy's name lives here?"

"His name is Kennedy. A newspaperman, I think."

MacBride's head jerked on his neck.

"Hotcha!" Rube Wilson rapped out. "I always thought that guy would wind up like this. And he had the crust once to tell me to my face that as Assistant District Attorney I was a blister on the heel of progress and would I please burst some day. Boy, I like this! Boy, how I like this!"

Patrolman Chatterson said to Hannah Mecklinborg: "What did he look like?"

She described him.

Chatterson swelled up, his eyes glittering. "I seen that mugg! I seen him! Just a few minutes after he committed the crime!" He leveled an arm. "At German and Hallam. He wisecracked me! I told him—he was hangin' around—I told him to move on and he wisecracked me! It was him, I'll bet. He said something like I had a bad disposition and it was because I drank milk that soured on my stomach."

MacBride let out a deep, rueful sigh. "That was him."

Chapter III

THEY stood in MacBride's office: Moriarity, Cohen and the skipper himself. They had just come in and still wore their hats and the three of them stood looking down at the shiny surface of the skipper's desk. They had, it seemed, not much to say. They were cops, the three of them; good cops, with fine records; but they were also human beings. Kennedy had for long been like one of them. Many times one or all of them had felt like socking the erstwhile newshawk, but that was neither here nor there; not now. They were after all plain men, ordinary men, with plain and ordinary emotions, and in the last analysis the law, even to its most militant members, is not so strong a thing that it can wipe out, instantly, these common emotions.

MacBride said at last, in a low, clogged voice: "The thing is—it's so damned out and out."

"Yeah," nodded Cohen.

"M-m-m," nodded Moriarity.

"He must have been gawd-awful drunk," said MacBride.

"Crazy drunk," Cohen said.

"Swizzled," said Moriarity.

They were silent again for a minute, and then MacBride, flexing his lips, warping his brows, opened the annunciator and said: "Kennedy's wanted. The newspaperman—Kennedy.... That's right. Five feet seven, about a hundred and twenty-five pounds. Light brown hair. Blue eyes. Sleepy-looking. Was wearing a light gray suit and a light gray hat. Most cops know him.... All booths, precincts, and patrol flivvers."

He hung up his hat, ran his palms from his temples backward past the tops of his ears; he said: "Well, that's that." He dropped into his chair—dropped hard, heavily, as a chain falls; and he slurred out of a corner of his mouth: "I always figured Kennedy'd wind up in some way out of the ordinary, but I never in cripes' world thought it would be like this." He looked unutterably weary. He moved his hand. "Oke, Mory, Ike. You guys line out and see can you find him. You know the places he hangs out. I don't have to tell you. And to think I damn' near got Flannery to say he'd take him back on the *Free Press*." He yanked open a drawer, hauled out a bottle of Canadian Club and took a stiff jolt straight. "Try to get him before the D.A.'s office gets him. That pain in the neck Rube Wilson—" He sighed, stood up, flung his hand. "Okey, beat it."

A description of the dead girl had been broadcast on the radio and by eleven that night an identification was made. Her brother made it—in the morgue—and then passed out. MacBride happened to be there at the time (he himself was on the walkabout, too, looking for Kennedy) and picked up the brother.

The girl's name was Naomi Penfields. She was twenty-one. "Young," MacBride mused aloud, bitterly. "They've always got to be young." They were the Penfields of Livermore Walk, in the West End. Harrod Penfields had died a natural death five years before. He'd left a sizable estate to his wife, daughter, son. The Penfields mansion was one of the show places of the West End. Alvina Penfields, the mother, was a recluse who, it was said, spent all her time writing monographs on dead languages. The brother, Bacon Penfields, had not come to by the time MacBride left the morgue.

Gahagan was asleep at the wheel but MacBride punched him awake and then climbed in back. Smoking his pipe, he sat in the corner of the seat, his arms folded on his chest. He told Gahagan where to go and while the car hummed through the spring night the skipper chewed on his scarred pipestem and wondered what he would do when he got hold of Kennedy. He did not exactly know what he would do. Kennedy had helped solve many a crime; more than that, he had actually solved many crimes that had confounded the whole Department.

But all that would be washed away. A cop may serve his shield for twenty years and if at the end of that time he commits a heinous crime, he must pay the penalty. MacBride had no complaint with this law. It was an inevitable law. But still—he had been in many tight places with Kennedy; he had saved Kennedy's life and Kennedy had saved his. But he knew his hands were bound. The case, actually, would not be in his hands at all.

"That one," he told Gahagan. "On the corner. With the green and white lights."

He swung out of the car, knocked open the door of the Tin Can Club with his shoulder and ran into Gus Winkler in the anteroom.

"Kennedy been in?"

"Hello, Cap. Kennedy?"

"Kennedy."

"Not for a couple of days. You want to see him?"

"Very much."

"If he comes in, I'll tell him you want to see him."

The skipper went to other places: the joints in lower Jockey Street and the tonier places in upper Jockey Street; the bars in Flamingo Street—*Enrico's,* the *Pig's Knuckle, Eddie's,* the *Sawdust Club;* the strictly Italian hang-outs in Rosario Street; the dance-halls of Exeter Square and the beer halls in Strauss Street; the Turkish bath where he knew Kennedy frequently went following a drunk and the bowling alley where Kennedy usually placed bets on the horses. No one had seen Kennedy that night.

Driving back towards Headquarters, MacBride found himself hoping that Kennedy might have run off to some far corner of the world, never to be found. And when he became conscious of this thought the iron-bound skipper sat up straight, colored in the darkness of the tonneau.

Moriarity was in the office.

"Well?" MacBride grunted.

"This." Moriarity sat on the desk. "I just by a fluke dropped in at Willie Murry's place, and sure enough Willie saw Kennedy at about a quarter to ten. He said Kennedy staggered in the place carrying a zither. 'Where the hell'd he get that?' I asked Willie and Willie said,

'Oh, he said he picked it up for a song.'"

"Kennedy can't play a zither!" MacBride shouted.

"That's what Willie said. Let me tell you. He said Kennedy came in, had a drink at the bar and wanted to know if anybody there could play the zither. Well, nobody could and then Kennedy asked Willie if he knew of anybody else who could play it. Willie said no, so Kennedy said prob'ly he'd best go to an employment agency."

MacBride covered his eyes with his hands, groaned.

"Sure," Moriarity nodded. "Kennedy told Willie he'd picked up the zither hoping he could find someone to play it. I said to Willie, 'Hell, if Kennedy really wanted zither music why didn't he do the sensible thing and try to find a zither player first?' Chances are that the zither player would have had a zither of his own, because zithers—"

"Zithers! Zithers!" barked MacBride. "Shut up, Mory."

"Well, I was just telling you."

The Assistant District Attorney flung open the door, came in and flung the door shut. He snapped:

"Any news of that rat yet?"

"What rat?" MacBride said.

"Kennedy, of course!"

MacBride said: "Call him a rat again, Rube, and I'll hit you with a radiator."

Rube Wilson nodded. "I know, I know," he said sarcastically. "You've got a tender spot in your heart for the palooka but it's not going to do him any good."

"I've got a tender spot in my heart for him, Rube, and who the hell said it was going to do him any good? I've got practically the whole Department looking for him. I can't do any more. But lay off the rat business."

"Anyone seen him?"

"Mory said Willie Murry saw him about a quarter to ten."

Rube Wilson grinned. "I'm going to hate to prosecute that onion for murder. Yes, I am, I am!"

"Sore, Rube?" MacBride said.

"Sure."

"Okey. We understand each other then."

"What do you mean by that?"

"I don't know. Look it up somewhere and tell me."

Rube Wilson's face darkened. "Flimflam on this, Skipper, and maybe I'll get around to prosecuting you some day."

MacBride stood up, rubbed his palms together. "Look here, Rube. You're being nasty now. We're looking for Kennedy and we'll get him, but take a tip from a guy and don't shoot your mouth off too much. You're like a lot of wise young assistant D.A.'s: eager as hell to make the headlines—"

"I make 'em, don't I?"

"Just take the tip, fella. Crack around too much and I'll drop a word in the right ear and if this thing does come to a prosecution you won't be in on the kill at all."

"Do it and I'll yell my lungs out to the papers."

"Make one peep and you'll land on your neck in the gutter, where you started from—a cheap, lousy ambulance chaser."

"Why, you big—"

"Shut up. Personally you want to make Kennedy take water. You want to make him writhe, play with him like a cat plays with a mouse when the cat knows the mouse hasn't a chance. It's personal with you, Rube. You hate him. You're sore. You're lousy sore. You can't take it. You're a dirty stink in the D.A.'s office because you brought a bad stink up out of the gutter with you. Six years ago you framed a woman with a guy in the Bedford Hotel. The woman's husband was your client. How do I know? Well, the guy you paid to help frame the woman was and is a stool pigeon of mine. We have an understanding: he gives me tips and I give him immunity. Think it over, Rube. And stop blowing off your mouth. And take the air. I hate your guts."

Rube Wilson flung out and Moriarity said: "That ought to hold the lousy buzzard."

Chapter IV

KENNEDY and one Ignazio Mirabelli stood on a street in the residential quarter of Little Italy. Ignazio played the zither. He was a very short, very fat man, with rosy cheeks, a rosy chin and large, merry eyes. His clothes looked as if they had been dragged out of a rag bag, but he played with a flair while Kennedy, holding his hat, caught coins tossed from windows and hallways. Ignazio's eyes may have been merry but they were also watchful, and the larger the coin the greater vigor he brought to bear in his playing.

"We have now, Ignazio," said Kennedy, "seven dollars and forty-three cents. Also a Chinese coin. Also some lead slugs. We might do worse than taking time out for a drink."

" 'Swatcha say she's ukkey by me, signore."

They went over to *Enrico's*, in Flamingo Street. Paderoofski, whose real name was Bennie Iammaranzio, was tending bar.

"Jeese now," exclaimed Paderoofski.

Kennedy said, with a gesture: "Signor Iammaranzio, meet one brother countryman, Signor Mirabelli, known as Ignazio, for short. He plays a thiz—a ziz—a thizzer—I mean zizzer— Oh, nerts, give me three rye highballs. Two for me and one for Ignazio. Iggy doesn't drink."

"Ha!" laughed Ignazio.

"I was gonna say, Meester Kennedy," Paderoofski said, "the Captain MacBride was in-a here look' for you."

"The skipper? Good old Skippy MacBride!"

"By God!"

Paderoofski stretched his neck. Ignazio turned around like a barrel. Kennedy was never disturbed by anonymous exclamations.

Rube Wilson left the doorway and came over and took Kennedy by the arm. Rube fairly quivered with excitement. He took hold of Kennedy's arm very gently, almost tenderly, and there was on his face a smile that would have been tender also had it not contained too much that was obviously Satanic. When he spoke again, his voice almost dripped with tenderness:

"Kennedy, you don't know how glad I am to see you."

Ignazio beamed with joy.

Kennedy teetered about. "Well, 'f it isn't Rube. Meet my palsy-walsy, Signor Mirabelli."

Ignazio made a deep bow.

"A man of parts," went on Kennedy, "and none of them spare parts. A wagabond minstrel, just an old wagabond but with a heart of gold. I must come up your place for a turkey dinner some night, Rube."

A high little laugh trilled from Rube Wilson's teeth. "Yes, you must, Kennedy—"

"Look here," said a tall, button-nosed man striding from the doorway, "I told you he might be here, Rube."

Kennedy clapped his hands. "Flannery! My old editor, Flannery! Me and my, but isn't this old home week!"

"Ha—ha—ha!" laughed Ignazio, clapping his hands also.

Flannery clipped: "Who's this monkey?" And then, with a stern, wintry eye on Rube Wilson: "You're not taking Kennedy till we get—till I get the lowdown."

Rube Wilson muttered: "Pipe down, Tom. Just over my office—"

"With a man from every newspaper in town camped there? What do I look like, last week's cream?" He snapped on: "Get a room here! Step on it!"

"Tom, listen—"

Flannery flapped his hands. "Nix. Get a room. I'll get a room…. Hey, Enrico! Got a room here?"

Rube Wilson bit his lip petulantly and Kennedy, seeming detached from the whole affair, crunched potato chips between his teeth. But Enrico had a room and into it Kennedy was herded by Flannery; and, as an after-thought, they hauled in Ignazio and his zither. Ignazio did not seem to know what it was all about, but being a polite little fat man, he kept smiling and bowing until Flannery snapped:

"For cripes' sake, Wop, lay off the setting-up exercises!" He had a choppy way of saying things, and his eyes wore a blue-white glare.

There was a couch against one wall and Kennedy laid down on it, propping his head high enough so that he could drink with a minimum of movement. Flannery yanked a chair across the room, planked it down alongside the couch; he sat down, planted his hands on his knees, elbows out, and glared down at Kennedy. Rube Wilson took a seat beside him. Wilson's narrow dark face showed chagrin, but there was also a ray of hope.

Kennedy said: "Awfully kind of you chappies to provide me with a private chamber."

"Let's have it," Flannery clipped. "Come on, spill it, get it out." He was an impatient man, used to having his way. "The dame—this Penfields dame—dish us the dirt and I don't care how dirty you dish it."

"Penfields?" Kennedy said, cocking one sleepy eye. "Oh, yes. You mean the Penfields. The West End Penfields. I'm sorry, but we've never—ah—met, y'know, socially."

Flannery rasped: "Cut out the tony accent, mugg!"

"Okey, Tom. Precious nerts to you, you big turnip. Do you know why I never liked you, Tom? Because you never split infinitives. It shows a peasantry of intelligence. Old Non-split Tom Flannery, the great horse's neck."

Flannery tightened his lips. "I don't give a good cripes what you think of me. That's not what I'm here for. The Penfields dame was beaten up so's she conked in your room, you fathead, and I want the story. Rube Wilson wants it, too, but so do I. Snap out of it, baby."

Kennedy sighed. "You annoy me, Tom. Go away. Git along, little dawgie, git along."

"Listen, you, Kennedy," Rube Wilson cut in. "It's a pinch, you understand. I'm pinching you for the murder of Naomi Penfields. You lured her to your room and then attacked her. I'm going to burn you for it, Kennedy, and I'm going to like doing it. I told you you'd come a cropper some day, and, boy, have you! Have you!"

Flannery silenced him with a hand; and then to Kennedy: "Come on, kid. It's open and shut but what I want is the story. I'm holding up the presses for it. Spill it and don't be a lug and clown around. You killed her. Okey, that's over with. Maybe you had a reason. But get it off your chest."

Kennedy sighed. He lay back and closed his eyes and his pale, wan face looked strangely like a death mask. His hair was tousled, his tie was out of place. He looked as if all the sap had been drained out of him, leaving nothing but a husk. And as he lay there, his eyes closed, his mouth lax, a tragic look began to creep slowly over his face.

Rube Wilson licked his lips hopefully and Flannery edged his chair closer to the couch.

Kennedy opened his eyes. "So you want my story."

They nodded.

A dry, Satanic laugh crackled feebly from Kennedy's lips. "Sure I killed her."

"Ah!" breathed Rube Wilson.

"Proceed," said Flannery.

Kennedy's face looked very haggard and his mouth sagged weakly, a strange glaze came upon his eyes. "Yeah, I killed her. I guess I kind of went nuts, Tom, but you know how it is: a pretty dame, a little booze. You know, Tom, I've been thinking that if you hadn't fired me, things might have been different. But there I was, out of a job, reckless, I guess, and I guess I didn't care much what happened to me."

"How did you kill her?" Rube Wilson asked breathlessly.

"Oh, I batted her in the jaw a couple of times and then I kicked her and then I guess I hit her with some things. I don't remember what I hit her with."

Flannery said: "Feel any remorse?"

"No. No, Tom, I don't. It's all like a dream, I guess. I just got her in my room and then I went out and then I thought it over and came back again and began to sock her. I guess I socked her because she was so damned pretty and because she tried to high-hat me."

Flannery frowned. "You sure went the whole hog, didn't you? You were a great newspaperman in your day, Kennedy."

"*Sic transit gloria mundi.* I was, Tom. I am still. I forgot more than you'll ever learn. I learned young how to split infinitives."

"Stick to the story," Rube Wilson chimed in.

"What," said Flannery, "was your real reason for killing her? I mean the one thing that finally drove you to it."

Kennedy sighed. "She did not know how to make a Martini."

"Hell, he's completely screwy!" Rube Wilson cried.

Kennedy cried: "I killed her because she was too beautiful for this world. This world is so crass and designing and so full of filth and tragedy. I killed her because—well, because she was a flower, a fair flower."

Rube Wilson rasped: "Screwy as hell!"

Kennedy sat up, held his head in his hands. "I knocked her around the room—knocked her round and round and kicked her and punched her and maybe I hit her with inkwells and things until she fell down and then I kicked her some more and then I chucked her on the bed and went out for a drink."

"Madman!" Rube Wilson chopped off. "When the fair young womanhood of our city—"

"Lay off the crap," Flannery said. "This is a story, a wow. We haven't had one like it in years. The public will eat it up and the *Free Press* will be the first to spring it." He turned on Wilson. "You heard that, didn't you?"

"Yes—sure, Tom."

"Well, remember it."

Kennedy was crying into his hands. Ignazio came over and put a hand on his shoulder.

Flannery grabbed a phone and called his office. "Jack, get this. It's a lulu." He rattled the story off, sitting back on a tipped chair, one hand in his pocket. His choice of words was good. He told a terse, dramatic account of the murder, building up on such details as Kennedy had given him.

"Don't forget my name," Rube Wilson said.

And Flannery said into the phone: "Assistant District Attorney Rube Wilson arrested Kennedy in person. Run a picture of Rube, one of Kennedy and one of the Penfields dame. Hop to it, Jack. It's the scoop of the century."

He hung up, rose and lit a cigarette. "Thanks, Kennedy. I'll send you flowers." And to Rube Wilson: "And remember, sweetheart, no two-timing. This is a *Free Press* story, exclusive. So long, Rube. So long, Kennedy. Tell me if it hurts."

Flannery went out and Rube Wilson said: "Come on, Kennedy. Get up. We blow."

"Oh, I don't feel like going Rube," Kennedy sighed. "I'm tired. Leave a call for me in the morning."

"Rat, get up!"

Rube Wilson was not big but he was wiry, strong. He hauled Kennedy off the couch and stood him on his feet. "We're blowing, son. The can for yours and am I going to lay into you in court! I've waited a long time for this, Kennedy. I've stood your razzing a long time." He paused, grinned, hot-eyed. "So I don't hear you making any cracks now. Why don't you? Or maybe you're figuring on me giving you a break. Are you?"

Kennedy's eyes were half closed, and he swayed to and fro on his feet. "A break, Rube? Uh huh. I wouldn't ask you for a break, Rube. I like you. You're a nice guy. Nice like a louse. Rube, I don't feel like going places. That's a fact. It's nice and comfortable here. Why should I go places?"

Rube Wilson jerked at his arm. "You're going—now! What do I look like, a sap?"

"Frankly, yes."

Rube Wilson started to manhandle him across the floor towards the door. Kennedy fought back feebly. Ignazio, very much concerned, and not knowing what it was all about, scratched the stubble on his chin. Rube Wilson was red in the face, still trying to get Kennedy to the door, and Kennedy was flip-flopping back and forth. Ignazio picked up the zither and brought it down on Rube Wilson's head.

Rube Wilson said "Ah" gently, and his eyes rolled as he sank to the floor.

"Jeese, boss!" Ignazio gasped, pointing. "I sock him! Look!"

Kennedy hiccoughed, bleary-eyed. "Ignazio, you are a true friend. On second thought, I don't like this place. Let's toddle."

Chapter V

MacBRIDE was eating a late snack in his office when the door banged open and Rube Wilson came in flame-faced and wet-lipped with rage and chagrin.

"Please knock hereafter," MacBride said.

"I'll knock!" Rube Wilson snarled. "I'll knock somebody's block off!"

"Mine?"

Rube Wilson drew in a long breath, cocked one eye. "I wouldn't be surprised, Skipper—I wouldn't be surprised a bit if you had a hand in this!"

MacBride took a long pull at a thermos of hot coffee and then said: "Fall in a corner somewhere, Rube. I've never seen it to fail yet that every time I try to eat a meal here in my office some half-baked fool comes in and spoils my digestion."

Rube Wilson had hurried and was still out of breath. "You and your lousy digestion! Do you know what?" He slammed both hands down on the desk. "I collared Kennedy! I collared him and got a confession out of him! Flannery was witness to it. That crazy friend of yours beat the girl to death and wasn't even sorry. I got the confession, I tell you!... And then what? Then I'm attacked. I'm socked on the head by some dago friend of Kennedy's and I'm out for an hour. When I come to, I learn that Kennedy's breezed. He breezed over an hour ago! And then you sit there and tell me about your digestion."

MacBride leaned back. Sudden anxiety had come into his eyes but his voice, when he spoke, was low, guttural. "Breezed, did he?"

"Breezed!"

"And he'd confessed, huh?"

"Absolutely! And I want this—now! I want every damned cop on the Force out after him. I got him all right—single-handed, and because I was just too soft-hearted the dirty palooka takes advantage of me. Signals to his pal and his pal lets me have it over the head. I'm mad, MacBride. I'm boiling over—over! I tell you Kennedy's lost his mind. He's a madman. He's crazy. Cuckoo! Screwy! And God knows how many more people he'll kill. The lust of blood is in him. He's become another Dracula. He laughed when he told how he killed the Penfields dame. It's the liquor. The liquor turned him into a maniac. It—it—"

He was out of breath. He stood toiling on his feet, his face crimson, sweat pouring down his cheeks. And there was a gray look on Mac-Bride's face. A look of fear. Liquor had driven many a man out of his mind. Kennedy was, always had been, an abandoned drinker. MacBride made no effort to conceal his fear. His strong body shook and his throat felt dry and in his heart there was a deep remorse. But he saw his job now—clearly. He pulled himself together.

His tone was crisp: "Rube, take it easy. You'll pass out again if you don't calm down. I'll handle this. I'll get Kennedy."

"I tell you, MacBride—"

"You've told me enough. All I need to know. I'm serious, Rube. I'll get Kennedy. I may have to shoot him—but—well—under the circumstances—" The thought gagged him, but his jaw clamped down hard. "Leave it to me. This is what I get for being a cop. Sit down, Rube. Draw yourself together. Who was the dago?"

"I don't remember. A funny little fat guy. Looked like a clown. Carried a zither. The zither was probably just a stall."

"Where'd this happen?"

"In a room at *Enrico's*. I had Flannery in as witness."

"So that's a *Free Press* scoop, huh?"

"Sure. I had to have somebody in. Enrico didn't know I'd been knocked out until an hour afterward. He said Kennedy and the funny little wop pranced out arm in arm, as if nothing had happened. I tell you, they're a couple of ghouls!" He fell breathless into a chair.

MacBride took down his gun and spring-holster from the clothes tree in the corner. He strapped on the holster, put on his hat. "Take it easy, Rube," he said grimly, and strode out. He drummed his heels down to the central room, where Otto Bettdecken, on duty at the desk, was eating a plate of ham and beans.

The skipper continued on towards the door. He had no precise idea of where he was going. But the streets would be dark, quiet, and he could walk hard, fast, and think. All his men were still looking for

Kennedy, so he could do nothing more about that. But he could walk, walk, revisit the haunts he had visited earlier in the night, and he might find Kennedy. He hoped he wouldn't. He hoped that if it came to guns, someone else would take Kennedy.

"Hey, Cap!"

That was Bettdecken yelling from the desk.

MacBride turned, scowled dourly at him.

Bettdecken was waving a fat hand. "Come here. On the phone—I just got—" He yelled into the phone: "Wait, you!… Hah?… No, wait!… Hey! Hey!" He hung up violently.

"What?" MacBride growled, reaching the desk.

"That was Kennedy. He called up to say—what he said was, 'Otto, tell that prince of fellows, Captain MacBride, that Kennedy, world-famous newspaperman, will be at home this evening, at 201 Furness Street, apartment twenty-one, if the able captain should wish to call.' He said that, just like I said it."

"He must be nuts," MacBride brooded.

"Hah?"

MacBride muttered: "Keep it under your hat till I get back."

He swiveled, strode across the central room and went dull-faced out into the street. He did not bother to get out his police car. At the next block there was a taxi and he entered it and told the driver where to go.

Chapter VI

THE address was at the other end of the city. Sitting in the taxi-cab, his hands sunk in his coat pockets, his legs out straight, the skipper stared vacantly at the meter. He did not notice its changing numbers, for his eyes were out of focus. Nor did he bother to brace his body against the frequent jouncing of the cab; he let the cab play with his body. There was a coldness round his heart, a sensation of time suspended in his brain. His mouth was set, grim, and his face looked wooden.

The cab stopped at last but MacBride did not stir. And finally the driver looked around and said: "This the number?"

MacBride muttered: "Huh?" He looked up, blinked his eyes. "Yeah," he muttered. He got out of the cab slowly, like an old man. Absently paid his fare. The cab went away and MacBride stood on the curb and looked at the small brown apartment house. He passed a hand feebly over his eyes. Then he shook himself. His shoulders drooped as he went across the sidewalk and entered a small lobby. There was no elevator.

He heard voices upstairs and as he climbed, his ears rang and there was an odd tightness in his throat. In the second floor corridor he found a small group—three women and a man. They turned frightened eyes on him.

"I'm a policeman," he said dully. "What's the trouble here?"

A woman pointed. "In there. There's been an awful racket. There's someone—"

The sound of some heavy object crashing silenced her and then another woman said: "It's been like that—only with yells and whoops. They won't open the door. Somebody's being killed, I think."

"Look out," MacBride muttered.

He stood before the door. He heard a thumping and a pounding. A crash of glass. A loud groan.

His fist pounded on the door and he said in a loud voice: "Open up! It's the police!"

But the noise went on.

He turned his head and said: "You folks get back."

They retreated a few paces down the hall and MacBride drew his gun. He held it near the knob and pulled the trigger three times. The sounds crashed in the corridor. The women held their ears. MacBride stepped back, drew up his shoulder and plunged it towards the door. The door whipped inward and the skipper straddled the threshold, his gun leveled.

"Cut it!" he barked.

The people in the corridor stood in a white, breathless huddle.

Inside the room there was a man on the floor. He looked very big, strong, young, and his face was bloody. Sitting on him was Ignazio. Ignazio had lost his ragged coat, also his shirt. He had only his pants on and his face also was bloody.

"Get up," said MacBride. "The law to you."

Ignazio got up. The very large young man did not get up. He was unable to get up.

Kennedy was lying on a desk trying to get a telephone number.

"You," said MacBride, "put that down."

Kennedy rolled over, still retaining the instrument. "Oh, so you came around. Good. I am delighted to see you, Skipperino. Only I wish you'd tell Otto to take the marbles out of his mouth when he's on the phone."

One trousers leg was completely gone. His face was streaked with red, his coat was ripped all the way up the back, and one of his eyes was blackened and closed.

MacBride entered the room. "Kennedy—"

"Sh! I think I'm getting my number.... Hello, is this the Richmond City *Times-Express?*... It is. Well I want to talk to Ridley.... Ridley? This is Kennedy.... *The* Kennedy, sweetheart.... Yeah. Listen, how about that job you offered me the other day?... I thought it would be.... Well, I've been thinking it over and I want double the salary you offered.... I'm ga-ga, am I? Listen, darling Mr. Ridley, would you like the lowdown on the Penfields kill?... You would. Well, papa has it. Papa has it all in the bag.... You will? Okey, double it is.

"Listen. I picked the Penfields girl up at Hallam and German Streets at about seven-twenty. I thought she was tight. I mean, awful tight. She had some liquor on her breath and she seemed scared to go home, so I went softy and dragged her around to my room and chucked her on the bed. Then I went out and after I'd walked a couple of blocks a guy ran up and stopped me. He was a big fellow, about six feet three, aged about twenty-seven. His name's Wallace Pringle and he lives at 201 Furness. He's a sculptor. Yeah, he sculpts.

"Well, he stopped me and said in a shaky voice, 'Is she all right?' I asked him who and of course it was the girl and I said I thought she was—she'd sleep it off. He was a little tight. I asked him if he knew of a chili joint around there and he said he did and showed me the way. He went in with me and we ate and drank and we both got tight. Only he was tight to begin with and he got very tight. He bawled too. He told me he was crazy in love with this Penfields girl, and when, at his studio, she told him she was through—because of his drinking—he tried to get her to stay. He told her she was always too sober to appreciate the finer things of life and then it seems he tried to make her take a drink. He forced some down her throat but spilled most of it on her.... Yeah, he told me this over the wine and chili. Bawled while he told it. So one thing led to another. I guess he got enraged.

"He said he tried to make her stay and she fought back and he socked her and then he went nuts completely and beat hell out of her. He finally tripped over something, fell down and the girl escaped. He said he followed her along the streets, but got a little sobered up and didn't dare to speak to her, fearing what she would say to him. Then she ran into me and you know what I did. The guy saw me take her in my place and then followed me when I came out and, as I told, accosted me. After the chili, he was so tight I had to steer him home. I got him to his studio and then left. I remembered what the building looked like and had an idea of the neighborhood, but it took me a hell of a while to find it again.

"Well, as I say, I left him. I was feeling fine myself and had a few more drinks and then I helped a guy out by buying his zither and then I picked up a little Sicilian named Ignazio Mirabelli, who could play it. We had a great amount of fun going about playing and making collections and then I heard about the death of the Penfields girl.

"An assistant D.A. who thought he was smart and a famous newspaper editor who thought he was clever wanted to hang the kill on me. So after a little clowning around Ignazio and I go out to hunt up the studio. Finally we find it. Well, I sat down and talked simply to Wallace Pringle and much to my surprise he wanted to fight. Well, he's a big lug, you know, and there was I. But Ignazio was there too. A great fellow, Ignazio. Pringle beats the living hell out of the both of us. Boy, you should see me, and Ignazio's no beauty either. But by a lucky break Ignazio's foot slips. And where do you think it lands? It lands smack on Wallace Pringle's jaw—and he's down. Then we sit on him and hit him with various objects. I think he's just coming to now.

"But wait. The arrest, by the way, was made formally by Captain Stephen J. MacBride. A certain assistant D.A. is going to feel red all over tomorrow and a certain high-pressure editor is going to have to take it and like it…. Listen, send me over a pair of pants, will you? I lost mine."

He hung up, lay back on the desk, stretched his arms and yawned. A smile, wicked and wise, crept across his bloody, haggard face. He laughed mockingly.

MacBride's low voice said: "Kennedy."

"There's your man, Skipperino. On the floor. I hope you don't mind if I don't get up."

"Rube Wilson told me—"

"I know what Rube told you. Rube and Flannery thought they were a couple of geniuses. Flannery's tongue hanging out for a scoop and Rube's hanging out for the big pinch. Well, I hated to disappoint them. So I gave them what they wanted. I gave them a big meal of it, old tomato—intending to serve up the razzberry dessert later. They'll get it for breakfast."

MacBride said: "Thank God, Kennedy, old kid! Thank God!"

"God and Ignazio," said Kennedy. "Iggy can do more things with a zither than play it. Ask Rube."

Ignazio bowed. He bowed six times.

Kennedy went to sleep on the desk.

Be Your Age

MacBride thinks he has his man, but Kennedy has seen murder in a woman's eyes.

Chapter I

THE police phaeton sped with a sleek, complacent dignity through the summer night. It hit River Road south of the railway bridge, turned west and followed the river's course, the long beams of its fat headlights rushing far ahead of it through the moist, lush darkness. Great balloon tires, limber shock-absorbers, made the broad cobbles of the river-front street seem smooth. Wharves, black warehouses, rangy sheds rolled and bulked past.

"I know it wasn't something I ate," said Kennedy the newshawk, "because I didn't eat anything."

He was sitting in the rear, wedged in the middle between Moriarity and Cohen. Cohen clapped him on the back.

"That never does any good," Kennedy said, shaking his head.

Moriarity looked at Kennedy in the darkness and observed with grave concern: "I read of a man that died once of it."

"Oh, he died only *once?*" Kennedy sighed.

Captain MacBride, sitting in front beside Gahagan, the driver, held his hand cupped over his charred and battered old briar. A hard straw hat was dipped down to his wiry eyebrows. His eyes were shuttered against the cross wind but he could see the dials on the dashboard and he muttered:

"Shake a leg, kid."

Gahagan stepped on it, the long car seemed to lift, swell and lunge forward. The canvas top drummed with a hard, brittle sound and the scattered lights popped past and soon the sheds and warehouses petered off, vanished, and the road beneath became a dim ribbon of pale cement. It rose slightly and ran along the river, but between it and the river were the trolley tracks of the interurban line.

But soon these tracks cut across the road and vanished in some

woods and then the highway bent nearer the river and followed it. Soon it reached a small town gaudy with colored lights that blossomed in the narrow street and flowered outward to several gay piers. There was a sandy beach, a boardwalk, and the music and the noise of an amusement park. The town was an amusement park. Silver Park. It was in the Sixteenth Precinct—the frontier of the law as administered by Richmond City.

Gahagan guided his car among rambling merrymakers. Girls in flowered pajamas or jerseys and sailor pants or in bloomers, and boys and men dressed any old way. The concessions were everywhere—noisy, strident with the voices of hawkers, whirring machines of chance, popping guns, a merry-go-round. A wild, a free-and-easy settlement.

Gahagan pulled up and braked and MacBride climbed out, almost falling over a fire-hydrant. He cursed under his breath, struck a match on the underside of his leg and laid its flame against the crusted bowl of his pipe. Moriarity and Cohen stepped to the sidewalk, eyeing with

approval the shapeliness of the strolling girls; and then Kennedy, still hiccoughing, fumbled his way out and wobbled across to a soft drink stand, where he got a glass of water.

A uniformed cop came into view and MacBride high-signed him. The cop came over, touching a finger to his visored cap.

"Where's it at?" MacBride said.

"You go between them two buildings. You'll strike a narrah boardwalk and— Hell, come on; I'll show you."

He led them. MacBride went at his heels. Moriarity and Cohen followed. Kennedy came last, a frail, emaciated figure in a baggy gray suit and a lop-eared gray hat. His progress was not as certain as the others', but he managed. For a minute the harsh music of the merry-go-round was close at hand, but soon, as they followed the narrow boardwalk out across the sand, the music faded. Small cottages, built like a boardwalk on stilts, branched off at intervals, each with a short walk of its own. The air was soft and warm and moist, and the early moonlight lay vaguely on the water. Soon they saw a group of men up ahead and the casual wanderings of a flashlight's beam.

"That's the place," the cop said, pointing.

MacBride turned from the main boardwalk onto a narrower one. The cottage was white, faded white, and its door was open and figures could be seen moving inside. The flashlight swung upward, steadied. MacBride blinked.

"It's me—MacBride," he said in a low, gruff voice.

A couple of cops and two precinct detectives were inside. MacBride stood in the doorway, leaning against one side, bracing his right arm against the other. His sharp, weathered eyes flicked the room—the broken furniture, the shattered glass, the twisted rugs. A small, fat man was rising. He was Feldman, from the Medical office. A small terrier came in but was instantly chased out.

"I guess I just beat you here, Cap," Feldman said.

"We picked it up on the short wave," MacBride said, his eyes settling on the dead man. "Who's he?"

Mara, the precinct detective, said: "Fuller. He was the daring young man on the flying trapeze."

Cohen said: "What did he do, get in the wild animal cage?"

"Pipe down," MacBride said.

There had been a fight here—a brawl. The dead man was covered with cuts and welts. One of his arms looked peculiarly out of joint. His face was a pulpy mass, his lips mashed.

MacBride said: "Who did it?"

Mara held his arms limply out from his sides, palms up.

The man from the Medical office said: "He sure was beaten up. Beaten and choked to death."

"Choked?"

"Beaten and choked."

"Who reported it?"

Mara said: "I'll get 'em," strolled to a curtained doorway, pulled the curtain aside and disappeared. The sounds of the mixed music at the amusement center came faintly through the darkness, mellowed by the darkness and by the distance. The smell of the river was near. Kennedy came in and flopped down on a shapeless cot, drawing his legs up, leaning back against the wall. His face looked worn, pasty, sallow—but it was nonetheless genial in a faintly satiric way. His bleary eyes drowsed.

"How's your hiccoughs?" Cohen asked.

"Better."

MARA reappeared, holding the curtain aside. A woman and a man came in from the other room. The woman was young, maybe twenty-five, and well built. She had on a kimono but it was open and you saw taut blue tights, a taut blue brassiere. Her hair was reddish brown, more brown than red, and cut like a boy's. Her legs were well shaped and solid, muscular, and she had a strong, smooth neck. She had a sullen, Slavic beauty.

Mara, said: "This is Sophie Zihala. This guy's name is Weymer."

"The woman find this?" MacBride asked.

"I did," Weymer said.

He was stocky, with a great chest bulging a white athletic shirt, and a pair of white trousers hanging on lean, tough hips. His stance was firm, solid. His arms were long, rippled with muscle, and his neck was stout, his head boldly chiseled, beginning to be bald on top. He had the poise of a lion, and the animal grandeur of a lion.

"I walked in and found him like that," he said, nodding towards the dead man but not looking at him.

"Where were you?" MacBride shot at the woman.

"Up there." She nodded towards the amusement center. "Eating some supper. He was with me," she added, sliding her large, dark eyes towards Weymer. "We were having supper."

"How'd you come to come out here?" MacBride asked.

"Came to get George," Weymer said. "He eats with us. He said he'd be up, but he didn't show, so I came out to get him. I found him here like this."

"Any idea who did it?"

"No."

"You?" MacBride asked the woman.

She shook her head, her features heavy, sullen, sensual.

"Did anybody hear the brawl?" MacBride asked, looking around the room.

"No," Mara said. "The places next door were empty."

MacBride looked at Weymer, who looked levelly back at him. "What time did you leave to come for Fuller?"

"I guess it was eight."

"Look at your watch?"

"No. The hula dance was just starting. It starts at eight."

"And what time did you tell Miss Zihala?"

"Well, I ran right back. After I took a look around here, I ran right back. How do I know what time it was? I guess about ten minutes later."

MacBride crossed the room, picked up one of Weymer's fists, then the other. They were hard, strong—and unscarred. Weymer mocked him with a brief half-smile.

"You were all in the same act, huh?"

Weymer nodded. "I did the heavy work."

"How long you all been together?"

"Two years. I joined them two years ago."

The skipper jabbed his finger towards the dead man. "Didn't this guy have a scrap with *any*body recently?"

Weymer was calm, complacent. He shook his head. "If he did, I don't know. Ask her."

She shook her head also. Then she said sullenly: "Not that I know of."

MacBride looked at Sophie Zihala, at Weymer. Weymer looked back at him, mocking him urbanely.

The skipper made a half-turn. "Get out a fingerprint man." And to Weymer and the woman: "You'll have to shift out of here for a while. Don't touch anything. A cop'll park here."

Kennedy hiccoughed. "Oh-oh, it's back again."

"We can shift next door," Weymer said.

MacBride said: "See it's no further."

Weymer shrugged, grinned complacently. "Why should I go any further?" he said, and strolled into the other room.

The skipper watched the curtains swing languidly back and become motionless; then he turned to the two precinct men, saying: "What was on your mind?"

"We figured," Mara said, "to see the guy that rents out these cottages tomorrow and find out who's rented 'em all, and if anybody's left."

"Who is he?"

"Name is Cuffey. Owns the whole damn' place."

"Why tomorrow?"

"Well, his office is closed now."

"Go to his home. Get him to open his office and go through his files. A single night can leave a trail cold as ice. This may still be hot.... Ike," he clipped to Cohen, "take Miss Zihala up to the place she ate at. Check up with the guy who served her and find out exactly when the hula dance went on and find out— Well, you know your onions. Go to it."

"Can I get a coat?" the woman said.

"Sure," MacBride said.

She got a coat and went with Cohen. At the door MacBride grabbed her hands, looked at them. She gazed up at him with heavy, languid, disturbing eyes. Her full lips were pink, soft but firm-looking. The skipper dropped her hands, dropped his eyes. He jerked his chin and Cohen took her out. Mara and his partner went too. One of the cops sat down and the other left.

After a moment Weymer came to lean indolently in the connecting doorway, the curtain thrust back of him. Controlled power lay smoothly along his arms and shoulders. He was in his thirties, even though his hair was thinning. He sucked absently at a cigarette, holding it to his lips with thumb and forefinger.

MacBride crossed to face him. "I'm going to ask you a point-blank question."

Weymer gave him a point-blank look.

MacBride said: "You got a crush on the woman?"

"What's it to you?"

"I asked you a question."

"I said, what's it to you?"

MacBride slapped his face. The cigarette flew from Weymer's lips and landed in a sputter of sparks on the floor. His eyes shimmered and he took a slow, smooth stride and ground out the butt with his foot. Then he looked up at MacBride.

"Kind of," he said.

The skipper nodded to the dead man. "Did he?"

"Yeah."

"Much?"

"I guess a hell of a lot."

MacBride grinned. "You're a cool customer, Weymer."

"You got to be, in my business."

"I'm not," the skipper said. "I'm a hot-head."

Weymer touched his face, smiled coolly. "I know that."

MacBride bent down, lifted the dead man's right hand. The knuckles were skinned, broken and caked with dried blood. The left hand was the same way.

Moriarity came in saying, "There's blood spots outside, Cap, but they only go a little ways from the door. The guy must have got wise and jumped down to the sand or something."

"Did you jump down?"

"Yeah. But you can't tell anything. The sand's loose and fine and there's a million people been tramping around there. He left no trail. Probably a lousy sneak-thief that this guy George Fuller surprised."

MacBride stared down at the dead man. "He sure must have been powerful and he sure must have known how to handle himself, to"—he pointed—"to smash up this guy the way he did." He looked up at Weymer. "Just about as powerful as you are, huh?"

Weymer was lighting another cigarette. "Yeah. George was pretty damn' powerful."

"Lucky for you your hands are clean."

Weymer looked absently at his hands. "Ain't it," he nodded.

Chapter II

MOSS CUFFEY was a little Irishman of about fifty. His hair and his face were red, but his face was redder than his hair. He was thin but he had a paunch, a round, odd little paunch, and he wore roomy coats in order to tone it down. The skin of his face was like a piece of rough canvas that has been painted red and then left in the sun to dry and crack. He was an untidy little man and his choice in clothes was terrible, though he practically owned Silver Park. He carried a huge watch in his breast pocket, its heavy gold chain hanging from the buttonhole of his coat lapel.

"I sent Lafe all around," he said, dropping into the huge swivel chair in his ramshackle office, tossing a ring of keys to the desk. "He went around to all the cottages. Folks are either in them or at work or the cottages ain't rented."

MacBride said: "Thanks."

Cuffey looked exhausted. "This fags me." Though he had done really nothing at all. He took a drink from a bottle and popped the bottle back into a drawer with magical speed. He screwed up his red, plucked-bird's face. "I don't want too much ballyhoo over this, Mac-Bride."

MacBride was standing with one foot propped on a chair, leaning on his knee. He looked at Cuffey. "What do you mean—ballyhoo?"

"Just—well, go easy. No sense making a big shout over the death of some second-rate slack-wire artist." He snatched up a nail file and plucked nervously at his fingernails.

"Talking murder," the skipper said flatly, matter-of-factly, "I never ask the murdered guy's social reputation or bank account."

Cuffey tossed the nail file to his cluttered desk, scratched the knuckles of his left hand. "No sense, though. Sure, you know your business, but I mean, I mean just don't kind of make a big ballyhoo about it. I own all this property—buildings and everything. I got my finger in the pie. I don't want this place to get a bad name."

"It never had a very swell name," the skipper chuckled; and then he scowled and was blunt: "You're talking crap, Cuffey. You know me. Murder's murder. Be your age, man."

He strode angrily from the office, whose door led him directly to the sidewalk. The smell of roasting peanuts came down the wind. He strode back towards the place where he had left Moriarity and Cohen. They were now in front of a concession where you pitched baseballs at a Negro's head. Moriarity was tossing wicked in-curves. MacBride watched him idly, then looked across at the merry-go-round. He saw Gahagan going round, leaning against a horse on which a girl rode. Gahagan's arm was round the girl.

The skipper broke it up when the merry-go-round stopped. "Stay in the car, you monkey," he muttered.

"I was just sayin' hello to a' old friend. I was just."

"Keep it going, Gahagan, and you'll go back pounding the pavement."

Kennedy drifted up holding a top balloon at the end of a string, humming vaguely to himself and looking blissfully tight. Cohen reached up and touched the balloon with the end of his cigar. It banged. Kennedy ducked, then swung around and jumped on Cohen's foot. Cohen yelped. Moriarity held his stomach and laughed; he laughed so hard that he staggered from side to side, bent-kneed. Cohen tripped him and Moriarity collapsed, knocking down a strange young woman.

"Fight! Fight!" somebody yelled.

"Drunks! Bums!" exclaimed the strange young woman. "Where was you brang up?"

Kennedy whispered to an infuriated MacBride: "Note the young lady's Radcliffe accent."

MacBride hustled Moriarity and Cohen away from the scene. "You guys'd try the patience of a gent! A person'd think you were out on a picnic instead of a murder case! Gradually, step by step, I think this police department is going to hell. I know it is!"

Kennedy rolled up, with his hat on one ear, his knees breaking ever so slightly.

"And you too!" MacBride barked at him, then glared around. "You're all like a lot of damned hoodlums." He clamped his dark, furious eyes on Kennedy. "And you—of course I might have known you'd get all liquored up again." He threw up his hands. "Boy, what support I get around here! What support!" He added: "And Moss Cuffey trying to tell me to ease up around here. The crust of him!"

Kennedy stuck out his arm sidewise to lean against what he thought was a post. It was not a post, and he pin-wheeled off the boardwalk, into the sand below. He lay back, clasping his hands behind his head.

"You fellows just run along," he said. "This is the first comfortable spot I've found since we came out here." He waited until they had gone and then withdrew a half-pint flask from his pocket. There was not much left, but he finished it and tossed the bottle away. "Bacchus, ever fair and young!…" he sighed pleasurably.

Five minutes later he rose. The boardwalk was about level with his chest and he had a hard time getting up; but he got up and meandered back towards the amusement center, humming abstractedly to himself. On the way he paused at a concession where you tossed darts at a lot of numbers painted on a large board. He won an imitation silver pocket mirror and left.

At the edge of the amusement center, he climbed a long, narrow stairway that ran up the side of a clapboard two-storied building. He opened the door, entered a room where an Italian boy was painting on Chinaware. He went through another door, opened it, entered a short hallway, went to the end of the hallway, opened another door and listed into a cozy, rectangular room furnished with two wicker divans, a lot of wicker easy chairs. He listed right across the room and landed seat-down, neatly, in one of the divans.

"Home," he said, "is the sailor, home from the sea, and the bootleg-ger home from his still." He pulled a cord that tinkled a bell somewhere distant. "Cripes," he mumbled, "what a pedestrian hunk of parody that was!" He lay back eyeing himself in the tiny mirror.

LULU BAILEY came in and said: "I thought you just left."

He nodded. "I did."

Lulu had a rough, good-natured laugh. "Boy, you sure look like you're headed for a hangover."

"Can you spare a pint?"

She laughed. "You can't buy anything here, Kennedy. But you can drink."

She left the room and came back with a bottle, glasses and a siphon. She was a hefty woman with a shock of dusky short curls, milky skin, and when she walked she had a habit of slapping her feet down, making her dress spin. She was on the other side of thirty and had the air of one who had been around and knew all the answers. Kennedy had known her when.

He said now, not eagerly: "About what we were talking about before, Lulu—this fellow Cuffey."

She drank. "Do we have to talk about him?"

"No, we don't have to talk about him. Let's talk about the weather."

"Swell."

"Okey. You were saying Cuffey's been here with Sophie Zihala."

"Yeah. It's a quiet place and not public."

Kennedy put his feet up on the divan and leaned back. "Is he that way about her?"

Lulu chuckled. "He's that way about any dame with a shape. He likes 'em bigger than him."

"Why'd he pass you up?"

She laughed outright. "He didn't. I told him to go sell his canned tripe where he had a market. Besides, I wouldn't do wrong by Buck."

"Who's Buck?"

"He's the lifeguard up the beach. He's my weakness. Besides, even if I was hard up I'd never fall for Cuffey. He's a pawer. I hate pawers."

"How long's he been coming here with Sophie?"

"Oh, on and off for a month."

"What do you make of her?"

Lulu stretched her arms. "I don't know, Kennedy. I don't make out I can read people, least of all women."

"You and me both. I just thought you might have an idea."

"Well, she's good looking in that kind of foreign way she has. Quiet, sort of broody, you know. She looks all animal to me but don't take that as a crack. I don't like her eyes. They're sort of spooky. But get me straight, Kennedy, I'm not saying anything against her."

"Did this fellow Weymer ever come in here?"

"Nope."

"George Fuller, the guy's dead now?"

"Nope."

"Do you think Weymer or Fuller knew the girl was running around with Cuffey?"

She looked at Kennedy. "You're asking a hell of a lot of questions, sweetheart."

"You know me, Lulu. Did I ever cause a comeback on you?"

She dropped her eyes and looked strangely pretty. "No, I guess you never did." She rose and went to stand by a window that overlooked the sand dunes. She said: "I don't think they knew. I was standing here one night and saw Cuffey and the girl come up across the dunes from the beach. I've got an idea I'm the only one knows they ran around."

"Why did Cuffey take a chance on you?"

She turned, smiled drily. "The guy knows I make my living selling hooch without a license. He owns this building. He never sat in here with her. He used a private door and they used a private room and the bum never paid for his liquor he drank off me. He knows the D.A.'ll send me up if he gets one more charge against me."

"You were always one for getting in spots, Lulu."

"Yeah." She laughed shortly. "Wasn't I, though."

He swallowed another drink and got to his feet, teetering over on one foot. "I'll be seeing you again."

"Listen, Kennedy, if you breathe a word—"

"What do you take me for, a rat?" He left with a sharp port list and floated among the concessions, benign, sleepy, unhurried. He made his way out along the boardwalk to the cottage. Fuller's body had been removed and there was a man there looking for fingerprints. He said the others had moved next door. Kennedy went next door and found MacBride, Moriarity and Cohen; Weymer and the woman.

"Did you sleep it off?" MacBride said.

"Yeah."

A little terrier came in carrying something dark in its mouth. It went to Weymer, put its front paws up on Weymer's knee. Weymer took a glove out of its mouth, grinned and tossed it out of the door.

"The pooch's a scavenger," he chuckled.

MacBride got up and went outside and returned with the glove. It was a yellow glove, fleece-lined, and it was smeared with some dark matter. He took out a knife and scraped at it. Then he lit a match and held the glove over it. Then he smelled the glove. He tossed it to Weymer.

"Try it on," he said.

"Why?"

"Try it on."

Weymer tried it on.

"Fits, doesn't it?" MacBride asked.

"Just like a glove."

"Get up."

"Huh?"

"Get up."

Weymer stood up, his smile cool mocking.

MacBride raised his fists. "Put up your dukes."

"What the hell—"

MacBride feinted with his left, struck with his right. He struck again and again. Finally Weymer squared off. His muscles rippled. He crossed deftly, smoothly, laid a clean jab on MacBride's chin and piled him across the room.

The skipper got up feeling his jaw. "That's what I wanted to find out."

"Find out what?"

"If you can box. You can."

Weymer laughed easily, the laughter rolling out across his curved lips. "Jeese, you're funny, Captain."

"I'm so funny, baby, that I'm going to pinch you. There's no marks on your hand. You could have used gloves to prevent that. You can box. Maybe Fuller couldn't. Catch on?"

"I caught on long ago—but you're still funny."

"Give me that glove."

MacBride passed the glove around. It was covered with dried blood. "We'll take the woman along too," he said. "Get some clothes on, lady—or you'll raise a crowd."

She rose with slow, muscular grace, her eyes brooding like a humid summer sky.

There were slow, heavy footsteps on the boardwalk and then a brawny, powerful man in white flannels, a white turtleneck sweater and a close haircut, came up to lean indolently in the doorway and pick his teeth.

"Which is the boss cop here?" he asked.

"Who are you?" MacBride asked.

"M' name's Buck McCarty. I'm the lifeguard around here. Are you the big smoke?"

MacBride nodded. "Yeah."

Chapter III

McCARTY spread himself on a camp stool, planting his big feet solidly, wide apart, slanting his big ruddy paws on his knees. He scowled with an appearance of great profundity at the floor, then scratched his cheek with a thumb; though the cheek was shaven, there came a sound like a file against sandpaper.

"Look," he said suddenly, raising an index finger. "Maybe I'm nuts, see. Maybe I'm goofy. Who knows? I don't. But like a guy now gets a' idea in the back of his head, well, he gets it in the back of his head, don't he? Am I clear kinda?"

"Well… kind of," MacBride said, not vigorously.

McCarty inhaled, muscling his eyebrows down over his eyes and bunching them above his nose. "I says to myself, I says, well, maybe you oughtta mind your own stinkin' business. I says that to myself, see? Then I thinks, well, s'pose you do and s'pose then years later you live to regret it. Then I says, well, I says, Buck, you go up and find the big boloney that's with the cops there. You. I mean, see? Though not exactly meanin' you're a big boloney, see?"

MacBride looked resigned. "I see. So you what?"

"Well, look, tonight I'm takin' a swim at about eight, maybe a little after. I ain't got no suit or trunks on, see? I have to wear 'em all day and I find 'em constrictin', so nights sometimes, if it's nice, I sneak in the water in m' birthday suit, so to speak, as you'd say. So there I was, up near the cove, where there ain't nobody usually. I hear somebody peggin' along and I go and swim out a ways and tread water till they get past.

"Well, it's quiet as hell along there and I can tell somebody's runnin' kind of loggy-like. Then I get a glim of a shape and it looks like a man and he's sort of ploddin' but runnin' too, I mean. Sort of, you know, like a guy tryin' to run in deep snow, if there was any snow. I can hear him breathin' like he'd bust his lungs and I stayed very quiet there and soon he passed and then disappeared round the point there. At the time, o' course, I don't think anything about it. Then I begin to hear about a guy bein' knocked off, and, hell, everybody's talkin' about it, and fin'ly, well, about twenty minutes ago, I'm shavin' when I think, boy, maybe that was somethin'! Hah?"

"You say it was about eight?"

"Well, mister, I guess it was." He thrust one arm out, revealing a gaudy wrist-watch. "I didn't have this on account of I take it off when I go in the water, but it musta been about eight and maybe, like I said, a little after, but not much. Because eight-twenty I like to hear Uncle Bob's Chums on the radio, and I run back from m' swim and get in m' shack just as it come on."

MacBride said: "Ike," to Ike Cohen, "you stay here. Mory," he said to Moriarity, "you come with me." He looked at Kennedy. "You stay here, for once, Kennedy, and keep from underfoot."

Kennedy was lying comfortably on a cot. "I intend staying here, old horsefly."

The skipper went out with Moriarity and Buck McCarty.

Sophie Zihala came back into the room slowly, a kind of lazy rhythm to the movements of her legs and body. She wore a shortsleeved blouse, a blue skirt, a black beret. She kept her sultry eyes on the floor. Weymer was eyeing her from beneath his big brows.

"You can sit," Cohen told her. "We ain't going yet."

She sat down.

Kennedy said from the cot. "You miss George Fuller, Sophie!"

She looked at him absently for a moment, then lowered her eyes again. Her expression did not change. She seemed remote, untouchable emotionally.

"What you ought to do, Sophie." Kennedy drowsed on, "is look around for some nice old guy with dough instead of fooling around with these ham trapeze artists."

"Funny," sneered Weymer, folding his arms, looking very majestic.

"Yes, Sophie, that's what you ought to do. Why, right around here there's any number of old guys would fall for you like a ton of brick. What do you get out of floating around the country to fairs and amusement parks? Look around. You'll find any number of unattached old guys, lousy with dough. Like Moss Cuffey, for instance, just as an example; though of course Moss Cuffey, I understand, has no use for women."

A flame seemed to move beneath the surface of her skin. Only one who looked closely would have detected the slight motion outward, inward, of her wide nostrils. Kennedy, for all his apparent sleepiness, had a camera eye.

Weymer laughed scornfully. "That guy! That little sawed-off shrimp Moss Cuffey? Ho-ho!... Listen to him, Sophie!"

She stared humidly at the floor, suppressing the movement of her bosom.

Kennedy said: "Hell, Weymer, you think because you're a he-man you're a big shot all around, huh?"

"With one hand I could break you in two, mister!"

"Don't brag about that, kid. I'm only a shell, a husk. Why, even Sophie could make a bum out of me."

Weymer growled: "Lay off her!"

"Boo," said Kennedy.

"Quit it, Kennedy," Ike Cohen said.

Kennedy turned his face to the wall. "Wake me up when they get back, Ike."

BUCK led the way along the dark beach. He said: "They got to build them cottages on stilts and them boardwalks account of every spring the river swells and all this sand is under. See that little knoll there? I got a shack up there."

"Where were you swimming?" MacBride asked.

"We're comin' to it."

In a few minutes he stopped. It was a part of the beach, he explained, where few people came. He liked it for that reason. The sand was moist and hard-packed here, and MacBride sprayed a flashlight around.

"Were you in bare feet?" he asked.

"Yeah."

MacBride knelt down. "Here's tracks with shoes on. Let's follow them a ways."

They followed them for twenty yards and Moriarity said: "D'you notice how the right foot turns way in? It don't look natural. It looks almost at right angles to the way it should be. See?"

MacBride nodded. They went on, following the tracks around the point and up a path. The footprints faded away here but the men continued to follow the path through sparse timber until it came out on another stretch of beach. Here they again found the footprints and followed them to the water's edge. "He washed here," MacBride said.

They followed the tracks along the beach and then into another path which led them through the timber again. The ground was hard here, but at intervals it was sandy also, or moist, and from time to time they found the familiar footprints. The path ended at the trolley line's right of way and they lost the footprints but found them again in a sandy gully beside the tracks. They followed the footprints through the shallow gully for a hundred yards, until they came to a small open-faced shed painted green.

"This is a car stop," Buck said.

Moriarity went on for a matter of twenty yards and then came back saying, "Nope. None up ahead there."

"He took a car here—a city-bound car. How often do they run?" he asked Buck.

"Well, from the city to Silver Park and back they run every fifteen minutes, but here, this part of it, there's a car through every forty minutes. There would ha' been one at eight-twenty and one at nine and then one at nine-forty. I know account of I used to be a motorman here once."

"It was the nine o'clock," MacBride muttered. "We'll see if we can locate the conductor on the nine o'clock."

"He'd be comin' out this way on his return trip at about I guess eleven or so. Lemme think." He thought, counting on his fingers, then said: "Eleven-fifteen at Silver Park."

MacBride grabbed at his watch. "It's five of now. Mory, you head down along the tracks. We'll go the other way. If you see the car coming along before you reach Silver Park, stop it. There's an old newspaper. Take it. Set fire to it and flag him and ask him. I'll be seeing you at the Silver Park station."

The skipper started off on the run, with Buck McCarty at his heels. He reached the Silver Park station a minute after the car had left. Fifteen minutes later Moriarity showed up, carrying his hat, mopping his neck.

"I flagged him," he panted.

"What did he say?"

Moriarity nodded. "I asked him if he seen a guy get on there that had maybe a limp or a funny foot and he said yes, the guy kind of swung his right leg stiff-like."

"Did he say he looked smashed up."

"He said the guy was blowing his nose in a big handkerchief as he got on and he didn't notice, he couldn't. These cars have only one guy that acts as motorman and conductor, so he didn't notice after that, he didn't look around."

"Where'd the guy get off?"

"He got off at the other side of Silver Park, at what they call the Grove Street stop."

Buck McCarty pointed. "It's only about four blocks up the line. You can see the little shed there when you get there."

"Okey, Buck," MacBride said. "You scram—and thanks. Come on, Mory."

They walked up the street, past the fringe of the amusement center, into a dark area where weeds grew between the street and the trolley tracks. Soon they came to the little green shed and MacBride clicked on his flashlight. In a couple of minutes they picked up the familiar prints and followed them to the highway, where they lost them. Five minutes later they picked them up on the other side and followed them through clayey earth to where Grove Street, coming down a hill, met the main highway. The footprints led to the Grove Street sidewalk, where they vanished.

"Well, that's that," sighed Moriarity. "I never found a way yet to follow footprints on pavement. The guy must be a native."

"If he is, it won't be hard to locate him, with that way he swings his leg. People notice a thing like that. Let's take a prowl up the street anyhow."

They took their time because now the closeness of the chase had gone. Until Moriarity pointed:

"There—he stepped off the sidewalk—then back on again."

"Well, he came this far anyhow."

The street was bordered with neat lawns, neat houses. They went to the top of it, stopped, and MacBride took off his hat and scratched his head. "It looks like it ends there. We'll go up to the end, then start back, every house. You take one side and I'll take the other."

"Swell. Come on."

"First. Wait a minute. There's a big place across the street with a sign out. Let's see what the sign says."

They crossed the street and stopped before a sign that hung from a tree and was illumined by a floodlight planted in the lawn. The sign said:

Summer Boarders
and
Transients

"Come on, kid," the skipper said. "It won't do any harm."

They climbed four steps to a broad, screened porch, opened a screened door and faced a wide, open door that said *Welcome* above it in faded gold letters. They strolled in. A small entrance hall had been converted into something slightly akin to a hotel lobby. There were a couple of leather rocking chairs and a small desk with a register on it. A plump, neat-looking old woman sat behind the desk.

MacBride took off his hat. "Madam, we're from the police. We wonder if you've got someone staying here, a man, who limps or sort of swings one leg."

She sat back, her eyes wandering. "Why"—she looked up, nodding—"I believe I have."

"Is he in?"

"I really don't know. I just sat down here to go over my accounts. I don't remember seeing him come in, but"—she started to rise—"I'll see."

MacBride restrained her with an upraised palm. "Just tell us what room it is."

She sat down again, looking scared.

"Don't be scared, madam," the skipper said. "We'll be very quiet."

"Up one flight—room twenty-two—in the rear."

Chapter IV

COHEN was sitting on a tipped-backed chair, absent-mindedly trying to do tricks with a piece of string, when Moss Cuffey, all puffed out like a pouter pigeon, showed up leading a large beefy man in blue coat and flannels. Cuffey doubtless intended his entrance to be spectacular, but Cohen, who was in the midst of a difficult string trick, the string laced between the splayed fingers of both hands, merely glanced upward, then proceeded with the intricacies of his trick. Kennedy didn't even wake up; he slept the sleep, if not of the righteous then of the carefree.

Having come through the doorway, Cuffey stamped down one foot, threw his narrow shoulders back, his fat hips forward, and frowned. His face looked vaguely like a Boston bull pup's. His companion came in and stood holding a Panama in his hand. He let large soapy eyes wander wearily about the room. A diamond glittered on the small finger of the big baggy hand that held the Panama.

"This," crackled Cuffey to Cohen, "is Alderman Pfeifferhaus!"

Cohen muttered, "Pleasetuhmeetcha," and twisted his fingers, screwed his lower lip in against his teeth.

"Alderman Leopold Pfeifferhaus!" sputtered Cuffey.

"I heard—"

"Well!"

Cuffey stamped hard.

The tipped-back chair on which Ike Cohen sat slipped, and chair and Cohen crashed; the trick, almost near completion, was ruined. He got up, sighed and wandered disconsolately into the kitchen. There was the sound of running water and then he reappeared with a tumbler.

"Yes?" he said blandly, and drank some water.

The blandness almost choked Cuffey. He made a ridiculous figure, with his skinny legs and arms, his narrow shoulders, his diminutive pot-belly. Alderman Pfeifferhaus cleared his large throat, said heavily but not unpleasantly, in the sonorous tones of a born bore:

"Ah-hum, Detective Cohen, my friend Mr. Cuffey has informed me that there's been a great deal of fussing about here that is tending to create an unfavorable impression in *re* his property, or properties, the same being his livelihood—"

"Yah-h-h-h—m-m-m-m-m—*humph*," yawned Kennedy, sitting up, stretching, then rubbing his eyes. "Boy, oh boy. I must have fallen asleep. I dreamt I dwelt in marble halls— Oh. M'm. New faces. Well, well, *well!* Alderman Pfeifferhaus!"

"Please, Mr. Kennedy!" Cuffey stormed. "We are here on important business!"

Sophie Zihala slid her sultry eyes from the floor to Cuffey's feet, then up his legs—almost to his face, but not quite. Her lips flexed a trifle and she slid her eyes down to the floor again. Weymer stood immobile, his arms crossed on his great chest, his strong legs spread, planted firmly.

"It is just this, Mr. Cohen," Pfeifferhaus said peacefully: "I wish to recommend that you don't make all this fuss Mr. Cuffey has been informing me about."

Ike Cohen looked irritated. "You'll have to speak to Cap'n MacBride about that. We're pinching these two people and yanking 'em to Headquarters."

"On what grounds?" Pfeifferhaus asked gravely.

"Suspicion."

"This is disgraceful!" Cuffey cried, throwing up his arms. "You look here, Cohen. I'm powerful around here. I own Silver Park and I'm not going to have a pack of you apes flocking around here and turning it upside down. Why are you taking Miss Zihala? It's been proved where she was when Fuller was killed and it's been proved that Mr. Weymer was there too except for ten minutes, which time it took him to walk down here from the restaurant and then run back. Understand, my man. I'm powerful. I'm a big man here. I won't stand for this. If you won't listen to Alderman Pfeifferhaus, by gawd, then I'll go right to City Hall!"

Cohen looked confused, angry. "It's no use talking to me, Mr. Cuffey. I take orders from the skipper. What he says, it goes."

Pfeifferhaus bowed hugely towards Cuffey. "I will talk to Captain MacBride, Mr. Cuffey."

Kennedy yawned again and stood up. "Hell of a lot of good that will do you."

"You keep out of this, Kennedy!" Cuffey spluttered. "This is no affair of yours. I know all about you. You're a lousy drunken sot and you're always sticking your nose into other people's business. I tell you I'm a big man here—powerful."

"Yeah?"

"Yeah! and I'll not see Miss Zihala—"

"You annoy me tremendously," Kennedy said sleepily.

"Yeah? Well, I'm glad I do. This happens to be my property and just one more word out of you and I'll throw you off it!"

Kennedy said in the same weary tone: "Listen, you pot-bellied tramp, you annoy me. What's the idea of the big fatherly interest in our lady in distress?"

"It's not that! It's everything! All this clowning around!—you and MacBride and the whole blamed crowd of you!"

"Calm yourself, Cuffey. You don't scare me and that line of crap you're tossing out doesn't get to first base. Why with every word you say, even when you mention her name—why do you damned near have to break your neck to keep from looking at her? And her frightened to hell of looking at you!"

Cuffey's eyes popped. "What are you saying!" he cried, while veins stood out at his temples.

"I'm saying, you pot-bellied fat-head, that you've got a yen for the girl—you're *that* way about her."

Weymer took one step, swung. Kennedy was lifted off his feet. He hit the wall. The building shivered. He crumpled and lay on the floor. Weymer, white-faced, started after him. Cohen clipped Weymer with a blackjack and Weymer stopped, stood stupidly in the middle of the floor, his legs sagging but still holding. He rubbed his hand across his eyes, backed up slowly until the wall stopped him. He stood there, still passing a hand across his eyes.

The girl sat clenching her hands together between her knees; her face was scarlet, bent low.

Cohen went across the room, picked up Kennedy and flopped him to the cot.

"Thanks, Ike. The guy can sock, can't he?"

"You ought to know."

Cohen pivoted, crossed to face Weymer. "One more step out of turn on your part, baby, and I'll open that head of yours."

Pfeifferhaus had paled. He said: "I had better leave. I—I will speak with Captain MacBride."

Cuffey had no reply. He stared transfixed at Kennedy. Pfeifferhaus went out, touching his chest as though indigestion disturbed him.

FOR three minutes no one said anything. Cohen, ready to act on a split-second's notice, shifted his eyes from one to another, back and forth, angrily and irritably. Then the tramp of feet came out of the darkness, grew nearer, came up to the door, and MacBride strode in. Instantly he bit Cuffey with a hard, windy glare.

"I just met Pfeifferhaus up the way, Cuffey. Next time you think running to an alderman is going to get you anywhere with me, have that head of yours examined."

"I just thought—"

"You just thought! I know what you thought! You thought because you own a lot of property here and swing a lot of votes that you're a big potato. That's over, Cuffey. That's over in Richmond City."

More feet were tramping nearer.

The skipper looked at Kennedy, on whose face was a trickle of blood. He roared: "Who the hell hit Kennedy?"

Cohen said: "There was a little rumpus over nothing. Weymer took a sock at him and I socked Weymer."

"Why'd Weymer sock Kennedy?"

Weymer said grimly: "He can't say things about Sophie."

Moriarity came in with a tall, heavy, bull-necked man whose one eye was blackened, whose lips were cut, puffed; whose dark eyes burned in their deep sockets.

Kennedy sat up. "Who's so-and-so?"

"His name's Bartelli. He's the guy beat hell out of Fuller."

Cuffey's eyes almost popped from his head.

MacBride tossed a stained glove to the table. "There's the other glove. Mory and I grabbed him in a summer boarding house on Grove Street. I don't know much about him. We didn't ask. We just grabbed him and bounced him down here. We asked him if he had a fight with Fuller and he said yes. He didn't know he'd killed him."

"I didn't know," choked Bartelli, his eyes rolling, settling hungrily on Sophie Zihala. "I didn't know, Sophie."

Kennedy stood up. "My, he knows her!"

Sophie stood up slowly and backed away until she was against the wall. She spread her palms back against it and stared with humid terror at Bartelli. Her breath began pumping from partly open lips.

MacBride said: "Bartelli, why the hell did you beat up that guy?"

Bartelli's eyes rolled towards the skipper. He pointed downward.

"You see this foot—this leg of mine? Fuller did it," he panted. "Once it was Bartelli, Fuller and Zihala—over two years ago. And I loved Sophie, and Fuller—he did this to me." He struck his leg. "Fuller did it! Fuller ruined me! It was in the part where I walked a tight wire at an altitude of three hundred feet—out at Moonlight Park. I used special shoes, which I would slip over my regular ones. I would wear my regular ones on the climb up the long ladder, and then when I was on the platform I would slip on my special ones. Fuller always gave them to me. This time I did it all the same. It was all right till I got to the middle, when I always did a somersault, landing on my feet on the wire again. This time I did it. I landed—but I slipped. I fell, this leg under me and"—he shook his head—"they never fixed it right. It took my heart out.

"As soon as I could I went away, for I was no good to the act and no good to Sophie. Later I ran games of chance at the concessions, all over, and met a woman and married her and she's out in Akron now and we have a kid. She's a good woman. I love her. Then one night we were sitting home and I took out, I don't know why, my old things—tights and slippers—and my special toppers. We were sitting by the fire. I laid them all down after a while and my wife smelled something and grabbed the slipper, it was too hot near the fire. Then I smelled it. Then I looked. The slipper had scum on it. My slippers— had been—greased. Something busted like a bomb in my head. I saw it all. *George Fuller!* He'd greased my slippers—that was why I slipped. That—that was why I came here and—you know what—I did."

"Why'd you wear the gloves?"

"I knew they'd hurt him more."

"How'd you come to toss one away?"

"It was while I was running away along the boardwalk. My shoe-lace got undone and I took off the gloves and tied it and then I thought I picked both gloves up again, but I didn't."

"It's murder, you know. Stop to think about that?"

Bartelli nodded, said hoarsely: "If it is, it is. I don't care. He tried to murder me and he only crippled me, which was worse. All right, it's murder. You know what to do about that."

"I know what to do about that," MacBride nodded bitterly, "but maybe I ain't going to like it."

Cuffey sniffled, frowned, cleared his throat. "I hope you're satisfied now, MacBride. You see how wrong you were. You ran around here like a chicken with it's head off, accusing people of killing people for no reason at all. I'll go down to City Hall and complain about that. Mark me, MacBride!"

MacBride muttered: "Nerts. Go to it." He wasn't thinking of Cuffey, didn't even bother to look at Cuffey.

"I am a big man here," Cuffey said, sticking out his chest, showing off like a kid. "I'll go to City Hall and have a long, long talk. Now," he said, bowing sharply, "I'm going."

"Go and be damned to you," MacBride muttered.

"Better hang on to him, Skipper," Kennedy yawned, twisted out of shape while he tried to scratch between his shoulder blades. He walked over, turned around and said to Cohen: "Scratch me between my shoulder blades, will you, Ike?"

Cohen scratched him.

Cuffey stopped in the doorway, his fists clenching. "I've had enough of your slurs, Kennedy."

Kennedy looked at MacBride dreamily. "Better hang on to him, Stevie, old tomato."

MacBride glared at him. "What've you got up your sleeve?" he demanded. Then he pointed: "It wouldn't hurt if you stuck your shirt-tail in your pants. You look like something the cat dragged in. Drunk. You need a shave. Your shirt-tail's out—"

"He's nothing but a drunken sot, a dirty rat!" cried Cuffey.

MacBride barked: "You let him alone! And," he added, dropping his voice, "hang around here a while." Then he faced Kennedy, his hard fists jammed on his hips, a wintry look in his eyes. He said: "Now are you just trying to horse around here and make trouble, or do you really know anything? I don't see how you could know anything, because ever since we came out here you've either been asleep or drinking out of a bottle."

Kennedy turned around and looked at Sophie Zihala. His eyes drowsed and the ghost of a satiric smile traveled languidly across his lips. "Sophie," he said, "did you have anything to do with greasing Bartelli's slippers that time?"

Her mouth looked warped, her eyes hot, smoky. "Of course not!" she cried in a low, husky voice.

"I mean," he went on, "did you know Fuller greased Bartelli's slippers?"

"You're mad!"

"Did Fuller tell you he was going to grease Bartelli's slippers?"

"Please!" she cried, stretching her hands towards MacBride. "He is making fun of me!" She sobbed once, hoarsely. "He—is making fun of me!"

MacBride growled: "Kennedy, you're drunk. What happened then has got nothing to do with this. You're drunk and you're screwy. Cut it out!"

Kennedy ignored him and turned to Bartelli. "Bartelli," he said, "when you beat Fuller to death, where did you go? I mean, how did you get down to the beach?"

"The boardwalk, like I said. I ran to the end of the boardwalk and down the steps there."

"You're sure you never left the boardwalk before you got to the end of it?"

"Sure I'm sure."

Kennedy sat down and rested elbow on knee, chin in hand. He mused aloud: "It's funny, it's like a puzzle with some pieces missing. I see things in my head and then they sort of fade. If I only had about three shots of rye straight now, I think it might clear me up a bit." He stood up and said: "Come outside a minute, Cap."

Scowling, MacBride followed Kennedy out to the boardwalk and Kennedy said: "Now, look. How well do you stand in with the District Attorney?"

MacBride gripped his hands together, held them up. "We're like this."

"Okey. Now I know a person the D.A. might send to the cooler if he got one more liquor case against this person. It so happens that this person may be able to shed a little light on dark doings. This person is in no way connected with this case, but if—ah—my client should talk a little, a certain other person might talk to the D.A. and my client might go to the cooler. I'm not going to drag this person in unless you swear, cross your heart, that the D.A. will not send my client to said cooler."

"How long'll it take you to get this—person?"

"Ten minutes."

"Shoot."

Kennedy headed for the amusement center.

Chapter V

HE returned with Lulu Bailey and as she hesitated in the doorway everyone in the cottage looked at her. Cuffey's mouth tightened. His hands were in his coat pockets but even so you could tell that his hands bunched and pressed against his hips.

"Hello, MacBride," Lulu said.

"Hello, Lulu, I haven't seen you since—"

"You raided a little hot-spot I ran in Jockey Street."

"That's right. How've you been?"

"So-so. You?"

"Swell."

Lulu came into the room and Kennedy lolled in the doorway. Kennedy said listlessly: "Cuffey and Sophie Zihala used to hang out nights in one of Lulu's rooms and Cuffey never paid for his drinks. Lulu wants to make a charge against him. I don't know offhand how much Cuffey owes her."

Weymer unfolded his arms and let them hang at his sides. His head went down, his cold blue eyes bit across the room at Kennedy. Dull red color came slowly into Sophie's face. Lulu looked a little troubled.

"Tell the Skipper, Lulu," Kennedy said, "what you didn't tell me."

Her eyes clouded, but suddenly she looked frankly at MacBride. "There's probably nothing to it, MacBride, but this is a case of murder and I was walking up and down, trying to get up enough courage to come down and tell you, when Kennedy just showed up. It probably means nothing at all, but—well, here it is: As Kennedy said, Mr. Cuffey and Miss Zihala used to come to my place.

"Well, one night, about two weeks ago, I overheard them. Mr. Cuffey wanted her to marry him, he told her how much he was worth and all that. After a while I heard her say, like this, 'But there's George Fuller. He's so mad about me. He'd kill us if I married you.' Mr. Cuffey laughed at that but she was serious. 'I know George,' she said. Then Mr. Cuffey said, 'Maybe we can get rid of George.' And then after a minute she sighed and said, 'I wish we could. I think there might be a way. I'm not sure, but I think George tricked a partner we had once—Tony Bartelli. Bartelli broke a leg and was ruined. I think

George did something to Bartelli's slippers.' Then I heard Mr. Cuffey say, 'Good! Drop Bartelli a line. Say you heard Fuller talking in his dreams about it.' And then Mr. Cuffey said, 'What about this other fellow—Weymer?' And she said, 'Oh, I think he's in love with me too, but he's not a madman like George Fuller.' That was all I heard."

MacBride said: "My gawd, you mean to say you held this back because Cuffey—"

She colored. "I've been in the cooler too many times, MacBride. I didn't have the guts to face it again. I just didn't. I knew if I was thrown in again—I knew it'd be the end of me, I'd go mad!" She cried a little. "You wouldn't understand."

MacBride spun on Bartelli. "What was all this song and dance about you and your wife sitting before a fire and all?"

Bartelli's head was lowered. "Some of it was true. Only I didn't look at the shoes again till I got Sophie's letter. Then I looked at them and held them over the fire. Then I saw. But I didn't mention the letter because I didn't want to drag in Sophie."

The skipper's bitter eyes swung towards Cuffey. Cuffey retreated into a corner and seemed to shiver there. But it was Weymer's ice-blue glare that cut him as much as MacBride's bitter one. Sophie was pressing her hands on her thighs and groaning in low whispers.

MacBride said: "Cuffey, what do you think of it? You know what this means, don't you? You get it, don't you, that you and the woman were accomplices, really, in this murder which this poor sap Bartelli committed?"

The woman made a terrified dash for the door. Moriarity reached out. She dropped Moriarity with a hard, unexpected blow. Cohen took a step and clipped her on the jaw. She wheeled away across the room and crashed against Cuffey. She gripped him, cried:

"You said you were a big man here! You told me you had pull at City Hall! Do something now! Do—something!" she screamed.

MacBride grabbed her by the arms. She whipped around and kicked him in the shins. He slapped her face hard with the heel of his hand.

"Cut it out, Sophie!"

She kicked him again and he slapped her again—harder. She cried hoarsely and fell on to the cot.

MacBride looked disgusted. He waved a hand peremptorily. "Ike, get to a phone and call the wagon. We'll run in the whole crew." And to Bartelli: "You're the only guy I'm sorry for, Bartelli. If you'd had any sense; you'd have known by one look in her eyes she's a killer at heart—only she doesn't do the dirty work herself. By gawd, Bartelli, I'm sorry for you!"

Cohen headed for the door but Kennedy shoved him back. "Just a minute, Ike. Just a little minute."

"What now?" MacBride demanded. "Ike, you do as I tell you—"

"Hold your horses, Skipper," Kennedy said. "This thing isn't straightened out yet. Think back. There were blood spots only a few feet from the door of the murder cottage. They ended there. You know that. There's not another blood spot on the boardwalk, beyond that. Bartelli says he never left the boardwalk, till he got to the end of it. He couldn't have been bleeding very much. You can see that outside of a black eye and a few minor scratches, the rest are bruises that didn't bleed. Bartelli didn't bleed much. I'll bet my shirt those blood spots outside the door are not Bartelli's."

"Whose are they?"

"I'll bet they're George Fuller's. I'll bet that when Bartelli ran off, Fuller staggered to the door, a few feet beyond, then collapsed and crawled back into the cottage, to lie on the floor. I'll bet you ten bucks."

MacBride said: "Suppose they are his blood spots. Suppose he did do what you say. The fact is, he's dead. The beating killed him."

Kennedy laughed. "Did it? Did it? What do you want to bet that it didn't?"

"I won't bet anything. What the hell are you driving at?"

"At this, old tomato. The trouble is that while you use a lot of leg motion, I get a little plastered and lie around and think and after a while things come to me. Bartelli had gloves on when he licked George Fuller. Bartelli admits he beat Fuller to death. Bartelli *thinks* he beat George Fuller to death." Kennedy chuckled sardonically. "He didn't, Stevie. He didn't. Remember, those blood spots are Fuller's. You can get an expert out to chip up the wood where the blood spots are, analyze the blood and you'll find it's Fuller's. Bartelli beat him to a pulp and then lammed. He stopped somewhere along the boardwalk to take the gloves off and tie his shoelace and there he lost one of the gloves.

"Now think back to the way you saw Fuller lying on the floor. You remember the finger marks on his throat. You must remember that Bartelli's gloves were soaked with blood. Okey. Did you see any bloody finger marks on Fuller's throat? No. Why? Because the guy that choked Fuller to death didn't have any gloves on and the guy's hands were not bloody!" Kennedy tossed a thumb casually towards Weymer. "Ask big boy over there if when he came to get Fuller for dinner he didn't find him in a bloody welter on the floor. Ask him if he didn't back down and finish Fuller."

Weymer folded his arms on his chest, smiled a cold hard smile in which there was no humor.

MacBride barked: "Hear that, Weymer?"

"I heard it."

"Well?"

"Well, what?"

"You're still inclined to be funny, huh?"

"I'm not being funny, Captain. I'm thinking what a shame it's going to be that I ain't going to get twenty thousand dollars."

"Where did you expect to get twenty grand?"

"I figured that with the twenty grand I'd take Sophie and we'd go far away. I was kind of gone on Sophie, but now I wouldn't touch her with a ten-foot pole. You were right about her eyes. I didn't notice it till a little while ago. She's bad medicine, but, cripes, she's something to look at. She was bad medicine for Bartelli there and she was bad medicine for George Fuller and she was bad medicine for...." He paused; then he said: "Here's where I chuck away twenty grand, Captain—"

"Hey!" Moriarity barked.

Cuffey was standing with a gun in his hand. Little pot-bellied Cuffey, whom all had forgotten to notice during Weymer's speech. His jaw trembled and the gun was small but deadly black in his hand. His eyes looked green, crazed, and his face was redder than his hair.

He panted in a small, taut voice: "As you are, all of you! As you are now! One move and I'll shoot to kill!"

"Pull at City Hall, have you?" MacBride said sarcastically.

"One move and I'll—Kennedy, get the hell out of that doorway!"

"Make me," Kennedy said, leaning indolently in the doorway. He looked wasted, sallow, toying idly with the imitation silver pocket mirror he had won at one of the concessions.

MacBride's hand rested on the lapel of his coat, but he knew he would not be fast enough to draw in time. He muttered: "Kennedy, you fool, get out of the doorway. This guy is nuts!"

"He's nuts and he's a pot-bellied little bad smell—"

"You, Kennedy!" MacBride roared. "Move!"

Cuffey's eyes were fixed on Kennedy. "Kennedy, get out of the way," he panted.

"Go to hell, sweetheart," Kennedy said languidly. "You annoy me."

Cuffey took a step forward, his eyes bulging, his hand tightening on the gun. Then he gave a little cry, ducked, flung his left hand in front of his face while his right hand jerked with the explosion of the gun. Kennedy did not budge. The bullet smashed into the frame of the doorway, an inch from his shoulder. MacBride and Moriarity and Cohen all fired at the same time. The three shots seemed interlocked. Cuffey wilted and crumpled to the floor.

Kennedy tossed the mirror in the air, caught it. "Not bad," he said. "You got it, didn't yo' all? Yassuh. Fiddling with this, I finally did it. The light back on the wall… its reflection in the mirror blinded palsy-walsy there for just one brief instant. Not bad, sez I, sez I, podner—not bad a-tall." He swallowed and sweat burst out on his face. "But if you think I was calm, cool and collected there for a minute, you are most certainly screwy. Whew!"

"Ike," MacBride snapped, leaning over Cuffey, "get an ambulance."

Cohen ran out.

The skipper stood up, gray-faced, bony-jawed. He stared at Weymer. "So you lose twenty grand, huh?"

"Yeah. I happened to come in the cottage as Cuffey was choking Fuller. Cuffey was grunting and pressing down hard. I said, 'Hey, don't do that.' Then he jumped up. But Fuller was dead. Well, I never cared a hell of a lot for Fuller, but I grabbed Cuffey anyhow. Then he offered me twenty grand. Why not? I said, 'Okey, mister.' I didn't think he could have beaten Fuller that way, so I asked him. He'd seen the fight. He'd been going along the boardwalk and passed the cottage and heard the sounds and he looked in the window. He watched. He saw Bartelli lam and he saw Fuller crawl out and then collapse. He dragged Fuller back in and finished him." Weymer chuckled drily. "I figured taking the twenty grand and—" He gazed across at Sophie Zihala. He shrugged. "I guess I got a break after all."

Sophie Zihala stared with glazed eyes at Cuffey. Hoarse little sounds, inarticulate, crept from her lips. Her body shook. Sweat poured down her face.

Weymer said, "I guess Cuffey never seen her eyes straight, either."

"Cuffey," Kennedy said, "was always interested in ankles anyhow."

"Pipe down," MacBride growled in a low voice.

The cottage was quiet then. Until Sophie suddenly clapped her hands to her eyes and screamed. And then her hands shot upward and tore wildly at her hair. Bartelli crossed the room, his eyes grave, his head shaking. He took hold of her hands.

"Sophie, don't," he said in a thick voice. "Please, Sophie."

She glared up into his face with wild, murderous eyes. And then she spat in his face.

Bartelli dropped her hands and looked stupefied, hurt. But then his eyes snapped awake, brightened, hardened, as though in this moment he saw the truth, what had always been the truth. His lips grew taut, his brows came together. He clenched his fist and glared down at her contorted, hateful face. His fist swung.

Bartelli knocked her out.

He Was a Swell Guy

It looked like suicide all the way, but when it broke it was a sizzler.

Chapter I

MORIARITY and Cohen were playing table tennis in the base-ment of Police Headquarters. It was a few minutes shy of midnight. A mild breeze puffed in through a window and frolicked half-heartedly with the wispy hair of Dutch Moeller, the fingerprint expert. He was eating a ham-on-rye and taking absent-minded drags at a bottle of Canadian ale. He seemed unmoved by the quality of game the two men were playing, and his reasons for being unmoved were manifest.

Cohen, going haywire, made a wild drive, and Captain Stephen J. MacBride, drumming his rubberless heels down the steps from the central room, arrived in time to receive the Celluloid ball briskly on his bold Roman nose. The skipper did not duck, he merely came to a stop, wrinkled his nose and took his battered brier from between large, rugged teeth.

"Horsing around again, horsing around again!" he growled, dark wind in his up-from-under stare.

Fat Dutch Moeller was shaking with silent laughter, his eyes watering. "Oh, boy!" he spluttered. "Right on the schno-nozzle!"

MacBride said: "I don't think that's funny, either." And to Moriar-ity and Cohen, "What has kept me all these years from tossing you two hoodlums back in harness is one of the mysteries of my life. The next thing I know, there'll be something else screwy down here, like a badminton court or a roulette wheel. Whenever I want you guys, you're not upstairs where you ought to be; you're either down here or up the street in the Greek's or you're—" He broke off, blew out an exasperated breath, then said with winded patience, "Get your coats. We're going places."

Moriarity and Cohen moved with alacrity and a simulated earnest-ness. The skipper swiveled on his heel and went up to the central room. He was a lank, bony man in a two-year-old gray suit and a hard straw hat. His hands were big-knuckled, lean and strong. He had a dark peppery mustache clipped close to a straight upper lip. His eyes were bold, blunt, his face ruddy-brown, with high cheekbones and a scrubbed look.

Gahagan was at the wheel of the black touring car parked at the curb. MacBride got in beside him and Moriarity and Cohen climbed in back.

"Step on it," the skipper said.

His explosions were of short duration and left little or no ashes behind. By the time, five minutes later, they crossed South Square, he turned around and said in a loud, good-natured voice:

"Hey, what d' you think my daughter did today? Won the Metropolitan Singles!"

"No!" exclaimed Moriarity.

"What d' you mean, 'no'!"

"I seen her play once at Fair Hills," Cohen said. "She looks a lot like her mother, don't she?"

"Yeah," said MacBride. "Except around the mouth. She's got my mouth. If she had a mustache, she'd look just like me. That is, in a way.... Gahagan, get over on the right side of the road for a change, before you smack a taxpayer."

THEY struck Napoli Street and went through the heart of Little Italy to India and down the darkness of India Street towards the waterfront. Three blocks north of the waterfront, where India makes a dog-leg twist, they drew up behind a precinct flivver parked at the curb. Farther along the curb was a police ambulance, its headlights tinted red, its spotlight slashed across the sidewalk and lighting up a corner of a vacant lot. Shapes of men moved about or stood motionless and voices made clean night sounds.

MacBride got out of the touring car and picked his way through rubble toward the group of men. A uniformed patrolman turned and his shield and buttons gave off quick little gleams. The ambulance doctor had just risen and was stamping his foot to get his trousers cuff down. There seemed to be no onlookers but those connected with the law. It was a fag-end of the city, not residential. A couple of precinct detectives were going over articles they had taken from the clothing of the man on the ground. Farther back, Kennedy, the newspaperman, was sitting on a rusty five-gallon oil drum and smoking a cigarette.

The skipper put his hands on his hips and looked down at the pale dead face of the man on the ground. His peppery brows came to-gether, one side of his mouth drew downward, bending his mustache with it. He looked up, squinted around at the circle of faces.

"Duke Collins, eh?" he muttered.

The ambulance doctor said: "That's what Kennedy says."

MacBride raised his chin. "Oh, you here, Kennedy?"

"In the flesh, Stevie. Weak flesh, but—"

"I knew this guy," MacBride said, jabbing a finger towards the body. "I knew him. When we were kids we used to live next to each other. I busted his nose once—but he was a nice kid. Well, he was a nice guy, too. But nuts on the ponies and dogs and cards. I think I seen him last about five years ago. Know what I always used to say to him? 'Duke,' I used to say, 'some day I got a hunch I'm going to pick you up dead. It'll either be by your own hand,' I said, 'because you're broke—or by the hand of some other guy because you cut corners on him.' Well, Duke laughed. He was in the dough then, and he said: 'I can't picture myself cutting corners, Steve. If I decide to do the dutch some day, that's my business. See they bury me in my dress suit, will you?' He was a nice guy, but nuts. Poor old Duke. Who found him?"

"Me," said Patrolman Kleinschmidt. "I was walking along River Road, about four blocks from here, when I heard the shot. It was about twenty to twelve. I figured it was up this way, so I picked up me dogs and came right up India, shooting me flashlight in the alleys on the way. I guess it was about ten minutes before I found him. He was curled up and I seen he was shot in the chest and I stepped in the puddle there and felt something hard under me foot and I fished out the gun, all muddy. He was dead. Then I rang in."

"See or hear a car around?"

"Nope, I didn't."

The skipper heaved a sigh, bent down. "Yep, I guess Duke gave himself the works."

"His shirt and chest are powder burnt," the ambulance doctor said. "It looks like he let himself have it and then pitched forward."

One of the precinct detectives said: "The rod's a .32 auto. Loaded but for one. I found the ejected shell. He had five dollars and sixty cents in his pants. No dough in his wallet. There was a pencil in his pocket with *Coronet Hotel* stamped on it. It's new and been sharpened only once—machine-sharpened."

MacBride muttered in a low, reflective voice, "Five bucks on him... five bucks. I seen the time he carried around a roll of ten or fifteen grand. Pin money, he called it. Let's see the gun." He took the gun, looked at it. It was still wet, still smeared with mud. "It's his all right. I remember the cracked grip. He wanted me to get him a license to carry it and I told him don't be an Airedale, old friends or no old friends. He laughed and said: 'Well, I don't need a license anyhow, Steve. The only guy I'll ever use it on 'll be myself.' He had it all doped out."

He hung around until they loaded Collins' body in the ambulance and headed off for the morgue. Then he climbed into the front seat of the touring car. Moriarity and Cohen got in back and Kennedy climbed in after them, saying:

"I hope you fellows don't mind."

"We'll drop you off at the *Coronet*," MacBride said. "And, hey, Kennedy—don't forget you promised to get Flannery to smear my daughter's picture all over the sports page.... Shoot, Gahagan. The *Coronet*."

"Why the *Coronet?*" asked Kennedy.

"See Duke's diggings. I think he's got an aunt out West and besides, I want to make sure I get that dress suit. Imagine! There he was living at the *Coronet*—"

"Uh-huh," said Kennedy. "He was living at the *State Hotel.*"

"What! You mean that one in—"

"Brick Street."

"But, hell, it's a dump, it's a dump!"

"It's a dump," said Kennedy.

"When'd you see him there?"

"About a week ago. Flannery sent me over to get a story on that terrible tempered Swede who busted a telephone booth to pieces when the operator gave him a wrong number three times in a row. And I ran into Duke there. His clothes looked okey but Duke himself looked like a ghost. It gave me the jitters to see him that way."

Chapter II

THE *State Hotel* was a narrow red brick building, five dusky stories tall, in the down-at-the-heel neighborhood that hems in Brick Square. The lobby was an unprepossessing room back of a plate glass window on which the hotel's name was inscribed in gilt letters. The desk was brown and pulpit-like and the clerk was thin, middle-aged, and looked embittered in a quiet, unaggressive way.

The room in which Duke had lived was discouraging. Small, narrow, it contained a single bed, a battered bureau. There was no closet. Duke's clothes hung on hooks screwed into the wall. The bureau drawers contained half a dozen shirts, underwear, socks. A set of silver brushes, gold cufflinks, black pearl studs, proclaimed a former affluence. The evening clothes had been tailored by a famous name, but they were dusty now, they had not been worn recently. Going over these things, the skipper wagged his head, clucked his tongue.

"You can say what you want, a thing like this kind of gets you. A guy that was handsome and a pretty swell egg, a guy you once saw flash ten grand like it was stage money—and now, this!"

Kennedy, leaning indolently against the wall, said in a drowsy, chiding voice, "The old skipper's certainly going lachrymose on us, fellows."

"Whatever you mean by that word you found in a book, Kennedy, I know it's a dig; but nerts to you, sweetheart! And another thing, I haven't found out yet who sent me that book, 'How to Be a Detective,' but I've got my suspicions."

He found some letters and read them. They were from a woman who signed her name Marjorie and lived in Topeka, Kansas.

"It's his sister, not his aunt," MacBride said. "That's it—his sister! I remember the family split up when he was a kid and the sister went to Kansas to live with an aunt. She writes like she liked him a lot. Maybe she'll want to bury him." He turned and squinted at the dress suit. "Ten to one I'll have to get that dry-cleaned."

"Is there any liquor around?" asked Kennedy.

"Let's see," recommended Moriarity, going to work. He found a pint bottle, half-full, and took a long swallow. "I don't like it," he said. He took another swallow, lowered the bottle, shook his head. "No, I'm afraid I don't like it."

Kennedy said: "Well, while you're being afraid, how's to let me not like it for a while?"

He drank at length and passed the bottle to Cohen, who drained it and observed, "No, I don't like it, either."

"Very, very inferior rye," Kennedy agreed.

MacBride said: "So help me, it's a wonder you birds aren't dead! Mooching all the time. We can't case a place any more without you monkeys don't right away start playing bottle, bottle, who's got the bottle." He jerked his chin towards the door. "Come on, let's get out of here."

Downstairs, he said to the night clerk, "Was Collins around tonight?"

"No."

"When'd you come on?"

"I came on at four. I had orders to plug his keyhole."

MacBride looked grave. "Behind in his rent, huh?"

"Three weeks."

"Tough, tough. Well, you won't have to, buddy. Collins is over the morgue."

The man closed his mouth, looked away. "I was afraid I'd go up some night and find him croaked in his room."

"Looked bad, huh?"

"Pretty low."

The skipper led the way out to the touring car, climbed in and said: "Back to Headquarters, Gahagan."

"Just by way of suggestion," Kennedy drawled, "it might be a good idea to run over to the *Coronet*."

"Why? He could have picked that pencil up in one of the writing rooms."

"Ixnay. They don't have them in the writing rooms. I know. They have 'em only in the rooms—three-fifty and up, with bath, some with shower; special monthly rates. I'd like to write this story, Stevie, but I'd like to build up to Collins' death. I've a hunch he was in a game tonight."

"Owing three weeks' hotel rent. That's bright!"

Kennedy was tranquil, a little sleepy. "You knew Duke better than I did, but I happen to know he was sentimental about his jewelry. I happen to know he had a ring set with a diamond. It was a ladies' engagement ring. He was engaged to a girl about four years ago and she died and after that Duke used to wear the ring on his little finger. He was wearing it when I last saw him, a week ago. He admitted he was broke and I pointed to the ring and he said with a kind of bitter, desperate little smile, 'That stays with me. Kennedy.' Well, sir, that ring was worth plenty potatoes and it wasn't on his finger when they picked him up tonight. If by any chance you should wax curious and ask me, I'd take a guess that he hocked it and went plenty heeled into a game. Okey. Then say he lost, took a long walk in the general direction of the river, but chose an empty lot and a bullet instead. A gambler's last fling. It's poetic as hell. Maybe he even took a suite at the *Coronet*, rounded up some card-conscious citizens—"

"Come on," the skipper interrupted. "We'll go over."

THE *Coronet* was one of the best hotels in the city. Whether you ate or danced or lived there, it ran into money. It was proud of its three dining-rooms, its food, its murals and its period suites.

The skipper said to the man at the desk: "I'm Captain MacBride from Police Headquarters and I'm wondering if a man named William Collins registered here within the past day or so."

The clerk referred to his files, shook his head.

"Ask him," Kennedy said to MacBride, "to show you who's living here now."

"Why?"

"Familiar names."

"The clerk let them look through a card index and it was in the Ds that Kennedy stopped, said: "Oakley Dowd. You remember him. He used to hang out a lot at the Livermore dog track and Duke used to hang out there too. Then Dowd went West. I didn't know he'd come back. It wouldn't do any harm to look him up. I see he's in 310."

It was Oakley Dowd who opened the door of 310. He was a tall, heavy man of about fifty, with a dramatic mane of tawny hair and flashing blue eyes.

"By George!" he boomed. "Well, knock me down with a feather! Well, as I live and breathe—Come in, MacBride! Come in! I haven't seen you since—since—well, since I can't remember when. And Kennedy! And—well, I don't know these two gentlemen, but—"

"Moriarity and Cohen," Kennedy said tranquilly. "The skipper's stooges."

"Come in, come in! It looks like old home week!"

Two other men were in the large, sumptuous living-room. One was short and fat with a hard, solid fatness, and with clipped black hair that sprouted straight up from his head like the bristles of a hairbrush. A swart dark hand held a highball. He was introduced as Mr. Kournados. The other man was thin, diminutive, with a wizened, middle-aged face.

"Tommy Birch," said Dowd in his lusty, driving voice. "He used to ride the nags. George Kournados and Tommy are going in with me on the dog track. Oh, I didn't tell you! I'm going to open the Livermore track. Well, how about some drinks? I've got some Scotch, rye, and some Bacardi."

"Just the first bottle you come to," Kennedy said.

"Rye for me," Moriarity sang out.

"Ditto," said Cohen.

MacBride said: "I'll skip it just now. What I came around about, Oak, we picked up Duke Collins in a lot in India Street, dead about an hour ago."

"Duke Collins!" exclaimed the fat man in a high unbelieving voice, spilling part of his drink.

Dowd reared back on his heels, stared incredulously at the skipper.

MacBride shrugged, said: "He had a bullet in his heart and about five bucks in his pants. I was wondering if you'd seen him around lately."

Dowd pointed to MacBride and said to Kournados: "He was wondering if we'd seen him around lately!"

"What did I say!" cried Tommy Birch in a charred voice. He pointed to Dowd, then to Kournados. "What did I say! I ask you, didn't I say—"

Dowd's hoarse, dropped voice broke in. "MacBride, I'm sorry as hell about this. Duke was in a game here today. He dropped ten grand with us."

MacBride sighed, nodded. "I thought it was something like that."

"He was down on his luck," Dowd pounded on in his heavy, husky voice, his mouth whipping dramatically from side to side. "I met him in the street several times since I got here. Then yesterday he said he'd like to get in a game. He looked drawn, kind of desperate, and I had a hunch he wouldn't make the grade. But he told me he had ten grand that said he could. He hocked a ring to get it." Dowd flung up his heavy arms, took a turn around the room, stopped, shook his head regretfully. "There's not much a guy can say, MacBride. Except that—"

"When he left here," Tommy Birch broke in, pointing to the door. "When he went out that door, I said: 'Boys, I got a funny feeling. I got a feeling that Duke is headed for the last roundup.' Those 're my exact words."

"What was it, stud?" asked MacBride.

"Stud," said Dowd.

"He was always a sucker for stud."

"We started in at about five this afternoon. At ten-thirty he was cleaned—flat."

Kennedy, lolling bonelessly in a wing chair, said over the rim of a rye highball, "I remember it was toward the end of the season at the Livermore track, about two years ago. Let me see. I was tight. No, I wasn't tight. Yes, I was. I mean about that night, late, after the pups had run, you and Duke and a couple of other guys got in a game of stud. Johnny Cruise was there, too. Sure. Johnny was running the track and the game took place in his office. I'm still a bit hazy on it, but I'll swear it was the night Duke dropped fifty grand in that stud game. It seems to me that was the game that licked him. I don't mean just that he was wiped out then. I mean that from that night on Duke never was back in the running again."

"Sure, sure; I remember that night," Dowd said. "Duke dropped fifty-five grand, to be exact."

"Let's see. There was you, Duke, Johnny Cruise, and another guy—what was his name now?..."

"You mean Joie Tell—"

"That's it, Oak. He hanged himself a month later."

"Yes, poor Joie."

"And with six thousand in the bank," said Kennedy.

"Poor little guy. I know, Kennedy. But he was morbid."

"Absolutely," nodded Kennedy. "He was a funny little guy. I remember he kept Johnny Cruise's books at the time. Queer little duck. Always worrying. He'd feel rotten if he didn't send his mother some dough each month. Always wanting to do the right thing. Always wanting to be on the level."

"Yep, Kennedy. That was Joie. That was Joie, all right."

Kennedy pushed himself up out of the chair, drained his highball and said: "I guess Duke should have known better than come up against you tonight. You were always his unlucky day, Oak."

"I guess I was. Yes, I guess I was. But I warned him. And when he came in here, and when I broke open a new deck of cards—" He turned to George Kournados, spread his big hands. "Remember, George?"

"Do I remember! Didn't I get sore right away?"

Dowd said to MacBride: "It just goes to show the state of mind Duke was in. When I broke that new deck, Duke says: 'Suppose you send down for a couple of nice brand new decks, Oak.' Well, any other guy—I'd have slapped him down!"

MacBride made a rasping, back-of the-throat sound. "I told him, I told Duke years ago he'd wind up that way! It's a game you can't beat, say what you want.... Well, I got to get along."

"Listen, Mac," Dowd said, dropping his voice. "Is there going to be any stink about this?"

MacBride shrugged. "It won't be my doing, Oak. I liked Duke a lot, but he asked for what he got. So long." He turned on his heel, headed for the door, barking, "Ike, Mory—come on."

Kennedy joined them and as they rode down in the elevator the skipper said: "Weren't you kind of riding Dowd?"

"Maybe, in a pointedly pointless way." He moved his frail, bladelike shoulders, blinked his tired eyes; but his bland, washed-out face did not change expression. As they wandered out into the lobby, he said:

"There was a little stench in the air that time—a hint, a suggestion that the stud game in which Duke dropped fifty-five grand was a little on the phoney side. Maybe yes, maybe no. Duke was a secretive guy, in many ways. When I mentioned that game a few days later, he smiled—and there was a funny look in his eyes and he made his lips very thin. But he said nothing."

Moriarity said: "If Duke suspected anything, don't you think he'd ha' been a dummy to walk into the lion's den again?"

"Maybe I'm just imagining things. Maybe he didn't know. But there was Joie Tell, who hanged himself a month after that game, for no good reason. An honest guy, a little weak, very conscientious, as weak people often are."

"But what you're driving at," MacBride thrust in, "is that maybe these two birds upstairs, along with Dowd, took Duke for a merry sleighride."

"I'm only intimating, old tomato, and you know yourself how screwy I am. But Dowd's going to open the Livermore track, and not from any moral or civic motives but because I like to bet on the doggies myself, I'd feel happier if I knew for certain that the track's to be run on the level. I don't bet on horses, I don't like cards, but I'm a weak sister when it comes to greyhounds. I see the cigar stand's closed. Just for fun, Stevie, ask the cashier if there were any charges for 310 from the cigar stand this afternoon, and what they were."

MacBride growled, "I wish you'd stop putting ideas in my head." But he went over to the cashier's wicket and in five minutes returned, saying, "Two packs of playing cards. Were you thinking that Dowd's crack about sending down for cards was a gag?"

"I was this way, that way, about it. Forget it."

They went out into the street.

"Now where's Gahagan gone?" MacBride demanded.

"Gahagan doesn't live here any more," Kennedy sang.

Cohen pointed. "Here he comes."

Gahagan came out of an all-night drug-store across the street, saw MacBride and the others grouped around the car, and broke into a run.

"What a time I had," he said, crowding in behind the wheel. "I remembered the wife asked me to bring home some iodine or witch-hazel, I couldn't remember which. So I tried to get her on the phone, and what a time, what a time. But I finally got her all right. Lucky I did, because it wasn't witch-hazel or iodine she wanted, it was carbolic acid, but she didn't want it after all account of she remembered she had some from the time I was supposed to bring home witch-hazel and brought carbolic acid instead."

"Well," said MacBride, "I'll stuff my pipe and maybe by the time we reach Headquarters I'll be able to make out what you're talking about—not that it matters."

Chapter III

THE skipper came hard-heeled into his office next day, banged his straw hat on the desk, grabbed a phone and presently was giving Mr. Flannery, editor of the *Free Press,* a sizzling piece of his mind. MacBride wanted to know precisely why Miss Gwendolyn Dorshinski, whom his daughter had beaten for the Metropolitan Singles, should have rated two pictures in the *Free Press* while his daughter had received but one. Besides, he added, Miss Gwendolyn Dorshinski had a face that only a mother could love, and a very broad-minded mother at that. Mr. Flannery explained ("Between you and me, old fellow") that Miss Dorshinski was an intimate friend of Miss Naomi Henderson, whose father, of course, was one of the owners of the *Free Press.*

The skipper blew up. "Favoritism! Rank favoritism! Okey, baby! When Henderson decides to haul off with that chariot of his and push it eighty miles an hour, tell him to come around to me with the ticket he gets. Tell him I'd love to see him!"

Hot under the collar, he refused to endorse two requests for leave of absence. He refused a rehearing of the case of one Guido Ricco, recently bounced back into harness from the plain-clothed Alien Squad. He refused to contribute to the traveling fund of the Police Glee Club on the grounds that what the department needed was fewer crooners and more policemen. For an hour he worked at his desk in a dull, relentless fury. Then he took some baking soda in a glass of water, felt better, and reversed all the foregoing decisions.

At a little before noon Kennedy meandered in with his hat beneath his arm and his pale, wayward hair a little windblown. He yawned, stretched, let his fragile, shadowy body down into an armchair and said indifferently:

"I've just been over to the *Coronet*."

"Dowd going to send flowers?"

"I didn't see Dowd."

"I had a wire from Duke's sister, Kennedy. They've got a family plot out in Topeka. I took her instructions around to the undertaker. He'll embalm the body and send it out. I'm having the suit dry-cleaned."

He brushed aside some papers over which he had been working and leaned forward on his elbows, his brows bent, one corner of his mouth yanked down and a hard, reflective light in his eyes. "You know, Kennedy—" He paused, raising a rugged forefinger, tightening the look in his eyes. "You and your insinuating around last night kind of kept me awake. I got to wondering if after all Dowd didn't take Duke for a sleighride. We know he did order a couple of decks of cards fresh from the hotel cigar stand. All right.

"Then say he met the bellhop that brought 'em up in the entrance hall. Well, he could have switched decks easily. I know marked cards ain't as easy to get away with as some guys think. But if you doubt a guy's cards are right and he sends out for new ones, ten to one you're off your guard, you wouldn't even look close. It sounds screwy, I know. But all this talk about Joie Tell and that other game—" He stopped, growled, "It's your fault, Kennedy. You start dropping ideas around and me, like a fool, I go around picking 'em up and losing sleep over 'em."

Kennedy chuckled dryly, one eyebrow lifted whimsically. "We do have fun, though, don't we, Stevie? But about the *Coronet*. I wanted to have a talk with the guy at the cigar stand but he wasn't there. He was canned yesterday. Now wait—don't break your suspenders. The management took him on two months ago, but only temporarily. That was understood. A week ago he was given a week's notice, and his time was up at midnight last night. No complaint against him. He was just let go. His hours were from three in the afternoon until midnight.

"Now we have only Dowd's word for it that Duke demanded new decks. A bad-minded bird like myself might suppose that there were no decks in the apartment at all and that Dowd, to cast away any suspicion that Duke might have of him, didn't order the cards till Duke arrived."

"Am I caught up with you, Kennedy?"

"I think you are. Our Henry Brandon, who clerked at the cigar stand from three until midnight yesterday, might have got chummy with Dowd. Sometimes clerks make mistakes in their accounts. An assistant manager at the *Coronet* was swell enough to help me. A very recent inventory showed twenty-three decks of playing cards on hand at the cigar stand. In going over the cigar stand's accounts we found this curious fact: since the inventory was taken there have been fifteen decks of cards sold, all noted down. Take fifteen from twenty-three and you have eight. Eight decks should remain. However, there remain ten decks."

MacBride was eyeing Kennedy levelly. "The answer being that somehow or other two decks got into the cigar stand's stock."

"Somehow or other," Kennedy nodded.

"And those two decks found their way to Dowd's hands."

"It's highly possible, Captain MacBride."

"It is, Mr. Kennedy."

Kennedy pushed himself up out of the chair. "As I said last night, if there's a dog track opened at Livermore, I like the greyhounds and I'm a sucker for betting on them. And I'd be mighty uneasy if I felt a long-fingered citizen was top-man there. But of course that's no concern of yours, so you'll probably—"

"Just a minute, angel child. Where does this Henry Brandon live?"

"I was on my way there. I just stopped by to pass the time of day with you—"

"Yes you did!" MacBride rose, grabbed his hat. Before putting it on, he pointed it at Kennedy, said: "If I find Dowd rode Duke to a fare-thee-well on finagled cards, that baby'll never open a track in this man's city. The gambling laws around here are lax, but I think I can find a way to make it hotter for Dowd than anything he'd like to sit down on." He slapped the hat on the side of his head. "What's the address?"

It was a three-storied frame house, one of a row of similar houses, in upper Church Street. MacBride and Kennedy got out of a police two-seater which MacBride himself had driven over. The neighborhood was quiet, decent, colorless, and the bell-button which the skipper pressed was in a small, clean vestibule. The door was opened presently by a short, stout woman, elderly, who wore horn-rimmed spectacles.

"Mr. Brandon live here, madam?" the skipper asked, lifting his hat an inch, then replacing it.

"Yes, he does."

"Will you show us where?"

She told him where the room was located and Kennedy followed him up a flight of the stairs to the second floor. MacBride rapped several times, but there was no reply, no sound behind the door. He bent down and looked at the keyhole. It was empty.

"He's out."

THEY returned to the lower hall, where the woman still lingered.

"He's out now," MacBride said, "and when he comes back I don't want you tell him anybody was here looking for him. We're from the police. You understand that, don't you, madam?"

"Oh, the police," she hastened to say, nodding.

"How long's he lived here?"

"Just about two months."

"Know anything about him?"

"Very little. He was always quiet as a mouse. I hardly ever saw him, except when he paid the rent. Weekly, you know. He didn't look very well, ever."

"Did he have many visitors?"

"I don't remember anyone ever asking for him. He was a very polite young man, but like a shadow, very timid."

"Well, remember what I told you—"

The front door opened and a man came in. MacBride was looking at the woman and saw the harried expression that appeared suddenly in her large, good-natured eyes. The skipper made a half-turn away from her, saw the man go past, caught a glimpse of the woman's eyes stumbling after him. The skipper said:

"Brandon."

The man had taken one step upward. He stopped and looked around, saying, "Yes?" curiously. He was young, tall and thin and stoop-shouldered, with a long, narrow face, very pallid, and large dark eyes.

"Brandon, I want to talk to you. Your room's as good as any place. Just a little police routine."

MacBride took him by the arm and hustled him up the staircase and Kennedy followed and in a minute they were in Brandon's small but neat bedroom. The skipper kicked the door shut with his heel, took off his hat and scaled it on to the bed. His voice was hard and direct but it was not brutal:

"Where'd you just come from, Brandon?"

Brandon looked like a man who had been spun around violently and then placed precariously on his feet again. "I—well, I was out looking for a job. I was laid off—"

"I know, I know. You were laid off yesterday. You worked two months at the *Coronet*, at the cigar counter. You finished last night and now you're out of a job. How much did you make a week?"

"Twenty dollars."

"Not much, is it? You can't do an awful lot of things on twenty bucks a week. What d' you pay here?"

"Six."

"How old are you?"

"Twenty-two."

"Got a girl?"

"I—I can't afford—"

"You'd like to afford it, though, wouldn't you?"

Brandon colored, dropped his eyes.

"Of course you would!" MacBride said heartily. "When I was your age I was a hellion, even if I say it myself, but I got married and my wife put a stop to that. You'd like a girl, though. And shows. Maybe a vacation in the country. Maybe you'd even like to get married. Or take a trip on a boat somewhere. It's the bunk living in a hall bedroom. You look like a lonesome guy. You are, aren't you?"

Brandon looked confused and his dark eyes danced agitatedly back and forth across MacBride's face.

The skipper hammered on, warmed to his work: "Suppose while you're working at the *Coronet* you meet a fellow and he's got a lot of dough. He buys butts and cigars and odds and ends, and then somehow or other, you don't know why, you tell him you won't be working there much longer. You're going to lose your job and with thousands out of work, hard up, you get to dread what lays ahead of you. It worries you day and night. Pulls you down.

"You see swell guys and dames swanking around the *Coronet* and you think of you and no job soon and it kind of gets you way down. But this fellow I'm talking about, he's nice, genial, and when you tell him you're going to be out on your uppers soon, why, he makes you a proposition. He offers you a sum of money to pull a little stunt. You don't like to do it, it goes against the grain—but in the end you come across. You're like any other guy up against it. You say you'll play ball. You take the offer."

Brandon's eyes were fixed feverishly on MacBride's face; he could not seem to tear his gaze away. His lips moved slowly. "What offer?" he croaked.

MacBride slapped his thigh. "All the foregoing hocus-pocus, son, is to show you that besides being a cop I'm a guy that can understand why people do the screwy things they do. You're no crook. I'll bet you wouldn't hurt a fly. But you were up against it, you caught a chance to grab yourself some rainbow and you grabbed it. Now weren't those cards you sent up to 310 yesterday afternoon finagled?"

Brandon gulped and his face twisted out of shape.

The skipper dropped his voice to a tone of familiarity: "How much did you get out of it, son?"

"I—I didn't do anything! I—"

"Son, don't be a horse's neck. Where'd you look for work this morning?"

"I went—well, several places."

"Name them."

"I can't remember."

"Name one."

Brandon grimaced.

Kennedy said, "Suggest a bank."

Brandon spun around, his mouth flying open, soundless.

MacBride grabbed him. There was a brief flurry and then the skipper had Brandon's wallet. The youth groaned and slumped to the bed.

"Okey," said MacBride, holding up a white slip. "Here it is. A receipt for a safe-deposit box, dated today. The South Side Trust Company."

They took Brandon over to the bank. The youth was stunned and moved in a dull stupor, and when he came out of the vault where the safe-deposit boxes were located, his feet dragged as though booted with lead and sweat stood out on his forehead. He gave MacBride a long brown envelope, and from it the skipper extracted four five-hundred-dollar bills.

He muttered, "So you sent two finagled decks of cards up to 310, son?"

Brandon, staring dully at the floor, nodded. Then he lifted his head. His eyes rolled. MacBride caught him as he fainted and carrying him outside, placed him in the two-seater.

"Listen, Kennedy," the skipper said. "Drive him over to Headquarters, will you? The air'll fix him. Drive him over and stay with him in my office. I won't be long. If he's still loggy when you get there, there's a bottle of brandy in the lower right-hand desk drawer."

"Where are you going?"

"You wouldn't have any doubts about where I'm going, would you, Kennedy?"

Chapter IV

OAKLEY DOWD opened the door of 310. He was dressed in a becoming sports suit of some rough, grayish material.

"Oh, hello, Mac!" he said in his heavy, gusty voice. "We just got in. We were out going over the dog track. It was a great day, a great day! Come in, come in. You're just in time for a cocktail."

"Thanks. I don't drink during the day."

"Well, well," said George Kournados in his high voice, "glad to see you, Captain MacBride. We were just out—"

"The country," said MacBride dourly. "Oak just told me."

Tommy Birch was working with a big cocktail shaker. "It won't be long now, Captain, till puppies will run at Livermore."

Dowd flung up an arm. "Get the skipper a cigar, Tommy. I know he likes cigars."

"Skip the cigar, too," said MacBride.

"Well, you'll surely join us in lunch, Mac. Tommy, call room service and—"

"And skip lunch," MacBride growled. "In fact, skip all this boloney, Oak." He banged his hat down on a table and whipped out: "If you guys think you're going to open that track, or do any other kind of opening around here, you're crazy!"

A shadow leaped out upon Dowd's ridged brow and he said: "What's got in your hair since I last saw you?"

Tommy Birch, who wore gray slacks and a tweed sack coat, set down the cocktail shaker and wiped his hands. Then he clapped them. "I recommend a round of drinks. Come on, Captain MacBride, break down to a liquid diet."

"Shut up!" Dowd's husky voice ripped out. "I want to hear what got in MacBride's hair." He pivoted heavily, thrust his big hands into his coat pockets and drilled the skipper with an aggressive, searching glare. "So we're not going to open the dog track?"

"You're not only not going to open the dog track, Oak. You're not going to do a lot of things. I'm even going to see what the chances are of getting you tossed in the can."

Dowd's glare was steady, unwavering. "For why?" he grunted.

"Look here, Oak. It was Duke's own funeral when he walked in here. I'm not crabbing about that. I knew he had it coming to him some day. That's all okey. But what I can't understand is a supposedly big shot like you, when Duke was trying for a comeback, deliberately cutting corners on him, ribbing him for his last cent and letting him walk out of here practically knowing he'd do the dutch. I don't know. Maybe I'm thick. Maybe I've been wrong all my life giving a guy a break when I had him down. Maybe—"

"Now wait a minute," Dowd broke in harshly. "Will you tell me what you're beefing about?"

"The marked cards, dummy, that you planted with the guy downstairs at the cigar stand and paid him to send up when you ordered them! We picked up the kid a little while ago, found he'd just planted two grand in a safe-deposit box, and he passed out with fright at the bank. I put him in the car and Kennedy ran him over to Headquarters."

A stupid, glassy look came into Dowd's eyes. He raised a hand, pulled it across his forehead. Tommy Birch was regarding him with squinted eyes. George Kournados was dabbing at his throat with a handkerchief, holding his chin way up, his eyes very wide. Dowd took a few heavy steps, dropped to a chair. He didn't seem to be able to say anything. He moved a hand in an aimless, meaningless gesture, then let it flop back heavily to his knee. He looked winded, sapped. And then he growled in a thick, halting voice:

"Seems to be—nothing I can—say."

MacBride clipped, "I'll want a statement for the records. You three guys get your hats and we'll go over to Headquarters where there's a stenographer. We'll take your statements and the kid's at the same time."

Dowd grunted. "Okey. You run along. We'll be over in half an hour. I'm expecting a phone call from Chicago any minute and—"

The telephone bell jangled and MacBride, who was nearest, scooped up the instrument in his left hand, said into the mouthpiece, "Hello.... Oh, Kennedy.... Of course it's MacBride.... What's that?... *What!*... You say that Dowd—"

The skipper flung the instrument violently away, threw himself to his knees as Dowd's gun exploded. His own gun came out and upward in one swift, incalculable movement. It roared twice. The walls of the room seemed to bulge and snap back into place again, vibrating.

Chapter V

WHEN Moriarity and Cohen came on duty that afternoon, the skipper, sitting at his desk, said, "Did you guys miss the time of your life today! Boy, did you!"

"Yeah!" said Moriarity. "Bettdecken was just saying—"

"There I was stewing around in Dowd's apartment, talking my nut off and wanting Dowd and his pals to come over here so I could get their statements. Dowd tells me to go along and he'll be over in half an hour. He's waiting for a phone call. And me like a fathead, I'm ready to fall for it. I thought the guy was just knocked glassy because we found out he'd finagled Duke in that card game. But how was I to know?

"So the phone rings and I grab it and it's Kennedy, over here with the lad, telling me—"

"That's what Bettdecken said," Ike Cohen interrupted.

MacBride leaned forward. "Dowd knew what that call was about. The minute I mentioned Kennedy's name, Dowd knew. The other two knew but they couldn't seem to do anything about it but look sick. But Dowd goes for his gun and both Captain and Mrs. MacBride are thankful he's a lousy shot. I ducked and went to town on him.

"It was my own fault in the first place. I went off half-cocked with the kid Brandon. He thought I was talking about Duke all the time. But Kennedy didn't get it straight until the kid got here with him and then Kennedy called me up.

"This Brandon used to know Duke over at the *State Hotel*. They got to know each other quite well and when the kid got the job at the *Coronet,* he moved nearer. Duke got pretty desperate—but it was more a matter of revenge than anything else. He'd bided his time a long while to get back at Dowd. He told Brandon the whole story— about how Dowd had framed him in that game at the Livermore track and how Joie Tell had committed suicide because he was in on the deal that trimmed Duke that night.

"So Duke arranged a game with Dowd and his pals at the hotel and he planted two marked decks with Brandon and when an order came down from 310, Brandon sent up the marked cards. Dowd and Kournados and Tommy Birch were taken over like you take a glass of water. They never in the world thought that those cards, coming up fresh from the hotel cigar stand, were phoneyed. So Duke took them for seventy-eight grand—wiped them out.

"But these guys were tough. And Dowd followed Duke out of the hotel. He saw Duke stop at the cigar counter to buy a pack of butts, but he didn't see Duke pass the kid two thousand dollars. Then Duke went out the side way and Dowd followed him, caught up with him half a block away and put a gun on him. He walked Duke clean to India Street, took his gun away from him and then let him have it muzzle-first and took back all the money. He went back to the hotel, in the side way and up the stairway. The other two muggs would have sworn up and down that he didn't leave the apartment after Duke left."

Moriarity said: "So then all that stuff Kennedy was saying about Joie Tell and the crooked game at Livermore—"

"Was true!" MacBride interrupted. "Duke was out for revenge and that'll make a swell story in the papers. He'd never peeped about that game. He bided his time. And by not peeping, he threw Dowd off his guard. And then he nailed him."

"And Dowd couldn't take it," Cohen nodded.

"Listen, Ike," said the skipper, leaning forward. "None of those guys can take it when they get desperate. Dowd couldn't take it. Neither could Duke; it didn't matter to Duke that he dragged in that poor kid at the *Coronet.* Man and boy I've known Duke for over forty years. A swell guy. But he was a rat, too. I remember I busted his nose for chiseling at marbles."

It's a Gag

Kennedy is the bait to lure killers into the open so that MacBride may follow the trail.

Chapter I

IT was ten past midnight at the *Athens Grill*. Miklos Sanaponolis was counting cash back of the cigar case. He was a fussy-looking little squat man, with small feet and small, plump hands, a round doll's head, shell-like ears and excitable brown eyes. His clothes were dark and tight and good and his *Grill* had a reputation. From time to time, while he counted cash, he raised and tossed a pettish look towards a booth halfway down the room, where a haphazard altercation was going on between a waiter and a woman customer.

Kennedy, the newshawk, was down at the end of the room trying to catch his waiter's eye, but his waiter had his eye on the waiter who was embroiled in the argument. The other waiters had gone home. Kennedy's hair looked like windblown straw, his thin, pale, washed-out face looked genial in a sleepy, good-natured way. He had tucked away some Welsh-rarebit and a couple of bottles of ale and it was in his mind to have another bottle of ale and then pull a fast one by going home to bed. When Sanaponolis joined the argument, backed up by the second waiter, Kennedy let slide the idea of a third bottle. He got to his feet, put on his faded fedora, got achingly into his threadbare topcoat.

He approached the disturbance, hiccoughing mildly behind a hand, and tapped his waiter on the shoulder. There was no use. The waiter was intensely interested in what was going on. Kennedy wanted simply to pay his check, go out, home. But he was not a forceful character ordinarily, and he teetered back on his heels, scratched his ear.

Then suddenly Sanaponolis pivoted, his little red mouth set, his short arm leveling towards the door, his stern brown eyes fixed on one of the waiters.

"Nicholas," he said, "go getting the polissman on the bitt!"

"Hoke," said Kennedy's waiter.

"Now hold on," said Kennedy, fumbling at Nick's elbow. "Please, before you get a gallery in here, how's to break this five spot and take out what I owe you? Come, like a good Grecian fellow."

"First, Nicholas," insisted Sanaponolis, "getting in a hurry the poliss!"

"Oh, please!" the woman begged.

Kennedy blinked.

She was a brunette with a neat velour tricorne lopped over one deftly penciled eyebrow. Her coat was mink and revealed nothing of her throat. She looked harried, desperate, high-colored. Her eyes were dark and luminous, her nose straight, her mouth full and no redder than it should have been.

"Please—please!"

"Nicholas!" squeaked Sanaponolis. "Doing as I am told you!"

"Axcuse me, pliss," Nicholas said to Kennedy, backing up, getting set to turn and dash to the door. "I'll being back in wan second, hokey—"

"Hold it," said Kennedy; and to Sanaponolis: "What's eating you, Mike? If you draw a copper in off his beat for something petty, he'll get sore—"

The woman cried explanatorily: "I'm sorry—sorry! I brought the

wrong purse along! I didn't realize it until just now—until I wanted to pay my bill!"

"Ha!" laughed Sanaponolis.

"It's true!" she cried, striking the table. "Do you think I'd hold you up for two dollars?"

"My God!" groaned Kennedy. He thrust his five-dollar bill at Sanaponolis. "Take hers out and mine, Mike."

"Pliss, Mr. Kennedy—"

"Go ahead."

"Oh, thank you, thank you!" the woman said.

Kennedy looked at her. "I'll see you home. I can't afford to toss two bucks away, so I'll see you home and you can give it back to me."

"Of course! I mean to!"

Kennedy wore a lopsided grin as Sanaponolis headed for the cash counter. "Mike's just easily excited," he said.

The woman had risen. "I can't tell you how I appreciate it. That terrible man would have called in the whole Police Department."

Kennedy picked up his change at the counter and followed the woman into the street. The wind, coming bitter and raw down Cherry Street, struck him, knifed him, and he shivered in his inadequate clothing, digging his hands in his overcoat pockets, hunching his frail

shoulders, so that he looked like a scarecrow.

"What's it, a cab?" he said.

"We really can walk. I live only four blocks away."

He was looking down at her feet and his eyes narrowed; he raised them briefly, fleetingly to her face. Her color was still high, her voice quick, uncertain, breathlessly dipped. Then they were walking. He did not offer his arm. They turned into Flint Street and climbed the grade, the wind behind them. Kennedy shivered as the cold bit into the small of his back. The street was empty, dark, the stone houses standing in cold, rigid formation, a distant street light clear and cool. The woman coughed, making echoes that seemed to go far away.

"Right here," she said, and led the way into the small, warm lounge of an apartment house. The dry, warm air encompassed Kennedy. "Do you mind waiting here a moment?" she asked. "I'm sorry I can't ask you up."

"I'll wait," he said.

She got in an automatic elevator and he saw by the indicator that it took her to the third floor. He sat down in a mohair divan, content that it was warm here, and lit a cigarette. The lights were dim and there was a radio playing, the strong movement of the wind outdoors. His eyelids drooped and the cigarette, hanging from his lips, sent skeins of smoke about his head. His head nodded, his chin sinking to his chest. He roused himself with a start, looked around. He rose, stretched, ambled up and down, pausing at times to listen at the elevator shaft and at the foot of the staircase. Then he returned to the divan.

A couple came in, buttoned the elevator car to the lobby floor, took it up. It came down a minute later and deposited two girls and a man who went out laughing over some joke. A man came down the staircase, turned up his coat collar, crossed the lobby and disappeared into the street. Two girls came in several minutes later and rose in the elevator.

Kennedy got up, looked at his watch. He had waited half an hour. He shrugged, chuckled ruefully. "Horse on me," he said. He looked aloft, muttered with smiling irony, "So I'm a Goodtime Charley, am I? Okey, sister. Okey." He saluted the ceiling. "Maybe Mike Sanaponolis was right. Discerning, these Greeks."

He made his way into the street, buckling against the bitter drive of the wind. As he headed towards the distant lights of State Street, he ruminated on the curious fact that the woman had worn no stockings and that she had worn pale blue bedroom mules, each with a small heel strap. Also, he seemed to recall, the skirt of the gown which showed below the bottom of her coat appeared very much like a blue silk, lace-trimmed dressing-gown.

His teeth chattered. He had a feeling that his cold bones were knocking together. It was too cold to go all the way home without a little stimulating stop-over. Miro's turned up conveniently on his way and he ordered rye straight and one drink led to another but he finally got home at three.

"You gotta hand it to Mike Sanipop—Sanipop—Sanilopopop— Well, anyhow, it's not the two bucks, it's the principle of the thing. No!" he amended, tossing his hat across the room. "I'm damned if it is! It's the two bucks!"

Chapter II

THE morning was bright, clear, windy. Tattered clouds hiked across the city and the huge weathervane atop the City Hall shivered and whanged. Newspapers sailed the gusty streets and business-bound pedestrians bucked head-on into the wind or went skittering before it. The harbor was deep blue, choppy. The fruit express went through the West Yards under a full head of steam. Ragged newsboys drummed cold feet on cold pavements, their faces beet-red, their hands chapped. Life in the great city moved at the double.

Up Flint Street there was trouble. The wind had tossed about quick, wondering whispers. Cops going in or coming out of that graystone doorway. Cars arriving. Men with cameras or tripods. A red auto truck with brass fittings. Men in white. A long black touring car, curtained, with the chromium-plated letters P.D. between its headlights. This was no way to begin a day.

The corridors in that seven-story building were busy with excitement. All the windows in apartment 302 were open wide, the wind kiting white curtains. The third-floor corridor was busy as a busy street, and MacBride, coming to the doorway, blew his nose and said angrily to a uniformed policeman:

"Vogler, I thought I told you to clear this hall up! Do I have to do everything myself around here?"

"I been tryin', I been tryin'—"

"A guy'd think this was a Midway or something. Come on, you folks, break it up, break it up. Vogler—come on, Vogler, get 'em moving, get 'em moving. Shoo! Shoo!" he blew out, waving his hands.

"I happen to live here!" argued a large, haughty woman.

"All right, madam—all right," the skipper said. "But you don't live in the hall."

"Of course I don't! It so happens that I've been trying to get into 303 for the past five minutes but this dumb cluck of a policeman keeps pushing me back."

"Vogler!" barked MacBride. "Let the lady in her place!"

Vogler stepped aside, muttering under his breath: "And I ain't a dumb cluck."

The woman said from the doorway of 303: "I just called you that, young man, because I don't use profanity in public." She slammed shut the door.

Two men came out of 302 with an inhalator and one snapped: "She don't need an inhalator. She needs a casket."

The living-room of 302 was crowded and the police photographer was getting shots of the bedroom. Half a dozen uniformed cops and a sergeant were there from the local precinct. Rube Wilson, the assistant district attorney, was talking rapidly to Jacobs, the medical office man, who stood with his sleeves rolled up. The apartment house manager, a gaunt, middle-aged man named Kramer, was polishing his spectacles. A couple of newshawks and two news photographers were ganged around the precinct sergeant. Moriarity was going through a desk and Cohen was in the kitchenette where the woman lay.

The dead man was in the bedroom, shot twice through the heart with a .22 automatic. Rube Wilson had the gun and Moriarity had found a box of Super-X long-rifle cartridges similar to those remaining in the pistol. They were lubaloy coated bullets. The dead man was fully dressed. He was about forty, tall and slender.

The woman, who had died by the gas route, was dressed in a nightgown and a pale blue dressing-gown. The news photographers wanted a shot at her but the skipper had put his thumbs down on that. No pictures of any kind.

"Now you fellows," he said to the newsmen and the photographers, "give us a break and clear out. Everything's balled up here. Go outside. There's no use hanging around, because there's no news yet and there won't be any pictures."

"When the Judge's secretary is found dead, Captain, that's news."

"Okey, okey. She's dead—and dead, she's news. But there's no Department hand-out yet. Now do as I tell you—beat it. When I get things straightened out, I'll give you a hand-out. I don't know who let you in, in the first place—"

"I did," put in Rube Wilson, the assistant D.A. "What are you giving the boys the bum's rush for?"

"Room—room, I got to have room here. Besides, if you don't keep an eye on these birds, before you know it they break out the cameras. Keep your oar out of my business, Rube. This is a police case right now and you're here as an observer."

"You trying to tell me my business?"

"No. Show you your place."

"Go air yourself."

"Listen, Rube. I've got no time to argue with you." He went past the slim, dapper D.A.'s man and ran into Jacobs, who was rolling down his sleeves.

Jacobs said: "The woman, well, she's been dead about nine hours. Gas killed her. She could have got the bump on her head from a fall while she was taking the gas. That porcelain stool was knocked over in the kitchen. That air-vent in the kitchen would have taken a certain amount of the gas out, but all the jets were on and there was plenty to kill her. The guy, of course, died instantly from those shots."

Moriarity came over to say: "Yup, it's her gun. Here's a license to carry it. The numbers tally. She let him have the two shots, I guess, and then she got cold feet about using the gun on herself, so she took gas. It's often the way these little house parties break up."

"What I can't figure out," said MacBride, rubbing the back of his neck, "is how nobody in this house heard those shots. You sure you asked all around?"

"I asked in ten apartments, all the ones around this one, above and below. Nobody heard the shots. If, as Doc here says, they're dead about nine hours, that'd mean the fireworks went off around midnight. Some of the people I asked were up at that time—up until one or half-past. I asked if maybe they heard something they thought was backfiring. But no, they didn't. No reports at all."

MacBride shook his head, growled: "I can't believe it. I mean, I can't believe two shots'd go off in here at that hour of the night, when the streets are quiet, and nobody hear them. How about radios? Were there any radios playing?"

"Yes. Yup, there was. People in 410 heard a radio playing."

"Even so," MacBride said, "you'd hear the shots above that, unless they were muffled somehow. But apparently this woman just took two shots at him—and if so, then they should have been heard." He crossed the room to where Kramer, the house manager, was standing. "Mr. Kramer, who reported to you about smelling gas?"

"No one. I didn't say anyone did. I smelled it myself. Coming along the corridor."

"And what time was that?"

"At eight—maybe a few minutes past eight. I was coming along the corridor. I smelled it."

MacBride nodded towards the bedroom. "Did you get a good look at the dead man?"

"Oh, goodness, do I have to look again? It upsets my—"

"I mean, you saw him, didn't you?"

"Yes, I saw him."

"Ever see him before—either in here or in the halls?"

"Never. I never said I did."

"Nobody's saying you did, Mr. Kramer. Can't I ask? Am I going to get anywhere if I don't ask questions?"

"Just about as far," said Rube Wilson on his way past.

MacBride turned after him but Patrolman Vogler was motioning from the doorway. "Cap'n," said the patrolman, "here's a lady says she seen a bum hangin' around the lobby last night."

"Madam?" prompted MacBride.

She was young, in her early twenties. "That is, I mean," she said, "when I came in with Sister, it was about half-past twelve, I saw a man sitting on the divan in the lounge. He had an old gray hat pulled down on his head and his overcoat, well, the collar was turned way up. He looked huddled in it, as if he was trying to hide his face. I didn't look close. That's all I saw. He looked like a tramp or something."

"You live here?"

"Yes. I live with my sister and brother-in-law, we live in 605, upstairs. Georgia Cavlin's my name. My brother-in-law is Homer Staffey; he is, you know, with the Acme Fertilizer Company, since Lord knows when, and I'm a manicurist. I do manicuring at the *Hotel Angley*. A tramp, I think, he was."

"Do you think you'd recognize him again?"

"If I seen him, yes. And if he was dressed the same, yes. I'd do anything to help."

MacBride cracked a dry smile. "Thanks very much, Miss Cavlin. I'll buzz you if I want you."

She flounced away and Vogler said under his breath, out of the side of his mouth: "I t'ink she's nuts, I t'ink, between I and you, Cap'n."

Moriarity called out: "Hey, look what I found. I found this down alongside the cushion in that armchair."

"What is it?" asked MacBride.

"A fountain pen."

"Any initials on it?"

"Lemme see. Yup. Yeah, there is. 'O.T.S.' Nice pen too. Maybe it belonged to the dead guy."

"Lemme see that!" Rube Wilson snapped. His small, hard jaw jutted as he rapped his heels across the room, snatched the pen from Moriarity's hand. He held it up, squinted at the initials, then took it over to a window, to peer closer. MacBride went over and stood alongside him. The skipper folded his long, bony arms on his chest, muttered under his breath:

"Judge O.T. Stillson?"

"What d' you think?"

"Well, she worked for him, and you don't find guys with those initials all over Christendom. I don't like the look of this whole thing, Rube. I think there's dynamite behind it or ahead of it somewhere." He dropped his voice still lower: "On the surface here it looks like the gal took a roundhouse at the guy and then did the Dutch herself, but I got to be convinced. She was Ozzie Stillson's confidential secretary and she knew a lot—"

"Steve," yelled Jacobs.

"Yeah?" MacBride left Rube Wilson and crossed the room towards the medical office man.

"I'm running along, Steve," Jacobs said. "Haven't had breakfast yet. I'll see the autopsy on the bodies is done right off the bat. Better call the morgue wagon. I'll see you—"

The explosion rocked the room. MacBride was thrown against Jacobs and both men crashed into Kramer, the house manager. One of the cops dived head-on into the wall and another stood rooted, his mouth wide open, a stupid look on his face. Screams burst in the hallway.

The skipper, spinning, stopped with his back against the wall. His face was gray-white, his lips hueless. He saw Rube Wilson draped over a chair. The front of Rube's clothing was gone and his body was streaked with red, you could not tell quite what his face looked like.

"I seen him," choked Moriarity. "I seen him open—that—pen he was holding. It was the pen did it. I seen him as he was opening it. It stuck kind of. He gave it a little yank— Good God, there ain't a hell of a lot left of Rube!" He shuddered, turned a shade more pallid. "Good cripes, and if he hadn't ha' took it away from me, I'd opened the thing myself!"

Jacobs said in a jittery voice: "Five gets anybody ten if Rube ever moves again." He gulped, turning yellow. "Did I say breakfast?…"

Chapter III

KENNEDY got up at eight-thirty that morning. Only half awake, he dressed and still only half awake, he left his Hallam Street rooming-house, groaning as the bright morning sunlight hit his eyes and the brisk wind belabored his body. The Brown Coffee Pot was nearby, and he sat at the long counter, still bleary-eyed with sleep, and drank three steaming cups of black coffee. His hat was unbecomingly turned up in front, down in back, and the collar of his jacket protruded above the collar of his topcoat. He ate a roll and a baked apple and meandered out into the cold again, pausing once to stare wistfully at a poster extolling the charms of Southern California.

When he drifted sleepily into the *Free Press* office, Flannery said down the length of a nickel cigar: "Shoot over to 847 Flint Street, Kennedy. Stupack's on it, but he's green, you know. See no tricks are missed."

Kennedy sat on the steam radiator. "Right now, you mean?"

"Instanter," Flannery clipped, writing furiously. "They go bang-bang-bang over there. First what looks like a crime of passion and remorse and then Rube Wilson gets his puss blown off. Tough. The guy had a swell career ahead of him, even though he'd pulled a fox pass or two in his time."

"As I remember," Kennedy nodded. "As a matter of fact, you and Rube tried to gang on me once—"

"In fun, Kennedy, in fun. Get going, get going. This is the biggest news break in months. Ozzie Stillson's secretary gassed. An as yet unidentified guy apparently knocked off by the gal. Then Rube Wilson— Breeze, Kennedy. The repercussions of this are going to be far-reaching, or I'm a horse's neck."

"Horse's neck? My, you're a champion of under-statement!"

"Get!"

Kennedy caught a cab in front of the *Free Press* building, closed all the windows as the driver geared off. He was still only partially awake, lounging with his hands thrust in his topcoat pockets, taking no interest in the morning scene. When the cab finally stopped, he found himself in the center of a shoving, murmurous mob. He saw many cars drawn up, an ambulance, a couple of internes, policemen shouting and gesticulating.

He groped his way through the mob, squeezed into the lobby and ran into young Stupack. Stupack said:

"No use, Kennedy. MacBride won't let us in."

"Where's it at?"

"Up in 302—but honest, Kennedy, there's no use."

Kennedy pushed on his way, pressed and twisted on his way up the staircase. He got as far as the second-floor corridor, and here a young copper blocked him.

"You go down where you came from, buddy!"

"I want to see Captain MacBride. I'm a close friend."

"Gag me, huh? Gag me? No guy gets up—"

A shrill scream cut the copper short and he wheeled around. Miss Georgia Cavlin was staring wide-eyed, pointing. Horror was in her face. She was pointing at Kennedy.

"Officer!" she cried. "Grab him! He's the tramp! He's a murderer! Grab him! I seen him!"

The cop spun back on Kennedy.

Kennedy said: "She has illusions of grandeur, brother."

"Officer, arrest that man!"

The cop grabbed Kennedy and lifted him off his feet.

"Leggo!" Kennedy complained "You'll break my coat!"

"I'll break your coat? I'll break your jaw!" He shook Kennedy violently. "Resist an officer, will you? Take that!" He cracked Kennedy on the head with his nightstick.

This served to make Kennedy wide awake and he said, "Listen to me, flatfoot. You bop me again and I'll make your life miserable for years to come."

"I'm making your life miserable right now, heel!"

He hoisted Kennedy through the crowd, using his nightstick to jab the reporter in the small of the back. Kennedy winced, groaned, squirmed. The girl was explaining in a high-pitched voice to a crowd of eager listeners. She had seen the tramp in the lobby. This was the tramp. Didn't he look vicious? Didn't everybody hear the way he talked to that nice, handsome policeman?

Kennedy was dragged, pushed and cuffed on the way up to the third floor. He looked a little dizzy now, and his tie had become undone, his hat had been smashed down over his ears. He didn't know whether or not his arms were still intact. He caught a glimpse of the number 302 on a door and then the door was opened and he was walloped into a crowded room.

"This," said the young copper, "is the tramp that young lady seen here last night."

Kennedy still looked dizzy. He was stumbling, but his jaw was set. Kennedy set his jaw very seldom. As a rule, he let time and events carry him along willy-nilly. But his jaw was set now, and before anyone knew what he was about, he scooped up a pedestal smoke-stand and broke it over the young copper's head.

"Kennedy!" barked MacBride, rushing to him.

The young copper collapsed.

"With bricks I could have done a better job," panted Kennedy.

"You can't do that!" ripped out MacBride.

"What do you mean, I can't? With the guy conked out, it looks as though I can. Can and did, Skipperino!"

The girl was at the door again, yipping: "Mr. Captain, that's the man! I swear it! I seen him in the lobby last night—"

Kennedy sighed. "These dames that try to make the front page usually wind up in the funnies. What's she stewing about, Stevie?"

MacBride had his fists planted on his hip-bones. "The young lady says you were in the lobby downstairs last night at around midnight, when these deaths occurred. She says you were trying to conceal—"

"I was here?" Kennedy asked curiously.

"That's what she says. Downstairs. Do you deny it?"

"Why should I deny it? How do I know where I am all the time? Was this the place I was in? Hell, I might have been—"

He stopped short, blinked, stood back on his heels. With his topcoat pulled lopsided and his hat crushed down over his ears, he looked more like a scarecrow than ever. But he was blinking, blinking his eyes fast. He moved towards the open door of the kitchenette, leaned in the doorway, stared down at the dead woman on the floor. He frowned. Mockery went out of his face slowly. He looked almost grave, but not too much so. His eyes steadied. He turned around, said:

"Who is she, Steve?"

"Edna McKie. Ozzie Stillson's secretary."

Kennedy's eyes drooped, slid around the room. "Sure," he said. "I was downstairs last night."

"What did I tell you!" exclaimed Miss Georgia Cavlin.

Kennedy said, "Are you a professional stooge, young lady?"

"You can't talk to me like that! I'll get my brother-in-law Homer—"

"Ah," said Kennedy, "she has a brother-in-law, too!"

MacBride snapped: "Cut it out, Kennedy!" He strode to the door. "Miss Cavlin, I'll see you later. Pardon me." He closed the door, swiveled. His eyes were steady, grave, hard, his voice low and blunt. "Now what do you know about this, Kennedy?"

"Well," said Kennedy, "first of all, Edna McKie owes me two bucks, but I'm no cad—I'll skip that."

Chapter IV

THE death of Edna McKie was something. The death of Reuben Wilson was something, too. The circumstances, according to one editorial writer, had about them something distinctly macabre. It was not the usual case of death and consequences. It was not open and shut. Nor was it cut and dried, even to a cynic.

For five years Edna McKie had been associated with Judge O.T. Stillson. Ozzie Stillson. He had not been on the bench for ten years. He swung a much more vital, potent gavel, as boss of the state political machine. He made no speeches, you never found his name on sponsored bills. But he pressed political buttons, he cracked the state-wide whip. Ozzie Stillson was a legendary figure to many a man in the street. Orrin Taylor Stillson, the man behind the political gun.

Kennedy could have filled a book with all he knew about the ins and outs of the state and metropolitan regime. But Kennedy did not write books. It was too much trouble and if he should put down in the book the things he suspected, his life, he knew, would not be worth powder to blow it to hell. He was no uplifter, he had no martyr's urge. Life was pretty good, even when it was pretty bad, and he somehow muddled along.

MacBride was stuffing his caked old brier with coarse, strong tobacco. The morning sun poured into his office. Kennedy was sitting on the desk, his feet dangling.

The skipper spat smoke from a corner of his mouth, said, "And you're sure she had on bedroom slippers and a nightgown?"

"I saw the slippers, Stevie. Not the nightgown. I did see the dressing-gown. I wasn't sure then, but when I saw it in her apartment this morning, I knew it was a dressing-gown. And she didn't have stockings on."

MacBride stared at the bowl of his pipe. "What would you make out o' that, Kennedy?"

Kennedy shrugged. "I don't know. As a rule, women don't chuck a fur coat over their night clothes and go out for a sandwich and a couple of drinks. Then she didn't have any dough along. The whole set-up, if you want my opinion, leads me to believe that she left her apartment in a hurry. I checked up with the Greek and he says she came in his restaurant about fifteen past eleven. He recalled that she looked excited when she came in. So if he's not handing me a line, and I don't think he would, that checks up with my theory that she left her apartment under steam. And why?

"Well, maybe she got a disturbing phone call—but you checked up on phone calls and found out that there were none, to or from, last night. All right. Try this angle. Somebody was there and she had an argument with him and got in a huff and slammed out. I remember when I walked home with her, she was nervous. That might have come from the brawl with the Greek, but when she asked me to wait in the lobby, I remember a funny look in her eyes. Then let's say the guy was still there—the guy you found croaked—when she went up to get the two bucks. From that point on, anything could have happened."

MacBride took his pipe from his mouth, leveled the stem at Kennedy. "Fella, I still don't see how those shots could have been fired without being heard. You would have heard them. Did you hear a radio playing?"

"Yes, I did. Pretty loud. I figured it was a party. But I'd still have heard shots."

"Yet Doc Jacobs swears the guy was shot around that time. And it's her gun. She had a bump on her forehead, but she could have got that while flopping around when the gas was taking her. That's logical enough. But the shots don't fit in." He waved his pipe, said doggedly: "Kennedy, it looks screwy to me! I don't believe she knocked that guy off!"

Kennedy said: "While I was in the lobby, the people that came in or went out—all of them used the elevator but one. This one came down the staircase, turned up his coat collar and left. If a fellow commits a crime in a building like that—if he takes an elevator down, there's no telling who'll be at the bottom when the elevator door opens. Taking the stairway, he can do better."

"What did he look like, Kennedy?"

"That's by me, old tomato. Tall and in dark clothes—that's all I remember. As to his face, no can do." He got off the desk, smiled crookedly. "But I feel like having some fun. It's going to appear in the papers that I got a good look at the guy, that I'll be able to identify him. Directly that appears, old horse, you're going to have to supply me with a bodyguard. Not to pal with me, but to cover me. Pick some fast, good shots. It will also appear in the newspapers that I had a long chat with Edna McKie but that details in *re* that chat are police secrets for the nonce."

MacBride said in a low voice: "Kennedy, don't be a fool."

"Calm yourself. This thing wasn't just frustrated love. This thing goes deeper."

"Deeper? How?" the skipper asked, putting his pipe between his teeth, shuttering one eye.

"Who owned that explosive fountain pen? Why were Ozzie Stillson's initials on it? Of course, we're assuming they were Ozzie Stillson's initials. What's the sense in assuming they weren't, when you find it more interesting to assume they were? You're sure they were O.T.S., Stevie?"

"Positive. Ask Moriarity. Mory found the pen." He rubbed his jaw. "I wish to hell we knew who the dead guy was. Ike Cohen's working on it now. There were no labels in his clothes and he didn't carry a wallet—or if he had one, it's gone. But they got a pretty good picture of him. One of the photographers propped up his body and the other guy snapped it. I hope something comes of it."

The door opened and Ike Cohen came in, tossed a butt into a cuspidor and said: "You ask me, Cap, and I'd say it was a set-up. Now look. I took the guy's clothes around to a friend of mine who's a good tailor. Well, look at this suit I have on. Just an example. He makes 'em for me at cost. But about what I began about: I took the stiff's suit and overcoat over to Louie and Louie goes over them and says the labels were taken out. He says just recently. He says there was a label taken out from the neck of the overcoat and from the inside pocket. The same thing with the guy's suit. And get this: Louie claims it was done recently because some shreds are still there where they took off the labels and there's a few tiny slices, like a guy used a razor blade to cut the stitches. The clothes were ready-made but they were very expensive, Louie says. And they're quite new. And by the cut and the material of the overcoat, he knows the brand. It's called Oxmoore-Tex. The overcoat, Louie says, is newer than the suit."

"That brand sold in this town?"

"Yes. I was coming to it. It's sold exclusive at Hoyt's, according to Louie."

MacBride said: "It could have been bought in any number of cities, but take the coat over to Hoyt's, Ike, and see if you can turn up anything."

Ike went out and Kennedy said: "What about Ozzie? Has he been in yet?"

"No." MacBride looked at his watch. "I phoned first thing this morning and they said he was up at Lake Moar, ice-fishing. They long-distanced him and he's on his way down."

"Who was with him?"

"I don't know. Couple of his crowd, I guess."

Kennedy said: "Ever meet his wife?"

"Nope, never have."

"You ought to some time. She's got everything and some guys maintain she's not close-fisted."

"What do you mean, bozo?"

"Hell. Skip it."

The extras were on the streets. The kids were hawking.

Chapter V

HE was dressed in rough, burry tweeds and an old Burberry and he did not bother to take off the Burberry but let his big frame land in the upholstered chair and flopped his big palms on the broad, heavy desk. His office was large, oak-paneled, and all the furniture was heavy, out-of-date but well-preserved. His face was massive, rugged, with a tell-tale looseness of skin only beneath his jaw; but the jaw itself was strong and there seemed no great flabbiness about him anywhere. His hair was white, crisp, close-cropped. Winded a bit, he stared at his big knuckles with fixed, preoccupied eyes.

"This is terrible, MacBride," he said. "I can hardly believe it's true. Edna was such a brick. I'd have trusted her with anything I owned."

The skipper said: "Your confidential secretary, wasn't she?"

"Yes."

"Knew a lot you knew, huh?"

Ozzie Stillson nodded.

MacBride said: "Mind letting me look at that fountain pen in your vest pocket?"

"Of course. Here."

MacBride took it, turned it round in his fingers. It was an exact replica of the pen which Moriarity had found and which had turned out to be an infernal machine. The initials were the same. Everything about the pen was the same.

"Got another pen just like this, Mr. Stillson?"

"No. But hold on. I did have. When I ordered that pen you have in your hand—oh, it must have been a year ago—there was some mix-up, and I received two pens, each alike, and with my initials on each one. Instead of returning the extra one, I gave it to Edna McKie—as a souvenir. What makes you ask?"

"The extra pen was the one that blew up and killed Rube Wilson this morning."

Stillson sat back in his chair, a breathless look about his face. "I can't understand that. I can't—"

"What we're thinking," the skipper broke in, "is that you were a marked man. It looks as if somebody got the idea of turning one of these pens into a highly explosive machine that would go off when you opened it. I say that because of the similarity of the pens. Offhand, I figure, you couldn't have told one of these pens from the other."

"You're right."

"So it figures. Did Miss McKie say anything lately about losing her pen?"

Stillson shook his head. He was a little dazed now.

MacBride cleared his throat, asked point-blank: "D'you have any trouble with her lately?"

"No." Stillson roused himself. "Of course not! I just told you that Edna—why, she was the most faithful—" He broke off, growled impatiently: "Don't be a damned fool, MacBride! That was none of Edna's doing!" He stood up. "Well, I think you'll have to excuse me. I have to shave, change my clothes. We'll talk about this later. I just got in, you know." He bent a stern, grave eye on the skipper, placed his fist on the desk. "Go to the bottom of this, MacBride. The bottom. Certain newspapers went off the handle with a story about unrequited love. That's nonsense. I believe Edna was murdered for another reason. I shouldn't be surprised if it develops that she was trying in some way to protect me. I feel it, that's all, MacBride. There are not many things in this world I give a living damn about. One of the few is my wife; another my daughter; and there was Edna. But don't give that to the newspapers. They'd slop it up. I hate slop, MacBride."

The skipper said: "Now what about her body? How about her folks?"

"I'll take care of burying Edna, MacBride."

"But her folks. After all—"

Stillson's fist pressed against the desk. "She hasn't any."

"Well"—MacBride shrugged—"you'd know, Judge."

"I'd know." Stillson nodded. "I'd know."

MacBride frowned momentarily. A wall seemed to have risen for an instant between him and Stillson.

WHEN the skipper drummed his heels back into Headquarters, Ike Cohen was in the central room.

"Say, I just this minute got in," Cohen sang out.

"What about it?" MacBride clipped, on his way.

"Hey, wait! About that overcoat!"

"Oh...." The skipper stopped, turned. He had been thinking about Stillson and the wall. "What about the overcoat?"

Cohen snapped a piece of chewing gum. "I went over to Hoyt's and had a talk with a couple of clerks and I think things are showing up. Well, it was a size forty coat, see. So I started by asking about size forty coats. They checked up on their slips and found that all this month they sold only six forties. So then I concentrated on that and worked down to a sale to a lad named Norman Grail. He had to have the coat altered and they sent it around a day later to the *Hobart Hotel*. I described the guy we found dead in the gal's apartment and one of the clerks says it sounds like the same bird. He said this lad Grail, when he was buying the coat, asked them to send it over in a hurry, because he'd just come up from the South and needed it. I called up the morgue, thinking I could take this clerk over, but they were working on the autopsy. Then I shot over to the *Hobart Hotel,* found out Norman Grail is still registered there. But I didn't want to go any further until I could check up more."

MacBride muttered: "Swell work, Ike. Go downstairs. I think Ben's got a picture of the stiff. If he has, get it and take it to Hoyt's and see if they recognize it. Phone me."

"Okey."

The skipper went up to his office, where Moriarity was snoring in a chair. MacBride kicked the chair, asked:

"You being overworked?"

"I just didn't sleep good last night. I had dreams. Whenever I eat hamburgers before going to bed, I have dreams. I toss all night. All night I toss."

MacBride, staring abstractedly at his desk, pushed tobacco into his pipe. "Mory, see if you can get a line on Edna McKie. Under cover. I don't want it known about. Pump Kramer, that apartment house manager. Find the postman that delivered mail around there. Ask him if he remembered especially any postmarks on letters for her. I'm thinking especially of letters from other states—or countries, even. Well, you know your onions. Go to it. But use your head, Mory."

He sat down, lit his pipe, and had smoked it down when the phone rang. It was Ike Cohen.

"Okey," the skipper said. "Meet me in the lobby."

He hung up, made a pass at the inter-office annunciator, said: "Tell Gahagan I want the car. Now."

WHEN he walked into the lobby of the *Hobart Hotel,* ten minutes later, he did not at first see Cohen. He craned his neck, cruised the length and breadth of the lobby, and was about to approach the desk when he saw Ike at the newsstand beneath the west mezzanine. Cohen was holding hands with the ash-blonde behind the counter. MacBride came up behind him, stepped on his heel. Cohen spun. The ash-blonde began primping.

"If I remember right," MacBride muttered, as he and Cohen headed for the desk, "it was just a year ago your wife sicked a private dick on you. What a swell situation that was! If you got to hold hands with a wren, at least do it in the dark."

The assistant manager said he would send a bellhop up with them, but the skipper said:

"Never mind, Mr. Golias. They only get in the way."

Norman Grail's room was on the tenth floor and MacBride took the key and Cohen rose with him in the elevator. The elevator boy, when he stopped at the tenth floor, explained the way to Room 1019. The skipper stretched his legs, the skirt of his overcoat scuffing his knees.

"It just occurred to me, Ike," he said over his shoulder. "If that stiff was Grail, why the hell didn't we find his hotel key on him? It wasn't downstairs at the desk."

"I gave up trying to figure this business out, Cap'n. It's okey by me just to follow my nose."

MacBride grinned. "So far you've had pretty good luck following your nose. Well, here's the door."

He unlocked the door, swung it open and strode into a large, modern bedroom. A man turned from a lowboy at the opposite side of the room and as he turned he swept a gun off the lowboy and cocked it, leveled it. MacBride stopped in his tracks, his hands far out of position. Ike Cohen started to twist, to go for his gun, but the man in front of the lowboy growled:

"Dummy!"

"Easy, Ike," MacBride bit off. "The lad's top man."

"That's quick thinking," the man grunted.

"Quick your Aunt Nellie," the skipper said simply. "With a gun staring me in the kisser, I know what to do."

"For a copper, that's bright."

"I'm bright, mister."

The man flattened on his feet. "Then keep your paws up!"

"They are up. Should I bust my fingernails on the ceiling?"

"You're tough too, huh?"

"Tough enough."

"Yeah? How'd you like your belly ripped open?"

"I'm not nuts about it, but if that's on your mind, fella, you're boss. Only why waste breath? How'd you get in?"

"That's my business."

"You're right."

"I suppose you think you're smart, walking in like this!"

MacBride said: "It's probably the dumbest thing I ever did."

"For a cop, you sure reason things out." The man shifted a matter of six feet, hunching. He was tall, hard-boned, dressed in a blue Guards' coat, a dark blue fedora. He looked able, deft. His face was lean, tawny, good-looking in a dark, threatening way, and he wore lightweight gray gloves. He said: "Get away from that door."

"Which way?" MacBride asked.

"Along that wall. Push the divan out with your knee, then you and your pal get behind the divan. And keep your hands up."

When MacBride and Cohen had done this, the man came over, kicked the divan back into place. They were hemmed in behind it. He stepped back a few paces, standing very erect now, more certain of himself. His hand was big, strong, and the gun in it was steady. His eyes were narrowed, hard, watchful. After an instant's deliberation, he backed up, caught the phone in his left hand and ripped out the cord. There was a tight, sullen twist to his mouth.

"Where's the key you came in with?" he snapped.

"In the door," the skipper said.

The man's eyes shimmered and he said with hard, cold precision: "I'm going to walk out of here now. I'm going to walk, get me. I'm going to lock that door from the outside and if you drug-store cowboys make a move before I get out, I'll let you have it hard."

He backed up to the door, reached behind him with his left hand, opened the door, felt the key on the outside. He backed out swiftly, silently, pulled the door shut. The instant the door was flush Ike Cohen, snarling "Drug-store cowboy, am I!" whipped out his gun and fired twice. The explosions battled in the room.

MacBride hurled the divan into the center of the room, leaped across the room, landed on the doorknob. He yanked the door open, for the man had not had time to lock it. A gun boomed in the corridor and the door-frame alongside the skipper's nose shook. Ike Cohen was diving for the corridor and MacBride, tight-lipped, batted him down into the room as a second shot rang out.

An instant later the skipper peered out. The man had vanished. MacBride broke into a run, turned a corner in the corridor as he saw the man jumping into the elevator. MacBride brought his gun up, but a woman had stepped out of the elevator. He could not fire. The woman put her hands to her face and threw herself against the wall. The elevator door slammed shut. As MacBride raced up to it, he saw the indicator moving rapidly. The car was speeding downward. He felt an utter helplessness in his bones, and seeing the number two indicator moving downward from the roof, he pressed the button. The door opened in a moment and he stepped in, snapped:

"All the way down. Fast! Police!" He showed his badge.

When he strode out into the lobby, a crowd was milling around the elevator bank. The operator of the other car was saying:

"He made me come all the way down. He had a gun!"

MacBride barked: "Where'd he go?"

The boy pointed. "Side exit."

The skipper was off, his coat tails flying. Skidding into the street, he looked up and down. The man was not in sight. No one was in sight. The side exit gave on to a narrow, little-used street. He ran up to the corner, where a welter of traffic was in motion; craned his neck, saw no sign of the man. Then he went back into the hotel, back to the elevator bank.

"He was bleeding," the elevator operator said. "His left hand, it was all bloody. Look at the floor of the car! He held the gun against my back! He made me—"

"Okey, son—okey," the skipper muttered. "Run me back up to ten."

"Yes, sir."

When MacBride strode back into 1019, Cohen was just getting up, blinking and rubbing his jaw. "What a nice guy you are!" he groaned.

"You would have dived right into his fire," MacBride growled. "I had to slap you down. He got away. But you winged him, Ike. He bled like a stuck pig.... Well, let's case the place."

What the man had been searching for, MacBride could not guess. He did not, at the moment, try very hard to figure it out. He had hit Cohen a solid smash and Ike was having a time pulling himself together. Meanwhile the skipper went through Norman Grail's wardrobe. Evidently the man had traveled light, for the skipper found only a suitcase and a small overnight bag. These contained wearing apparel. There were no letters, no papers of any kind. A gray suit hung in the closet and two pairs of shoes were on the closet floor. The suit bore a Havana label and several of the shirts also bore Havana labels. One shirt, apparently new and yet to be laundered, bore a Miami label.

"This guy Grail came from the South, Ike."

"A big man from the South?"

"Havana labels here."

The lowboy drawers were empty. The writing desk was empty. But on the glossy side of a small, rectangular blotter MacBride found *Edgemere 7707* written in ink. He took the blotter and went downstairs to the lobby.

"When did Norman Grail check in here?" he asked the desk-clerk.

"Just one week ago today."

"Let's see his signature."

The writing on the white registry card strongly resembled the writing on the blotter.

"For the time being," MacBride said, "I want 1019 locked. No one's to go in it—no one, understand. I'll get an officer around and station him there. The phone's ripped out, but you can fix that later. Send a bill to the Department for the damage we did to your door."

He rang Headquarters and told Otto Bettdecken to send a reserve over. Then he went up and got Ike Cohen.

Chapter VI

THE *Stokehold* was a smart bar in upper Jockey Street and catered in great measure to the carriage trade. It ran to a lot of black marble and chromework, trick indirect lighting; and while the nautical flavor was slightly cockeyed—fish swimming past lighted ports and a flunky strolling around in a chief engineer's uniform—the cocktails were reputedly the best in town and Nina Gianfranco sang a mean string of hot-country torch songs.

Kennedy hit the *Stokehold* during the cocktail hour. He looked a little haggard, as though he had been doing a lot of running around. He also looked windblown, which was not unusual. And he was still cold and only mildly tight. A man came in a few minutes later and took a small table in a corner. This man was small, well-built, well-dressed, and of inconspicuous physical attributes: he was Sam Galya, a Headquarters crack shot whose specialty was offhand firing.

The bar was crowded, lively, and a sad-eyed lad was rippling the ivories with some intimate love songs. The women were outstanding examples of how the smart woman should dress. Kennedy found the atmosphere warmly buoyant. He preferred rye.

He was on his second drink, hunched amiably at the bar, when a tall, elegantly dressed dark man came up and leaned alongside him, saying: "How's every little this and that, Kennedy?"

"Oh, hello, Lew. You like this place, too, huh?"

Lew Gentilli shrugged broad, muscular shoulders, showed hard white teeth in a slow, amused smile. His black mustache was clipped very short and followed the straight line of his wide upper lip. He was a former lawyer who had been disbarred and had become a private detective in a big way: no small change.

Gentilli said in a low, rounded voice: "I see by the late editions that you're on the inside track of our latest crime-with-a-vengeance case."

"Is that what they said?"

Gentilli chuckled. "As if you didn't know!"

"I write news, Lew. I don't read it."

Gentilli dropped his voice: "I'd like you to meet somebody. Or rather, come over and sit with us. You know her casually."

"Do I?"

"Mrs. Stillson."

"Ah, Mrs. Stillson."

Kennedy drained his drink, paid up, and followed Gentilli among the small black tables.

Thalia Stillson would have stopped the glance of any right-minded man. She was in her middle thirties, tall enough to wear any kind of clothes, slender, striking, finished. Her hair was rich dark bronze, built to the shape of her head, and on it she wore a brown crush hat with an oval-shaped brim and a single feather whipped across the crown. There was about her face a breathless, about-to-take-off air; high-strung.

She said: "I was angry when you gave up doing those theatre reviews, Mr. Kennedy. Why did you?"

"I was only pinch-hitting, Mrs. Stillson."

He sat down. Gentilli sat down, placing his elbows on the table without leaning on them, folding his large, smooth hands. He ordered a round of drinks.

"Mr. Kennedy—" Thalia Stillson leaned forward, her eyes and voice throaty, anxious. "This terrible thing about Miss McKie! I loved Edna like a sister! Look what I've done!" She nodded to Gentilli. "I've engaged Lew Gentilli to solve it. You know, Lew and I have known each other a long time. I feel obligated to do something about it, Mr. Kennedy, because I'm afraid—I'm afraid those criminals meant to kill Ozzie, my husband! I'm afraid they'll try again!" Her throat pulsed and her eyes widened. "It's dreadful! Horrible!"

Gentilli dabbed at his lips with a napkin, said in his low, composed voice: "Thalia and I have been talking it over, Kennedy. I thought you might be able to put me on the right track."

"Yes!" said Thalia Stillson breathlessly, leaning forward. "The papers make it pretty plain that you know something about it. They say you had a conference with Edna just before the crime. They say you saw a strange man in the lobby of her apartment house at about the time of the crime." Her wide, lustrous eyes searched his face anxiously. "You will help us, won't you?"

Kennedy was slouched in his chair. "I've promised the police to hold everything, Mrs. Stillson. I'm sorry."

"But think of me!" she cried. "I'm Ozzie's wife! I'm really more concerned about his welfare than the police are! Oh, dear, the police, the police! They take so long, they botch so. Don't be a stick, Mr. Kennedy."

Kennedy mulled over his rye highball.

Gentilli leaned forward from the waist, his nape straight. "You know the police, Kennedy. I don't have to go into that. They mean well, but they're a big machine and it takes a big machine a long while to get going. Why not play ball with us? It means a lot to Thalia—you can see the state she's in. And"—he shrugged—"it might mean a lot to me. I'm doing what I can for Thalia gratis—"

"You're a dear, Lew," she said, touching his hand.

He went on to Kennedy: "But she doesn't expect you to do it for nothing. Why not break down? Why not let us in on what you know, old man?"

Kennedy took another pull at his drink, used the glass to make wet

316 The Complete Cases of MacBride & Kennedy, Volume 3

whorls on the table. He dropped his voice as he looked with veiled eyes at the woman, then at the man. "I can't. I'd like to, but I can't. There's dynamite in what I know, but we need a spark to set it off. We're working on it now. It'll take a few days. The cops made me promise and you know what cops are if a poor guy like me breaks his promise."

"Oh, it's ridiculous, ridiculous!" choked Thalia Stillson. "It's my husband who is in danger!"

Kennedy finished his drink. "I'm very sorry, Mrs. Stillson. I'm just on a spot. And I'm scared stiff. And between you and me, I haven't told the cops everything—"

Gentilli broke in: "Then why not tell us? Why are you holding something out on the cops?"

"I've found, Lew, that it's not wise to tell the cops some things until you're dead sure. When I check up a little more, then I'll spring." He stood up. "Right now, if certain people knew what I know—" He drew his index finger across his throat.

Thalia Stillson reached out a hand, cried in an urgent voice: "Don't go! Please—"

Gentilli put her hand down, muttered: "Okey, Kennedy. Thanks."

Chapter VII

THE skipper looked up as Ike Cohen came into his office. "Ike," he said, "that number on the blotter we picked up in Grail's room was Edna McKie's telephone number."

"Another dead end, eh?"

MacBride rubbed his jaw. "Except that it adds definitely to the fact that Grail and the McKie woman were tied up. I sent Kozinski out to check up on that bird took a fall out of us and Kozinski just phoned in. He said he cased the neighborhood around the *Hobart Hotel* and found out that the mugg caught a cab two blocks away, in Malone Street. The cab driver was a fellow named Goetz. He said there was nothing strange about this guy when he hired the cab. The guy got in and told him to drive to Sadler Square and he did. When the guy got out, he looked pretty sick—white as a sheet. Goetz asked him what the matter was and the guy mumbled something and kept his left hand in his overcoat pocket. Turning around, the guy bumped

into a pedestrian with his left side and yelped, made a face. Goetz
thought it was funny but it was not until Kozinski was checking up
that Goetz began to put two and two together. I sent a squad out to
visit all the doctors around Sadler Square and case the neighborhood
generally. You seen Kennedy?"

"Nope."

The skipper wagged his head. "I sent out Sam Galya to watch him.
I only hope Kennedy stays sober. Sam phoned in once to say that he
was getting fallen arches keeping up with Kennedy. Kennedy is doing
a lot of slamming around town. The guy is on to something and I
wish he'd show up. He worries me, damn him—and I know he can't
stay sober— Oh, hello, Mory. I thought maybe you'd taken a trip
somewhere. "

Moriarity said: "You asked me to check up on the McKie woman,
didn't you? Well, I checked up. Can I check up and be around here
at the same time?"

"What are you beefing about? I just passed a remark. When you
eat hamburgers at night, you get touchy next day too, don't you?"

Moriarity looked irritated. He growled: "Ah-r-r, it's my wife's sister.
I phoned my wife to ask how her cold was and she said her sister was
coming to spend two weeks with us. It'll drive me nuts. She's screwy,
the sister is. She's an athlete. She boxes. She boxes all over the place.
We have friends in, and she wants to box. Last time she gave me a
black eye and busted the china closet. Phooey!"

MacBride drew his hand across a tight grin, then said: "And how
about the McKie woman?"

"Oh, yes," said Moriarity, snapping out of it. "Oh, yes. I had quite
a time locating the mailman on that route. He had a day off. But I
finally found him and he says, yes, he does remember having letters
for her that had foreign postmarks. Just about a month ago, he says,
there was a letter with a Cuban stamp on it for her and he asked her
for the stamp, because his kid was collecting stamps, and she gave it
to him."

MacBride said to Cohen: "Ike, this guy Grail and the woman were
old friends, old pals. We're sewing that up. Shoot, Mory."

"Well," Moriarity went on, "she's been living in that apartment for
three years. I checked back to where she lived before and it was in a
boarding house, a nice place, in Provost Street. She lived in that place
for three years and two months—well, she was living there a year or

so before she got the job with Stillson.

"First she was his steno, and then when she was made his confidential secretary, she moved to the apartment in Flint Street. Woman by the name of Emma Oliphant runs the boarding house. Says Edna McKie was a hard worker, very conscientious about everything. Didn't seem to have many acquaintances. In fact, avoided making them.

"Mrs. Oliphant says that when Edna came there to live, she was sure she came from some place out of town, because she didn't know her way around the city. But Edna never said where. As a matter of fact, the impression I got from this old Oliphant dame was that Edna was a mysterious kind of gal; lonely as hell but dead against making up with anyone."

"What else?"

"Well, that's all. Then I called up my wife." He began to look desperate again, his jaw hardening. "And she said—"

"I know about that, Mory," the skipper broke in. He put his tongue in his cheek and said: "Maybe for the two weeks she's here we can keep her in the jug for disturbing the peace. The sister, I mean."

"For cripes' sake, don't put ideas in my head!"

The skipper stood up. "I think you've put an idea or two in mine though, kid," he said. He got into his overcoat, slapped on his hat and strode out of the office.

LIGHTS were on in Ozzie Stillson's paneled office and the big, middle-aged man was at work on some papers, a huge cigar in his mouth. When MacBride entered, Stillson leaned back, rubbed his eyes vigorously, said:

"News, MacBride?"

"Breaks here and there, Judge. Little breaks. We've identified the guy who was found dead with Edna McKie. That is, we know his name's Norman Grail. At least, it's the name he was registered under at the *Hobart Hotel*. We got our lamps on another guy mixed up in the case. He was going through the late Grail's hotel room. He got the drop on me and one of my men and scrammed but we winged him. This lad Grail came up from the South recently and we've reason to believe he came from Havana and was an old acquaintance of Edna McKie. Whether he was a friend, we don't know. If you want to put your cards on the table, Judge, how much more would we know about Edna McKie?"

Stillson shrugged his heavy shoulders, made light of the query. "You overestimate my knowledge of the poor girl's private life, Captain. She only worked for me."

"Granted. But she was your confidential secretary and a man might readily suppose that you'd know a good deal about her background— her companions, for instance; where she came from; things like that."

"I only know that she served me faithfully."

"Where'd she come from originally? Where was she born?"

"Somewhere out West, I believe. I'm not sure. I never asked. You must understand, MacBride, that when she first entered my employ she was only a stenographer. I later raised her. Why? Because I think I'm a judge of people. I liked her. I had an instinctive trust in her." He dropped his hard elbows to the desk, brought his white brows together. "Are you trying to make it out that she was trying to pull something on me?"

"I'm trying to find out something about her," the skipper insisted doggedly. "I have no doubt that she was killed. I don't care if it was her gun that killed Grail, I don't believe she did it Because nobody heard the shots. Those shots were muffled. She would never have muffled them. The explosive fountain pen is evidence enough that an attempt on somebody's life was to be made. Because of the similarity of the fountain pens—yours and the one you gave her, which was turned into the business that killed Wilson—a man would say that you were to be the victim. She had the pen. It's logical to assume it was through her the pen could have been loaded and later easily placed on your desk—"

"I don't believe it!" Stillson broke in angrily. "You'll never convince me that Edna would plan to take my life. She had no reason to." But for an instant there was fear in his eyes, a queer look about his mouth. Then he struck the desk with the flat of his hand shattering this illusion. "Absurd, MacBride!"

"On the surface, maybe," MacBride said in a cool, level voice. "But if we knew more about her background, we might be able to reconstruct something."

"I know nothing about her background!" Stillson growled, again slapping the desk. He shuffled his papers. "If you don't mind, I'm busy!"

MacBride remained motionless, his eyes leveled on the man. After a moment Stillson stood up, bulking in the room, a harried, haggard look in his eyes.

"Be good enough to go along, Captain," he said. "All this has upset me terribly." There was a strange pallor in his face. "I don't mean to be angry with you, but your statements, or rather your insinuations about Edna irritate me. Good evening."

WHEN the skipper got back to Headquarters there was a small group of men gathered in the central room, among them Moriarity and Cohen. MacBride stopped. Moriarity turned to say:

"Hey, Cap, listen to this." He nodded to a small, timid man who wore a derby, a black beard and small spectacles. "This is Mr. Schultz, Cap. Tell the captain, Mr. Schultz."

Mr. Schultz cleared his throat. "Well, Captain, in the newspapers it says about fountain pens, about these fountain pens and about that big murder or what it is. I have in Low Street a jewelry store, a small one, not big, and in the papers I recognize the picture of the lady was dead, or killed, or whatever. By my store comes this lady three days ago, it was raining, and looks over my fountain pens. She wants a particular kind and in a little while she finds it, a big one, like for a man. Then she wants I should put initials on it and I asked her what kind and I show her a book with initials and she finds the kind she wants. O.T.S. is the initials. Then she explains to me how a very good friend gave her a fountain pen and she lost it—oh, my, she says—and this is one she wants, just like the one she lost, account of it might look to her friend she was careless, losing the one he gave her. So this one just like the one she lost, he would not ever know."

MacBride asked: "And did she get it?"

"Captain, sir, how could she? It would be ready today, only she is dead! Here, I brought it along."

It was, MacBride saw, an exact duplicate of the one which had blown up and the one which he had seen in Stillson's possession. He turned to Moriarity, said:

"Hers was stolen. Either at the office or in her apartment. It was returned to her apartment either by Grail or by the guy Ike and I ran into at the *Hobart Hotel*. If that's the case, then the McKie woman was the one put on the spot. It gets screwier every minute. There's no rhyme or reason about it. I just about had it figured out that the McKie woman was getting set to plant that fountain pen on Ozzie's desk and then got in a jam herself. Now that's out—because she'd never gone to a reputable store to buy another one."

At seven that night Detective Kozinski came in to report that he had covered all the medical offices around Sadler Square and that nothing in connection with the wounded man had been found.

At half-past eight Sergeant Otto Bettdecken burst into the skipper's office and shouted: "Sam Galya's been wounded in a gunfight in Schick Street! Oppenheimer phoned in. Sam drilled one guy clean but was knocked over by some others."

MacBride was on his feet, anger and anxiety in his eyes. "That means they snatched Kennedy!" he ripped out.

"You took the words right outta my mouth," Bettdecken said.

Chapter VIII

THE light must have been about a million candlepower. Kennedy didn't know. But it felt like it ought to be a million candlepower. There was no sense in keeping your eyes shut, because that light came right through your lids. Open or shut, it was just the same. You were blind. You couldn't see a thing. It was worse than pitch darkness, a million times worse. Because this way, it hurt. The light boiled right through your eyes and fried your brains. You sat in a straight-backed chair, your arms lashed to it. All the liquor you had drunk that day sizzled through your pores.

"Like it?" said the thin voice, playfully.

Kennedy moistened his lips. "Kind of bright, isn't it?"

"Like you ought to be."

That was the thin voice again. Kennedy didn't know what any of them looked like. There was the thin voice; there was the low, hard, resolute voice; there was the husky voice of one who did not say much, except now and then some attempt at coarse humor. Three of them. He thought he liked the thin voice least of all.

Said the husky voice: "Ha, I bet he seen many a guy git a light like 'at over at Headquarters shoved in his puss all night long. I bet he don't like it, I bet. Anybody wanna bet?"

"Pipe down," said the low voice.

The thin voice carved itself neatly near Kennedy's ear: "Pal, when you shoot your jaw off in public, you ought to be prepared for the worst. Now open that trap of yours. It was loose enough in the first place. Loosen up now. What do you know? What do you know that ain't ripe to publish yet? That's what you're here for, to spill what you know. Spill it!"

"I don't know anything."

The low voice said: "You ought to know better than cough up a gag like that. You've been around, bud. You ain't green."

"You're informing me?" He licked his lips. "You know what?"

"What?" said the low voice.

"You guys stink."

"Smile when you say that," the thin voice taunted.

Kennedy smiled and said: "You guys stink."

He rocked in the chair as a hand clouted him on the side of the face. It seemed his eyes jigged in their sockets like white-hot coals. Another blow struck him at the back of the head. Bright, fiery pinwheels spun before his eyes. His tongue felt swollen.

The husky voice hacked out a short laugh. "Ain't he a glutton for punishment though? Tsk, tsk!"

The thin voice came very close to Kennedy's ear and was satanically intimate: "You know, palsy-walsy, that it don't hurt us a bit to sock you around. Are you going to open that stubborn jaw of yours or do we have to take you completely apart?"

Kennedy mumbled: "We have to go over that again?"

Silence followed. The light poured into his face, through his face. He was sure it went right through and out the back of his head. When his head drooped, they held it up. When he tried to twist his head free, they socked him and held it up again. Sweat streamed down his body beneath his clothing. He was sure he didn't have eyes any more. The terrible light was all inside his head.

"How about it?" the thin voice asked.

"No can do," Kennedy muttered.

The low voice said reasonably: "Don't be that way, guy. What did Edna McKie tell you before she died? You had a talk with her. What did you talk about?"

Kennedy shook his head wearily. "Nothing. I lent her two bucks."

"Now there's a mugg for you!" brawled the husky voice. "Damn me, if there ain't a mugg for you! He lent her two bucks! Tsk!"

"I lent her two bucks," mumbled Kennedy.

The husky voice guffawed: "There he sits with his bare face hangin' out lendin' her two bucks!"

"Two bucks," murmured Kennedy, nodding.

"Talk sense," insisted the low voice. "Because if you don't, it's your funeral. Now what did she say? What did you know about her? How much do the cops know? We're going to find out, pal. I mean it. Who was this guy Norman Grail?"

"I don't know."

"The hell you don't. Where does he fit in?"

"I don't know."

"Give me the names of the people the cops suspect."

Kennedy licked his lips. "I don't know. The cops don't suspect anybody."

"But they don't think it was murder and suicide, do they?"

"No."

"You mean they don't think she shot Grail and then committed suicide?"

"They think that was a gag."

"What do you think?"

"I think it was a gag too."

"Who do you think killed Grail and the woman?"

"Offhand, I'd say you did."

"You sure believe in free speech, don't you?"

"You asked me," Kennedy said hardly above a whisper.

"And I ask you this: What did Edna McKie tell you before she died? What name did she mention?"

Kennedy sighed. "Nothing. No names. I lent her two bucks—"

"My Gawd!" exploded the husky voice. "We're back on that now again!"

The thin voice sliced in: "Listen, Kennedy, I think you're trying to be funny. I think you're trying to hand us a birdie. Do you by any chance think you're tough?"

"With this Brawn Trust around here, no. What would it get me?"

"You're still being funny!"

"Boy, you are easy to please for humor."

"See," said the husky voice, "you just can't stop him from bein' funny."

"Hold his head up," the low voice said. "We'll burn it out of him. I think I'll have a nice long cool drink of ice water."

"Me too," said the husky voice. "A nice—long—cool—*cold*—drink of sparklin' ice water. M-m-m-m-m! Ah! M-m-m-m-m!"

Kennedy licked his dry lips. For half an hour they did not address him, but whenever he tried to duck his head, one of them held it up again, so that the fierce glare engulfed him. He was weak as a cat. His body was a welter of sweat. He wished he would faint. He tried hard to faint. But he couldn't. He remained sufficiently conscious to be aware of the awful agony.

"How about it now?" the low voice asked.

"We've been over it, over it," Kennedy murmured weakly.

"Suppose you tell the truth now."

"Did."

"Are you crazy, or do you like that light?"

"I'll go crazy, if you keep this up."

"That's an idea," said the thin voice.

Kennedy coughed. "I'll tell you what happened. I killed her. I killed Grail, too." He chuckled dryly. "She was really my wife, you know. I married her when she was taking in floors to scrub. I was just a poor plumber's assistant at the time. Then Grail came along. He took her from me. It wasn't that that made me mad, though. Grail swiped my assistant-plumbing tools. That drove me to it." He giggled.

"Nuts, he is," said the husky voice. "Ga-ga, he is."

"I think he passed out," said the low voice.

"Round one," said the husky voice.

"I'll bring him to," the thin voice promised.

"Ha," the husky voice laughed. "Round two comin' up!"

The low voice said: "I think I better change this bandage on my hand."

Chapter IX

THE skipper came back from Schick Street with a wicked glint in his eyes. Gahagan drove the car, jumping the red lights with his siren, cutting corners on the inside. It was a demonstration of how not to drive safely. MacBride paid no attention. When he strode into the central room at Police Headquarters, Moriarity and Cohen were there.

"Galya was only winged," stated the skipper in a hard, savage voice. "The guy he plugged was a bum named Biff Ressler, a cut-rate heel that I've been kicking around on and off for six years. He should be doing time now. I picked a crack shot all right. I'll bet Ressler never twitched once after Sam Galya hit him. So what? So Ressler can't talk. So nuts for that. The car was a Hup sedan, license K-9192. Sam put a hole in the back of it, he says. Three guys lammed with Kennedy. It happened fast—outside *Rotolo's*. Dark as hell there. Kennedy came out and the four guys fell on him. Galya did the best he could."

The skipper went up to his office, unlocked a lower desk drawer and took out an extra gun. He loaded it. It was of the same make and design as the one he carried regularly in his shoulder-holster. Into his overcoat pocket he poured a handful of cartridges. He opened the annunciator and spoke in short, terse sentences. "Call all cars...." He stuffed his pipe meanwhile. "All precincts...." He wanted all reserves out. "A dark Hup sedan... license K-9192. Look for a bullet hole in the rear of the body... garages... parking lots... all parked cars, anywhere. Quiz any known companions of George Biff Ressler. Drag 'em in and hold 'em en route." It was in the nature of a general alarm. He lit his pipe, strong smoke foaming about his head. The dispatcher, aloft, was relaying the skipper's orders.

Moriarity and Cohen came in and Moriarity said: "Well, do we go to town?"

"We mark time here a while. I've got things moving. The first smell I get, we go to it." His eyes darkened. "I'm afraid those guys'll be the death of Kennedy. If he knew something, that'd be all right—he could come across after they beat him some time. But he don't know a thing. He can't tell 'em a thing. And they won't believe that."

He took an angry turn around the room, his hands restless. "Kennedy can't stand it. The guy's a shadow. I carried him up the stairs where he lives when he was tight one night and it's like carrying a kid. And that's what I'm afraid of tonight. Rotolo said he was pretty tight, and when he's tight he thinks he can take it.... Go downstairs, Ike, and tell Gahagan not to leave the building. He's making passes at a gal up the block and twice I've had to send up after him. Once more and I'll tell his wife."

Moriarity left and a minute later Bogardus looked in. "Lew Gentilli, the private dick, 'd like to see you, Cap'n."

"Gentilli? Send him in."

Lew Gentilli strolled in, smiled, said in his slow, deliberate way: "Haven't seen much of you lately, Steve."

"We don't cover the same territory, I guess. Sit down. What's on your mind?"

Gentilli laid his gloves on the desk, laid his black velour hat on top of the gloves. He looked debonair, and sitting down, he was careful to pluck up his trousers legs an inch or two, so as not to bag the knees. He lit a Turkish cigarette.

He said: "I was wondering what progress you've made on the big was-she-pushed-or-did-she-fall case. What would you call it? A kind of double play: McKie to Grail to Wilson. Tough about Rube. He had a few brains that he might have learned to use later on."

"Rube was all right. He went off handle at times and we were always riding each other—but the guy worked hard. What's your interest in the case?"

"Didn't Kennedy tell you?"

"No."

"I ran into Kennedy at the cocktail hour at the *Stokehold*."

"I haven't seen Kennedy," MacBride said, "since about noon. Didn't you hear about the shooting tonight in Schick Street?"

"No."

"Some guys shot up Galya and lammed with Kennedy. I've got a general alarm out."

Gentilli frowned concernedly. "Tough, Skipper. I remember Kennedy made some provocative statements in the papers. As a matter of fact, I tried to bribe him to tell me the lowdown this afternoon."

MacBride brought his brows together.

Gentilli smiled coolly. "Mrs. Stillson got panicky and hired me. She's afraid something will happen to Ozzie. Dealing with a panicky woman is no soft snap. I'm worn out. She seems to have a large opinion of my ability and thinks I can do more than the police. I've tried. I thought you might give a little coöperation, so I dropped around."

"What kind of coöperation?"

"Let me in on the stuff you're holding back from the papers."

MacBride tamped down his pipe, gave Gentilli an up-from-under look. "So Mrs. Stillson hired you, eh, Lew?"

"I've known her and Ozzie quite a while. I wouldn't say exactly 'hired.' She asked me to work on it. She's afraid that the death of the McKie woman was only the beginning and that Ozzie might be next."

"What makes her think that?"

Gentilli shrugged. "Newspaper talk, I suppose. And she's by nature a high-strung woman. I'd appreciate it a lot if you'd let me in on some of the dope you've got."

MacBride chuckled ironically. "Dope. Hell, Lew, to be frank with you, we don't know a thing. All we know is that the dead guy's name is Grail and that some other guy, who we winged, was interested in Grail's hotel room. The guy got away clean. Then some muggs shoot up Sam Galya, who was covering Kennedy. Sam kills one, the others get away—again clean. We don't know a thing. We ought to get a medal for not knowing anything. I sent out a general alarm for Kennedy and I'm praying it turns up something. The newspaper talk was Kennedy's doing. He thought it would be a swell way of making some nervous parties show their hand. Well, they didn't fail him. But Kennedy knew nothing. It's a gag."

Gentilli clucked his tongue ruefully. "Kennedy was always one to get himself in hot water for a gag." He stood up, sighing. "I thought you'd be able to give me a steer, Steve. I thought we might be able to get together on this." He shrugged, picked up his hat and gloves. "Sorry."

"Me too, Lew. By the way, there's lipstick on your neck, in case you want to wipe it off."

"Oh." Gentilli chuckled, took a handkerchief and wiped the lipstick off. "I got it in the neck, eh?"

Chapter X

TIME no longer meant anything to Kennedy. As a means of reckoning, it ceased to exist. Hours, days or weeks might have passed, for all he knew. Fainting; coming to; fainting again. All the moisture seemed to have been drawn from his body. His mouth was like a desert. Thin voice. Low voice. Husky voice. They all took turns. Until he knew that if ever he lived after this, he would again recognize these voices, anywhere, at any time.

There was silence now—one of those lulls during which the white glare poured through him. And then he heard a bell ringing. Feet moved. The bell stopped ringing. Later the feet moved again and it was the low voice now:

"We're to let him go."

"What!" boomed the husky voice.

The low voice growled: "We're to let him go."

"And why?" asked the thin voice, doubting.

"Come in the other room a minute."

The feet went away and a door closed and after a while the door opened and the feet came back. Kennedy felt a slap on his cheek.

"Okey," the low voice said. "You're going."

One of them blindfolded Kennedy and then there was no light. Only darkness. And the darkness was so dense that it pained him horribly, like screws being twisted into his head. They unbound his arms and lifted him up. His knees gave. Strong arms did not permit him to collapse. His hat was slapped on his head. They practically carried him, but he felt his feet dragging on the floor. Then someone actually carried him down a flight of stairs.

Cold air struck him and he inhaled great gusts of it and it hurt his lungs but he kept on inhaling it. The blackness was less painful now. He was piled into a car, felt the cushion give beneath his not great weight. The self-starter ground. The motor sent its eager pulse through the car. There was motion, driven wind. The cold wind laved his body and his numbed senses. He was fighting now to clear his head.

Later, the car stopped. A body alongside him moved, hands grabbed him.

"I got him," said the husky voice.

He was hauled out of the car and now he was able to stand on his feet, though his legs shook and his body swayed.

"This is to remember us by," laughed the husky voice.

The world shook and Kennedy knew complete darkness.

When he came to he was lying in weeds against a board fence and he was chilled to the bone. He saw the stars above him, cold, radiant particles in a dark sky. No moon. The wind was making the dry weeds click. He lay there for a few minutes, moving his eyes, remembering. Then he got to his feet and leaned against the fence. Old dark buildings were across the way and there was the smell of the river. He shambled to the end of the fence and saw the railroad yards, the river lights beyond. He was stark sober now. He could not recall having been so sober in a long time.

Moving off, he hunched in his topcoat, tried to put some measure of rhythm in his footsteps. He turned into Flamingo Street and followed it upward, seeing soon familiar lights. There was *Enrico's* sign.

He went into the bar, said to Paderoofski:

"One large drink of rye, Paderoofski, my friend. Apprise me of the date and time."

"Shoo t'ing, Meester Kennedy. She is Sahrday, being twalve o'cluck axcept for tan minoots. In tan minoots she be twalve o'cluck and den she be Sahnday, shoo 'nough."

Kennedy picked up the drink of rye. "Paderoofski, bless your soul."

"Shoo," laughed Paderoofski, "I dun't t'ink so."

"To you, keed."

"By me it's ukkey, t'ank you so much. I'm sure."

"It seems like years, Paderoofski, and it's been only several hours."

"Tsk, tsk, ain't it so! I'm find it so myself, by damn! Wotta hell—she's whatcha call life, Meester Kennedy."

"Fill her up, philosopher."

"Say, dassa name I'm like! I t'ink I name my new bambino dat! How you spal dat name, axcuse me?"

A police siren screamed somewhere in a distant street. Kennedy paid no attention to it. He polished off six drinks and felt as if some of his old aplomb had returned. To make sure, he took another drink, then left. At Flamingo and Russell, two cops came out of a rooming-house.

"Well, he ain't in there," one said.

"Nope. Let's try across the street."

"Pardon me, officers," said Kennedy, passing between them and turning up Russell Street. He walked for fifteen minutes and entered Police Headquarters by a side entrance. No one was in the corridor there. He took the back stairway up, looked into the reserve room and saw three plainclothes men playing cards. They did not look up. He shrugged and went on upstairs and wandered into MacBride's office. This was empty. But the office was warm and a clock ticked comfortably on the wall.

Kennedy sat down in the swivel chair, put his feet on the desk and lit a cigarette. He thought of taking a good sleep but after a moment he tried one of the desk drawers and found a half-empty bottle of brandy. He had no prejudice against drinking brandy after having drunk rye. There was a glass convenient and he settled down to an satiable, meditative communion with the bottle.

Half an hour later the door opened and MacBride came in long-legged, his face drawn, dark circles under his eyes. Behind him were Moriarity and Cohen, dead for want of sleep. The skipper stopped in his tracks and wild joy leaped to his face.

"Kennedy!"

"Hi-de-hi," Kennedy drawled. "Also, hi-de-ho."

"Thank God!" groaned Moriarity. "Now I can go home to bed."

And then the skipper looked suspicious. One eye narrowed. "My bottle, eh?" His jaw hardened. "How long have you been here, Kennedy?"

"Half an hour or so."

"Half an hour! Damn it, I've been downstairs fifteen minutes! Nobody said you came in!"

Kennedy shrugged. "I didn't want to disturb anyone, so I came in the side way."

The skipper snatched up the bottle. "I'll bet you've been hobby-horsing around town and getting tight while Ike and Mory and me have been running our legs off looking for you! You monkey's uncle, do you realize I turned in a general alarm for you? Answer me or I'll slap you against the wall!"

"My, my—such temper," said Kennedy languidly. "It is true I have been traversing some faubourgs tonight, but it was because I was left in some weeds alongside a fence by the railroad yards. Some loving young lads took me for a buggy ride—"

MacBride's hands landed on the desk, his rigid arms braced his wide shoulders. "Spill it, kid! Where are the guys?"

"You've got me, Steve. They blindfolded me when they took me to this home. Then they turned this high-powered light on me. It blinded me. I never saw one face. Only voices—I heard only voices. I must have fainted about six times. They always brought me to, thoughtfully."

"What'd they want?"

"Give you one guess."

"I thought so."

"And of course I had nothing to tell them. So they took smacks at me from time to time—and then that pretty light. One thing I know—Grail wasn't mixed up with them. They couldn't figure Grail out. One of those babies must have had something wrong with his hand—he spoke about changing a bandage—"

"Ike!" yelled the skipper. "You hear him! The guy we met at the *Hobart!*"

"What guy at the *Hobart?*" Kennedy asked.

MacBride explained.

Kennedy nodded. "It's likely the same chap. Well, then after all this light business and the questions and the slaps and after I'd fainted half a dozen times—then a phone rang. The guy with the bandaged hand went into another room to answer it. When he came back, he said to the others, 'We're to let him go,' like that. So that means there was somebody else in it—somebody who phoned and told them to let me go. Why, I don't know. Unless he had evidence that I'd been gagging them all along and really didn't know anything. So they blindfolded me, took me out, rode me a ways and then tossed me out."

There was a look in the skipper's eyes that seemed to well outward, as though a vision were sweeping up within him. He chopped off: "What else do you know?"

"Nothing."

"I mean, did you learn anything before you were snatched?"

"No. I got interested playing hide and seek with Galya. It was great fun. Once or twice I damned near lost him, but that lad's good. I met Gentilli at the *Stokehold* some time during the proceedings. Lew Gentilli, the private dick. He's working for Thalia Stillson and they wanted me to divulge what I knew. Boy, is he a looker!— Oh, yes, I did find out she was a nurse once."

"Can I go home now?" Moriarity asked.

MacBride pivoted. "You cannot! We just begin now! Go down and tell Gahagan to bring the car around front! Brother, I'm going to town!"

Chapter XI

THE police car drew up in front of a large apartment house on the top of Post Street. It was one of the highest points of the city. From it you caught a glimpse of the harbor lights. The wind blew a gale here, loud and cold. It plastered the skipper's coat against his hard, lean back.

"You guys wait down here," he said, holding his hat to his head.

He turned, strode across the wind and entered the lobby. A middle-aged man in uniform stood outside the open elevator door.

"Judge Stillson's apartment," the captain said.

"Who will I say is calling?"

"Never mind that. I'm from the police."

"Yes, sir. Penthouse A."

MacBride entered the car and the middle-aged man drove the car up to the last stop, opened the door. It led into a private foyer. The car went down and the skipper pressed the button alongside the paneled door. A small, fat butler opened the door.

"Is Judge Stillson in?"

"Who shall—"

"Captain MacBride."

"Step in, please."

MacBride waited in the rectangular entrance hall and in a moment the butler returned, bowed. The skipper went down a corridor behind the butler, followed his bow and gesture into a large living-room across which Stillson, drawing on a dressing-gown, was advancing.

"Captain, how do you do."

"Hello, Judge."

"I daresay you have news."

MacBride was frowning, his voice was brusque. "Yes and no."

"Sit down, please."

Stillson did not look at him. The Judge's eyes looked haggard, wandering; they seemed to have no connection with his polite, formal voice. There was a strange pallor on his face, an indecisive look about his usually firm mouth.

MacBride did not sit down, explaining: "I'd like to see Mrs. Stillson, Judge."

"Eh?"

"Mrs. Stillson."

Stillson pawed absently at his jaw, then shook himself. "Oh, yes. Well, sir, she's not at home just now. Out. Some affair. She wanted to break the engagement, but I assured her it would be ridiculous to do so. Can I help you?" he asked, his eyes darting back and forth across the rug at his feet.

"I don't think so. Do you know where I can find Mrs. Stillson? I just want a few words with her."

"The *Ambassador*. The Winter Carnival." He roused himself again. "Look here, what's your object?"

"Routine, Judge," MacBride clipped. He backed up, dipped his head. "Sorry I had to disturb you."

Stillson rubbed his jaw, stared curiously, vacantly at the rug. He looked very old and bewildered at that moment.

The skipper left wearing a troubled frown, a warped, frustrated mouth. He chewed his lip on the way down in the elevator and as he climbed into the front seat of the police car, he said:

"The *Ambassador*, Gahagan."

Kennedy asked from the back seat: "What news of mice and men?"

"None. Maybe there'll be some of rats soon, baby. Shake a leg, Gahagan. You're not in a parade."

The Winter Carnival was being thrown in the main ballroom of the *Ambassador*. The skipper got in touch with the headwaiter and asked him to summon Mrs. Stillson to the anteroom. The head-waiter went away and returned in a little while saying that Mrs. Stillson had left about an hour before. He remembered: a gentleman had called for her. A tall gentleman, dark.

"Oke," said MacBride, and returned to the car.

"I ought to been home in bed hours ago," Moriarity complained.

"Shut your trap," the skipper said, climbing in; and to Gahagan: "Buzz over to 94 Edgewood Terrace." And over his shoulder: "You got no pride, Mory. All you think about is the clock. If you got no sleep last night, it's your own fault for eating hamburgers. Try spinach some time."

"Hell, I'm no vegetable-what-you-call-it-arian."

It was a ten-minute ride to Edgewood Terrace, which overlooked Edgewood Park. Number 94 was a building with a center garden, an entryway recessed deeply between two tall wings and a horseshoe driveway of cement. Gahagan parked in the driveway, in front of the pillared entrance.

MacBRIDE went alone, spoke for a minute to the elevator man and was then taken to the sixth floor. He stretched his bony legs down the carpeted corridor past mellow wall lights, came to a paneled door numbered 616 and used the bronze knocker. Inside there was the sound of a radio tuned down low.

Gentilli opened the door. He held a highball in his hand. His eyes dropped for an instant, then lifted and he smiled.

"Hard at it, eh, MacBride?"

"Ask me in."

Gentilli took a pull at his highball, looked over the rim of the glass. Then he said, shrugging: "Sure. Glad to have you."

Lew Gentilli's place was small, smart, done in excellent taste. Thalia Stillson was standing before a living-room mirror using a vanity. She had on an evening wrap. Her back was to MacBride.

"I believe you know Mrs. Stillson," Gentilli said. "Captain MacBride, Thalia."

She turned smoothly, smiled brightly. "I've always wanted to meet you, Captain MacBride."

He said stiffly, in a low voice: "How do you do, Mrs. Stillson. I came here on purpose to meet you."

"Really," she said, looking pleased.

"I wanted to know just what your object was in hiring Lew."

"Oh, but don't you know? Ozzie's in danger!"

MacBride's lips flexed. "Why didn't you come to us? Lew's all right in his line but I never knew he was heavy on tracking down criminals. In fact, he used to represent criminals, when he was a lawyer. He used to make great speeches about the under dog—an under dog, according to Lew, being a guy that shoots people in the back in the dark." His voice was hardening.

Thalia Stillson looked puzzled, a little apprehensive.

Gentilli grinned. "The Captain's off again. Every once in a while he goes oratorical in a big way. Don't take him seriously, Thalia."

"Counsel's advice," muttered MacBride; and then he dropped his voice threateningly: "Kennedy's back."

"Oh, good!" cried Thalia Stillson, clapping her hands soundlessly. "Oh, how good!"

MacBride was bending a hard stare on Gentilli. "Every time I see you, Lew, there's lipstick on your neck!"

Gentilli's hand started up, paused midway, and then he dropped it, digging the skipper with a contemptuous sidelong look. Thalia Stillson had colored, the flush racing over her face and throat. Her eyes shimmered with a green, unearthly light.

"I must go," she said. "I really must go home. I'm happy to have met you, Captain MacBride—"

"Wait," said the skipper.

"But, really, I must—"

"Wait."

Her lips tightened nervously and seemed to pulse tautly against her teeth and the shimmer heightened in her eyes, her breast rose on a slow inhalation and did not instantly recede.

Gentilli took three long strides, set down his glass on a table, swiveled and said darkly: "If you're clowning, Skipper, I don't think it's funny."

"I'm not clowning, Lew. Why did you take Mrs. Stillson from the ball at the *Ambassador?*"

"That's no business of yours. Thalia and I are old friends."

"What's the degree of friendship?"

"Oh!" squeaked Thalia, putting pink fingers to her cheeks.

Gentilli's jaw set and shot over to one side. "I'm liable to take a fall out of you, MacBride!"

"Grow up, boy. You're big but I can take you if I have to." He turned to Thalia Stillson. "How long have you been married to the Judge? Six years, isn't it?"

"Why—yes."

"Up until that time you made your living as a trained nurse, didn't you?"

"Ye-es."

"As I recall now. Judge Stillson's first wife died about seven or eight years ago. Were you the nurse on the job?"

"I was. I took care of her for a year and a half. What has all this got to do—"

"It might have a lot."

She cried out angrily: "I tell you I am going home!"

"Madam, you're not."

Gentilli smiled wearily, said in a pacifying voice: "Look here, MacBride. Why act like this? Be reasonable."

"Never mind turning on the personality, Lew. You can chuck it out the window."

"All right," Gentilli snapped. "I'll chuck it out. And one more crack out of you and I'll chuck you out! If you think you can drag your flatfoot methods in here and get away with it, you're out of your head!"

"Don't get angry, Lew!" cried Thalia Stillson, who was angry herself. "I'm going home," she said to MacBride. "I am going to tell the Judge just how you acted—"

"The Judge is not my boss, Madam."

"He's the boss of a lot of people who don't realize it!"

"Madam," the skipper said gruffly, "you can tell the Judge anything you want, but just now you're not going home!"

"Oh!" she squeaked; and again: "Oh! Oh, oh!" in a high panicky voice. "You're so—so—*impossible!*"

MacBride turned on Gentilli, barked: "Who's in that next room?"

Gentilli looked, nodded towards a closed door at the other end of the living-room. "That room? No one."

"I heard somebody in there."

"Nonsense. That's my bedroom."

"I didn't ask you what it was. I asked who's in there!"

"I tell you, no one's in there!"

MacBride said offhand: "Take a look."

Gentilli strode across the room, grabbed the knob and snapped angrily over his shoulder: "I tell you no one's in here!" He opened the door, groped just inside it for a moment, then switched on the lights and looked in, around. "Take a look yourself," he said.

The skipper crossed the living-room, stood in the bedroom doorway, saw that it was empty. He started across it towards the bathroom when he heard a door slam elsewhere. Spinning around, he saw that Thalia Stillson had vanished. He cursed, ran towards the corridor door, flung it open and looked down the corridor. He heard the elevator door bang shut as he raced towards it. The car had started down by the time he arrived. Looking over his shoulder, he saw Gentilli watching him from the apartment doorway. MacBride ran towards a red globe of light, opened the steel door leading to the fireproof staircase and plunged downward. But at the floor below he stopped, gritted his teeth, turned and climbed back upward and came out again in the sixth-floor corridor.

Chapter XII

GENTILLI'S door was open on a crack and the skipper banged into it, knocked it wide open. Coming towards it on the run across the living-room, with Gentilli helping him into his overcoat, was the man the skipper and Ike Cohen had met in Grail's hotel room. The skipper saw the man's bandaged left hand and in his right hand he saw a gun. He saw the gun explode and knew instantly that he was hit. It was like being hit with a club and it shook him. He himself fired while the other gun's echoes were still hammering in the room and his shot hit the man in the leg and knocked it from beneath him. He went down like an axed tree, piling against the skipper's legs and uprooting him.

Gentilli stepped in and drove his fist between MacBride's eyes and MacBride spun as he fell, cracking down on a low coffee table. His hat flew off. The bandaged man was beginning to crawl towards the door. Gentilli had dived towards his desk and was ripping out a drawer. MacBride, landing on his back on the floor, shot offhand at Gentilli, splintered the drawer, made Gentilli jump away. But Gentilli set his jaw and made another try for the drawer. MacBride fired and hit him high on the shoulder, again driving him away from the drawer. Gentilli tumbled.

MacBride heaved around and up to his knees, saw out of the corner of his eye the crawling man raise his gun. The skipper flung himself flat and two shots went past him, shattering a wall light. As he fired at the man, a chair, hurled by Gentilli, hit him in the back and blew the wind out of his lungs. Gentilli came after the chair, landing on MacBride hard, kicking him, scrambling for the skipper's gun. The gun flew away, high, landing in the middle of the room. Gentilli heaved away after it and MacBride made a pass at his foot, tripping him. As Gentilli fell, he kicked backward and his foot clipped the skipper on the jaw, jarred his brain, fogged his eyes.

The man with the bandaged hand was lying face down on the floor, panting, groaning. He had got almost to the corridor door but could not seem to go farther. Gentilli was at the other end of the room, clawing towards the gun which had been knocked out of MacBride's hand.

The skipper got to his feet, saw Gentilli get his hand on the gun. MacBride went for his spare gun. It was in his left overcoat pocket. And then he knew where he had been hit—the left arm. He could not make it. He could not raise his left hand high enough to slip it into his pocket. Blood was covering it. A lump shot pistonlike up into his throat and his scalp stiffened as he saw Gentilli get the other gun, jump up and swivel around. Gentilli's eyes were blazing with a dark fire and his teeth were bared.

MacBride did not duck. There was no use. He did not even try to cover his face. His face looked gray, hard like granite, and his hair stood on end, his eyes were glued on Gentilli.

The two interlocking explosions came not from Gentilli's gun. Gentilli shook, looked stupid, struck with awe. His wrist bent limply and he dropped his gun, folded his arms across his chest and pitched forward, plowing into the thick carpet.

MacBride turned around. He saw Ozzie Stillson standing above the inert man near the doorway. Ozzie was holding an automatic in his hand. He had picked it up from the useless hand of the man on the floor. He had come in dragging his wife with him.

His big face was pale, it looked out of shape when he said in a cluttered voice: "I did it, MacBride. I shot him."

MacBride passed a hand across his face. "Orchids to you, Judge."

Thalia Stillson lay crumpled in a dead faint behind the Judge.

MacBride crossed the room, bent, turned Gentilli over. Gentilli was breathing, murmuring. The skipper tore open his vest and shirt. Then he stood up and said:

"I think he'll live for a while."

"I don't want him to," the Judge said in a shaken voice. He staggered forward, raising the gun again.

MacBride got in front of him. "Maybe I catch on, Judge, but I'm an old copper."

He took the gun out of Stillson's hands.

There were running feet in the corridor and Moriarity and Cohen rushed in, their guns drawn. They stopped short, looked around. The Judge swayed, sank heavily into a chair.

"Hey, Cap'n," Moriarity yelled. "I thought you were just going to pay a call!"

"So did I. Call an ambulance."

Kennedy came up and leaned in the doorway, stared negligently at the men on the floor. "Well, they say life goes on and on, but that's another gag. *Sic transit gloria*, Gentilli—and a hey-nonny-nonny...."

Chapter XIII

SUN of a bright winter noon streamed into the Judge's paneled office, lay in a bar across his desk. He lounged heavily in his chair, unshaven, his big shoulders bulking alongside his ears, a slab of hair lying across his forehead.

MacBride stood with one arm in a sling, eyes downcast, a bitter grimness round his mouth.

"It's the way of life sometimes, MacBride," the Judge said moodily. "I loved Thalia too much, I guess. I didn't know what to do. I would never, if it had not culminated as it did last night, revealed what I knew. I don't know what I would have done—but never that. You know the daze I was in. I was trying to make up my mind. When you love a woman, it's so hard. I knew all along, from an hour after I got back from Lake Moar, that Thalia was involved.

"Edna McKie was a strange woman: she had a high sense of loyalty. Five years ago she loved a man in San Diego. Her husband. She loved him so much that even after she found out he was a thief and a criminal she could not leave him. Until he left her. It was on a train one night. He left her holding the bag—a bag full of stolen jewels. She got out of that after a trial and because of extreme leniency on the part of the man from whom the jewels had been stolen. Her husband fled the country and she came East, knowing she had to start all over again. She did."

"How do you know this, Judge?"

"She told me her whole story when I offered her the position of confidential secretary. Her conscience made her do it. I told her the story would be a secret with me and gave her the job. A few days ago her husband—Grail—showed up in town. She told me. She was through with him—that was all past. I offered to do something about getting him out of town. She said no, she'd take care of that. He drank quite a bit, I understand.

"About two months ago Edna came to me one morning and told me that she had put a sealed envelope in safekeeping with the bank where she kept a small account. She said that she had left instructions with the bank to turn the envelope over to me in case of her death. I was worried. But she laughed and said, 'Oh, just the usual papers.'"

His lips stiffened. He opened the top drawer of his desk, drew out a large brown envelope, extracted from it a typewritten letter. Grimacing, he passed it across the desk.

"It's self-explanatory," he said. "Read it. I picked it up at the bank as soon as I got back from Lake Moar."

MacBride knit his brows, bent stern eyes on the letter. It read:

Dear Judge,

I have thought and thought about this and finally I have decided to do it this way—to write down certain things in a letter and leave it in safekeeping, to be handed over to you in the event of my death, if the circumstances surrounding my death should appear to be of a mysterious nature.

Doubtless my concern regarding your welfare has been and is too great, but that is the way it happens to be. This is very blunt: your wife and Lewis Gentilli conspired to kill you. I never trusted your wife and I took steps towards watching her movements. It was only because I felt such a great loyalty towards you.

I managed one night to gain entrance to Gentilli's apartment, moved by a dread I felt, a superstition, that he was a dangerous man, the more so to you because of his constant association with your wife. I know you accepted him as a friend and that made me all the more fearful. While I was in his apartment rifling his desk, I heard his voice in the corridor. I closed the desk and hid in a closet. I heard him and your wife come in.

Their conversation turned to you and first one and then the other wished you were dead and your wife said that with the legacy you would leave they could do so many wonderful things. Then Gentilli said to her, "Want to take a chance on hurrying the old boy on?" After a minute or two she said, "I can't think of any safe way." They had drinks then and after a while they went out. I left also.

Next day I confronted Gentilli. I didn't go to you because I couldn't hurt you and I didn't dare to do anything that might bring on a trial, because of my past. Also, I had no witness to what I had heard. But I told Gentilli to stay away from your wife. I told him what I had heard. He was horrified. I left, knowing that they would never dare harm you. Then I began to look at my own position and so I have written this letter....

MacBRIDE let the letter slip from his hand to the desk. The Judge did not look up. MacBride did not look at him.

"So they figured it would be a good idea to get Edna McKie out of the way."

Ozzie Stillson nodded slowly, said: "Grail's turning up merely complicated matters. He had no connection with it. He merely got in the way of it."

MacBride nodded. "I know that, Judge. I got that from Gentilli's confession. It was"—he took a breath on it—"your wife who stole Edna McKie's fountain pen one day while she was in the office. The fellow Cohen and me found casing Grail's hotel room was a lad named Ramsey from Detroit. He used to be in the chemical business before he left the straight and narrow. Gentilli had once got him out of a rap and it was Gentilli who approached him about a trick means of killing somebody. First they thought of fixing up a vanity case, but then Gentilli happened to remember about the duplicate pens. Your wife had told him about them. So Ramsey said that would be a swell bet and your wife stole it one day. Ramsey was to get a big cut and he was to carry out the whole thing himself; fix and plant the pen on Edna.

"He watched outside the apartment house night before last and when he saw Edna McKie leave, he went up and went to work with his skeleton key. That was the first thing that started us off on a wrong track—the McKie woman leaving her home so abruptly at that time of night, just throwing a fur coat over her dressing-gown and night clothes and not even waiting to see if she had any money; probably forgot about it until she got the check for drinks at the restaurant— I can understand it now. Her husband, Grail, drunk, probably forced his way into the apartment on threat of a scene; but she wouldn't stay there, just beat it any place. When she came back with Kennedy, she was afraid Grail was still there.

"Anyway, Ramsey got in and ran into Grail, and was he surprised. Grail hit him first and floored him for a minute. Then Grail found Edna McKie's gun and when Ramsey came to, Grail was having a drink and covering Ramsey with the gun. Grail was pretty drunk and kept Ramsey covered quite a time, taunting him. But Grail took one drink too many and got shaky and Ramsey kicked the gun out of his hand, grabbed it up and covered him. He got a bath towel, soaked it in water, wrapped it around his hand and the gun and shot Grail twice, the wet towel muffing the shots.

"While he was standing there Edna McKie came in, ran at him and he turned and knocked her down. Knocked her cold. But he couldn't figure out where Grail fitted in, though he found his hotel key, his wallet and some cards with Cuban addresses. To fox the police, he cut out the labels in Grail's clothes. Then he couldn't find the fountain pen and this was the last straw. He hunted high and low and never thought of looking in the chair, under the cushion, where it must have fallen during the scuffle. So he dragged Edna to the kitchen, smacked her again and turned on the gas jets. He was the guy Kennedy saw going out. Later, he went to Grail's hotel room to see if he could find out anything more about him. He didn't. All this was told me in a confession by Gentilli. His gag about your wife hiring him to track down the killer of Edna McKie was the result of nervousness—they were afraid Kennedy knew something. Then Ramsey and some other hoods snatched Kennedy. It was your wife who dressed Ramsey's hand."

The Judge made no movement. After a while he put his hands over his eyes and his body began to shake with silent sobs. The skipper put his hand on the Judge's back but did not say anything. There was nothing he could say. He pressed once, sighed, strode grimly from the office.

He rode back to Headquarters in the back seat of the long, curtained touring car, his teeth clamped hard on the stem of a cold pipe. It was windy out, bright with sunlight. Papers flew. Kids on their way to school waited at crossings. The faces of the traffic cops were wind-reddened.

"Watch those kids, Gahagan!" the skipper barked.

Kennedy was hanging around when MacBride strode into his office, hung up his coat, slapped his hat on top of it. Moriarity was sitting in a corner, with his head in his hands.

"What do you want, Kennedy?" the skipper growled.

"News, dearie—news."

MacBride dropped heavily into his chair, said in a low, bitter voice: "It's not pretty, bozo."

"You would tell me?"

"Ozzie looks a hundred years old—"

He told Kennedy about it.

Nothing could ever amaze Kennedy, who always took the best with the worst. He drawled: "And a gag really started the ball rolling, huh?"

"A gag," MacBride nodded.

He looked up at Moriarity, who was still standing spellbound by the story. One of Moriarity's eyes was a deep shade of purple.

The skipper grunted: "Hey, has your sister-in-law arrived?"

"You catch on quick, Cap'n, don't you?"

Publication History

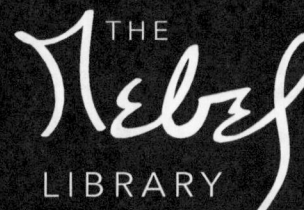

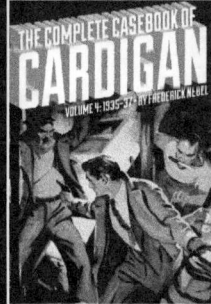

THE COMPLETE CASES OF MacBRIDE & KENNEDY

IN FOUR VOLUMES

BY FREDERICK NEBEL

Crimes of Richmond City

CAPTAIN STEVE MacBRIDE was a tall square-shouldered man of forty more or less hard-bitten

Dog Eat Dog

WHEN CAPTAIN MacBRIDE was suddenly transferred from the Second Precinct to the Fifth, an undercurrent of whispered speculations trickled through the Department, buzzed in newspaper circles, and traveled along the underworld grapevine.

It was a significant move, for MacBride, besides being the youngest captain in the Department—he was barely forty—was known throughout Richmond City as a holy terror against the criminal element. He was a lank, rangy man, with a square jaw and windy blue eyes. He was brusque, talked straight from the shoulder, and was hard-

INTRODUCTION BY DAVID LEWIS

Coming This Fall From Altus Press

The Law Laughs Last

TOUGH precinct was the Second of Richmond City, lying in the backyard of the theatrical district and on the frontier of the railroad yards.

A hard-boiled precinct, touching the fringe of crookdom's elite on the north—the con men, the night-club barons; and on the south, the dim-lit, crooked alleys traversed by the bum, the lush-worker and poolroom gangster. On the north were the playhouses, the white way, high-toned apartments, opulent hotels, high hats, evening gowns. On the south, tenements, warehouses, cobblestones, squalor, and the railroad yards. The toughest precinct in all Richmond City.

Law Without Law

KENNEDY chuckled. "So you're back in the Second, Mac."
"See me here, don't you?"
"Ay, verily!"
The old station-house, blown up during the last election, had been rebuilt, and the office in which Captain Stephen MacBride sat and Kennedy, the insatiable news-hound, stood, smelled of new paint and plaster. Something of the old atmosphere was lost—that atmosphere which it had taken long years to create: dust, age-colored walls decorated with news clippings, "wanted" bulletins, likenesses of known criminals.

Two days ago MacBride had been

New Guns For Old

POLICE Captain Steve MacBride was on leave. He had it coming to him. As one of the main factors in the scouring of Richmond City's corrupt municipal government, he was due some little respite from the shield and the gun. With the raising of a self-seeking Mayor